Jennifer Foehner Wells

Blue Bedlam
SCIENCE FICTION

Remanence/ Jennifer Foehner Wells. – 1st ed.
ISBN-13: 978-0692669617
ISBN-10: 0692669612

Also by Jennifer Foehner Wells

Novels
Fluency (Confluence Book 1)

Short Fiction
The Grove
Symbiont Seeking Symbiont

Anthologies
The Future Chronicles—Special Edition
The Future Chronicles—Alien Chronicles
The Future Chronicles—Z Chronicles
The Future Chronicles—Galaxy Chronicles
Dark Beyond the Stars

For my fourth grade teacher, Mrs. Plog,
who first encouraged my love of reading and writing.

"The heavens themselves blaze forth the death of princes."
—William Shakespeare, *Julius Caesar*, Act II, Scene 2

"Fuck a doodle do."
—Dr. Alan Bergen

SYNOPSIS
of
FLUENCY
Confluence Book 1

For more than sixty years, an alien ship drifted in the Greater Asteroid Belt just beyond Mars. It hid in plain sight, never moving, never receiving resupply, its intentions unknown. Dr. Jane Holloway was a linguist savant, expert at making first contact with isolated human societies. She was recruited, along with five NASA scientists and engineers, for a mission to explore the city-sized ship, with the goal of uncovering its technological secrets. They assumed the ship was empty.

As Jane analyzed language fragments, a symbol opened and expanded into a hologram, revealing its meaning to her. She conversed with the voice of an alien who welcomed her, but was otherwise reticent and remained hidden. Jane awakened from this experience unsure if it was real, a dream, or a hallucination. The crew continued to explore, but Jane opted to stay quiet rather than confess what she feared might have been space madness.

After two of the crew stumbled upon a room full of slug-like creatures and xenon gas, Jane received instructions from the alien, allowing her to save her crewmates.

Her colleagues had lots of questions. She confessed she had made contact with an alien and offered proof to her colleagues by leading them directly to a fully automated medical facility to receive treatment. Walsh, the commander of the mission, was wary about Jane's silent interactions with the alien, Ei'Brai.

The mental bond between Jane and Ei'Brai grew stronger. She was undergoing medical treatment with engineer Dr. Alan Bergen when she sensed something was amiss with the ship. She reconnected with Ei'Brai and demanded to know why the ship had come to Earth and why it was uninhabited, except for him.

He disclosed that his crew, from a race called the Sectilius, had been lost to an unknown silent agent. They'd come to warn Earth of impending danger and recruit humans to fight in an intergalactic war. Someone had wanted that mission to fail.

While Jane was unconscious, her comrades discussed the situation. Walsh believed Jane was compromised, putting them all in danger. Tom Compton began to behave strangely, fueling Walsh's argument. They decided to retreat.

When Jane returned to consciousness she realized Compton's odd behavior was a symptom of the agent that had wiped out the Sectilius. As they backtracked, it became clear that the xenon gas leak had triggered a metamorphosis of the slugs, which had encased themselves in pupa and were hatching into hordes of venomous creatures. The crew was cut off from escape.

Before long, they were surrounded, fighting to survive. When Jane tried to protect Compton, she was separated from the others and badly injured. Ei'Brai mentally inhabited Compton's catatonic body and used it to carry Jane to safety, then cut power to the deck-to-deck transport so no one could come after her. Bergen was injured and doggedly searched for Jane. The rest of the crew retreated to the capsule.

Ei'Brai placed Jane in a regeneration tank and drugged her. He tried to distract her, but his methods violated a human cultural taboo, outraging Jane, making her more determined than ever to escape. She feared that her colleagues were either dead or had left her behind.

Jane broke free, donned sectilian battle armor, and searched for her colleagues. She found Bergen holed up, barely surviving, near death. She got him to safety and decided to confront the alien face-to-face.

She approached Ei'Brai's inner sanctum and discovered that he was a massive, cybernetically enhanced squid. He revealed that everything she'd endured so far he had engineered as a test. Due to the way the sectilian government had programmed his computer interface, he couldn't move the ship without another person aboard as his democratic check. He needed a ship captain, and he had chosen Jane as the most suitable candidate.

She was reluctant to take the job. He threatened to injure Bergen if she refused. She called his bluff, countering that she would destroy his life support if he were to hurt Bergen. They came to terms. She agreed to take the position with stipulations.

Jane, Bergen, and Ei'Brai worked together to get to the bottom of the nanite infection that had wiped out the Sectilius and infected part of the human crew. Their only option was drastic. Jane took command, maneuvering the ship to rescue her colleagues, who were drifting through space in the capsule. She issued an order that annihilated the nanites.

Jane made contact with Mission Control on Earth to arrange to send the rest of the crew home. She explained to Houston that she intended to take the alien ship and return Ei'Brai to the sectilian home world in order to investigate the mass genocide that had killed the original crew and to search for other kuboderans stranded throughout the galaxy.

1

When the first blow hit the ship, Kai'Negli was thrown across his enclosure with a violence he'd never known in his long life. He thudded into the wall of his tank so hard he lost consciousness for a moment. When he came to, he reeled with pain and consternation.

He had incurred soft-tissue damage, for sure. He'd regenerate, but it was a blow to his ego to be treated with such blatant contempt.

His limbs curled in impotent rage and he went immediately to assess the damage to the ship. Some of his equipment was failing from the impact, but he was able to determine that there was a breach on the starboard side—a gaping hole in the protective envelope of the ship. If there had been sectilians still alive onboard, thousands would have met dusk from explosive decompression.

He was incredulous. This was a science vessel. It was unthinkable to damage a functional ship so wantonly.

He itched to retaliate, but of course he had no recourse and they knew it. Without a commanding officer he was powerless to do anything but endure this insult. They'd made their point. Perhaps they thought he'd change his mind under threat.

He would not.

He set several thousand cadres of microscopic escutcheon squillae to move into the damaged areas. It would take years for them to close that gap, harvesting material from other areas of the ship molecule by molecule. But if anyone could guide them to such a feat, it was Kai'Negli.

Then he saw it. Red light in his peripheral vision. He rotated his funnel to change direction and froze in place, his eyes widening. They wouldn't dare.

A laser was shining through the opening they'd created in the hull of the ship. They were slicing open his enclosure.

He trembled with horror.

How could they even contemplate such an action? Because he'd refused them? They would kill him for that? Why not just let him be? Move on?

He had to verify it with his own eyes. He jetted closer to that end of his habitat. Without the tough exterior of the ship in the way and the escutcheon to re-form over the cuts, there was little to impede the laser. The line they were scribing was moving fast and water was already spilling out of the opening.

He marshaled every squillae in the area to converge on the line already cut to re-bond the material. They moved en masse but most were caught up in the flood of escaping water, carried away to be lodged within shards frozen in the vacuum of space.

Nothing could save him. He had nothing left. He was powerless to stop them.

Perhaps they expected him to capitulate now, but he would never cooperate with thugs like this. This kind of behavior was beneath him.

He watched the laser mercilessly cut across the barrier between himself and the void. Cracks began to form in the transparent material as the pressure of the water pushed against the weakened areas. He could hear the tank creaking and groaning under the strain.

He never would have guessed he'd meet dusk in this manner.

Suddenly it gave way.

He didn't even fight the rush of water.

The sluice hurled him through the line of the laser itself. He barely registered the pain of amputation as he flipped end over end, his remaining limbs reaching out and finding nothing to cling to. He was thrown clear of the ship, his mantle fluttering with no water left to push against.

The last thing he saw before dusk settled over him was the *Portacollus* initiating a jump sequence and leaving him behind.

2

Jane Holloway's heart slammed against her rib cage as microseconds ticked by. She could see the leading edge of the swirl, smudging the stars beyond into indistinct commas of light. They were almost to the tunnel. Her vision blurred as the wormhole generator deep inside the ship roared to a crescendo, dominating her consciousness, linking machine to living flesh through Ei'Brai. She could feel it resonating in her bones.

Almost…there…

Absently, she felt her body lean against the straps, eagerly pushing toward the wormhole as if she could make the ship get there faster somehow. Pain pulsed in her head with every heartbeat. It felt like her brain could split in half. She did her best to ignore it. It wasn't important. She focused all her concentration on the jump.

Jane breathed shallowly, stubbornly clinging to consciousness and the mental link with Ei'Brai. She'd felt the rest of the crew wink out ages ago, though she knew it had only been tiny fractions of a second. It felt like forever.

A seemingly endless stream of calculations—distance algorithms, wormhole formulae, coordinates in space— flowed from Ei'Brai through her, then the ship's computer, and finally the drive in a seamless and nearly instantaneous cascade of incomprehensible data.

She could not let go. If she did, the wormhole jump would fall short and they'd have to add another one to the route. That was the last thing she wanted to do. The fewer jumps they had to endure, the better.

Ei'Brai's consternation grumbled through her. The end of him and the beginning of her was indistinct. He didn't know why jumping with her was so difficult, but every jump so far had been like this—grueling, with her barely making it to their destination conscious. He blamed it on her inexperience, on her otherness, but he didn't really know the cause.

He'd never jumped with any species aside from sectilians before he'd jumped with Jane. Human minds, as he often reminded her, were very different from sectilian minds—less organized, more tangentially driven—which under certain circumstances might be construed as a good thing, but not when jumping. It could be that or any of a billion other factors. She might never know.

A ring of stars before them turned to streaks, smudged by the gyre of the wormhole as it moved to envelop them. Through the lens in the center were the distant stars on the other side, many light-years away. She held her breath as the funnel sucked them in. There was a long moment of utter chaos during which no thought could find a place to stick.

Then, relief. They'd arrived…somewhere, anyway.

She sagged back in the oversized command chair, breathing raggedly, one critical question on her mind. She sent the thought to Ei'Brai, who had already receded from her to watch the computer analyze star maps. "Did we reach our destination?"

He didn't reply immediately. He put her on hold, a mental gesture, as if he were sticking up a finger as he watched data scroll by.

They'd left Earth weeks before to begin a sequence of jumps toward the heart of the Milky Way galaxy. Their trajectory would eventually take them to the Sectilius system and the sibling worlds of Sectilia and her moon Atielle, where Jane would turn over the ship to its rightful owners. When Jane had taken command of the *Speroancora*, she'd pledged to take Ei'Brai home, and that was what she was doing. Once there, she hoped to find out who had orchestrated the genocide that had killed Ei'Brai's original crew. She also hoped the *Speroancora* would be used in the search for the kuboderans stranded all over the galaxy. Jane and her human crew would join in that mission, if the Sectilius would have them.

She'd never imagined the journey would be this difficult but that didn't matter. She'd gladly face ten times worse for the opportunity to meet sectilians in person. She needed to go to Sectilius like she needed to breathe. She had to see it for herself, meet the people for herself, for reasons she couldn't fully comprehend.

Finally the strand of tension between herself and Ei'Brai broke. "Yes," he said. "We have arrived at the target destination." She felt him go limp, drifting, as he let go of his own anxiety, letting exhaustion take him. She did the same.

"Jane?" Ajaya's voice and gentle touch broke through the heavy blanket of sleep.

Jane opened her eyes to find Ajaya Varma leaning over her, her hand on Jane's arm, with a kindly look on her weary face.

"What?" Jane stammered. "Oh. I…" Her mouth was dry. She needed a sip of water.

"We all fell asleep, Commander," Ajaya said kindly, in a manner probably meant to obviate Jane's embarrassment. No one used the sectilian term Quasador Dux or Qua'dux except Ei'Brai, though Ron called her QD sometimes in a jocular way. Only Ajaya used the term Commander. Ajaya would feel the need to dignify Jane's place as the leader of this ship, but apparently the alien title still felt odd on Ajaya's tongue, despite the fact that she'd made great strides in learning the language.

Ajaya straightened from her position stooped over Jane and glanced back.

Ronald Gibbs stood behind her, rubbing his eyes sleepily. "Alan must have woken first. He's probably off exploring Tech Deck again."

Jane pushed herself up, her body stiff and painful. She'd been slumped at a strange angle in the command chair. She had no idea how long she'd been like that. Too long, judging by the muscles protesting in her neck.

Ei'Brai briefly checked in to confirm what Ron had said. Alan was on the deck that housed the engines, drives, and various electrical systems and water-processing systems. Alan called it Tech Deck, eschewing the longish Sectilius name for it: Tabulamachinium. They could have called it engineering, but Tech Deck was fine. It was probably better than "TMI deck," which was what she'd been calling it in avoidance of saying the name. She'd thought that was a mildly amusing name. No one else had.

Jane frowned and wiped at her face, hoping she wouldn't find drool there. She wished Ajaya would call her Jane. Mark Walsh had been the commander, but he wasn't there anymore. He was safely back on Earth, along with a much-rejuvenated Tom Compton.

Ajaya said, "You were positioned awkwardly, such that your airflow was restricted." She paused, her lips pressed together.

Jane wondered what Ajaya wasn't saying. Then Jane's sleepy brain caught up. Ugh. How embarrassing. She'd been snoring, not getting enough air. She sighed and shrugged at the ache in her neck and shoulder.

Ajaya grimaced. "I felt it would be better to wake you and get you to your quarters and a proper bed where you might get more restful sleep."

"Thank you, but I think I've slept enough. There's work to be done." Too much work. She felt an urgency to accomplish as much as she could before they reached Sectilius. She wanted to turn over the ship in the best condition possible.

Ajaya shook her head. "You need to rest, Commander. The jumps are taking a physical toll on you."

Ron moved closer, a wry look on his face as he rolled his shoulders. "There's always work to be done." He came up to stand behind Ajaya as though lending his support to her argument. His large, brown hand came to rest casually on Ajaya's shoulder.

Jane stifled a yawn, nodded her agreement to Ajaya and Ron, and headed for Tech Deck. She'd rest a little as soon as she finished this next task. A batch of squillae had recently completed production, and she needed to distribute them as soon as possible. These sectilian nanites, programmed to repair and maintain every ship system, made it possible for such a small crew to manage the city-sized vessel. Normally the ship would replenish and distribute the tiny machines automatically, but since they'd been forced to destroy every last one of them to survive, she'd taken on the task of personally dispersing them to the most critical areas herself. It would take a full year to manufacture them to the level they'd been at before she'd obliterated them. It left the ship vulnerable and that wasn't okay. This was her ship, at least for now, she thought wistfully. She had to optimize its condition.

As she walked through the corridors, the need for sleep pressed on her. She stretched her arms out and twisted her head to one side and then the other, trying to push the sluggishness back, wake up more fully, and get rid of the creaky feeling in her neck that kept making her wince. Duty had kept her on her feet long past the point of sanity.

Her somnolent brain drifted as she went. Echoes of the former Qua'dux Rageth's memories crept to the forefront. She could see the empty corridors as they were, but also as they had been in Rageth's time, full of bustling people—a mixture of short, stocky sectilians with corded muscles and willowy atellans from Sectilius's moon, Atielle. They all shared an angularity—high, geometric cheekbones and froths of bushy curled hair ranging from light gray-brown to medium brown. She wondered what thoughts had been lurking behind their somber expressions. Then she could see those thoughts in Rageth's mind too, funneled through

Ei'Brai's perception of the crowd. They all had been filled with purpose, just as she was, driven to complete their myriad goals. These sectilians were gone, but surely someone had survived on the sibling planets. She couldn't wait to meet them.

3

Alan Bergen ran a practiced hand over the wall, seeking the spot where a light touch would trigger the opening mechanism. Around him there was a barely perceptible hum of machines and that faint, peculiar odor that he smelled only on Tech Deck—wintergreen and burning paper. The odor had come to represent an overall sensation of curiosity, excitement, and frustration for him.

The chamber he occupied was less room and more corridor, though the walls terminated at roughly two and a half meters of height, so that there was a huge volume of shared air overhead. These walls meandered in a maze of undulating lines, arranged with these door-sized drawers set at regular intervals, containing the most important mechanicals on the ship. At first he'd found the layout irritating, but then he realized there was a method to it. It wasted no space and all the turns and cul-de-sacs allowed a kind of privacy that would be welcome when working with complex mechanicals in a busy ship.

Under his hand the mechanism engaged, and Alan straightened, watching the drawer slide smoothly from the wall. In his left hand was a device he affectionately called the Viking. It was an MCA or multichannel analyzer. He was using it to detect a number of things, though his primary interest was gamma radiation, the presence of which he hoped would clue him in to whether or not there was a fusion drive on the premises.

Since the first jump had taken them out of their native solar system, he no longer had the luxury of sending data to Houston to have his compadres look over and verify the conclusions he was making. There was no one to argue with about what was the best next step to take. He was on his own.

For that reason, he was forcing himself to go slowly and to work methodically. He could talk to Ron about some of this stuff, but Ron was an electrical engineer and computer specialist. He had little training in theoretical physics. The dude was brilliant in his fields, but he couldn't really talk fusion with Ron. Well, he could, but not extensively.

He probably should talk to the Squid. He would get up to speed a hell of a lot faster with help from the tentacled bastard, but at this point he'd rather figure it out on his own. It meant something to him, this process of discovery. Occasionally Jane rounded them all up for shuttle-pilot training or bridge-console training or a nepatrox hunt, but overall his time was best served figuring this shit out. What could be better? This was every engineer's dream.

He did feel a lot of pressure to learn as much as possible as fast as possible. They'd arrive in Sectilius space in just a few days. Who knew what would happen then? Everything was going to change and he wasn't looking forward to that. He wasn't done yet. He needed more time. He'd begun to feel almost a possessive feeling about the ship. Tech Deck was *his*. He didn't want to hand it over to the Sectilius—he wanted to keep it for himself. Being there was the best thing that had ever happened to him. It was the culmination of a lifetime of dreaming. He loved every single minute of the process of understanding how it worked.

One of the things that surprised Alan the most about the *Speroancora* was that very little of what he studied was incomprehensible. Overly complicated sometimes, yes, but not defying human understanding. Science fiction led the average person to believe that when a spacefaring super race finally deigned to pay Earth a visit, their tech would be mind-blowingly superior. So far that wasn't the case—okay, aside from the artificial gravity, the wormhole generator, and the fusion reactor he was looking for. But he suspected that if he looked at the math even those things would be within human reach. They'd be comprehensible, he was sure of it.

There was no reason to believe that the Sectilius had necessarily invented all of those devices themselves. They may have appropriated that tech from other cultures in their galactic wonder alliance. Maybe no single planet in that alliance was any farther ahead than any other, but the sharing of the technologies got them all farther faster. The only handicap humans had, as far as he was concerned, was the fact that they hadn't known until now that there were others out there.

A lot of this stuff—the nanites, the ship's computers, the medical equipment—human science was on the cusp of making happen or already had. And the sectilian shuttles— while awesome—were only a few steps ahead of the kinds of things NASA was imagining creating in the next few decades. It would take another hundred years, maybe less, for humans to reach the same technological milestones the Sectilius had with this ship—two hundred if he was feeling particularly pessimistic.

What the Sectilius *didn't* have was also notable. Number one: no magic shields to protect the ship from external roughhousing. The escutcheon was a kind of shielding made up mostly of nanites. The concept of an energy barrier to protect the ship was a sci-fi crutch, a good storytelling device that had no practical application in the real world. There were no magic weapons either. This was a science and diplomatic vessel, so all it had were a few missiles and a couple of laser cannons—nothing he couldn't have built in his garage back home.

The most magical thing they had—anipraxia—they'd discovered that. They hadn't created it. They exploited a biological resource that benefited them.

The Sectilius weren't a super race. They weren't thousands or millions of years more advanced than humans. That simultaneously amazed, confused, and reassured him.

It was reassuring because it meant that no one out there was necessarily *smarter* than him...or humans in general. That was actually pretty profound. The big-dumb-object-in-the-sky idea didn't necessarily have to mean that humans were the dumb ones.

The consensus at NASA prior to the launch of the mission to the Target had been that it would probably take decades to unravel the alien science. He wasn't convinced that was the case. In fact he thought that if the bigwigs could just efficiently cut through the bureaucracy bullshit they could probably be building their own versions of the *Speroancora* and her shuttles within a year or two with the specs Jane had given them when she sent Walsh and Compton home.

And when they did, they'd streamline all of it. Everything about this ship seemed overly complicated. Nothing was straightforward. He'd mentioned that to Jane once and she had looked surprised, disagreed, saying that once he had met and spent time with the Sectilius, he'd understand the ship on a much-deeper level. He'd narrowed his eyes and blinked at her but refrained from saying anything else about it. She'd never met one either, and yet she acted as though she had. He didn't think the Squid counted, but maybe he did in her book.

He sighed, his right hand going to the back of his neck. He hoped she was okay. This whole jumping through wormholes business seemed to be taxing her to the reaches of her endurance, and yet they pushed on relentlessly. It had been almost seventy years since the Squid was stranded in their solar system. What harm would it do for her to rest a few days? But no one wanted Alan's opinion on that subject.

Bergen frowned as he stared at the neat arrangement of components in front of him, willing his subconscious to come up with something…anything for this device. But unfortunately all he could think of was spaghetti and meatballs. That was probably his stomach's fault. He wondered absently how long it had been since his last bland meal. It was easy to lose track of meals and sleep without light cues or other people around to prod him.

He had all the data Jane had sent to Earth with the *Speroancora* shuttle. He studied it for a few hours each night before bed, reconciling the principles it outlined with the hardware he was physically in contact with every day. So far, he'd had a few really great eureka moments—those were the best. One of the things holding him back was his limited understanding of Mensententia. So he studied, observed, and took data. It was all coming together that way—a deeper understanding. It was pretty freaking awesome.

There were definitely multiple layers of command and control integral in every system he studied that had something to do with Ei'Brai. The neural-electric pathways that ran throughout the ship were connected to the aquatic beast cybernetically and the Squid had implants inside his body that communicated directly with the ship. It gave Bergen the eerie feeling that the ship was an extension of the Squid. That he was always watching them. Add that to his telepathic feats, and Alan just wasn't a big fan of their host.

It wasn't the difficulty involved with understanding. He'd never shied away from a challenge. Rather it was a pervasive feeling he couldn't shake that the Squid obfuscated everything on purpose somehow, to keep him from understanding. He had no evidence to that effect, but he wouldn't put it past the Squid to do such a thing, not after everything they'd been through.

Jane would say he was being ridiculous, but he felt that a healthy dose of skepticism whenever the Squid was involved was warranted. He just didn't trust him. He was in the minority there, too.

He recorded his data, made the necessary notations in his laptop, checked to be sure the data had uploaded from the Viking to his laptop properly, slid that compartment closed, and moved on to the next one. This one was larger, wider—probably three meters wide. He remembered this compartment from when he went through the entire deck doing spectral and thermal analysis. This segment was very different from many of the other ones. There was a round drum inside. The drum took a specialized tool to open—a tool he hadn't yet found anywhere on board, though he'd found many other tools. It was on his list of items to manufacture with the 3-D printer.

He took a step closer. *Hold on.* Something was different this time. All around the drum, amber lights were glowing. He narrowed his eyes. There was a definite low hum coming from this device. He tentatively put his hand on the outside. There was the slightest vibration. Something inside the thing was spinning or rotating in some way. What might they use that would require a centrifugal setup?

He knelt down so he could give it a full 180-degree sweep with the Viking. He was up to his armpit in the device when a sudden sound behind him made him jump, banging his elbow in just the right spot to trigger his funny bone. He almost dropped the instrument—which would have been disastrous since he only had one.

Pulling himself from the guts of the device, he staggered backward and upright until he bumped into the wall, cursing a blue streak as he swung his head around to see what had startled him. Some part of him was almost certain that one of these days a nepatrox was going to come up behind him and take a bite out of his ass.

It was Jane. He hadn't even heard her coming.

That was kind of weird, because even though he consciously worked most of the time to exclude Ei'Brai from his thoughts—which was freaking exhausting—there was still always an element of supra-cognitive awareness. He didn't have a clue what it was about, but he'd come to realize that he was just sort of aware whenever one of the other humans was nearby, especially if they intended to speak with him. He'd been taking notes on it for a while, which he intended to pass on to someone at some point. No idea who.

He set the Viking down on the nearest flat surface and straightened, shaking his arm, which had gone painful, numb, and tingly.

"Jesus, Jane! Give a guy some warning!"

Her eyes were wide and she looked like she was swallowing a smile.

Dammit.

"I'm sorry, Alan." She gestured in a way that encompassed the cavernous room and pointed to somewhere on the other side of him. "I've just come for a fresh batch of squillae."

He tried not to smirk in response to her persistence in using the word squillae even when speaking in English. It was the word in Mensententia for nanite, but the literal meaning was shrimp and it just made him want to laugh every time he heard it. He blew out a breath and sagged a little bit, cradling his arm, as his heart rate slowed. She was just passing through and probably hadn't wanted to talk to him. He was just in her way.

Mental note: add this encounter to the Journal of Bizarre Telepathic Bullshit. Could be significant. She didn't seem to have known he was here either. Further note to self: try really hard not to read anything into that.

"Yeah. Of course. Sorry. I don't know why I'm so twitchy." He damn well did know, but he wasn't going to admit that to her. "How did the jump go?"

She nodded. "It was successful."

He nodded too, inanely. Was he turning into a bobble-head? "Good, good. How many more now?"

"Just two more," she said gravely. She pointed at the large drum behind him. "How are things going here?"

He thumbed back at the open device. "This? Well, you know..." He didn't really know what to say. Did she expect some kind of progress report?

She half smiled and bobbed her head like she was uncomfortable too and ready to be on her way.

He couldn't keep himself from watching her as she approached the open device. He realized it would be a tight squeeze for her to get past and moved to close it so she could slip by more easily. She put out her hand to wave him off, but suddenly her expression went strange and she stumbled.

Alan lurched to brace her. She leaned into him for a moment. When her eyes met his, they were wide. She looked around as though she were searching for something she'd lost.

"What is it? What's wrong?" he asked her. He found himself looking around too, though he wasn't sure why or what he was looking for.

"Oh...I just...I don't know." She looked confused.

He took on a stern tone. Someone had to get through to her. At this rate she was going to stroke out or something. "This is about enough, Jane. You're pushing yourself too hard. You need to get more goddamn sleep."

"No, something is..." She shook herself and turned away from him, back the way she had come. There was a panicked expression on her face.

He let her go reluctantly as she moved away. He took a few steps after her, wanting to say more, but feeling completely impotent.

She reached the point where she'd been standing when they'd first begun this bizarre conversation and she stopped suddenly again, swaying.

He leapt after her and put his arms around her. "Jane," he said gruffly.

"No, it's…" She swiveled in his arms, and her eyes locked on the open device. "Oh," she mumbled. "It's from the jump…"

His eyes darted from her to the drum and back again. This device had something to do with the folded space-time they used, the artificial wormhole technology? A limited understanding dawned on him—and then grew exponentially. He'd relaxed his mental guard in his concern for Jane. The information that she was unlocking was passing out in the open between the three of them: him, her, and Ei'Brai.

He almost slammed closed the conduit that allowed the information to pour through, but stopped himself. He was too damn curious to pass up the chance to understand the device, even though it felt like cheating.

He looked at Jane with awe as he realized the level at which she understood the mechanics inside the device. They were completely open to each other now, as they hadn't been in ages. She registered his admiration, and the dimple on her right cheek deepened and her clear, gray eyes brightened. He liked that.

She was pleased that he noticed. He also registered that she was cautiously enjoying his embrace. There was hope in her mind—a breathless anticipation. That, added to his own feelings, which were igniting... Okay, that was an understatement. He was fucking en fuego. It was intense to feel her feeling him, feeling her—it all seemed to roll up into something more. Something...was snowballing...

He scooped her to him, tightening his hold slightly and extending their contact to cover more surface area. He bent his head over hers and feasted on her lips.

"Yes," came borne on a mental sigh of gratitude from her mind to his—via the Squid, he couldn't forget, "this, Alan, but...just this. Let's go slowly."

He tried not to let his body go stiff, because he did understand her. Suddenly he understood better than he ever had before. In that moment, she was so tired she couldn't hold back. She was raw. She was enjoying his touch, his company, the comfort he offered. For the first time he had a real insight into her inner turmoil—the desire she felt for him, the curiosity about what being with him would be like, and the need to remain aloof and professional to maintain both order and the respect of Ron and Ajaya—all were at war within her.

She'd given him a glimpse of her inner workings, and he wouldn't disrespect that by pressuring her for more. Her inner life was just as complicated as his. What he got from this unguarded interaction with her was that if he could continue to show patience, he would eventually be rewarded in spades.

So even though his loins ached—which she acknowledged with chagrin—he just held her, moving his lips over hers, one hand roaming up and down her spine in a soothing motion that went nowhere near either a bra clasp or the round swell of her ass. He savored the moment and kept his lust in check.

She sighed with contentment against his lips and broke off the kiss, leaning into him more fully, her head coming to rest against his chest. Her mental state was suffused with dreaminess, and he slowly realized she was no longer in touch with reality. Her mind spun crazy webs of disjointed thoughts. He looked down, not really surprised to see her eyes closed and lips parted. She'd relaxed into their warm embrace and had instantly fallen asleep.

He huffed with disbelief and wondered what the hell he should do now.

He glanced back at the device with wonder. The thing was an artificial-wormhole generator. That in and of itself was freaking insanely cool.

But there was more. His heart thudded. There was an interesting side effect when the device was active, as it was for hours in preparation in advance of a jump, as well as for hours long after a jump had been achieved: the device created an electromagnetic field. Normally, when the enormous drawer housing the device was closed, it was locked inside a Faraday cage and therefore wouldn't emit the EM field. But he'd opened it while it was still active, exposing them to it.

This EM field, he now realized, disrupted the reception of the quantum entanglement that allowed anipraxis with Ei'Brai. It was hard to translate Jane's very alien way of understanding the tech to the way he had been trained to interpret the science, but it seemed that when the waves hit the organs in the brain that made anipraxia possible, they acted on those organs as if they were measuring the spin of the electrons, effectively disrupting the connection. That made sense because of the spooky way quantum entanglement worked—observation defined what state the entangled electrons were in, not allowing them to stay in a state of superposition—therefore creating a static outgoing signal and not allowing new throughput.

It was jamming the signal. It made the Squid's telepathic Wi-Fi drop out. That was why Jane had been so disoriented. It wasn't just sheer exhaustion, though that had played a role. She'd been kicked out of Ei'Brai's anipraxic network.

If this device could do that... His thoughts raced as he considered the possibilities. He'd have to do some testing to figure out the specific frequency—easy enough to do with a wideband antenna and a spectrum analyzer. Once he did, he could reproduce it. And that meant he could actually relax without feeling like he was being watched by a squirmy, aquatic peeping Tom. That would free up some much-needed mental energy so he could focus on what was most important—mastering the alien tech.

He looked down on Jane, limp in his arms, and kissed her forehead before swooping to lift her legs out from under her—like a fucking hero—thinking about how she'd carried him around not so long ago. It was about damn time he got to return the favor.

Her lips curled up in a sleepy smile before she threw an arm around his neck and nestled her face against him. She'd heard his thoughts. She liked them.

"Thank you," flitted briefly against his mind and then away as she went deeper into sleep, completely relaxed. His own lips quirked up on one side as he began to walk, carefully, hoping the slight limp from his cybernetic leg wouldn't disturb her.

She trusted him.

Ei'Brai was there in the background, a distant brooding presence. Alan got the feeling that the Squid was just as exhausted as Jane seemed to be. Ei'Brai didn't say anything, but his attitude was also one of gratitude. He was also glad Jane was resting. So the Squid was sensible about something, anyway.

Alan grunted. She was heavier than he'd imagined. He hoped like hell that he'd be able to manage carrying her all the way back to her quarters without mishap. The last thing he wanted to do was thunk her head into a door frame like he was in a bad slapstick routine in a terrible sitcom. He wanted to keep the moment sweet. He needed, just one fucking time, to feel like the good guy.

He looked over his shoulder wistfully in the direction of the wormhole generator, then strode into the deck-to-deck transport, feeling happier than he'd felt in a very long time.

4

Ei'Brai's anxiety was not on par with any emotion that humans or sectilians could understand. It was an emotion uniquely kuboderan, based purely on magnitude alone. A kuboderan was capable of simultaneously holding dozens of possible outcomes in his or her mind at once. When faced with a dearth of knowledge about an upcoming situation, the possibilities could become overwhelming, even paralyzing. The fact that he was powerless to affect the outcomes, stuck as he always was in his aquatic environment, was something he and every other individual of his kind struggled with when forced to watch his or her terrestrial mind-mates go off into the unknown. Approaching Sectilius was having this very effect on him, and it seemed magnified somehow. It was troubling, the difficulty he was having reining that sensation in.

He was keenly aware that his mental state affected his human crew, so he constrained his apprehension to the strictest measure he was capable of. To that end, he employed rigorous exercise regimens and enforced a strict sleeping schedule, rotating his three cerebrums through rest phases to maintain optimal working parameters at all times. He'd gotten sloppy before, had developed bad habits during his long solitude. That could no longer stand. He must act in a manner worthy of the rank Ei—now more than ever.

The final jump placed the *Speroancora* at the edge of the Sectilius system. Normally he would have placed them far closer to their destination, but jumps were safest when endpoints were calculated for vast empty space. This strategy went back to an earlier time when jumps were more erratic—as they were with Jane. The distance also gave Quasador Dux Jane Holloway the opportunity to rest and recuperate from the taxing effects of the jump before she and the other humans went down to the surface.

Upon entering the system, they began broadcasting hailing radio signals, according to standard sectilian protocols. No answering signal was received on any channel. He monitored them all. Indeed, even as their trajectory took them deeper into the system, no stray communication signals of any kind were received.

Sectilia and her moon were silent.

Doubts churned in his mind. He was careful to keep them from the Qua'dux's notice, though he couldn't truly hide them from her. Was he putting her in abject danger? Could he bear it if she were injured or worse? And if the worst should come to pass, would he find himself stranded once again? He was certain he would go mad if that occurred. But what other course was there? Worse was the idea that he would most likely be forced to give her up. He couldn't refuse if the Sectilius decided to replace this crew. He'd be forced to adapt or face harsh consequences. He'd experienced significant crew changes many times in his life, but this was so radically different.

He would miss her.

He found some solace in the fact that the humans derived much pleasure from the simple act of observing the sights as they traversed the system. And he too could see them now with fresh eyes after so much time away. But was it fresh eyes, or had he just…forgotten them? Had it been so long that they would feel new? Or had he blotted these memories out during his long solitude to protect himself from the pain of remembering? Something about the disparity in his memory troubled him, but there were too many other anxieties on his mind to single that one out as significant.

As they passed a large hydrogen-helium planet, so critical to the stability of an inhabited system, each of the humans gazed with awe at its swirling surface through the large viewscreen on the bridge. Without compromising more than a few moments of time, and with the Qua'dux's blessing, he treated them to some of the most arresting views of that planet—its swirling storms and the endless layers of gasses of varying color and density.

Dr. Ajaya Varma gasped when the ship rose up out of the plane of the ring around the planet, displaying the striated band of rock and ice to its best advantage. The entire planet had an insubstantial, ethereal quality to it. It gleamed.

Dr. Ronald Gibbs remarked aloud, "Human eyes have never seen our own gas giants like this. It's…bizarre, isn't it? To see this in an alien system when Jupiter and Saturn have only been seen as images taken by drones?"

The Qua'dux and her crew made it a habit to spend their waking hours on the bridge as Sectilia slowly transformed from a pinpoint of reflected light in the distance to a lush blue-green sphere orbited by three smaller spheres, two of which were barren rocks, and the third of which was a diminutive and less verdant version of Sectilia herself—Atielle, their initial destination.

As the *Speroancora* passed the orbital plane of the fifth planet in the system, the ship's passage triggered a buoy to emit a warning. A red light bounced in the peripheral vision of his ocular implant. The Qua'dux felt his attention shift and instantly merged with him to assess the message.

The buoy identified itself as a quarantine beacon, placed by the Unified Sentient Races, the consortium of worlds whose primary objective was to work together against the terror of their common enemy: the Swarm. The buoy warned that trading with Sectilius was forbidden and that going deeper into the system would incur penalties and sanctions. The system was monitored remotely via extensive, redundant relays. The USR would lift the ban when it deemed Sectilius was no longer a threat to the rest of the galaxy. Until such time, it strongly advised them to leave the system.

"Have you ever seen anything like this buoy before?" the Qua'dux asked him.

"Never," he replied.

"Let's send in a drone to see if it has any firepower," she said.

He did. He determined it was just a messaging system.

She didn't hesitate. "Ignore it. We know the risks. Besides, surely they don't mean to prevent Sectilius ships from going home."

They encountered three more such buoys as they drew closer, each one with similar messages. None of them contained ordnance of any kind.

As the distance closed, he could not help but reach out to the full extent of his ability, seeking communication with his own kind. It had been readily apparent for some time that no intact ships were left orbiting either planetary body, and yet he held out hope that some individuals might have survived an oceanic crash landing, to subsist in the oceans of either world, awaiting rescue.

It was soon apparent that was not the case. No kuboderans remained, though at any given time in the past there might have been dozens of his kind in orbit.

The Quasador Dux monitored his thoughts as he searched, her own hopes high. When he abandoned the search, despondent and stricken with grief, she came to him in person.

She leaned her body against the transparent material that separated them and splayed her hand out over the glass, as though she were reaching out to him. She shared his pain.

For a moment it seemed unbearable that he could not touch her, for he wanted to experience the warm twining of bodies that she called a hug. He had observed this behavior among the humans and it seemed so...reassuring and natural. He wondered if wild kuboderans touched each other that way and suspected that they did. That kind of comfort would be welcome now. She smiled at his whimsical thought and promised that one day she would do just that.

She watched him gravely as he wrestled with his emotions. This discovery was another confirmation of loss. Though the deaths had happened long ago, he couldn't file them away so quickly.

Ei'Brai reached out an arm and carefully laid some suckers over the spot where the Qua'dux's hand rested. When he refocused on her, he saw a wet trail on her face that had originated in her eye. A uniquely human expression of sympathy. A strange quirk of their physiology, to be sure. Yet saline tears sacrificed for his lost kin seemed appropriate.

She understood him, silently. He was surprised at how much that eased the pain. Sectilians rarely shared such feelings with kuboderans. The former Qua'dux had been an exception. He'd never thought he would find another friendship like this in his lifetime. Yet here she was before him, brought to him by the *Providence*.

She stayed well past the onset of her discomfort. She communed with him even as her lips turned pale, her body shivered to make itself warm, and her teeth clattered together. Finally he sent her away, and guilt lay over the distress, that he had let her linger so long.

Eventually he set the pain aside, to feel it to its depth later, when there was more time for leisure, and plotted a course to put the *Speroancora* in geosynchronous orbit around Atielle over the residence of the issue of the esteemed Quasador Dux Rageth Elia Hator.

Both planets remained silent.

As they took up orbit high above the stratosphere, Ei'Brai detected only small numbers of sectilians on both planets in scattered pockets. The populations of both worlds had been decimated.

At this distance they were little more than faint mental signatures. There were a few mind masters who were somewhat stronger, but none who had the range of the kuboderans. He did not detect anyone he had previously connected to, which would have made communication feasible.

He had hoped to be able to use anipraxia to make introductions for the Qua'dux and her crew, but that would not be possible. That could make her journey more perilous. Yet he had faith in her skills and he counseled her to be forthright and straightforward with everyone she might meet. She patiently endured his admonitions, despite the fact that this was her field of expertise. He appreciated her forbearance.

They were prepared as well as could be expected under the circumstances. They would be outfitted with everything that could be thought of to protect them.

It was the things that could not be anticipated that worried him.

5

Jane swallowed a bite of a nutrition square. She'd gathered the others over a meal to discuss their upcoming arrival at Atielle. Jane sat at the head of an oblong table in the vast cafeteria-style room they used as a crew mess. Alan sat on one side with Ajaya and Ron on the other, the two so close to each other their arms occasionally brushed.

Her primary concern was unraveling the issue of the yoke before they left the ship. It was a complex amalgam of devices and software that controlled Ei'Brai, preventing him from moving the vessel without her consent and presence on board. They would be leaving him alone up here, and if something should happen to her, he would be trapped once again, as he had been in their solar system. That wasn't okay with her. She wanted him to have more latitude in a worst-case scenario. Alan had been looking into the issue already, but it was complex and hidden, even from her, for security reasons. She felt she couldn't depart until they found some way to decrease the yoke's power at least somewhat. She asked Alan to make that a priority in the coming days.

They'd already gone over the issues of the breathability of the air on the moon, which wasn't going to be a problem, and the foreign microbes, which they'd all already been exposed to without any negative impact on the *Speroancora*.

They'd deliberated the size of the Sectilius system's star, the fact that it was slightly larger than Earth's, and that Sectilia and Atielle were closer to their star than Earth was to Sol and what that might mean to them while they were planetside.

Ron joked, "But I didn't pack my sunscreen."

They'd also discussed how to handle potential reinfection with the rogue squillae some of them had been affected by when they first boarded this ship, and the safety measures they should take to prevent that problem from recurring. So far all scans for the specific signals squillae emitted were negative. There was no indication that any nanites were extant on Atielle. Given the volumes that would have been in use before the squillae plague, they should have been detectable if still present. That didn't mean they couldn't exist in small pockets, even if someone had managed to obliterate them on a large scale. As a group they worked out how to enact several levels of prevention and control just to be safe, including a small set of nanites, programmed to work defensively, for each individual.

With those details set, it was time to discuss the problem of the weather conditions on Atielle. The conversation was going about like she'd imagined it would.

"The entire planet is having a monsoon season? You're sure about this?" Alan asked incredulously, the food in his hand seemingly forgotten.

Ron frowned. "How's that even possible?"

Ajaya put down a food cube she'd been about to nibble on. "Surely there is some kind of temperate zone where we can touch down and travel overland?"

Jane sighed. "Unfortunately, no. Atielle is small, about one-third the mass of Earth, though its surface area is roughly twice that of our moon. It's orbiting Sectilia, which is a much bigger planet than we—"

"We'd call it a Super-Earth," Alan said and put down his food like he'd lost his appetite.

Jane nodded. "I think so. Its mass is nearly nine times the mass of Earth. Its gravity is greater—"

"Yes, but its gravity isn't nine times the gravity of Earth!" Alan interjected.

Jane raised a hand to forestall further comment so she could finish a thought. "True. The gravity of Sectilia is just under one and a half g." She'd found that a bit odd until Ei'Brai showed her how planetary density and radius worked to create surface gravity. The concept didn't seem to stump anyone at this table, so she went on. "Atielle's orbit is closer to Sectilia than our own moon's is to Earth. And there are three other moons which exert some gravitational force on it seasonally, as their orbits converge in proximity—this pressure and friction leads to a lot of volcanic activity. There is sporadic volcanic venting which creates uneven heating. The atmosphere destabilizes as hot and cold pockets of air continually collide—this results in a monsoon season that lasts for months."

"Without breaks?" Ajaya asked.

"The breaks in weather are very short windows and unpredictable. Minutes or hours," Jane replied.

Alan shook his head and blew out a heavy breath. "Jesus."

No one was questioning her choice to go to Atielle first, rather than Sectilia. That was good. Her official reason for going to the moon was to pay respect to the descendants of the former Quasador Dux and to have a soft introduction to the culture without a lot of pressure.

The real reason driving her there was more amorphous than that. Rageth Elia Hator was in her head. She had this woman's memories, put there by Ei'Brai along with a command-and-control engram set that connected her to him and the ship. He'd done this when he'd selected her from among her crewmates for the position of Qua'dux. It was a way of transferring power and wisdom that went deep into the cultural construct of ship life, so very different from life planetside. The average sectilian would never experience anything like this. It was a special gift bestowed upon a select few.

Rageth's memories were filled with sentiment and a strong sense of home. It was like a beacon calling her there. She'd tried resisting it, but whenever her thoughts turned to landing near the capital city on Sectilia some intuition told her no, that was the wrong choice. She had to go to the moon where she would be surrounded by people she could trust. It didn't make a lot of sense, but she'd learned long ago that she shouldn't ignore her intuition when it spoke that strongly. So far Rageth had never steered her wrong. These things, like many of the things that involved Ei'Brai, would be hard to articulate in a way that the others could understand, so she was glad she didn't have to try to just now.

If they did decide to visit the larger planet, they'd have no choice but to go in power armor. Adjusting to that kind of gravity for any duration would be exhausting—it would effectively increase their weight by roughly forty percent and create tremendous pressure on their joints and muscles.

It was a painful process every atellan who moved to Sectilia transitioned through slowly and with a lot of additional conditioning, both biochemical and physical training over time. It wasn't something to be taken lightly.

She and her crew couldn't present a strong first impression if they were fighting debilitating fatigue the entire time. They'd do it if they had to, but she hoped they'd get the answers they needed on Atielle.

Their mission was to return Ei'Brai to his people and tell them what they'd gleaned about the nanites, though she assumed the Sectilius already knew these things by now. After seventy years it seemed likely that the Sectilius had long since begun some kind of rescue operation for the stranded kuboderans and were in the process of rebuilding their fleet. Another ship would likely be a boon. The rogue nanites were probably just a memory by now, a problem long since solved, but they wouldn't know until they got there.

Ron leaned back in his chair and put his hands behind his head. "It is what it is. How do you want to proceed, QD?"

※

Jane strapped herself into the generously sized pilot's seat in the shuttle. She forced herself to take a deep breath, blew it out slowly, then glanced at Ron in the seat next to her. The air was a comfortable temperature, but she felt clammy from cooled perspiration. She wished she could just skip landing the shuttle and go straight to the part where she got to meet sectilians.

She wasn't a pilot. Ron, and even Alan, had undergone far more training in that department as part of preparations for the original mission to the Target. However, Ei'Brai had placed that engram set inside Jane's head, a set of skills, memories, and blueprints that theoretically included everything she needed to know to pilot this vessel. It made her the most qualified.

Jane had chosen Ron as her copilot because he had logged more real flight hours than the other two—back on Earth, in *Speroancora* shuttle simulations, and actual practice flight. Behind them, Alan and Ajaya silently strapped themselves in to the one-size-fits-most seats, both trained to step in, if necessary. The four of them had pored over the schematics. They had gone over every control together and had done a few practice runs in this shuttle, between jumps, throughout the cross-galaxy journey.

Those forays had helped Jane cement the connections between the alien memories and the implanted engram. Once the shuttle was moving, she found herself making automatic choices—much like driving a car back on Earth. That had put her mind at ease to an extent. She hoped her instincts would work equally well in an environment with gravity, atmosphere, and plenty of rain.

Ron quirked an eyebrow at her, and his lips turned up in a reassuring smile. He'd be right there as her backup, to help her monitor everything, ready to catch her if she fell. "You ready for this, QD?" he asked, grinning like a kid on Christmas morning.

Jane grimaced at Ron. "Ready."

Ron guffawed at her expression. Jane glanced back at Alan and Ajaya. Alan was nodding his head at her and Ajaya was double-checking her gear.

Ron's expression grew more serious. "All right, then. Preflight checks are complete. Let's do this thing." He reached out and flipped a switch that began the process of starting the engines.

Jane nodded and began her part of the process. She spoke aloud, because that seemed right. "Gubernaviti Ei'Brai, terminate synthetic gravity in chamber 245 and open the cargo door."

She felt the gravity go, and the door lifted. Before them a new world curved away with a halo of blue and gold at the horizon. It gave way to black space, pricked with millions of dots of light in a denser arrangement than she'd ever seen. They were no longer in the spiral arm of the Milky Way galaxy, looking at the flat disk from the edge on, as one would on Earth. They were closer to the galactic core, where the stars clustered together. These stars seemed larger, more luminous—and there were many more of them.

The tables had turned. She was the alien visitor in someone else's system now. She hoped the Sectilius hadn't developed xenophobic tendencies since the squillae catastrophe.

She eased the craft forward, moving it clear of the *Speroancora*, and swiveled the shuttle to face its parent ship. Atielle tumbled under them and Sectilia loomed large and distant in the background. The *Speroancora* looked right here against the blue-and-green world feathered with wisps of white cloud cover.

Swooping translucent structures slid over *Speroancora's* hull, resembling fins gleaming in the light of her home system. The immense ship looked more like a sea creature than it ever had before—an artistic homage to the gubernaviti within.

And deep inside that ship, Ei'Brai looked upon it with her, through her eyes.

Remove the terror of the unknown, give a thing meaning, call it home, and you can see all the grace inherent in it.

Her eyes felt full. She looked up and blinked, hoping the tears wouldn't spill down her cheeks.

She had needed to see the ship this way. It seemed likely that the next time she went aboard, she'd be a guest. The Sectilius would reclaim their wayward vessel and from here on out, the humans would be at their mercy. Jane's short time as Quasador Dux would conclude. She was surprised to realize she didn't want that. The *Speroancora* was starting to feel like home.

She glanced at Ron. He looked as dazzled as she felt. "She's a beaut, QD. No doubt about that. It's the right thing to give her back, but damn, I sure wish we could keep her." He looked down at the controls in front of him, and she returned to the matter at hand. Descent.

It might be a simple matter on other worlds, but not here, not now. Atielle's atmosphere was teeming with fragments of broken-up ships and satellites. Over the decades, derelicts the size of *Speroancora* or larger must have collided with each other or natural and artificial satellites, creating a self-perpetuating cycle. Now these billions of pieces were in slowly decaying orbits. It was a three-dimensional minefield, replete with torrential rain and excessive wind gusts—not simple at all. And all of the navigation satellites had been destroyed by the debris cloud. There would be no autopilot on this descent.

Jane laid her hands over the controls and engaged the flight path Ei'Brai had planned to skirt the largest obstacles. He had analyzed the weather patterns to determine the safest time to descend through the troposphere. They had a narrow window between thunderstorms, and sitting here gaping at the ship was wasting those precious minutes.

They approached on the night side of the moon, near their preferred landing site. They'd stood by, waiting for a break in the weather for some time. It was nearly dawn in that location on the surface. Jane was glad they'd been able to approach early in the day.

Atielle grew in size, and they dropped through the outermost layers of the atmosphere without incident. There was no air resistance at this distance and there was only a momentary spike on the shuttle's instrumentation as they punched through the magnetosphere.

As they passed through the thermosphere, Jane saw a few orbital satellites at a distance. She wondered if any of them were still functional. Had the Sectilius detected their arrival? Would someone meet them on the surface at the landing site near the Hator compound? Some of these satellites had been part of a defense grid, but as they were in a sectilian vehicle, they had nothing to fear from them, even if the defense drones were still active.

As they approached the mesosphere the external air pressure began to rise. They'd be hitting denser air soon and would need to reduce velocity so they could deploy the wings.

"All systems ready, QD," Ron stated.

"Engaging reverse thrust," Jane said and set a timer to fire the forward thrusters.

"Fifteen-point-four vastuumet per aepar, and slowing…" Ron called out.

Ron reached out to key the deployment of the wings. It was time to convert from a space vehicle to an aeronautical vehicle. Jane moved her feet into position to use the new controls that would be needed. The shuttle vibrated as the wings extended, then reverberated with a loud thunk as they snapped into place.

Alan was up, peering through a small window. "I have a visual on port wings," he announced, sounding like a kid in a candy store. She heard him cross to the other side. "And starboard. Wings have deployed."

"Thank you, Alan," Jane said, with a slight smile. She'd already checked them herself with cameras mounted to the outside of the ship for that purpose, but she knew he wanted to not only see it for himself, but to contribute. "Strap in. This is going to be a bumpy ride."

"Roger that," he answered. There was a loud snap as he refastened himself in.

The shuttle's handling changed as its flight surfaces bit into the thickening air. A faint glow built as the craft's thermal shielding dissipated heat caused by friction with the atmosphere. She still couldn't see the surface. The dense cloud cover of the underlying layers of atmosphere far beneath them blocked her view. Ei'Brai monitored the weather conditions between them and the ground in real time, streaming that information to Jane and Ron.

"Tropospheric conditions are rapidly changing now. There is some rotation developing, Qua'dux," Ei'Brai intoned.

"Damn it," she muttered.

Ron sent her a sharp look. "This could get rough. We can make it, but it's up to you. Should we abort, QD?"

From the back Alan voiced, "What's wrong?"

44

Jane frowned and ignored him as she tapped a control to bring up more information about the storm from the shuttle's sensors. Alan had been letting Ei'Brai in a little more lately, from time to time, but still didn't want to link with him and the network consistently. She heard Ajaya patiently explain to him about the weather.

Dark and ominous clouds flowed in swirls below them. Here and there flashes of lightning crackled as the storm gained some steam. Weather on Atielle was chaotic. Based on Jane's imprinted knowledge, this storm wouldn't stop a sectilian from completing the descent. The shuttle was built for this. These same types of shuttles would have routinely passed between Sectilia and Atielle for transportation and trade no matter the moon's weather.

But she wasn't sectilian and she didn't have any experience piloting through this mess. It made her nervous.

Ron heard that thought and turned to her to address it aloud. "That's all true, but we could wait weeks and still not see a better opportunity than this unless we decide to wait four months for the dry season to start."

She sensed Ron's eagerness to get on with it. Ei'Brai and Ajaya echoed the same sentiment to varying degrees. They were right. She was going to have to do this or wait for months, twiddling her thumbs.

"Okay, then. Here we go," she said, and gritted her teeth. She searched for the spot with the thinnest cover. She set a trajectory for a thirty-degree descent through that location. Ei'Brai confirmed her flight plan with minor changes. Jane adjusted the controls to reflect his suggestions and locked it in.

They descended through a layer of wispy, white, vertically trailing tendrils.

"Noctilucent clouds, maybe?" Alan mused from the rear.

No one answered him.

The layer of storm clouds was coming at them rapidly. Her fingers tightened on the control wheel. She just had to follow the flight path.

Some great distance away, a red plume shot up from the gray clouds and lingered for a few moments before fading.

Ron's jaw was bulging with tension when she glanced at him. "That was a sprite," he said, and she noticed his dark fingers clench and unclench before he reached out to tap another monitor. "It's a form of lightning that goes up instead of down." Several more sprites popped up around it, leaving what almost looked like jagged red streaks of paint that rapidly faded away.

"It's lovely," Ajaya murmured from the back. No one else spoke. Jane thought it was lovely too, but it also looked dangerous.

The air around the vehicle grew misty. A red ring popped up out of the clouds in front of them, and a second later another column of glowing red light shot up from the center of it, directly in their flight path.

Jane instinctively jerked on the control wheel to avoid flying through it. She wasn't fast enough. Red plasma flowed over the shuttle in a crackling wave of light and electricity. Every light and screen inside the shuttle went dark.

A meager amount of illumination came in from the windows, primarily from the unearthly orange-red glow of the heat shielding. The interior of the shuttle was dimly outlined in black and white.

She could hear her own jagged breathing dragging painfully through her throat. Cold panic flooded her body.

They were tumbling through the atmosphere of an alien
planet with no control over the vehicle.

The interior lights came on a split second later. Then the dashboard lights and monitors lit up. The shuttle shuddered.

Jane struggled to determine how far off course they'd gotten. She had to re-establish their flight path.

"Everything's back online. All systems nominal," Ron reassured her. His hands danced over his side of the dashboard. "On Earth aircraft are made to tolerate lightning strikes. This shuttle can handle them too. It was made to react this way. We're fine. You got this."

She was too busy to reply.

A proximity sensor began to alarm. They'd gone too far off their safe route. Something was close. Too close.

Before she could assess the object's trajectory and move evasively, something collided with a loud thud against the underside of the shuttle then skittered off to clip the port wing. The ship bucked.

The controls became jerky under Jane's hands. She activated a stabilizing subroutine meant to compensate for wing damage. It didn't do much. They'd gone into a wobbly spiral.

Ron's voice raised in intensity. She could see in her peripheral vision that he was leaning forward against the straps, all his concentration on readouts and controls. "Damn. We've just lost the starboard engine, but we're okay. We're okay."

Losing an engine was not okay, but they could land with only one. Engines weren't necessary for landing. The real concern was how they were going to get back to the *Speroancora* at the end of this visit to Atielle.

Jane gritted her teeth and struggled to get the ship back on course. "Keep an eye on the proximity sensor," she told him. "The storm must be flinging some debris at high velocity. It's more dangerous than we anticipated."

She activated an external camera and had it zoom in on the damage on the underside of the craft. The debris had punctured the fuselage at the point of the starboard engine, destroying it, and left a trail of destruction in a jagged line across the vehicle before striking the port wing. There was a chance the portside engine had taken some damage too. That would be bad. Very, very bad. How would they get back to the *Speroancora*?

She realized dimly that Alan had joined the anipraxic network. She saw his intent and heard the clack as he released his harness.

"I have a visual on the port wing!" he yelled. "We've lost about a quarter of it. It's hanging on and flapping around, creating drag."

"Alan, sit down and buckle in!" Jane shouted. "It's not safe!"

Ei'Brai sent her a new flight plan that changed their course. Their present heading would take them into a hailstorm that had just formed. The shortest route to leave the hail behind required a turn. She eased into it.

The controls were sluggish to respond.

They hit a patch of turbulence in the beginning of the turn. There was a short shout that was cut off by a heavy thud behind Jane's head. There was no time to check on her passengers.

A flashing red light and loud beeping recaptured her attention. It was the portside engine's heat sensor. The object they'd hit earlier must have damaged the thermal shielding just under the port engine. It was getting too hot. The temperature already exceeded safe levels and was rising rapidly. "Engaging fire-suppressant mechanism on the port engine!" Jane yelled.

Instantly they were engulfed in gray clouds.

The cabin was filled with the sounds of air buffeting the craft. An updraft rocked them to starboard. Jane scrambled to make adjustments and keep control. Her heart pounded as her body shifted, the harness biting into her shoulders, hips, and pubic bone.

Hail began to pelt the craft. Visibility quickly became poor. She tried to get another look at the underside of the shuttle, but the camera was already covered in ice.

Time slowed down.

"Shit!" Ron yelled.

Jane hovered over the dashboard, watching the temperature spike in the portside engine, despite the fire suppressant. The mechanism must have been damaged by the hit they'd taken. Then the engine went critical.

"The portside engine is on fire!" she yelled to Ron.

A glance at Ron revealed him frantically checking readouts and adjusting controls, his eyes wide. He turned to her. "It's gonna blow!"

She hesitated for a moment, and in that moment Ei'Brai urged her, "You must."

Another gust rocked the craft. The shuttle vibrated so hard it knocked her teeth together painfully.

She flipped open a panel and turned the knob inside until it clicked into place. That released the latch on a second, recessed panel. She flipped that open. Multiple alerts from various systems screamed in competition for her attention. Inside this deeper compartment were two handles, separated by a handsbreadth. She hooked her thumb around one and her middle finger around the other and squeezed.

It barely budged. She wasn't strong enough.

Good God, they were about to blow up.

Her hands weren't as large as a sectilian's or atellan's. She released the restraining straps of her harness and lunged at the dashboard in a single flowing movement, wrapped both hands around the release mechanism for the engine. She squeezed, bringing the two handles together with a click she felt rather than heard over the chaos. She pulled on the joined handles with everything she had. The craft bucked under her. She fell to the floor.

The shuttle went into a wild roll. Without the safety harness, she tumbled from one surface to the next along with the vehicle. She curled into a ball as her elbows and knees whomped painfully into the ceiling.

She reached out for Ron as she fell past him. His strong arms grabbed onto her and stopped her ungainly summersaults. With his help she was able to grab a strap of her harness and pull herself into the seat as the ship continued to career out of control.

There was a roaring in her ears. As soon as she stabilized herself, she reached for the starboard engine release. The shuttle thundered around her. The starboard engine wasn't functional, and the weight imbalance would make it impossible to glide to the surface. They were going to crash if she didn't release it.

Thankfully this release was just a few inches closer than the other one had been. She grasped the handles together and pulled. They came out of the tailspin, though they were upside-down and diving at a seventy-degree angle toward the ground.

Pea-sized hail pelted the windscreen.

The control wheel was stiff under her hands. "Come on!" she screamed, pulling back with all her strength. "Ron—fire reverse thrust in one-second bursts. We have to change our attitude."

"Firing!" Ron answered. The ship bucked with each burst. The small boosters in the bow weren't meant to be used at this altitude, but they were able to reorient the ship.

Jane regained control and returned them to a glide. She immediately put them into an S-pattern to control the speed of their descent.

Her heart thudded and she gulped air like a drowning man. They were safe for the moment, but she couldn't let go of the panic. "Scan for atmospheric debris." She tried to sound calm, but there was a sharpness in her voice. Her hands started to shake. She ignored that.

"I'm not picking anything up, but I think the hail is probably interfering with the scan," Ron replied.

Alan's voice came echoing from the rear compartment, harsh and ragged. "That's the least of our worries. There's ice forming on the port wing. It's rapidly turning into a brick. Bricks don't fly." She sensed him move, slowly, like he was hurt, to the other side of the small cabin. "Same to starboard."

Jane heard Ajaya speaking to Alan in hushed tones. Hopefully she was administering any first aid that was needed.

Ei'Brai was plotting a new course.

"We're losing altitude fast," Ron called out.

Jane pulled back on the control wheel. It had little effect. She concentrated all of her efforts on changing course by minute increments in order to move out of the hail. "I see that. Why aren't the wing deicers working?" she yelled. The windscreen was rapidly losing visibility.

She heard a click from the rear. Berg was buckling himself back in. "Because they cycled the deicing fluid through the engines to gain heat. For all we know, it's watering the atmosphere."

Jane knew that was wrong. There was a valve in the line to keep the deicing fluid contained in an emergency engine-ejection situation, but she had momentarily forgotten about the heat gain from the engines.

Ron called out, "I'm trying something now. Might help. Marginally." His fingers danced over the controls. He turned to her. "We're going to have to come in a little bit faster than you'll want to, QD."

Instinct told her that he was right. She nodded. Her fingers clenched the control wheel so tightly her fingertips blanched.

They broke through the clouds. It was raining and well above freezing at this altitude. The first rays of light were creeping up on a gray horizon framed by steaming calderas, smoking peaks and rugged, rock-strewn valleys. She stared at the unfamiliar terrain laid out before her with a gnawing sense of disquiet growing in her stomach.

Suddenly it hit her, and she cried out, "We are so far off course I don't know where I'm going to land! We'll never make it to that airstrip!"

"Just stay out of mountains, trees, and populated areas!" Bergen yelled.

"What a great idea! I never would have thought of that without your help!" she yelled back, swallowing a hysterical laugh at the insane predicament they were in.

She was flying on sensors alone. She stared at the screen that showed a three-dimensional representation of the landscape rapidly surging up to meet them.

Jane clamped her jaw tight. The entire shuttle was shaking violently.

She glanced up. The windscreen was awash with rain. The ice had nearly melted, but visibility hadn't improved much because the rain was torrential.

A thermal lifted them a few thousand feet, which gave her a few extra moments of breathing room, the first stroke of luck they'd had yet. She allowed herself to breathe again.

"Okay, QD," Ron said gently inside her head, "I'm here to help you any way I can. You're doing great. Let's put this thing down."

Ei'Brai reached out and extended his own calming presence, as well as access to all of his knowledge of Atielle's terrain from the ship's computers.

She didn't have time to worry anymore. She had to do it. The ship was more responsive now, and for the moment, the rain had let up. Only a few small drops beaded up and streaked over the windscreen from the force of the airflow.

She felt Alan and Ajaya join her to lend their support and focus, eyes and ears. It was not distracting or discordant. It helped. It steadied her. Instinctively they formed a silent pact to do what they could to assist in their own survival. All of their attention as a group was centered on that same goal, and not a single stray thought encroached on that primal focus.

The landscape looked remarkably Earthlike from this altitude. It was mountainous and rocky but there were patches that were lush and green.

There were hundreds of miles of terrain to choose from in every direction. Out of all of the possible places to land the craft, the best site came quickly and easily to her. Jane selected a long, wide, marshy valley to cushion their fall. She did not ask for anyone's approval, yet it seemed as though everyone agreed it was the best spot.

She took a turn around the valley to assess it from every angle, then went in for the final descent.

Ron triggered the sledlike landing gear to deploy under the craft.

The ship vibrated as she pushed the nose down to lose altitude and at the last second pulled it up again to allow the rear of the craft to touch down first.

Silently Ajaya admonished them all to stay relaxed, to not tense up.

Jane did her best to comply. She held her breath.

Jane rocked in her seat, teeth knocking together hard, brain ricocheting inside her skull, spine ramming into the seat cushion, as they slid violently across the valley floor.

Mud and vegetation flew up over the windscreen. The craft spun a quarter turn. They jerked hard against their harnesses and the shuttle nearly tipped over on its side as it came to a sudden stop.

They were still.

Jane sat there panting with her eyes closed. Her fingertips tingled. Her body was heavy despite the low gravity on this moon. She didn't want to move. She felt nauseated and cold. Her hands were trembling so she laid her palms over her knees and just breathed.

Ajaya was the first to speak. Her voice seemed distant to Jane. She said, "Is anyone hurt?"

Ron rubbed his hands over his face and replied, "I'm cool." He unlatched himself and stood up, bouncing on the balls of his feet, probably testing the feeling of the gravity. "Hoo-wee! That was some ride!"

Jane stared at him blankly and swallowed hard. Her stomach was churning. She was afraid to move for fear it would erupt.

"You okay, QD?" he asked. "You look a little pale."

Her tongue was dry in her mouth. She was afraid to open it. She nodded once and that little bit of jiggling cost her. Bile rose in her throat.

He patted her knee and moved toward the rear compartment in long, hopping strides. Jane closed her eyes.

"Can you give me a hand, Ronald?" Ajaya asked.

"Yes, ma'am," he answered. "Oh, shit."

Jane heard a sharp intake of breath. That was Alan. It was enough to rouse her from her stupor. She numbly unlatched herself and rose, swallowing convulsively. She was dizzy. Her eyes were rolling around. With effort, she focused on her three companions.

Alan was arching his back, grimacing in pain. Ajaya and Ron were helping him. His leg...

Jane bounded to the hatch and slammed her hand on the open symbol. It responded instantly. She felt like she was dreaming. The gravity was light, barely pulling on her, and everything around her was a swirling blur. Momentum kept her moving forward and she started to fall through. She scrabbled at the hatch for something to hold onto, breaking nails, scraping the skin of her hand raw, and finally caught herself as she fell to her knees, half in, half outside on the gangway.

She couldn't hold it back any longer. She heaved up the contents of her stomach. When she was finally able to stop, she stayed there with her face against the cold metal of the gangway, gulping air and struggling not to sob.

"Oh, God," she groaned and pushed herself back up on her knees. She brushed tendrils of hair from her face, worked up some saliva and spit, then wiped her mouth on her shoulder.

Her heart was beating out a slow heavy thud in her chest. *Alan.*

She staggered to her feet.

Inside, Ajaya had efficiently turned one of the crash seats into a makeshift examination table by activating its sleep mode and jacking the whole thing up as high as it would go. She had found a place to hang a high-powered lamp which was focused now on the messy juncture between what was left of Alan's leg and his cybernetic implant. Ron stood nearby, handing her things.

Alan twitched and gritted out, "Jesus! Holy mother of…" He trailed off into incoherency and bit his lip. His skin was pale. His shoulders trembled.

"One more moment and I'll have the bleeding under control. Bear with me, please," Ajaya said soothingly to him as she bent over him with a sectilian triage kit. She'd been studying sectilian medical technology and had become quite proficient with it.

Instinct pulled Jane forward. It had been foolish to indulge in a moment of weakness when Alan needed her.

"Do not come any closer." Ajaya spoke softly, but authority rang clear in her voice. "I have a very small sterile field here. We cannot risk contamination of the wound."

Jane swayed, and a stab of guilt hit her like a gut punch.

Alan's hands were balled into pale fists. His voice ground like glass. "Son of a—" He inhaled with a hiss and slammed one of his fists into the seat beneath him. "Damn it, Ajaya, hook up the filaments and let them do their fucking job!"

"Nearly there. I'm packing the wound with gel now." Ajaya straightened and turned. Her eyes swept over Jane but landed on Ron. "Ronald, if you'd be so kind?"

Ron moved to Ajaya's side, and together they eased the synthetic limb back into position. Immediately she could hear it hissing and whirring. It made a sound that might have been a vacuum pump engaging. Jane remained by the open hatch, feeling foolish.

Alan relaxed before her eyes. His shoulders sank back to the chair. His hands unclenched. His head rocked back and forth. "Aw, yeah. That's the good stuff."

Ajaya laid her hand on his brow. "Stay put. Let's let this machinery do its work."

His voice was full of relief. "Yes, ma'am." His head flopped to the side to look over at Jane. "Sorry about the horror show. Didn't know you were squeamish."

She shook her head. Her mouth tasted foul. "I'm not. I guess...just..."

"A word, Commander?" Ajaya said from her side.

"Of course," Jane answered. She followed Ajaya and tried not to drag her feet. Her head was clearing but she felt a little weak. She really wanted to sit down and let her blood pressure equalize.

When they got to the rear of the shuttle, Ajaya turned, worry pulling on her delicate features. "Are you ill? What just happened?"

Jane hung her head. "No. I don't know. It was just...a lot. I'm just a linguist."

Ajaya continued to scan Jane's face until she seemed satisfied that it was nothing serious, then nodded and turned to grab a fresh flight suit and a packet of wipes out of a protruding compartment. "You should get cleaned up."

Jane took the things from Ajaya gratefully. The wipes felt cool and soothing as she swabbed her face and hands with them. The blood was rushing back to her head—in particular to her face, which now felt hot and was probably red. She was acutely embarrassed at her reaction.

Everyone probably thought it was because of Alan's leg, but it wasn't. It was because she felt like she'd narrowly avoided killing them all. Sure, she'd trained extensively for all of this and she knew how to handle herself in a crisis, but that had been the closest she'd ever come to death, and the thought that she might have taken all of them with her while she crashed and burned was overwhelming.

Vomiting was particularly humiliating and wasn't something she'd done often. As she eased out of the flight suit and drew on the fresh one, she saw that Ron and Ajaya were carefully cleaning up Alan's blood, which had splattered all over the inside of the craft. A memory surfaced of the time, at the age of ten, that she'd first gone to live with her grandparents in Minnesota, the day when they had driven her mother to the airport to see her off on a journey. The drive was hours long. Jane had been gutted over her mother's departure and coped by losing herself in a book. She had dived so deeply into the story, she hadn't noticed the discomfort of car sickness rising until it was too late. She had begged her grandfather to stop the car, but he couldn't or wouldn't in time. The mess she'd made that day resulted in her first taste of her grandfather's rage. It hadn't been the last.

She tried to mentally shrug away the image of a sad, lonely little girl who'd lost everything and everyone she'd ever loved sitting on an icy sidewalk at a rest stop in rural Minnesota, hugging herself and crying while the grandmother she barely knew used piles of brown paper towels from the restrooms to wipe out the car, followed by scoops of snow to try to scrub it clean. Her grandfather's face had been beet red and shining in the bright sunlight bouncing off the snow. The remainder of that drive had been long, wet, and cold—and not all of that coldness had been temperature related.

But she was warm and dry now and no one was angry with her.

The trauma of landing the craft had led her to lose her lunch. That was mortifying, but not too strange considering the circumstances. She hoped to never repeat anything like that landing ever again.

Jane glanced at Ajaya and Ron as she pulled on her boots, catching a long, lingering look pass between them. Jane's eyes widened for a half second before she forced herself to look away. Ron and Ajaya had been spending a lot of time together and clearly were getting more friendly. Shared extreme experiences had a way of bringing people closer together. It was natural. It was also none of her business. They were keeping whatever was going on private and she didn't blame them.

Ei'Brai caught the thread of her thoughts and was instantly alert and probing. She sensed him skimming Ajaya's and Ron's minds and pushed him back a bit so she wouldn't breach their privacy. Ei'Brai was intensely curious about human interaction, which was natural, given the circumstances. However, she was, at times, uncomfortable with the voyeuristic nature of his personality. She understood it—he was confined and forced into involuntary solitude. They were still working out how to navigate that.

She moved back toward the front of the craft. Ron and Ajaya were finishing up the cleaning and Alan was lying there with his eyes closed. She felt foolish. Ron gestured for her to join him as he took a seat on the gangway, arms and legs sprawling out. "If you're feeling bad about what happened, don't," he said.

She eased down next to him, trying not to bounce as she settled onto the deck. "Why? Is that something pilots do after a rough landing?"

He glanced her way, eyebrows raised, a hint of a smile twitching on his lips. "No. Not really."

"We're alive," she said and held out her hands in a helpless shrug. "At least we're alive."

"Word," Ron said. "You did the best you could under terrible conditions. None of us could have done any better. Just keep that detail in mind. Don't be too hard on yourself."

"I'll try." They were in a bad way now. Without engines they couldn't move the shuttle to their destination or back to the *Speroancora*. They'd have to cross to the nearest settlement on foot and ask for help. It wasn't an ideal first-contact scenario. And she couldn't forget what she knew of Atielle—that the nepatrox that had plagued them aboard ship dominated this world, allowing the sectilians to carve out a survival existence in small colonies. Traveling out in the open overland, not knowing the terrain, would be very dangerous.

She looked out at the landscape. It was a new world, never before seen by human eyes. She was ready to see something beautiful, astonishing—she was ready to be rewarded for the harrowing ordeal behind them and the one that was likely to come.

She saw…stagnant muck, choked with straggly water plants. She smelled decay and foul odors tinged with sulfur and metal. The acrid tang of bile still lingered on the back of her tongue. She wanted some water but was afraid to put anything in her stomach just yet.

It was hot—at least ninety-five degrees Fahrenheit and very humid—the air felt thick and heavy, which seemed odd juxtaposed against the light gravity. The sky was dark and overcast. The rain they'd just been outrunning was on its way. Below her right knee, she heard a deep, sucking burble and a muffled splash as the marsh belched up some kind of gas.

A deep sigh filled her lungs with that funk, and she let it out with a trace of a bewildered laugh. She leaned against the side of the hatch and chuckled. She tried to contain herself. She pressed her lips together in a line but the mirth exploded from her suddenly. She laughed so hard she started to feel weak. Tears traced down her cheeks. She doubled over and just let it out. It didn't make sense, but it didn't have to. It was a release.

Behind her, Ajaya hovered over Alan, taking his blood pressure, ignoring her laughter.

Alan grumbled, "What's so funny?"

Jane pulled the sleeves of her suit over her hands and wiped her face. "We're alive."

Alan grunted.

Ron patted her arm like he wasn't sure what else to do. "What's next, QD?"

8

Bergen frowned and watched Ajaya tidying up inside the shuttle. She was taking her time and being methodical about it and he knew why. It was more than just keeping things orderly.

It kept her mind off of Ron and Jane traipsing through the swamp by themselves, where they would face God only knew what—not to mention the mind-numbing boredom he and Ajaya were about to endure until the two returned, hopefully with help and at least one of the engines for him to repair. That was assuming that the airbags that protected the engines after release had inflated properly, that their location beacons were functional, that they'd be repairable, and that he'd be in any kind of condition to execute those repairs.

As it was, the cybernetic limb was releasing a freaking lot of happy juice into his leg while it regrew and repaired the connections between its components and the synapses and sinews of what was left of his leg. Some of that joy juice was getting into his bloodstream. He was feeling a bit weird. He didn't like it. Slowly turning into Darth Vader was not all it was cracked up to be.

"How long do you think we'll last before we go fucking nuts?" he asked Ajaya, and threw his arm over his face to block out most of the pale light streaming in through the windscreen and side windows. He wasn't tired, but he was thinking about sleeping anyway. The drugs would make it easy. It would pass the time.

Ajaya sidled up to him. "We," she announced, "are not going to go 'fucking nuts.' *We* are going to stay busy."

"Speak for yourself, sister," he grumbled. "I didn't bring my needlepoint. In case you forgot, you yourself ordered me to stay flat on my back until my leg is healed."

"You're very funny," she quipped, but there wasn't any humor in her statement. "There's plenty we can do to keep our minds occupied at the very least. Why are you so morose?"

"Really? You're really asking me that?" He peeked out at her from under his arm.

"I am," she said archly and leaned against the back of the bucket seat next to his.

He didn't reply.

"You know," she said, "you should have more faith."

He snorted.

She looked very prim. "Six of us left Earth. We went farther than any human had ever gone before. We explored a vessel from another part of the galaxy, and despite the hostile environment, all six of us survived."

"Oh, am I getting a lecture now?" he asked.

"Indeed you are," she replied.

He huffed. "Great."

She went on, "Jane was chosen to lead us across the galaxy and though it was difficult for her, she was able to make that journey happen seemingly through sheer force of will. Then she piloted a shuttle through reentry onto an alien world under brutal conditions—something she had no experience doing—and yet everyone on board survived again." Ajaya paused. "Alan, Jane is resourceful, capable, and extremely intelligent. I have every faith that she'll be back in no time with a solution to this problem."

"Are you done?"

"Yes, I believe I am," she said pertly then busied herself with something.

Ajaya's words rang in his ears. They were all true. But he couldn't voice his actual thoughts and fears: that eventually Jane's luck would run out and they'd either die with her or be stranded and at the mercy of either the Sectilius or the Squid. He didn't know which would be worse. He was glad his arm still partially covered his face so Ajaya couldn't see the emotions warring for control of it.

"I'm going to take a nap," he said, his voice thick and pinched.

Ajaya squeezed his shoulder and returned to work. "Okay," she said softly. "And when you wake up, you will connect with Ei'Brai and begin to study everything you need to know about the engines to be able to repair them."

He'd already studied those engines extensively, but it was a good idea. He was bound to learn all kinds of things. And if he connected with the Squid, he'd be connected to Jane too. He'd know in real time how things were going with her. Except he wasn't sure if he wanted that. What if something happened to her while he was forced to sit and watch, powerless to help? *Again*? The whole thing was fucking nuts.

He felt like Rapunzel, stuck up in her tower waiting for her stupid macho knight to ride up on his stupid horse and rescue her. Her *and* her ridiculous long-ass hair. Fucking

Rapunzel. She'd probably had a bum leg too. That chick needed to get a buzz cut, grow a pair, and start taking care of business.

"Did you hear me, Alan?"

Alan shut his eyes and ground his arm over them to blot out more light. "Oh, I will, will I?" he challenged, just because.

"Yes. Jane left me in charge."

He sighed.

9

"Do you think they'll send anyone to investigate the crash site? If anyone was awake when we landed, they would have seen a bright orange streak in the sky, right?" Jane asked Ron and passed him the pouch of water they'd been sharing.

Ron squinted at the horizon between the two low mountain peaks ahead of them before squirting a swallow into his open mouth. "Sure hope so." He scratched his head. "Of course, they might have just thought it was space junk burning up in the atmosphere. They probably get a lot of that."

"True." Her boot stuck momentarily, held down by suction. She jerked it loose and bounded forward with a splash, nearly toppling face first into the muck before she caught her balance. She was still adjusting to moving in the lower gravity.

Her boots were laced tightly to her ankles and legs, but seconds into their trek, her socks had been soaked, and her toes felt wrinkly. Silty sludge had seeped in through the tops of the boots and lacings. Her toes squelched with every step. She was hot and sweaty already.

There were wide swathes of dense, tall grasses, very green, throughout the marsh. They seemed almost like archipelagos in a shallow sea. But trying to walk over or through them was more difficult than sticking to the watery areas, dotted with scummy-looking algae and leafy plants resting on the surface.

Despite the fact that they could cover more ground with each step due to the lower gravity, fatigue was building up. There was nowhere to rest out here. They had to make it to higher ground before they could stop. The sun was hidden behind the clouds and it had been raining lightly for a while, but it was still uncomfortably hot. "Any idea how much farther to the settlement?"

He glanced at a sectilian instrument in his hand. "In sectilian or human measurement?"

"Human," she replied.

He looked like he was converting in his head. "Just over four hours at this rate." He stopped suddenly and pointed. "Hey, I think I just saw a fish!"

Jane looked where he was pointing but saw nothing. "Could something actually live in this environment?"

"Stranger things have happened," he said and resumed his springy forward motion.

She silently agreed.

For the millionth time she wondered why no one had answered their hails. Could an entire civilization collapse in such a short time? Someone had survived the genocide, but would it be primitives that greeted them? Could all remnants of their advanced civilization have been lost in the last seventy years? And what would she do if that was what she found?

Ei'Brai was with her, but quiet. He didn't have any answers. *I continue to hail,* he said, *in hopes that they do monitor intermittently.*

"Mud skippers," Ron said.

Jane peered at him quizzically.

"Mud skippers could live in this kind of environment, I think. They're some kind of fish-reptile-like animal. I think they have both crude lungs and gills."

"Ah," Jane said.

She'd seen a few different kinds of insects. There were midges that hovered just above the watery mud. She'd also seen a bright-blue insect that resembled a hybrid between a praying mantis and a dragonfly skimming the surface of the marsh and clinging to reedy plant stalks. These blue bugs looked curious as they watched her and Ron trudge by.

Jane had also seen some furry animals flying overhead that made bleating sounds, possibly something similar to bats or maybe flying squirrels. She didn't think they had feathers, but it was hard to tell for sure.

Evolution had taken similar but clearly different paths here. It was a very strange sensation to see species that could have evolved on Earth, but hadn't. The evolutionary tree on this planet terminated in different branches.

"I wonder if they ever had anything like dinosaurs here," Jane mused aloud.

Ron didn't answer because at that moment the sky opened up and dumped on them. The rain was cold and quickly chilled the air. They had on protective gear—clothing that repelled water which included a hood. But unless she kept her head bowed, water ran down the sides of her face in rivulets. She could feel it drip from the loose tendrils of her hair down onto her collarbone, running under her shirt—and sometimes it just pelted them sideways. So, while the clothing itself stayed dry and relatively warm, there was cold water constantly chilling her skin, though her feet were still immersed in warm, muddy water.

Her hands and the tip of her nose quickly grew cold. She wished she'd eaten something before the deluge began. She was expending a lot of energy, slogging through the muck, and hadn't ingested any food in some time. She could use some calories to warm up.

Ron suddenly stumbled and sidestepped into her. She reached out to grab him as an animal thrashed and splashed in the water underfoot. She caught a glimpse of something large and silvery with a purple sheen as its long body broke the surface for a second and then trailed away, water rippling just underneath. Ron looked at her for a moment. "Well, that answers that," he said and shook his head and then trudged on. Jane was more tentative with each step after that, and kept her eyes on the water looking for evidence of other creatures that might be…hungrier.

Finally, the sludgy water turned to mud, and the mud progressively grew more solid until it gave way to wet, rocky soil. They started to feel the ache in their calves to indicate they were climbing a gentle incline.

They ate some food squares as they walked. The rain hadn't let up. They crossed many rivulets running past them downhill, and there was evidence of erosion all along the hillside. There were also many gaping holes that seemed to go deep underground. She assumed they were animal burrows. Visibility was poor and that was troubling. Jane hadn't forgotten about the nepatrox.

Ron held a device that contained all the information they needed about the terrain and the route to the nearest settlement. It also had a heat-detection scanner, but that was only useful if an object was considerably warmer than its surroundings, so insects and other cold-blooded animals were virtually invisible unless very close and very large.

They'd seen many small animals on the device since the rain started—animals they couldn't see with their eyes. They seemed to be good at hiding, which made sense because large packs of the voracious nepatrox were always a threat. Jane assumed they were just under the surface in the tunnels they kept seeing. So far, there'd been nothing big enough to be worrisome.

They'd seen no evidence of accommodations for people of any kind. But it was unusual for atellans to live outside of a dense grouping of residences, most of which were large multifamily dwellings or at the very least connected to other homes. So unless they found some kind of cave, they were in for a long trek in the open. There were very few trees. Those that were present were fairly small and grew in contorted shapes with sparse branches. There was no shelter to be found beneath one.

As they hiked along the low slope between two foothills, Jane kept scanning for some kind of shelter where they might try to dry out and eat something more substantial, but she hadn't yet seen anything that would work.

Ron stopped walking and grew very still, staring at the scanner. Jane was a few paces behind him. She didn't speak aloud, but connected to him through Ei'Brai.

What Jane saw in Ron's mind made her carefully slip her hands into one of the many pockets on her clothing and pull out a palm blaster. It was a sectilian weapon. Not gun shaped in the slightest, it was a convex disk with loops around one side for slipping over fingers and a small digital sight that she placed between her index and middle finger. She threaded it carefully over one hand and gripped it in her palm. One full rotation of its dial with a fingertip of the opposite hand would energize it, and squeezing it at two specific pressure points with her fingers would trigger a concussive blast. Ron already had one in each palm.

Jane eased her second one out and primed them both. There were similar weapons built into sectilian battle armor. She had used them before on the *Speroancora*. They were a devastating weapon when used against anything that was low density—like organic matter—but did very little to anything dense and solid—like the walls and hull of a ship, which made them the preferred type of weapon aboard starships. She remembered how the concussive force had penetrated the cracks in the nepatrox's shells and made them explode into goo and shell fragments.

Ron held out the scanner so she could see that around the two fuchsia dots that represented the two of them, there were green dots of various sizes encroaching from every direction. Some were very small, some of them were similar in size to Jane and Ron, and some were slightly bigger. Jane glanced up at Ron and sent him a thought. "Do you think those green dots are atellans?"

He replied, mind to mind, relayed instantaneously through Ei'Brai. "Sentients are supposed to show up as pink. But it might not be accurate, since it's only referencing heat."

Jane nodded. "Let's keep walking as if we don't know they're there. They could be simply observing. If they get too close, then we go back-to-back in a defensive formation. Be certain they're hostile before firing. Does that sound reasonable?"

"Affirmative." He slowed his gait and they walked on, side by side.

They hadn't gone far when they heard a shrieking cry, only slightly muffled by the steadily pouring rain. The cry echoed over the rocky terrain, and soon it seemed to be coming from every direction at once and growing louder.

Jane shuddered. She knew that cry. She'd heard it aboard the *Speroancora* just before the nepatrox attacked. The scanner showed the green dots closing in on the pink ones. Though they couldn't see them yet, there was little doubt now as to the identity of these creatures.

Jane looked wildly in every direction for a place to shelter and hide. All she saw was a twisted tree, growing at a crooked angle from the slope at least thirty feet away. Ron looked at her, looked at the tree, and mentally agreed it was their best option at the moment. It was the only available way of putting some distance between them and the predators, of getting any kind of tactical vantage point.

Ron didn't bother to say what was on both of their minds: *Then what?*

Jane remembered how running had stimulated the nepatrox's prey drive during their encounter on the ship and did her best not to break into a sprint, though it felt like the hounds of hell were at her heels. Those same instincts and thoughts echoed in Ron's head.

They continued on toward the tree, stiffly ambling at a fast walk.

There was a sudden burst of thought from Ron: "Too late! Run!"

Then she heard the flapping. The hissing. The prancing paws on the rocky surfaces of the hillside.

Jane bounded forward, her strides elongating, gaining more vertical height and forward thrust with each footstep than she could on Earth. Just before they reached the tree, she pocketed the palm blasters so that she could climb.

The tree was similar to a conifer. It had only small tufts of needles at the tips of its gnarled branches. Jane hoped the nepatrox couldn't climb it, but even if they could, only a few at a time would be able to. She and Ron would be able to pick them off. Ron motioned for Jane to climb first. He took up a protective stance to cover her while she got started.

She reached out to grasp a low branch to test its strength. She didn't know if it would hold an adult's weight, but she didn't have a lot of choice. She wrapped her hands around it, kicked up, and swung a leg over—much easier in lower gravity.

An unearthly scream pierced the sound of rainfall. It sounded like an inhuman battle cry. Ron backed into her, his shoulder brushing against her thigh as she hung upside down trying to pull herself up onto the branch. She didn't weigh as much here, but she didn't have any recent experience at tree climbing, and the branch was smooth and covered in something slimy.

She looked up. The scarlet-shelled, no-neck nepatrox surged into view. The fluorescent orange-and-magenta hinged flaps that flanked their wide mouths seemed comically bright in the dim light, flaring to make them look larger and more menacing. They were apex predators that were more numerous than atellans on this world.

78

They were pressing Ron back. "Come on, QD, you just shimmy right on up there." Then came the concussive thud and resultant splatter as Ron used the palm blasters against the animals that got too close.

Her fingers kept losing purchase. Her hood slipped back. She turned her head and gripped harder, digging her nails into the bark as she tried to flip her position on the branch.

Her eyes widened. There was one coming from the opposite side of the tree from Ron, slashing its barbed tail around in the air. It was bigger than any nepatrox they'd seen on the ship. Its mouth opened, revealing rows of jagged teeth. The brilliant mouth flaps ruffled and vibrated around its head, displaying the creature's aggression and intent. It was too close.

It was about to strike her in the face.

10

Alan's nap didn't last long.

He was snoozing away when a loud thunk reverberated from one side of the shuttle. He snorted awake and half rose before the aching heaviness in his left leg stopped him from swinging it over the side of the reclined crash seat.

Ajaya moved silently to the starboard window and peeked out. After only a moment she ducked and turned, sinking to the floor, her eyes wide with disbelief. "Oh, dear. We've got company," she said.

Alan's eyebrows drew together. He started to get up to see for himself.

"No. Don't." Ajaya crawled toward him and gently pushed him back down. Her tone was firm, but she spoke barely above a whisper. "You need to stay immobile while the leg finishes the binding process. We're fine. They can't get to us. We're safe in here." Ajaya had turned on the reassuring doctor tone she used when she didn't want to alarm anyone.

Alan was starting to freak out. "What the fuck is out there, Ajaya?"

She inhaled sharply and held that breath, her face drawn. "Nepatrox."

He let out a barrage of curses when an impact rocked the shuttle.

Ajaya's eyes went wider. Her fingers were suddenly clamped over his lips. *They are attracted to sound, remember?* she mouthed.

How could he forget? He knew better than anyone what the critters were like. He looked down at what was left of his ruined leg and snarled silently, his fingers curling into fists. Nepatrox had done this to him.

He felt an intermittent pressure, like a gentle tapping, on his brain. He opened up and let Ajaya in. He sensed Ei'Brai in the background, busily working on something else. Before she could say anything, he mentally said, "Get out all the weapons we have."

She stared at him, blinking. He could hear the echo of her thought. *We shouldn't need them.* But then her head bobbed solemnly and she turned away to gather them, moving silently, deliberately.

Out of the corner of his eye, Bergen saw movement and turned his head. The unhinged jaw of a nepatrox mouth—with the wide flaps to either side flapping away—greeted him through the window. The beast had climbed up on the wing. It was bigger than any of the ones they'd seen on the *Speroancora*. The brilliant flaps folded back in on themselves as the mouth closed and the monster head butted the window. The shuttle shuddered.

Leg be damned. He was on his feet and gimping into the cockpit as quietly as he could. He triggered the release that retracted the wings. It would make some noise, but it would also make it harder for the nepatrox to pound on the windows, which were easily the weakest point on the shuttle.

Then he shut off all of the lights inside the vehicle to further obscure the view inside. As the shuttle retracted its wings, the nepatrox scuttled off and fell out of sight. No more reenactments of "Nightmare at 20,000 Feet" necessary.

Ajaya rejoined him, her lips drawn into a thin line. She handed him a couple of palm blasters.

He took them silently. His leg throbbed. He felt a little lightheaded. He'd lost some blood when the device was shorn off. But the tiny display on the inner calf of the unit showed that the device was reattached and stable now. He wasn't in a lot of danger from that anymore. Just some.

There were a lot of drugs in his system. His head felt thick. He should have been lying flat on his back, but who could do that with monsters at the door?

Deprived of the wings to climb up on, the nepatrox began to launch themselves at the windscreen. Thankfully, they couldn't find purchase. They scrabbled fruitlessly on the aerodynamic cone at the front of the ship, leaving slimy smears behind as they slid back into the swamp.

Alan rolled his eyes and beckoned Ajaya to the back of the tiny ship. There was no sense in letting the ghouls see their prey if it could be avoided.

The damn things were smarter than they looked.

Alan wondered about the nepatrox sense of smell. Or was their hearing just that acute? The animals switched tactics and began lunging in groups at the ship.

Ajaya braced herself in the rear corner as the animals impacted the shuttle and it lurched over the watery landscape.

Alan did the same in the opposite corner. He shook his head with disbelief. He sent a thought to Ei'Brai that he needed a stronger link with Jane. He wasn't a bit surprised to hear an edge in her mental voice. He'd had a growing feeling that things weren't going well on her end either, though the connection had been very limited.

She wasn't paying much attention to him. That irritated him more than it should have. But whatever. He was human.

Throughout his brief conversation with Jane the shuttle was being shoved around in the marsh, sometimes twisting in violent turns as the beasts hit it from both sides nearly at the same time. There had to be dozens of them out there, all of them fully mature and well-fed brutes.

Ajaya went pale and her chest heaved as one particularly loud impact pushed them up on just one sled. For a brief moment it felt like they were suspended in midair. Every loose object in the shuttle skittered to one side.

Jane was saying she was sorry she couldn't help…

He didn't hear anything else she might have said. Another loud thud and the ship fell over to crash on the port side. Luckily, he'd been in the corner on that side, so he didn't move far and his leg stayed relatively stable. Ajaya, on the other hand, tumbled onto him, letting out a scream that she cut off immediately. He helped her right herself.

"I'm okay. You?" she sent in an urgent thought. She looked anxiously at his leg.

He swallowed thickly. His vision was swimming and he felt nauseated, but he sent back a confident, "Fine."

She looked shaken. She was staring at the windscreen, which was now partially submerged in brown water that sloshed around as the critters pawed at it and attempted to look inside.

"It's okay," he reassured her. "It holds air in a vacuum. It'll keep water out."

But he stared too as one of the monsters pawed at the seam where the windscreen met the fuselage of the ship. He was actually more worried about being tumbled around. They were in a precarious position. The ship was bottom-heavy. Hopefully they'd fall back onto the sleds, but he wasn't sure if the angle would allow that. If he got tossed around, he was also at real risk of losing the leg again. Ajaya might not be able to reattach it fast enough before he bled out. He started having all kinds of dark thoughts.

Ajaya gasped, pulling him out of his internal maelstrom of doom.

He turned to see what she was looking at. A tiny stream of water was running into the cockpit from the spot where the crazed creature pawed at the edge of the windscreen.

Another couple of animals slammed into the windscreen then. The dim light coming from the front of the vehicle went out as the windscreen was sloshed with mud and churning bodies. The impact shoved the shuttle several feet. Water sheeted off the windscreen as the front of the vehicle suddenly tipped up. Every loose object slid along the port wall—that was now the floor—toward the rear of the shuttle. Dirty water ran toward them too.

Bergen tried to reconnect with Jane, but he couldn't get through to her. He opened the connection with Ei'Brai to its fullest extent. "Come on, Ei'Brai. Tell me you're gonna zap these freaks with a precision laser that you've been keeping close to the vest…"

"I apologize most sincerely, Dr. Alan Bergen, but I'm powerless to assist. Would that I had such devices at my disposal."

"Where's Jane?" Alan demanded. "I can't connect to her."

"Qua'dux Jane Holloway is injured and unconscious but is safely en route to an atellan compound. However I can connect you with Dr. Ronald Gibbs, who is currently conscious."

They were slammed again, knocking them askew. The windscreen surged higher into the air. They had to be at about a twenty to twenty-five degree angle from level now.

"We're sinking!" Ajaya cried out loud. Being quiet hardly seemed to matter at this point.

Alan surged to his feet, grabbed Ajaya's arm, and pulled her up too. Adrenaline was in control now. "Other side of the fulcrum," he declared and hobbled up the slope to the other end of the shuttle, dragging Ajaya behind him. They clung to the seat backs just behind the cockpit. It didn't change anything.

"I have alerted Dr. Ronald Gibbs to your situation. He is attempting to communicate your predicament to his hosts. I have switched my outgoing beacon to a distress call that will alert them to your coordinates, should they pick up the signal."

"Fuckity fuckity fuckity fuck!" Alan bellowed. "Why did we have to land on Dagobah?"

"What can we do?" Ajaya asked him. She sounded relatively calm.

Their end of the ship dipped a little bit as another animal slammed into it.

He didn't know what to say. He was in a state of complete and utter disbelief.

That was when he heard it.

On the other side of what would normally be the floor, a nepatrox had managed to get into the empty engine compartment. It was scratching and scrabbling at the circuitry and components inside there.

Alan started to shake with choler. "No!" he roared. "That's *my* shit! Don't mess with my shit!"

Without thinking he slipped the palm blasters over his wrists and fingers and staggered to the midpoint of the ship to jab at the control overhead that would trigger the exit hatch. It instantly opened. He climbed up over the sideways crash seats until he was balanced on the one nearest the hatch. He popped his head outside. He didn't see anything up on top of the ship.

"Alan! This is not a good idea. Come back," Ajaya called from inside.

He got a leg up and eased out onto the uppermost surface of the shuttle. He kept his body weight spread out as he slid closer to the sled rail until he could peer over and see the exposed underside of the shuttle. He could see the tail end of a nepatrox sticking out of the empty engine compartment.

He heard Ajaya scrambling behind him, and then she grabbed onto his good leg with both hands, steadying him. "For the record, I object to this course of action."

He didn't bother to reply. He had the tail end of that goddamn monster in his sights. He blasted the shit out of it until all that remained in the engine compartment was a lump of charred, stinking meat.

Then he fired on every other nepatrox he could see. He thought about sliding to the other side, toward the top of the shuttle, but moving his weight to that side might tip the shuttle onto its roof. That would be bad. He did see a couple of the monsters sink into the quagmire near the rear of the ship, and that made him feel a little more cheerful about their situation.

When no new critters came into view after a few minutes, Ajaya patted his leg and said, "We've stopped sinking, I think. Just come inside where it's safer. We should eat something."

Reluctantly he agreed. Sliding back inside wasn't as easy as getting out had been. He cursed like a sailor when he bumped his bad leg. It was throbbing now that he was starting to calm down.

He eased down on the spot where the wall met the floor. It was the best place on this end to sit comfortably. He didn't want to tempt fate by putting weight anywhere near one of the windows.

Ajaya handed him a food cube and a pouch of water then sat next to him. They ate in silence. Ajaya was asking Ei'Brai more-specific questions about what had happened to Ron and Jane and the atellans who had rescued them when Alan heard movement outside the craft. It sounded like something was climbing the exterior. They were back.

His teeth ground together. He listened carefully, wondering if he had the energy or the stupidity to climb back up there again. Then a very civilized knock drummed on the hatch.

Alan and Ajaya looked at each other in amazement.

A voice rang out from overhead. "Scaluuti?"

Ajaya stood and called out, "Scaluuti!" She clambered up over the seats and pressed the button to trigger the door to open. "Scaluuti!"

A face like a hatchet leaned over the hatch after it opened up. Heat rolled in. The ears on this inhuman face pulled back dramatically, and its eyes widened. It rattled off an impressive amount of Mensententia. Alan lost track of what was being said, but Ajaya was nodding and replying and motioning to him.

The face disappeared and there was a lot of talking and other commotion outside. Alan started to feel really tired.

Suddenly Ron dropped through the opening. He and Ajaya had a little reunion. Alan closed his eyes so he wouldn't have to see it.

Hatchet face dropped in too. The three of them helped Alan up and strapped him, with great difficulty, into his reclined crash couch. Apparently Ajaya didn't want his leg to get dirty or wet outside. And she didn't want it to be wrenched badly as they righted the shuttle. He was too woozy to disagree.

11

"Ron!" Jane cried out loud in a panic, forgetting that sound only enflamed their hostility.

Ron swiveled and blasted the beast just before its barbed tail struck Jane.

Adrenaline surged though her. Every muscle tensed. And even though she hadn't climbed a tree for decades, muscle memory kicked in.

She pulled herself up on the wet branch until she was astride it and scooted quickly over to the trunk. From there she was able to stand, hugging the trunk with one arm for stability, and reach for the next branch overhead to pull herself onto it, pausing only to wipe the slime off onto her clothes to try to keep her hands from slipping.

When she was sure she was out of reach, she palmed the blasters again, primed them, then mentally signaled Ron to join her while she covered him.

She went into a trancelike state as she alternated between the blasters looped over each hand. She began to fall into a rhythm, deftly re-priming after each shot, sighting the next beast she would obliterate, and firing. It became a smooth, practiced motion. She carefully aimed through the sights between her fingers so that she wouldn't hit Ron or the tree as she picked off one after another.

Ron was much taller and far more agile. He made short work of the climb. The tree creaked under his weight as he joined her, and the top dipped a bit lower to the ground. Soon he settled on a branch on the opposite side and resumed killing the beasts himself.

They kept coming. She worried that the power supplies inside the blasters would fail before all the monsters were dead, and she experimented with aiming at angles that might let her hit more than one at a time. Ron shared her concern and was doing the same.

A few of the larger beasts darted in, grabbed a nepatrox carcass, and pulled it back out of Jane and Ron's range. She could see their silhouettes through the veil of the rain, hunched over, feasting on their fallen brothers. They were wily. They'd learned to stay back and take advantage of an easy food source rather than put themselves on the front line and risk being killed themselves. She'd seen this behavior before on the ship. It turned her stomach.

"Um, Jane? You there?" Jane heard inside her head. It was Alan. He sounded nervous.

She leaned out precariously on a branch, her nails deeply imbedded in the smooth wood. The top of the tree swayed lower to the ground for a moment. "Yes?"

"We've got a minor problem here..." Alan said.

"Okay..." Jane replied.

"It seems we've got visitors," Alan said wryly.

Jane adjusted her seat on the slippery branch and grimaced. It was getting painful. The tone of Alan's thoughts did not suggest he was bearing good news. She hoped they hadn't somehow offended the atellans already. "Oh? Atellans found the shuttle?" she asked hopefully. Perhaps there was a chance at rescue, if they could communicate their position to the atellans…

Alan sounded pained. "Not exactly. It's our old pals. The nepatrox."

Her attention on her own problems lapsed for just a second as she refocused on Alan. In that moment a large animal lunged at the tree trunk, clambering up a few feet before falling back upon the mass of its companions. Its weight caused the top of the tree to plunge toward the ground.

Jane yelped and wrapped both arms around the trunk in a desperate hug. Her face slid along the surface of it, coating one nostril and the edge of her mouth in slippery slime. She snorted and spit as the top of the tree bobbed.

The mass of animals below leapt every time she swung close to the ground, and more of them attempted trips up the trunk, sensing that they might dislodge their prey. All Jane and Ron could do was hold on for dear life as the small tree flopped erratically.

"Jane? You there?" Alan asked. He sounded irritated.

Jane managed to wrap her legs around the trunk to brace herself so she could get one arm free to fire. She sighted along the trunk and blasted whenever a scarlet beast came into the viewfinder. To Alan, she quickly spared a thought. "Okay. Well, just sit tight. You should be safe in there."

"Oh, sure." His voice was edgy. "We're just cozy in here while they push the entire goddamn shuttle around and slam themselves into the windscreen every few seconds."

"Alan. I'm sorry I can't help you. I've got my own problems right now." She let the connection between them widen, so he could see, for just a moment, what she was seeing, hearing, feeling.

She sneezed violently and broke off the connection with Alan. She suddenly plummeted to within a few feet of the ground. The barb of a nepatrox's tail caught Jane in the side, hooking itself in her clothing and flesh, tearing it.

Jane screamed in pain and terror as her skin was sliced. She was wrenched around the circumference of the trunk under the pendulous weight of the animal as the barb caught fast in the waistband of her pants. The branch scraped her cheek raw. Time slowed down. As the tree bounced back into the air, the animal went with it. The extra weight slowed the motion considerably.

They hung there for a moment, precariously suspended about seven feet above the gnashing jaws of the enraged throng of animals. Barbed tails whipped around them. She felt the hot breath of one as it snapped its jaws inches from her face. The reek of decay made her squirm.

The barb ripped free. The nepatrox fell. The tree sprung back violently and slowly returned to a gentle sway. The animals shifted their focus from climbing the lower trunk to leaping for the low-bobbing branches.

She fleetingly wondered if they were smart enough to combine the two strategies. She hoped not.

Ron worked his way closer to Jane.

She gritted her teeth and inhaled sharply. The jagged gash burned and now she was bleeding freely. Drops fell with the rain onto the beasts beneath them. That seemed to whip them up into an even higher state of frenzy. She looked down into a sea of hideous upturned faces framed in flapping fans of sunset colors. When her eyes went unfocused from the pain, it almost seemed pretty. Like a field of flowers swaying in the breeze. Nasty, vicious flowers…

"How bad is it?" Ron asked her softly.

"Bad," she whispered back and squeezed her eyes shut. The prickling and burning sensation seemed to ripple through her entire torso. When she wiggled her toes, she realized with dismay that they were already starting to feel stiff. She'd gotten a bigger dose of the neurotoxin the nepatrox used to paralyze their prey this time. It was acting more quickly. She hooked one foot around the other, hoping she could keep them in place even after her legs were immobilized.

Ron settled his body into a secure configuration, wrapped over and around several branches, and worked fast. He ripped open her shirt to the armpit. He opened his pack and punctured a tube of sterile sectilian healing gel and quickly spread it over her wound.

She was starting to feel weak and sweaty despite being soaked through with cold rain. She stopped watching the animals below and closed her eyes, leaning her uninjured cheek against the bark of the tree to conserve her strength. She wondered how long she could hold on. The skin on her arms prickled with goosebumps. She couldn't move the muscles in her feet or calves anymore.

Ron continued to work on her, carefully closing and covering the wound with large adhesive bandages which stuck despite her skin being wet and clammy. A small miracle. Then he wrapped himself around her to protect her with his body.

She protested weakly. She didn't want him to be put at more risk when her chances of survival grew slimmer every moment.

The tree vibrated. She could hear the creatures scrabbling around at the bottom, jockeying for a spot around the base of the tree.

"Hold on, QD," Ron said.

She felt his body tense. She felt the tree lurch and sway dizzyingly. She kept her eyes clamped shut and focused on holding on with her arms, because below the waist she could no longer tell what was happening to her body.

Scratching sounds. Sickening movement. Thuds. Cracks. Booms.

She shivered.

In her head she heard her father crooning as he held her—no longer a baby, but a sturdy child who liked to play "baby." Her father would make up new lyrics to time-worn lullabies, and sometimes he would swing her around while she screamed with laughter. She found herself humming softly to herself. She felt unhinged. "Rock-a-bye Janey, in the treetop. When monsters stalk, the treetop will rock. When the bough breaks, young Janey will fall. And down will fall Janey…"

Her body trembled so hard she seemed to rattle. She held back a sob.

Ei'Brai blanketed her mind with calm reassurance. She let herself swim in that feeling, and what was happening to her body receded. She let him take control. He could segment the pain away. He could continue to hold on as long as her body was able. He would not leave her as long as she needed him.

He met her in the cool, dark place where they often spent the twilight moments before dreaming, relaxed, reviewing the day's work, enjoying each other's quiet company.

"Quasador Dux Jane Holloway, I find your dearth of appendages appalling," he stated in his driest tone.

A laugh bubbled up out of her. "I could do with a few like yours. You'd have no trouble holding onto that tree."

And he wouldn't. He'd just twine a few of his sinuous arms around the branches and have several more free to do other things.

Except he couldn't. Because he couldn't breathe air. They were forever separated by that barrier.

His mood turned more somber. "I would be glad to sacrifice a few arms, cede them to you, if I could, to keep you safe."

"I know you would," she said softly.

"You must never stop. You must never lose hope," his mental voice growled in a sort of challenge.

She heard the pulse of his distress call, focused in a cone, directed on the nearest settlement to Jane's location on Atielle's surface. So unlikely to be heard. But he would never give up while there was a chance.

He grew quiet for a moment. He was using all of his powers of concentration and could spare none for her. Something had caught his attention. She instinctively moved back toward herself.

She felt the warm feathery touch of his mental presence brushing against hers right before he relinquished her body to her. The pain came screaming back. Her fingertips tingled as though they were falling asleep. Her lips felt numb and there was a sharp, acid taste on her tongue. Her body was wooden and cold. As she centered into the space behind her own heavy-lidded eyes, she saw what Ei'Brai had been looking at.

A dilapidated all-terrain vehicle was pulling up next to the tree.

12

"Not a minute too soon," Ron whispered.

Jane's head wobbled. Her eyes slowly refocused on Ron.

Water beaded on his tightly curled hair. There were multiple abrasions from his forehead to his cheekbone. Bloody drops of water trailed down that side of his face. The muscles of his jaw visibly bulged with tension. His eyes narrowed as he watched what was happening below.

The creatures immediately turned toward the new potential prey, swarming over and around the battered vehicle as soon as it came to a stop. A panel on the side of the vehicle lifted up, obscuring Jane's view of whoever had arrived. She heard concussive blasts. The creatures began to explode in an ever-widening arc that had its origin beneath this open panel.

Jane labored to take a deep breath. It was harder than it should have been. She tried not to let that scare her. Help hopefully had arrived. Ei'Brai remained close, a reassuring presence.

Two people emerged from under the vehicle's open panel, holding the small palm blasters that Jane recognized. Other panels lifted from the sides of the vehicle and soon six individuals were in full view, a mixture of both the willowy atellan type and the stockier sectilian body type. Three of them used palm blasters. The other three carried makeshift weapons—crude spears and clubs which served the same purpose—systematically killing nepatrox.

Tears of relief streaked down Jane's cheeks.

Ron's voice was thick and rough. "You okay, QD?"

She tried to form words but her mouth wouldn't work. She sent a thought instead. "As long as I keep breathing, I believe I will be."

"Don't you worry a bit. I'll make sure you keep breathing."

When it seemed that most of the creatures had been dealt with, one of the individuals swept his or her arm, palm out, in an arc from thigh to over his or her head, calling out, "Scaluuti!"

Ron returned the greeting and the gesture. "Scaluuti!" he shouted. "Casgrata!" He looked at Jane as though he needed confirmation that he'd pronounced the words with the right inflection.

She couldn't muster anything more than a weak thought of affectionate approval.

Ron's brows pulled together in concern.

Her vision was becoming blurry. She closed her eyes. She was virtually locked in. She could hear what was going on around her. She could feel people handling her body, but she couldn't help herself. She was at their mercy.

She gathered that one of the atellans stayed at the base of the tree on guard and the remaining five climbed the tree to help hand her down. Ron was speaking to them in his broken Mensententia. He was doing fine, but this was not how she'd wanted this to go. She'd wanted to arrive as a strong leader, fluent in their language, a broker of peace. Instead, they'd found her broken, unable to even beg for assistance.

Jane wished that the rest of her crew had been able to unlock Mensententia as easily as she had. They found it a slow, difficult process. It was overwhelming when each potent connection was made. As a result, the others tended to prefer to skim the surface of the language—to memorize the translations of individual words, rather than go through the mental struggle of truly unlocking the language from their genetic code to integrate it fully into their cognition.

The hands on her were gentle, and the voices of the atellans seemed to awaken some of Rageth's latent memories of home. The atellans were confused by the humans' appearance. Because of the quarantine of both Sectilia and Atielle, no aliens had ventured into this solar system in decades. They kept asking where she and Ron were from and then being confused by the answer. Ron was using the word Earth.

When Ron began to use the word Terra instead, their consternation only increased. But they could see the gravity of Jane's situation and didn't belabor the point. They settled her into the vehicle next to Ron and were soon underway.

Jane had been set at a semireclined angle. Ron had his hand encircling her wrist, presumably to check her pulse periodically, and she was sure he was keeping a close eye on her. She could hear the atellans discussing their strange, sudden appearance. They spoke freely. Maybe they felt sure Ron couldn't understand them, or their culture dictated that it didn't matter and it was perfectly normal to speak of another this way in their presence. Jane was pretty sure it was both.

All of them seemed to think it exceedingly strange that Ron couldn't speak fluent Mensententia. One thought they were mentally handicapped sectilian mutants—refugees from the squillae plague. Another thought she and Ron were shipwrecked and touched in the head because of the post-traumatic stress of a crash landing. Someone else piped up that a crash landing could have given them both brain injuries. One noted that Ron had been trying to indicate that Jane was his leader.

She was able to open her eyes from time to time but she couldn't see much. Her vision swam in and out of clarity. When she could see clearly, she mostly saw the worn, dirty ceiling of the vehicle and the back of three atellan heads. Despite the uneven terrain, the ride was smooth.

She focused on breathing and that seemed to help. They were safe. She hoped Alan and Ajaya were safe too. Ron had tried to communicate about the shuttle. He would continue to do so. There was nothing more she could possibly do. She gave in to exhaustion.

13

"Well now, well now, *well now*...aren't you an interesting creature?" said a voice with a deep timbre.

Jane didn't want to open her eyes. She could sense bright light behind them, but her lids were so heavy. She lay there, listening as the owner of the voice walked around her, chattering about her appearance, the deep voice booming.

"So...round...and such exaggerated...femininity. The lines of her body are positively spheroidal in places. She is quite diminutive compared to the male, but clearly shares the same genetic base. Be sure to record the gender dimorphism in your notes."

A smaller, higher voice piped up. "Can we draw that conclusion, Medical Master Schlewan? We only have two specimens to observe. Don't we need a larger data set?"

There was a long pause before the masculine voice replied. "Eh? Oh, quite so, quite so, *quite so*. It is but a hypothesis, yet not so very unusual. There may be more individuals spread across the continent that we don't know about yet. Let us hope for such a discovery to study them further. Poor souls. I hope someone gives them succor. It is quite dangerous outside of the compounds these days. She and her companion were well armed, too." The voice sounded weary and tinged with sadness.

The younger voice sounded shy. "My friend Chiba has spoken with the male. They've taken him and gone off to search for two more aliens trapped inside a shuttle in water."

Jane tried to stir then, but her limbs felt so heavy.

"In the ocean, you say? Quite some distance." The voice clucked. "Well, it is unlikely they will survive then. Unlikely, unlikely, *unlikely.*"

Someone lifted Jane's wrist, and a cold instrument pressed against her forearm. The older voice said, "Tinor? Come closer. Do note the interesting variation in skin tone between the two specimens. This one clearly evolved on a world or part of a world with less exposure to solar radiation and the other with more. This is a permanent coloration, though certainly it may range a bit seasonally. I suspect they make cholecalciferol upon exposure to sunlight in their skin, as we do. See?"

"Yes, Medical Master Schlewan. So, they do not make melanin on demand like us?"

There was a huffing sound from the older voice. "I suspect not. It must be a different metabolic pathway. Perhaps a different configuration of the chemical structure. We must, must, *must* take a skin sample from each and preserve them carefully. Small. Painless, of course. We have not the resources to elucidate these structures now, but one day we will again. You will find that these kinds of things are important to document. Remember this, young Tinor. One day, when you are as old as I, you may be a great scientist of the new republic we are building. It may become valuable to know how to introduce a gene that will permanently darken or lighten the skin of an individual for reasons we cannot predict now. For all we know it could cure a skin affliction or prevent a disease. Mark my words. Knowledge is everything and genes are powerful. These strangers are not so different from us—but they are different enough. There is much to learn from them, wherever they may be from. Much, much, *much* to learn."

"Chiba said the male claims they are terran, Master. Could that be true? If they are, shouldn't we..."

"Nonsense, nonsense, *nonsense!*" the older voice erupted. "A terran—*if* they exist—would speak properly, eh? Now! Did you get a good look at her reproductive anatomy? We must do a full study..."

Jane felt a waft of air on her face as a blanket lifted from her body, and there seemed to be a warm hand at her hip, tugging at her clothing. Suddenly Jane's eyelids didn't feel quite so heavy. She inhaled sharply and her eyes flew open. She struggled valiantly to move her limbs and managed to flail around a little bit.

"Oh!" the high voice exclaimed. It belonged to a reedy individual in a green, flowing tunic who had a narrow face and high, angular cheekbones. Tinor sported curly medium-brown hair and tawny skin. Jane had been thinking Tinor was an adolescent female, based purely on the voice she'd heard. Now she wasn't sure. Tinor was much younger than Jane had thought. Children were considered genderless until puberty in sectilian culture. If she spent any time with this child or any other, she'd have to remember to use the third set of pronouns, the gender-neutral set, or risk making a fool of herself.

Jane's gaze flew to the third person in the room. Her gender expectations were confounded again. This person seemed to be older, but despite the heavy frame and densely muscled physique of the shorter individual at the foot of her bed, something about the face, the softness of the eye, and the posture made her second-guess herself.

Then Jane noticed that the person's hair was arranged in an intricate many-strand plait that started at the hairline in front and interlaced, hugging the skull, all the way back to the nape of the neck, ending in multiple puffs of dense, curly, white hair that contrasted with the individual's light-brown skin. Noticing this hair arrangement jogged one of Rageth's memories. Jane was now certain that Medical Master Schlewan was either a woman or a trans woman, which, for all intents and purposes, meant the same thing. Gender wasn't hugely important to the Sectilius except for reproduction.

"Scaluuti! Scaluuti! *Scaluuti!*" The look on the woman's face was pure delight and inquisitiveness. She still held the blanket aloft but had taken a step back.

Jane croaked a greeting in reply and reached for the blanket. Her arm was heavier than it should have been, considering how little gravity there was on this moon.

Master Schlewan settled the green blanket back over her and frowned. "Are you cold, stranger?" She turned to Tinor. "Go fetch another blanket and some soup for the stranger."

"I...am fine, thank you," Jane replied, her voice barely above a creaking whisper.

Jane took in her surroundings. She was in a sparsely furnished room that had an institutional feel to it. Nearly everything in view was a sickly green color—bedding, walls, the clothing of the people. It could easily have been a room on the *Speroancora*, though the lighting felt different, softer and warmer. That was both strange and comforting at the same time.

The woman settled her hip on the side of the bed. "Not fine. No, no, *no*. Not yet. My, but you were caught up the proverbial tree without a wind-whip! You are fortunate to have survived the wilds, but you are quite safe now."

"Wind-whip?" Jane inquired, her voice strengthening.

"Ah! A local idiom. A wind-whip is a primitive weapon from our past. Makes a cracking loud noise to bring attention to one's need of assistance. The sound travels and travels. I suppose that's why they called it that. I've heard that they are making a comeback, as we have had some difficulty manufacturing power cells since the plague. Do you know of the plague?"

Jane nodded. She tried to push herself up to a sitting position. Master Schlewan did not assist, only watched her curiously. Jane didn't get far. Her limbs were working again but they were stiff and sore. She slumped back to the bed, her muscles burning. "The plague is why I'm here."

Before Master Schlewan could reply, Tinor burst through the door, sloshing soup from a deep bowl. "Medical Master Schlewan! They've brought back two more aliens! They were in a Sectilius shuttle craft. Cornu class. They've towed it back."

Jane breathed a sigh of relief. That had to be Alan and Ajaya. They were safe. She instantly felt much better.

"Do the strangers need medical attention?" Master Schlewan asked, gracefully moving to take the bowl, which resembled an overlarge, greenish plastic coffee mug.

Tinor looked like he or she hadn't considered that. "I'll find out!" The child dashed off again.

Master Schlewan turned back to Jane and handed her the warm bowl, which was full of a brothy green soup with un-identifiable ingredients. "I think you must have a story to tell."

Jane smiled wanly. The soup smelled delicious despite the fact that she didn't know what it was made from. Her stomach growled. She hadn't eaten for a long time.

"Eat well and rest while you can. Gistraedor Dux Pledor Makya Sten will be eager to meet with you, especially if these two newcomers are preadolescents like the young man who accompanied you," Master Schlewan admonished.

Jane started to disagree, to say that her three companions were adults, not children, but that would have required a great deal of explanation. She needed to save her strength for the meeting to come with Gis'dux Pledor Makya Sten.

She jerkily raised the bowl to her lips self-consciously and sipped. She hadn't been given a spoon so she could only assume this was how the soup was consumed. It was in-tensely herbal in flavor with a gingery bite that tingled on her tongue. Multicolored bits seemed to be evenly sus-pended in the matrix of the soup. A few came with each sip. Some were crunchy like nuts, others soft like noodles, others more toothsome. It was filling. She drained the bowl.

Master Schlewan looked pleased as she took the empty bowl from Jane. "I'll return to rouse you and check your vi-tal signs before your audience with the Gis'dux." Schlewan left the room.

Jane felt warm and sleepy. With effort she turned on her left side and let her eyes drift shut. She dreamed.

Jane felt light, buoyant. Gradually she became aware that she was underwater. It wasn't troublesome to find herself there—it seemed quite natural. She looked up through the crystal-clear water to see white light sparkling through the blue depths overhead.

There was a light touch on her arm, a friendly gesture. Her long hair swished languidly in front of her face as she turned to look. She smiled. Ei'Brai curled a tentacle carefully around her wrist, keeping the razor-sharp barbs turned away from her flesh, so he wouldn't hurt her.

Warm thoughts brushed against her mind. He pulled her into his version of a hug. It amused him, this human gesture, but he liked it too.

She embraced him, her face resting close to one enormous eye that was of approximately the same size as her entire head. Her hands smoothed over his slippery mantle and she was careful to only apply light pressure, so she wouldn't impede his breathing. More of his limbs wrapped around her—one around her waist, another coiled around one leg.

A protective membrane slipped down over his eye. He looked drowsy, and she knew that he trusted her. They trusted each other now. A cool current washed over them, but she felt warm.

He wanted to show her something. She felt him squeeze a large quantity of water through his funnel, jetting them in bouncing surges toward the ocean floor, arms still holding her close.

It was a reef, alive with activity. Vividly colored fish darted in and among the living rock. Anemones' tendrils waved in the current. Everywhere she looked there was movement and color.

Then she saw one...and another. Little shimmering things. Her eyes widened. Iridescent quicksilver and gold with speckles of bright colors—tiny limbs with impossibly small suckers and barbs, miniature replicas of Ei'Brai's.

She clapped her hands together with delight and laughed, bubbles gurgling from her mouth and shooting up over her head.

Soon there were dozens of them, darting from nooks and crevices all over the living reef, tiny mental voices squeaking an enthusiastic chorus of welcoming hellos. She reached out a finger and one tethered itself there, staring with wide, curious eyes at its father's friend. They crowded around her, lifting strands of her hair in their jewel-like tentacles, daring each other to touch her skin, to hug her fingers the way their father hugged her limbs.

She glanced at Ei'Brai. There was a brightness in his eyes that was like a smile. He was so pleased to introduce her to them.

But as she watched, a shadow passed over his body. The water went dim.

Her pulse quickened. She suddenly realized she'd forgotten her scuba gear. She twisted, trying to find where it had gone, frantically pushing the hair out of her face as it obscured her vision.

Her lungs burned for air. The gloom deepened. The water seemed colder than before. Her chest ached. Her fingers tingled.

She pushed on Ei'Brai's arms, gently at first, then with increasing desperation, until she was flailing and thrashing, his barbs cutting furrows into her flesh. The water bloomed with her blood, red-black clouds in the twilight. She felt no pain, only cold.

She gasped reflexively, trying to pull in nonexistent air. The salt water burned as it went in. It made her feel heavy. She tried to cough it up, but couldn't.

I'm drowning, she thought, even while she knew that didn't make sense.

It was happening to her this time. She couldn't stop it. She could never stop it.

She sent panicked thoughts to Ei'Brai to release her so she could try to get to safety, but he was oblivious, disconnected, unresponsive. He couldn't hear her. Was something wrong with him?

One great whoosh of water through his mantle would send them rocketing to the surface. Why would he abandon her when she needed him most?

✹

She woke with a gasp, her heart thudding painfully in her chest. She was alone. She considered connecting with Ei'Brai just to reassure herself he was okay, then decided that was unnecessary. It was just a dream. She closed her eyes again and slept deeply.

14

Jane's gait was stiff. Master Schlewan said that exercise would improve Jane's circulation and help her liver clear the toxins more quickly. Jane was a little concerned about that comment. Her skin had taken on a yellowish cast. She wasn't sure what that meant, but she didn't think it was good.

Master Schlewan had helped her dress and briefly allowed her to see Alan and Ron, who both seemed to be in reasonably good shape, before escorting her up. Jane had been offered a wheeled chair, but she'd declined it. Now she was wishing she hadn't been so stubborn. Of course, she hadn't known it would be so far.

She moved slowly beside Master Schlewan, who did not comment on their progress, as they slowly worked their way up a low-grade corkscrew ramp that wound around the circumference of this end of the building. Schlewan was surprisingly quiet, given how garrulous and curious she'd seemed to be before.

As they climbed, the walls around the outside of the ramp gave way to floor-to-ceiling curving windows with views of the surrounding landscape. She realized that what she'd thought had been the ground floor was probably several stories underground. Light sifted down around this perimeter from the upper levels all the way to the bottom through special channels in the windows. It was an impressive use of solar energy, Jane thought. These people did not waste things that were free. It was a very sectilian characteristic to maximize the use of natural light in this way.

Each level had an opening to the rest of the enclave and was bustling with people of all shapes and sizes. The building she was in was fluid in shape and slung low on the landscape like a stack of irregularly shaped pancakes connected by enclosed catwalks to other organically shaped stacks of pancakes. The enclave was easily the size of a city, but entirely contained and interconnected, separate from the outside. If viewed from the right angle, it seemed to go on and on, swirling buildings spaced out in a regular pattern.

"No elevators?" Jane said and grimaced.

Master Schlewan smiled. "Oh, yes, yes, *yes*, there are some, especially near the elder-community spaces, but walking is good for us and since we dare not ramble about outside the compound, this serves as our major form of exercise. Use of the elevators is generally frowned upon unless the need is dire. It is an egregious overuse of community energy."

Jane nodded. Schlewan's comments cemented in Jane's mind the community-centered culture she'd seen in Rageth's memories. That hadn't changed, at least.

From time to time they passed openings into the circular rooms that occupied the space interior to the ramp. Most of these spaces were dominated by classrooms, already full of quiet children studying at long tables. Jane noted that their heads were bowed over various forms of paper and books—

not some form of high technology. In fact she hadn't witnessed any form of advanced technology in use since their arrival to the compound.

Finally they reached the top of the ramp and the first door that Jane had noticed within the compound. Jane slouched against the wall and breathed deeply for a moment to collect her strength.

Schlewan opened the door and motioned Jane inside. "I will return in time with the wheeled chair. Please go in and introduce yourself to the Gistraedor Dux."

Jane nodded gratefully, then straightened and pulled the sleeve of her green tunic over her right hand to wipe the sweat from her face, not caring that it was probably bad manners. She didn't want to show up to meet the leader of the enclave looking weak, wan, and sweaty.

She wasn't in the best state for a first-contact meeting. She'd have to pull from someplace deep. She gritted her teeth, then went in.

It felt like she passed through a wall of humidity. Her nostrils filled with the earthy scents of moist humus. She squinted. The room was intensely bright and warm.

Every surface was encrusted with plant life. The floor was a maze of scaffolding which held layers of horticultural specimens of various brilliant colors. Overhead was a translucent dome that glowed with diffuse sunlight. Jane remembered that they used mirrors on the roofs of the buildings to intensify the sunlight collected.

Where was Sten?

She turned to look at Schlewan, who was now just a squat, dark outline in the doorway. Schlewan gestured toward Jane's left and let the door swing shut with a shush and a soft thud.

Jane took another moment to collect herself then continued on, actively attempting to transform into the person she needed to be to make this interview go as well as possible. Everything might hinge on the next few minutes.

She walked around the circumference of the room until she heard voices speaking in Mensententia—the halting sound of Ajaya's tentative attempts at the language as well as a deeper voice that drawled patiently and with exaggerated enunciation. The walkway expanded into an open space with workbenches and stools of various heights and configurations.

Perched atop one stool was Ajaya. Directly opposite her was a tall, narrow atellan whose hands were occupied with tools over a deep-purple plant specimen. She quickly surveyed this individual's appearance to determine gender so she'd use the correct set of pronouns. A shapeless mass of light-brown crinkled hair shot through with silver and something about the fit of the garment made her think male. She hoped she was right.

The atellan must have caught Jane standing there staring in his peripheral vision because he swiveled to face her. His head cocked to one side, projecting a very birdlike pose. Jane strode up to him, to stand just before him, and coolly looked into his eyes as a greeting before saying, "Gistraedor Dux Pledor Makya Sten. I am pleased to make your acquaintance."

He blinked slowly, looked back to Ajaya, and then refocused on Jane. "Your name, mistress?"

There would be no formal niceties to smooth the way. Sectilians were more direct than that.

She steeled herself to drop the bomb. She glanced at Ajaya, who was frowning worriedly.

"I am Quasador Dux Jane Augusta Holloway of the *Speroancora*."

Pledor stood. Jane knew this was more a manifestation of his disbelief than any kind of deference to someone of equal stature.

"Did you say the *Speroancora*?" he said calmly, his words still measured and heavily pronounced for clarity.

"I did, Gis'dux Sten. My crew and I are of terran origin."

Pledor's ears pulled back dramatically from his face in a gesture of surprise that left his facial skin taut and his eyes bulging. Sectilian ears were only slightly different in set, shape, and proportion compared to human ears, but they possessed more mobility, and because they were set into faces that were so angular, they appeared to stand out far more.

Jane continued, "We have come to return the ship to the Sectilius people. Our shuttle was damaged upon landing. We will need some assistance in reaching the proper authorities. I am grateful that you have come to our rescue and offered us sanctuary. Before we move on to meet with your government, we would like to take a brief journey to contact the descendants of Qua'dux Rageth Elia Hator at the Hator complex. I believe it is near here."

Pledor reseated himself after a moment and bent over the densely mounded plant in front of him, snipping off a few stems. He seemed to be pruning the plant into a flattened shape. His withdrawal was not offensive or a dismissal, Jane hoped. He seemed to be deep in thought.

She hadn't been offered a seat, but she wouldn't be. The Sectilius way was to do what was needed. She needed a seat, so she took one. She chose to sit a few feet from Pledor on the same side of the workbench. Ajaya glanced between them, worriedly. Jane held herself stiffly erect, but surreptitiously leaned her back against the bench. She tried to relax and wait patiently.

Pledor spoke. "Some of your preconceived notions are incorrect, Qua'dux. Allow me to edify you about where you find yourself. Sectilius is literally divided once again. This is a postapocalyptic state without centralized governance. Every compound on both worlds is governed in its own way. Rumor has it that parts of Sectilia herself are now feudal, though we have no way to confirm this, you will understand. If you wish to return this ship, I've no idea who you would return it *to*. Nor do I think anyone will want it, except to salvage parts from it, save perhaps the Hator descendants themselves who have a strong, seemingly genetic bent toward space flight."

Jane opened her mouth to speak, but closed it again as Pledor went on.

"There is one thing you possess which we have great need of, and with that you may barter for any of the things you desire, including passage to the Hator compound, though nothing will get you to Sectilia except for the *Speroancora* itself. A shame you chose to land here first. Sectilia would have been an easier landing for you. Rather wasteful to make landfall here for sentimental reasons."

Jane inhaled slowly. Things were getting tricky. She needed to tread carefully. "What do we possess that you have need of, Gis'dux?"

"Power cells." He turned to eye her. "But of course you cannot know." He gestured with a wicked, sharp-looking pruning shear toward Ajaya. "Your medical master speaks like a pubescent child, but she was able to reveal that you retain power cells at fully operational capacity both within your shuttle and aboard your ship in orbit."

Jane swallowed and sent a warning glance to Ajaya, who shook her head. He'd said "your ship" and "your shuttle," which meant that he believed she owned the right to them, no matter their origin. That was a heavy realization.

His speech was measured. He did not speak without meaning every single word. He wasn't going to commandeer anything, though he dearly wanted these things, that was clear.

Jane wanted to ask more questions but she was loath to appear stupid. She considered carefully what to say. "We do have power cells and can spare some of them. Do you have the ability to maintain them? Otherwise it would seem to me to be a short-term solution to your problem."

"You're quite right. There is a prohibition against squillae manufacture by general consensus because of the plague, so we are unable to rehabilitate spent cells. But we are still moving forward. We are now in a preindustrial state. We need the power cells to build defenses around a mine so that we can harvest primitive fuels from beneath the surface. That will be more sustainable in the short term, if imprudent in the long term. Our main concerns are safe transportation to salvage materials to build the enclosure and to traverse the distance to the mines. It was a salvaging team using some of our last remaining functional power cells that happened upon you in that tree."

Jane moistened her lips. "I see." An implication of something that was owed.

He twirled the shears in the air with his long, thin fingers and glanced at Jane. "You should know that there are those on the council who called for your execution and the usurpation of all of your possessions."

A poorly veiled threat. Internally, Jane blanched. She hoped that hadn't shown on her face.

She stood as Sectilius culture demanded, ignoring the pain shooting through her joints and the fatigue weighing her down. She stated flatly, "I'm worth more to you alive than dead, Gis'dux."

He didn't look up. He muttered, "That remains to be seen."

She continued to stand, to give gravitas to her next statement. "I have the ability to renew some of your fuel cells so that they will take a charge again and hold thousands of charges for future use—but I will only do so if our very modest needs are met."

Pledor put down the shears slowly and eased off his stool to face her. For the first time his expression showed a hint of emotion. Eagerness. His eyes bored into hers with an almost hawklike intensity.

Jane stayed motionless, staring back impassively.

His voice came out breathless. "Process thirty units to prove your assertion and I will grant you everything you wish."

Jane dipped her head. "I will need access to my shuttle and my entire team."

His eyes flicked over her. He knew the engines were gone. They weren't going anywhere. "Of course. But perhaps a brief rest and a meal are in order, Qua'dux? I regret that we could not offer you the use of a sanalabrium in your time of need. You understand we cannot spare the use of a power cell unless it is a matter of great urgency."

A reminder that she was worthless until she proved herself to him.

Her eyes narrowed. His body language seemed to be saying that he was about to dismiss her, despite the fact that there were so many issues left unresolved between them. She guessed he didn't want to waste the time in case she turned out to be a fraud.

"It is of little consequence," she replied. "I am quite well enough." It was a lie, but he wouldn't call her on it. He'd just offered her time to nap and eat. He knew she was ill.

Pledor resumed clipping away at his plant, his whole body moving in a jerky motion that made Jane think of a crow.

Jane leaned against the stool to allow the air to cool and clear a bit. Her eyes felt scratchy and she was breathing harder than she should have been. After a few quiet moments, she said, "If you don't mind, I will retire now and take my medical master with me?"

He looked up as though he'd just remembered Ajaya was still there. He waved the shears in the direction of the room's great door. "Of course. I'll send someone with a cart of thirty power cells to assist you in a few hours, Qua'dux."

Jane walked away without looking back, making her legs and feet glide over the floor as best she could. She hadn't gone far when sweat broke out on her upper lip and scalp.

She heard Ajaya tread quickly to catch up with her. Jane didn't acknowledge Ajaya's presence until she was certain they'd gone far enough to be out of sight. Then she turned welling eyes on Ajaya's concerned face.

Ajaya wrapped an arm around her shoulder without a word and helped her to the door. On the other side, Master Schlewan waited with a wheeled chair. Jane fell into it and closed her eyes, too tired to even speak. By the time they reached the medical chambers, she was ready to collapse in the bed and retreat to the oblivion of sleep.

15

Alan stood with his hand kneading the back of his neck, frowning. The four of them had tromped down to the basement of the building where the atellans had towed their beat-up shuttle. Now they were hanging out inside the shuttle, refurbishing Sectilius batteries, while their atellan escorts remained just outside. Jane was telling them about her meeting with a Geezer-Dux, or something—the local leader.

Alan was pretty skeptical about all of these doings, especially since Jane looked like death warmed over. The Sectilius were supposed to be superior technologically, but they'd fallen backward into a preindustrial state, except for a few remaining power cells that they used sparingly. That sounded fishy and he said so.

Jane sighed. Then she admitted, "I don't fully understand it either. I think it's really complex. They were very nearly wiped out by the squillae plague. That's got to take a toll on nearly every aspect of society. They no longer trust technology in a lot of ways, which makes sense, though they seem to crave that old way of life. They also lost an entire generation of their great thinkers—engineers, architects, mathematicians, philosophers, artists—and they lost all ability to communicate over distance, which is hampering the rebuilding process. There appears to be a huge gap between how they want to live and how they can live. I suspect we'll find out more when we prove we can do what I said we can do."

Alan switched one power cell out for another. They could do it. Then what?

Ron cleared his throat, and his eyebrows shot up. "Yeah, I think some of the sisters around here are looking for some…ah…" He chuckled, then went on, "…fresh genes, if you know what I mean."

Jane's eyebrows drew together.

Ajaya grabbed Ron's shoulder. "Ronald Samuel Gibbs—are you telling us they've propositioned you?"

Alan let out a barking laugh. "You too? Wow. That's awesome, dude." He high-fived Ron.

Ajaya suddenly looked cross and glanced from Ron to Alan and back again. "Do you mean to tell us that you took them up on their offers?"

Ron held up his hands. "Not me! I didn't touch anyone!"

Alan continued to snicker at Ron's expression until he noticed Jane's gaze boring into him. "Me either! They're handsy—that's all! I can't understand a word they're saying, but they keep sneaking up on me and going straight for the good stuff!"

"Inbreeding could be a problem in each enclave if they haven't made any attempt to prevent it," Ajaya mused.

"I don't have any idea." Jane flipped a lever on one of the seats in the rear row to turn it around so she could sit, like that was the last straw and she was giving in to exhaustion.

That immediately cut any amusement Alan was feeling to shreds. He was worried about her. She already had a tendency to work too hard. Now it was visibly showing. She couldn't hide it. He didn't like that one bit. Alan checked the progress of the power cell in the refurbishing compartment and returned to more serious conversation. "Given what you just said, how do you think they'll feel about the fact that we used nanites to rebuild these?"

Jane frowned. "He has to know. I think he wants the power cells so badly that he's turning a blind eye to that fact."

Alan pressed on. "What if he thinks we're using some human tech that isn't nanite related? He doesn't know anything about us or our level of technology. They might think we could be superior in that department. Will this come back to bite us in the ass?"

Jane blinked. "I hadn't thought of that." She let out a breath. "Well, you've programmed the nanites to stay put now, yes? None of them will have left our bodies or the shuttle. There won't be any on the power cells when we give them back. There won't be any evidence of how the batteries were reconditioned."

Ajaya said, "If it's our only bargaining chip, we don't have a choice. We're marooned here."

Ron put an arm around Ajaya. "We should move on as fast as we can. I get a weird vibe from this place."

Alan leaned against the wall. "So we've heard from one local leader that no one wants the ship and/or the Squid back. Our first priority should be finding the engines. Assuming all the preservation features worked during the drop, at least one of them will be repairable. It's going to be a big job, though."

Jane nodded. "Agreed. We've got a tracking system. Once we've given them the refurbished power cells, I'll ask for ground transportation to find the engines."

Ron looked at each of them in turn. "Then what?"

"While you and Alan are working on the engines, I'll visit the Hator enclave, briefly. There, I'll get another opinion about the ship. If Rageth's descendants are of the same opinion without prompting, I'll believe it's true. We'll return to the *Speroancora*."

Alan couldn't help himself. He had to know what was next on her agenda. "And then—?"

"The Sectilius aren't in a position to do the right thing, so we'll have to do it for them. We'll go looking for stranded Kubodera. To save them. Get them back to their home world, at least, so they don't have to die out there, separate and alone. I feel that we owe that to Ei'Brai."

Ajaya nodded as if that was the most logical thing to do. "We could use some additional crew members."

Jane looked pensive. "I agree, but I get the feeling that Gis'dux Sten won't want to spare even a single individual. From the conversations I've overheard, the goal of everyone in the enclave is reproduction and education—essentially rebuilding what was lost. They are very focused."

The shuttle's interior went quiet. Everyone seemed to be lost in thought. Their projected future had just changed drastically. Honestly, he liked this new mission a lot better.

Ajaya cleared her throat. "Commander, while we are here, will you please consider utilizing the triage compartment? It may improve your health and will at least give me a better assessment of your condition."

Jane cast her eyes down. Her jaw clenched. Quietly, she said, "Yes, I think I'd better."

16

Jane looked out the window of the primitive carriage she occupied. For the first time since they'd arrived, she could see Sectilia beyond the rushing gray clouds. It dominated the sky. It looked very much like home except for the unfamiliar shapes of the continents. She wondered what life was like there. Certainly it was very different from life on Atielle.

She'd given Gis'dux Sten thirty functional power cells a few days prior, and yet, after it was confirmed they all held a charge, he wouldn't spare one for her to use in a ground car, so they were forced to journey overland the old-fashioned way, Sectilius style. It was frustrating because they were moving at about the same speed a human would leisurely walk at, and she was anxious to get there, especially after waiting to travel for a few dark days while Atielle was in Sectilia's shadow.

It was hot. The air was heavy with moisture. It added to her discomfort. Bumping along in a primitive carriage was painful on her tender joints. Her overall health was much better, but she wasn't fully recovered yet and she was certain Pledor knew that. She couldn't imagine why Pledor had insisted on this method of conveyance except as another way to test her, to push her to her limits and to remind her that he really didn't care about her or her mission.

Tinor was acting as Jane's companion for the journey, which was another odd choice, Jane felt. The child was ecstatic about leaving the enclave for the first time. Pledor had also assigned a few adults, but they were positioned in front of, and on top of, the carriage—or serving as outriders.

The beasts of burden pulling the conveyance were an animal that looked very much like a cross between a rhinoceros and a hippopotamus. They were enormous. Jane couldn't even begin to imagine how much they must weigh or what it must take to keep them fed.

When questioned, Tinor said there were two reasons why the suesupus, literally translated as working pig, were domesticated. First, their tough hides were impervious to nepatrox stingers. They were also instinctual enemies of the nepatrox and would do fierce battle to keep their sectilian caretakers from being hurt. As a result, the nepatrox tended to shy away from them and leave such a procession alone. The second reason was that they were hardy in many environments. They had no trouble pulling a wagon through bogs or over rough terrain, both of which were common on Atielle.

Jane noticed that, compared to the adults, who tended to be more reticent, Tinor was free with sharing information, probably due to the fact that the youth was at a transitional life stage between childhood, when curiosity was tolerated, and adulthood, when it was actively discouraged as being rude.

It sounded mercenary even in her own mind, but Jane would probably get a lot more information from Tinor than from any adult she could try to question. As Jane conversed with the child, she was careful to use the gender-neutral pronouns reserved for sectilian children who had not yet declared their gender: *iad* in place of he/she as the subject of a sentence, *ium* instead of him/her as the object, *ius* for his/her as the possessive determiner, and so on.

It was fortunate that Tinor had already gained fluency in Mensententia, though iad was at only the very earliest stages of puberty. They'd been underway for over several hours when a driving rain began to fall that would muffle the sounds of their voices. Jane didn't want Tinor to feel self-conscious because adults were listening.

Jane turned away from the window and waved at Tinor to get the child's attention. "Tinor, I would like to apologize in advance if I ask you anything that makes you uncomfortable. You must tell me, plainly, if that's the case. As an outsider, I cannot always know what is acceptable in your culture. Do you understand?"

Tinor brightened. "Oh, yes. Master Schlewan told me that I should treat you like another child in need of education. Of course, that does seem odd because you are a Qua'dux, but you are not of these worlds and I imagine your world is very different. Will you tell me about it?"

"Of course I will. But first, can you tell me, do your people know who caused the squillae plague?"

Tinor frowned. "That was long before my birth. We learned about it in school."

"I know. But someone caused it. Someone programmed the squillae to hurt the Sectilius. Do your people know who did it?"

The child looked confused, as though it had never occurred to ium to ask that question. "It is done. It cannot be undone."

"No, it cannot." Jane paused, thinking how to rephrase in a way that Tinor could understand. "Do the adults in the Sten compound have punishments for children who've been naughty?"

Tinor's eyes widened. "Oh, yes. They punish us by taking away our favorite pastimes. We learn and do not repeat these mistakes." The child's mouth twitched. "Mostly."

Jane nodded. "So, no one has sought to punish the person who did this to the Sectilius?"

"How could they? We've been quarantined by the Unified Sentient Races. They destroyed the plague before everyone died, but their methods left us technologically crippled."

That spoke volumes. The Sectilius believed the squillae plague had originated from somewhere outside their solar system. The child had probably inferred that just as Jane had. As to who would gain from setting the plague in motion, Jane sensed that was beyond Tinor's grasp, so she wouldn't trouble the child further by asking that question.

Jane knew next to nothing about galactic politics. She knew that the Swarm, a colossal insectoid species that traveled through space devouring the ecosystems of entire worlds, was the biggest threat to life in the galaxy, but it surely wasn't the only one—though according to Ei'Brai, there was little squabbling among the Sentients themselves. He had no interest in anything that occurred outside the scope of his ship, so he had nothing to say on the topic of the greater galactic political atmosphere.

Tinor had pulled out a toy composed of a chain of six flat bricks connected by ribbons that twined around each brick in a pattern. As the youth tilted a hand one way and then the other, the bricks seemed to topple down the chain. It was mesmerizing, but Jane quickly realized that Tinor never let loose of the top brick. It was an optical illusion. Jane had never seen a toy like it on Earth.

Jane pointed at the toy. "What's this called?"

Tinor didn't look up. "Atielle's Ladder. It's named for the way my people used to get to Sectilia. One day we will get there again. Master Schlewan thinks it will be in my lifetime."

Jane's heart skipped a beat and one of Rageth's memories suddenly hit her hard enough to make her gasp. The atellans had a space elevator. If that was still operational, it would solve the problem of returning to the ship without having to fly through the debris field, though they'd need at least one functional engine.

Tinor peered at her curiously.

Jane smiled at the look on the small face. She adjusted her seat, though there was no way to get actually comfortable. "Does anyone ever think about the Kubodera?"

The child's face scrunched up. "Ship navigators? Not really. I mean, just in school. They come from a secret planet. No one here knows where that is."

"Do you think they survived the plague?"

Tinor shrugged and flipped the toy over. It worked exactly the same way from the other end. So far the atellans she'd met didn't have a lot of empathy for others. That was strange because she knew that Rageth had had that trait, though that may have come from being connected to others in an anipraxic network. The experience of anipraxia alone might have taught that level of emotional intelligence.

Something made her push a bit harder. Maybe it was the fact that she knew Ei'Brai was watching. "What if they are out there, alive? Untouched by the plague? Alone and stuck, drifting in various corners of the galaxy?"

Tinor inhaled sharply, as though the question irritated ium. "That is terrible for them, I suppose."

"Isn't it our duty to rescue them?"

"Why should it be our duty? We didn't put them there. Leastwise your duty, Qua'dux. You come from another world."

"True. But I know one. He's very nice. He misses being with other people like himself."

"They are people?"

"Yes."

"Then maybe they need rescuing. I don't know. Why can't they help themselves?"

Jane looked out at the rain again and inexplicably felt like crying. The Kubodera couldn't help themselves because the Sectilius had made it impossible for them to. It was painful to hear this kind of offhand comment from a child.

The outriders had moved closer to the carriage, probably because visibility had been reduced due to the rain. There was a suesupus and rider just a few feet outside the window. The massive beast kept its head down, occasionally sniffing the ground and then snorting loudly, its breath rising in a cloud of steam in the cold rain. Otherwise, the animals were relatively quiet.

Jane stayed silent for a long time. She didn't understand why, but she was stricken with a feeling of bitter disappointment. She hoped that the people at the Hator complex thought differently than this child had been raised to feel. Jane hoped that it was only an ethos of self-preservation because of the cultural setback, or the vagaries of youth, that brought on this thoughtless attitude.

She'd come here seeking allies. So far, she hadn't found any. It made her feel inexplicably lonely. She should have brought Ajaya with her, instead of leaving her behind to help Alan and Ron. Ajaya had wanted to come. She could have used her support.

Jane was formulating another question to ask the child when the carriage stopped. Jane looked outside and saw a rider dismounting. There were shouts, muffled by the rain.

Tinor opened the carriage door and peered out. Iad slipped back inside, hair glistening with raindrops. "We're here!"

Jane heard some dull mechanical sounds and thuds, and then the carriage lurched forward again and the patter of the rain on the roof stopped. Another moment passed and the carriage stopped again. Tinor leapt for the door and slid out before Jane could say a thing.

Jane stood and carefully eased out. She looked around. They were in a dim, cavelike structure without windows. There were some artificial lights and some illumination to one side that looked as though it was transferred from the levels above, similar to what she'd seen at Sten's compound. It was dimmer, but that would be from the dismal weather.

The suesupus stomped and snorted. The atellans who had escorted them from Sten's stronghold ignored her to tend to the beasts. Some were already escorting them away down a wide corridor. Tinor was nowhere in sight. Jane stayed near the carriage to keep out of the way. She didn't want to be stepped on. She forced herself to remember that this was a different culture. Things were done differently. Better to stay put than to wander off.

A willowy figure glided around the side of the carriage. Her crimped, flowing hair was full and barely held back from her slight, angular face in a semblance of a haphazard braid. She swept Jane with a gaze from head to toe, but remained impassive.

Jane didn't need to be told that this was one of Rageth's descendants. She looked very much like her. Tinor bounced around behind the woman.

"Scaluuti, Quasador Dux Jane Augusta Holloway. I am Gistraedor Dux Jaross Rageth Hator."

Jane returned the greeting. "I am honored. Thank you for admitting us to your home."

Jaross dipped her head and turned, saying, "Let us have some refreshment and your story, Qua'dux."

17

The child's words echoed from every quadrant of Ei'Brai's multiple brains. *They are people?*

His Qua'dux's answer—so swift, so pure, so emphatic. "Yes."

He withdrew from the Qua'dux's mind until only the most tenuous connection remained.

He didn't know what to do with himself. Sectilius was his home. These were his adopted people. Disbelief ate at him. His limbs felt heavy and lifeless. They'd forgotten about him and his kind. They cared not a whit what had happened to any of them.

That...hurt him.

He hadn't felt anything like this level of pain in so long. Not since the unending grief during his years of banishment. It was so strong it manifested in his body. He ached. His muscles twitched with tension he couldn't shed.

Would his dead shipmates have mourned his loss if their roles had been reversed and the plague had killed the Kubodera instead? Or would they simply have been frustrated by their inability to jump using his mind?

Was he just a tool? Was he a beast of burden like the suesupus that pulled Jane across that accursed moon?

The questions stirred up feelings he didn't like. He'd thought he knew the Sectilius. He'd thought he understood them, as a people.

They are people?

His limbs thrashed in his sterile, empty cage. This could have been his tomb, if it weren't for a terran woman named Jane Augusta Holloway.

He sucked in water, expanding his mantle to its fullest point, and shot himself to the other end of the ship. Instead of the exercise soothing him, it fueled his anger. He jetted himself again and again, grief blinding him until he slammed into the wall of his enclosure.

He barely registered the physical pain. The existential dysphoria was too great. He remained there, his limp body flattened against the glass, trying to feel anything but anguish and weak enervation.

They didn't want him back.

He wouldn't ever again be left in their care and he was glad. What a nightmare it could have been if he and all his kind had been forgotten, then reclaimed, only to be discarded again as they salvaged all of the ships like the *Speroancora* to build some primitive structure.

If Hator wanted the ship, he would mutiny. He would never serve another sectilian. He couldn't accept that fate after this grievous insult. He'd rather die.

Over the distance he felt Jane. He saw what she saw: water falling from a sky he'd never seen except in her mind and Rageth's memory.

He felt Jane's sadness. She cared for him. The child's words had upset her too.

He drifted. His limbs hung weakly around him, slack with spent emotion.

He took in his environment for what it was: a prison.

And even as he recognized that, he calculated a course correction to avoid a collision with stray debris—Jane had left the ship's computer with an order to give him that level of control—unlike the Sectilius, who, in death, had left him powerless and stranded for decades.

He snarled at himself angrily. He'd actually thought they might reward him for coming home. He'd hoped to be re-named—to leave the middling Ei' in his past and become Kai'Brai, earning his place in the most respected rank a ku-boderan could hold.

They are people?

He rejected the Sectilius and all their trappings—their ti-tles and their procedures and their confinement. He was not their chained beast. He was Jane's companion, Jane's friend. She treated him as an equal, as a colleague. He would will-ingly serve with her for the rest of his natural life.

This trip to Sectilius had been a fool's errand.

He would never again be the same.

18

Alan surreptitiously kicked one of the tires while he waited for the atellans to show up. The tire was that same green as everything else originating in the Sectilius system, but it was a tire and it didn't look much different than a tire would on Earth. The vehicle had sixteen of them, in fact, arranged in four rows of four. So, yay—the Sectilius had also invented the wheel.

The conveyance actually strongly resembled an amphibious all-terrain vehicle he'd seen once from World War II— proof that form followed function no matter where you were in the galaxy. It was slung low to the ground like a rectangular barge on wheels, and the side-opening doors lifted up, like a DeLorean, which he admitted to himself, begrudgingly, was fucking cool. There was a hoist in the back. He hoped it would be able to manage the load.

Pledor had agreed to let him, Ron, and Ajaya take a scavenging team out in this vehicle to retrieve the engines they'd dropped from the shuttle. Alan was eager to get his hands back on those, but he was also salivating to get a look at this vehicle's innards.

Ajaya might be curious about how human internal organs compared to their sectilian homologues, but he wanted to see how human machine guts compared to sectilian machine guts. He'd showed up early in the ground-level garage where they'd originally been brought in, dragging along Ron and Ajaya, mostly for translation purposes since his grasp on Mensententia was the worst of all of them. Now they were waiting for someone to come do some kind of maintenance check before they got under way.

Which never happened.

A couple of Sten's people showed up, climbed in, and started the vehicle—which was insanely quiet, goddamn it. He wanted to see if there was just one electric motor in there or one for each axle...

They were staring at him expectantly with those blank, hawklike faces. He sighed and climbed in the back, grumbling under his breath as he pulled the door down behind himself.

Ajaya looked at him, her eyebrows raised, "I'm sorry?"

He sighed. "Oh, nothing. I was just hoping to see the flux capacitor."

Ajaya looked skeptical. Ron chuckled.

And they took off.

It was a gloomy day, like most days seemed to be here. It was drizzling but there was light on the horizon. It might clear off. The atellans had the engine's homing device up front. So he just sat there and stared out the window. He didn't know what he'd expected from the Sectilius ahead of time, but this sure wasn't it.

It was supposed to be exciting meeting aliens, but so far these folks were pretty anticlimactic. They were so, sort of, disinterested in them.

Well, except for the women who kept trying to get in his pants. But that was too damn weird to be erotic. They were so cold about it. No preamble, no coy invitation, just sneak attacks to feel up his junk. He could be walking down a corridor on a way to a meal and out of nowhere a hand would be clamped on him. It was fucking embarrassing.

He found himself pushing these women away and looking around wildly to see if anyone had observed the insane interaction. Of course no one ever seemed to notice, and Ron said the same thing was happening to him.

At first Alan had thought it was kinda funny, but it had happened so much that now he was just in a perpetually wary state, keeping his distance from everyone and carrying stuff around awkwardly to keep his privates armored against invasion at all times.

He was now very sorry for every bra strap he'd ever flicked as a twelve-year-old boy. For every unnecessary brush against a woman's breast. For every time he'd stared at a woman's shapely ass as she walked away. Was this how women felt when that happened? Like a piece of produce being squeezed to see if it was ripe enough? Jesus. It was fucking nuts and their culture just ignored it.

Jane and Ajaya hadn't complained so he was guessing this was not a phenomenon that they were experiencing. He hoped to hell not. Ajaya stayed pretty close to Ron. Alan thought that she was probably fending off quite a few of these advances. Alan needed a female warrior coming to his defense too.

He sighed out loud.

Ajaya was scrunched in between him and Ron. She patted his knee and said, "Is it really that bad?"

He flinched and then rolled his eyes. "Yes. Yes, it is." He looked over and caught Ron's gaze. Judging by the wry look on Ron's face, Ron knew exactly what he was thinking about and didn't find it funny anymore either.

Alan's stare drifted from Ron to the dirty window on the other side of the vehicle. He saw a flash of red and sat up. There was a pack of six or seven very large nepatrox racing at a right angle to the vehicle on that side. Alan turned and there was another group coming down out of the hills from the other side, clearly bent on attacking.

"Fuck!" he yelled.

One of the atellans turned around and sent him a waggle-eared quizzical look, then turned back to face front.

Ajaya was talking to the atellans in Mensententia. He caught the gist of it. This happened all the time and they weren't worried. They were certain the vehicle was well balanced and couldn't be overturned. It had been engineered with the nepatrox in mind.

One of the beasts leapt at a tire with its mouth open. The vehicle shuddered but kept moving forward at its unhurried pace. The nepatrox was twisted grotesquely and flung beneath the other wheels. The vehicle ground over it with a sickening lurch and a distinct crunching sound that made him frown in disgust.

Another threw itself at the window next to Alan and then rolled away, leaving a muddy streak behind. The same was happening from all sides. It was very unsettling but the atellans were unconcerned. He guessed they were used to it.

Ajaya asked them about that. She interpreted for Alan. The atellan driver basically said, "We are the most sentient

144

form of life on this planet, but we are not the dominant form of life."

Atellans were pussies. These nepatrox were everywhere, eating anything that moved, and keeping these people living like rats in cages. The Sectilius weren't aggressive or competitive enough to deal with the problem properly. It was a miracle they'd survived as a species, really.

But that was why they'd come to Earth, wasn't it? The Sectilius were looking for allies in an intergalactic war—for people with more balls to fight the big, bad insect monsters. They were hoping that humans would turn out to be all the things that they weren't.

There was one thing Alan was certain of. Humans would never put up with this shit. If this were his planet? He'd devote his entire life to making sure those fuckers went extinct.

19

Jane followed Gis'dux Jaross Hator up a curving ramp that seemed to be carved from bedrock. Jaross wasn't in a hurry and for that Jane was grateful. Since she was still nursing residual joint pain, she was glad of a slower pace.

Tinor was too excited to be contained. Jane was unsure of how to handle that. She'd seen that children were mostly humored at Sten's compound except when it came to studying, so she didn't intend to admonish ium unless Jaross took some offense. And having Tinor along was useful, because the child's curiosity was met with openness, rather than reticence. Children were humored in this culture in a way adults were not. Education of youth was a general cultural goal that unified the Sectilius. That was helpful for Jane's purpose.

Tinor fingered the green-coated stone wall thoughtfully. "This is a very old place," the youth said with reverence and then skipped ahead up the ramp out of sight.

Jane hadn't gotten a look at the outside of the compound because the carriage's small windows never afforded a view, but she knew what it had looked like in Rageth's memories. It was very different from Sten's stronghold. This was an ancient building, built into the side of a mountain before the atellans had their technological revolution. It had been modernized centuries before, but many elements of the past remained.

Rageth had loved that about this place. For her, the connection to the very foundation of the planet made her feel peaceful and at home. That same feeling resonated with Jane now, and the sensation seemed strange—this was not her home, and yet it was very familiar.

Jane's memories had merged with Rageth's in a disconcerting way. They were not comprehensive. They were sporadic in nature and seemed to fill in gaps haphazardly, only when something triggered them. Once triggered, they suffused her with feelings that she recognized, but did not own. It was very like *deja vu* in a way. It made her want to pause and try to explore the fleeting sensations.

Jaross kept step with Jane, silently. But once Tinor had been out of sight for a few moments, Jaross asked, "Has the quarantine been lifted? I have not heard news of this. News travels very slowly here, as I'm certain you've gathered."

Jane grimaced. "I'm sorry, but I don't know anything about the quarantine aside from the warning buoys we encountered when we approached the planet."

Jaross's ears pulled back slightly, though her overall expression remained unchanged. "You've not come as an envoy from the Unified Sentient Races?"

"No..." The ramp opened into a grand atrium. Jane stopped and stared. One of Rageth's three-dimensional clay paintings was displayed on the large wall opposite. It had to be at least twenty by twenty feet.

It depicted Ei'Brai in a natural environment. The expression on his face had an intense look that Jane didn't recognize, and yet his many arms twined around him gracefully in what Jane knew to be a relaxed demeanor. The wall behind him was bright with the blues and greens of a sea, adorned with flowing strands of kelp and colorful sea creatures.

Suddenly Jane was struck with the feeling of painting it—she felt the scaffolding and the harness Rageth wore, the way she pushed herself to complete the piece throughout a brief leave from the ship during a resupply mission. Rageth painted until her arms trembled and ached, until she fell into bed each night and slept like the dead only to wake a few hours later, driven to paint more.

Jaross came to Jane's side. Her voice was warm in a way Jane had not yet heard from an atellan. The sound of it buoyed her. "I see you are enjoying my ancestor's work. Her name was—"

"Quasador Dux Rageth Elia Hator," Jane whispered without thinking, so entranced by the memory and the beauty of the painting that she forgot to remain on guard.

Jaross took a step back from Jane, indicating surprise though her face remained impassive. "You knew her? Before the plague?"

Jane dodged the question. She wasn't sure if the Gis'dux would understand without a lengthy explanation. "She is why I'm here."

Jaross wouldn't be misdirected. She was also very perceptive. Her voice was flat with certainty. "She was lost to the plague. You command her ship."

Jane expelled a breath she hadn't realized she'd been holding. "Yes."

Jaross moved to stand close to Jane again. "You must have come a great distance. Did you know the kuboderan as well? Do'Brai?" Jaross indicated the painting. All of her attention was focused on Jane.

"I do know him. He lives. He has been renamed. He is called Ei'Brai, now." Jane watched Jaross carefully. She felt like she was perched on a powder keg and didn't know why.

Jaross turned away from Jane to stare at the painting again. "He survived the plague," she said. "His enclosure was unaffected? His own squillae untainted?"

Jane looked at Jaross sharply. Ei'Brai had squillae too? That had never occurred to her. He'd never mentioned it. What purpose had they served? Jane widened her connection with him to send these thoughts and questions, but he didn't respond. He was likely busy with something critical, or perhaps interacting with the other three humans. Still, it was unusual and it troubled her.

Jane glanced up to see Jaross was waiting for her reply. "Oh...yes. It is sealed off, entirely self-contained. There is no exchange between the two environments. His enclosure is an island, isolated within the greater ship."

Jaross cocked her head. "Then there are likely others."

Jane nodded. "Yes. I suspect there are."

"A difficult fate."

Jane declined to comment. She had a lot to learn about life on Atielle and about Jaross. She already suspected that Jaross would be more sympathetic than Pledor had been, but she could not predict what that might mean to her mission yet.

The sounds of a commotion echoed up the ramp behind them. Jaross turned and stepped back. Jane copied the movement, careful to keep adequate space between herself and Jaross. She hoped that it wasn't Tinor getting into some kind of trouble. Jane had no idea how she would handle that situation if it arose. She was unsure of Sten's expectations in regard to the child. Was Jane watching Tinor or was Tinor watching Jane?

A deep voice boomed with excitement from behind them, but the cavernous nature of the compound obliterated the words and Jane couldn't make them out. Footsteps thundered up the ramp. People were yelling for someone to halt.

Jaross's ears pulled back sharply and she took another step back. Jane followed suit. She began to feel alarmed. Whatever was happening, it was unusual even to Jaross. Jane glanced into the atrium. Those who had been seated now stood and everyone had stopped what they were doing to look their way.

Jane turned back to the ramp in time to see a giant of a man burst around the curve into the open. He glanced around wildly, gray-white hair sticking out in frizzy tufts around his head. He stepped toward Jaross, extending a meaty hand almost questioningly, then he swung toward Jane and stopped in his tracks.

He looked Jane up and down with wide eyes. His mouth worked, but no sound came forth. He took a step back, directly into the path of two of Hator's people who'd been running up the ramp behind him. They collided, and the guards stumbled before grabbing ahold of him. He didn't resist. He just stared mutely at Jane.

"What is this?" Jaross demanded. "Who are you and why do you disturb the peace like this?"

He never took his eyes off Jane. "You. It was you I felt. You…aren't sectilian."

Jane glanced at Jaross. Jaross raised a brow.

The man went on, seemingly unaware of the fact that his arms were held tight by the guards. "You're an outsider. Yet you command a kuboderan. It is you, isn't it? It has to be you. I felt you."

Jane frowned. She wasn't sure what was going on.

Jaross spoke. "This individual is the Quasador Dux Jane Augusta Holloway. I have only just made her acquaintance. May we have your name? Or shall we throw you back outside with the rest of the animals?"

The man huffed and shook off the guards, who stepped back and watched him with narrowed eyes. The man drew himself up to his full height, which was impressive. He had to be at least seven feet tall, and he was not lithe like Jaross. He was burly and sinewy, built like an ox.

"I am Ryliuk."

"Scaluuti, Ryliuk...?" There was a definite question left hanging at the end of her statement. When Ryliuk didn't expand on his name, Jaross's lips tightened.

He ignored that and turned to Jane. "What ship do you command?" he asked.

Jane's gaze slid uneasily to Jaross, whose face was impassive now. "The *Speroancora*."

"Ah... That would be Do'Brai, would it not? He lives! I never met him."

"It's Ei'Brai now, actually."

Ryliuk's lips parted in a huge smile, revealing large, perfectly aligned teeth. "Even better! I pledge myself to you, Quasador Dux Jane Augusta Holloway, and to your gubernaviti, Ei'Brai. I humbly ask you for sanctuary. Can you find a place for me among your crew?"

Jaross took a step back. "That's treasonous. Your place is here, Ryliuk. Who are your people? Where are you from?"

His smile fell. "My people are dead. My pledge has always been to the Kubodera, not the Sectilius. I am a mind master. Your rules do not apply to me, Gis'dux Jaross Rageth Hator."

Jaross's gaze glittered. She turned away from Ryliuk dismissively to focus that hard countenance on Jane. "Do you accept the pledge of the mind master?"

Jane swallowed. She was afraid of making a cultural blunder that could cost her dearly in the long run. She had not come here to make enemies. She would have to tread carefully. Jaross was already angry.

Jane lifted her chin and was careful to focus her attention on Jaross only. "I do not know him. I will interview him and take your advice on the matter before I make my final decision. Is this acceptable?"

Jaross's gaze seemed to soften. "Indeed. I believe we were about to take refreshments?"

Jane inclined her head in acknowledgement.

Jaross whipped around briefly to say, "You may join us, Master Ryliuk."

Ryliuk's head dipped. "Of course."

Alan watched as another nepatrox gave up the chase. There was only one left following them now. He'd been mentally preparing himself for an epic battle with the monsters when they got out to pick up the first engine, but one by one over the last thirty minutes the nepatrox had peeled off and headed back into the hills.

He would have liked to think that perhaps the nepatrox had grown tired of chasing them or that the terrain was unfavorable. Maybe they figured there was easier prey somewhere else. But Alan knew these creatures to be relentless and determined. He didn't think they would give up so easily—and that made him nervous.

The vehicle came to a stop. Before them was a wide, marshy area that gave way to a lake. The sun had come out for a brief visit. In fact it looked like it hadn't even rained here recently.

Alan sat up. The single nepatrox outside was gnashing its teeth and flapping its hinged mouth flaps. He tried not to watch. He was glad he couldn't hear or smell it. He looked all around outside the vehicle but didn't see the shuttle's engine anywhere.

The atellans seemed to be disagreeing about something. Alan looked at Ajaya. She held up a finger, listening intently.

Finally Ajaya interrupted the atellans, asking a question in Mensententia.

Ajaya frowned as the atellans explained something to her. They spoke so fast Alan only caught a few words out of every sentence or two—not enough to be sure what was going on. Then Ajaya leaned back in her seat, a look of disbelief on her face.

Alan pressed her. "What's going on?"

Ajaya blinked. "I think they're saying one of the engines has moved since we left the compound this morning."

Ron looked alarmed and began scanning the surrounding countryside.

Alan felt his eyes bulge. "Moved? That kind of weight? What the...? How?"

Ajaya shrugged. "They say they don't know."

Ron said, "Another clan probably found it."

Alan nodded and clenched his fists, whispering a string of his favorite obscenities. Someone would have to have run across it, known what it was, and then come back for it with a winch. No way did they just pick up and carry off a shuttle engine. That thing was able to generate escape velocity. It was huge!

Now all three of them were on the edges of their seats, hanging on every word the atellans uttered.

"That's not what they think happened," Ajaya whispered. "They think an animal found it."

Alan peered out the window, but couldn't see the last nepatrox anymore. What could be out there that even a nepatrox was afraid of? He wasn't sure he wanted to know.

The vehicle jerked forward again.

"What kind of animal are they talking about?" Ron asked.

"Good question. That can be hard to decipher. These young atellans have a penchant for abbreviations, acronyms, and the like. It makes it a bit difficult for me." Ajaya grimaced.

Ron rubbed his nose. "What? Like LOL? ROFL?"

"Something like that."

Alan rolled his eyes.

The all-terrain vehicle cut across the shallow lake and climbed up a steep incline on the other side. Here it was rockier. There were lots of tufts of spiky grasses sticking out from every crevice.

When they reached a flat plateau at the top, the atellans stopped the vehicle again. They spoke in low voices and occasionally gestured toward the terrain before them in a vague fashion. Alan looked to Ajaya impatiently.

Ajaya rose from her seat and moved to the front to look out the windshield. "Oh, my word," she whispered.

Alan followed. He only had to look for a second, and then he fell back into his seat, scrubbing his face with his hand. "Fuck a doodle do."

There was a wide, dusty plain below, ringed by low hills. In a few places there were muddy patches with a small amount of shallow standing water. Dozens of enormous beasts shuffled around the space.

In the middle of that carnival of circus animals? An engine gleamed in the midday sunlight, with dirty deflated balloons from its descent draped on and around it.

"Suesupus," Ron said. "But that's a domesticated animal. They're like cows or horses, aren't they?"

Ajaya shook her head. "I could be wrong, but these look much larger to me." She asked the atellans more questions. After a lot of back and forth, she sat down on the bench seat they shared with a heavy sigh. "They're the wild cousins to the domestic suesupus. It's the same species, but they are about as close to the suesupus we saw as wolves are to domesticated dogs. The atellans breed theirs to be smaller and more docile."

Ron asked, "What do they want to do now?"

"They want to go back to the compound."

"That's the plan for getting the engine back? Leave? After we came all this way? They don't give a shit whether we can get back to our ship or not. They have no idea if Pledor will let us come out here again. And as hard as it was to get him to allow us this trip, I have my doubts." Alan squeezed the back of his neck so hard it began to hurt. His voice was loud enough that the atellans turned to look at him curiously.

Ajaya raised her eyebrows. "What do you propose we do, Alan?"

"I don't know. How hard can it be to spook them? Make them run off or something?"

Ajaya relayed that. The two atellans looked very grave and started gesturing a lot. She translated their answer. "I think they're saying the suesupus get very erratic when disturbed. Trampling is a very real possibility under those conditions."

Crushed under the foot of a beast the size of an elephant wasn't his preferred way to go. "What about luring them away?" Alan said.

Ron looked thoughtful. "A preferred food? A mating call? An infant distress call? That could be tricky, but it could work."

Another round of translation. Ajaya said, "Their preferred food is out of season. They don't have any recordings of these calls you suggest in the vehicle, but there should be recordings like that in some archives back at the compound."

Alan leaned back thoughtfully and weighed the options. "Would they be aggressive toward a solitary man?" He waited patiently for the translations.

Ajaya's brows pulled tightly together. "They don't know."

"Well, I give the sectilian education system an F in zoological studies." Alan heaved a huge sigh, then leaned over to unlatch the door. It opened and a wave of heat hit him in the face. The air was heavy with humidity. He shed the jacket he was wearing, climbed out, then started down the hill. He was going to make something happen for a change.

Jaross guided them across the atrium, through another corridor carved from stone, and into a sparsely furnished room dominated by a simple green table and an assortment of chairs. The light here was all artificial and far dimmer than it had been in the atrium.

Jane stood calmly to one side until she was sure what was expected of her, carefully watching for subtle body-language tells that might inform her where she would be expected to sit.

She was momentarily confused when Jaross took a bowl and cup from a small side table and set them down, then turned away. Then Jane realized that Jaross was assigning seats by laying out places for them in a triangular pattern: Jane and Ryliuk on the one side with several feet of distance between them, Jaross alone on the other side, facing them. Jane stepped to her place and waited, keeping the others in sight directly or indirectly, until Jaross seated herself. It could be tricky to know who might be meant to defer to whom in situations like this.

Once seated, Jane allowed herself to glance into the bowl. It contained food cubes, which surprised her. Jaross had a generator of some kind, at least for some functions, possibly only for guests. The cup was similar to those they used on the *Speroancora*, tall green plastic. The beverage inside was garnished with a shoot of a leafy herb.

Jaross broke the silence without preamble. "You have come from Sten. Do you have a contract with him?"

Jane inhaled sharply. "A contract? I'm not sure what you mean."

"You are using Sten's animals. You arrived in his carriage and bring his child with you. He did not give you these things freely. Gis'dux Sten is shamefully uncooperative."

Now Jane understood. "We traded for the use of them. This compound was our original destination, but things didn't go according to plan. Our landing was rough." Jaross's blunt opinion of Pledor was somewhat refreshing, though Jane knew to be careful not to imply that she approved or disapproved of either Pledor or Jaross's assessment of him.

"You intended to come here? For what purpose?"

Because I had to. Jane wasn't sure what to say. She didn't know how to express the urge she'd been feeling. For the part of her that had freshly received Rageth's memories, it was almost a nostalgia, a longing for a homecoming. She assumed the sensation would fade with time, but for now, she couldn't visit the Sectilius system without stopping at the Hator compound any more than she could have visited Florida without stopping in to see her grandparents.

Jane wished Ei'Brai weren't so disconnected. He could help her navigate awkward situations like this one. She glanced at Ryliuk while she thought a moment.

He nodded. "She has known your ancestor through the kuboderan. Part of the process of accepting command is knowing the predecessor. It is a way to honor the departed, whether dead or retiring. The Qua'dux was drawn here."

"Oh?" Jaross seemed to be intrigued by this. She leaned forward. "How extraordinary. Ship culture must be so very different."

Ryliuk suddenly looked a bit sad. "It is indeed, Gis'dux."

Jane said, "We didn't know if the *Speroancora* was an isolated target or if other ships or even Sectilius were affected. I wanted to bring news to Quasador Dux Rageth Elia Hator's family about her final days. I wanted to tell you that she was respected by her crew and that she was relentless in fighting to save them."

Jaross looked thoughtful.

Ryliuk said softly, "You can do more than tell, if you wish."

"What do you mean?" Jane asked. She felt a little spurt of fear.

"I can connect you."

Jaross stood slowly. "I have heard of such things. But we haven't had a mind master here for generations. They—you—are so rare."

"I have reluctantly been a farmer for these many years, marooned here without my preferred…company. I want to return to my old life. I will happily grant you this small thing if you will consent to it."

Jane realized he must be much older than he looked if he had been alive before the plague. It struck her that she didn't know for certain what the sectilian lifespan was.

She felt very uncomfortable. This life had been chosen for her by circumstance. She'd become accustomed to having Ei'Brai inside her head, to sharing a limited mental space with her crew, but she didn't know what to expect from Ryliuk and that alarmed her. Would it be the same intimate kind of relationship that she had with Ei'Brai? Or would it be more like what she shared with Ron, Ajaya, and Alan, through him?

Ei'Brai? Where are you?

Jaross lifted her drink to her lips, sipped, then said, "My aptitude scores showed I would have likely followed in my ancestor's footsteps had that been possible. I admit I am curious."

Ryliuk looked from one to the other. "Do I have your consent?"

Jaross returned to her seat. "Yes."

Jane moistened her dry lips. "Yes."

She was prepared for it. Ryliuk gingerly stepped into her frontal lobe where her peripheral thoughts resided, but made no attempt to go further. His thoughts were not greedy or impatient but indicated he was simply happy to connect with another this way. It was more intimate than speaking aloud, but not as deep as the contact she shared with Ei'Brai.

"Are you comfortable?" he asked mentally. "You seem unsure, though it is hard for me to tell—your mind is very different from a sectilian or kuboderan mind. I will withdraw if that is your wish."

"No. I—this is fine."

"I will now connect with the Gis'dux. She is very receptive, but has never experienced anipraxia. We must be patient." Out loud he said, "It is important to stay relaxed."

Jaross blinked slowly. "Of course."

And then they were there. Inside Jaross's mind. And for the first time Jane knew what Ei'Brai had meant about how different the human mind was. Ryliuk was disciplined. He only shared thoughts that he wanted to, so Jane was less aware of his thought process.

Jaross's thoughts were all there for them to see. She was unaware that she was sharing them or that she had any control over the process. They weren't fragmented like human thoughts. And they didn't zoom like Ei'Brai's did. They were dense, orderly, and insatiably curious. Jaross contemplated every aspect of the connection, cataloging how it felt, how it worked, how it had already changed her perception of herself and others. She was analyzing it in an almost scientific way.

There was a round of greetings. Then Ryliuk showed Jaross some basic precepts. He was patient. He had clearly done this before. Jane wondered, so that he could hear, if he had been a teacher. He smiled and said that he had.

After that brief orientation he asked the Gis'dux to simply remain receptive and allow Jane to show them the things she wanted to. Jane concentrated on sharing the memory of the creation of the painting in the atrium.

When the memory had been transmitted, Jaross inhaled sharply. The connection broke as she returned to vocalized speech. "That was astounding! For a brief moment, I felt as though I was inhabiting her mind. I can feel her…" Jaross broke off, searching for words.

Jane finished the sentence for her, gently. "You can feel her mood, her outlook, her sense of self."

165

Jaross's face was transformed to bewilderment. She stood and placed a hand on her forehead. "I apologize. I didn't anticipate this kind of emotion."

"No need," Ryliuk said in a neutral voice. "Your response is natural." He stayed seated while Jaross paced the room. He sipped his beverage and tossed a food cube into his mouth. Jane did likewise, but watched Jaross worriedly. This was the first time she'd seen any kind of strong emotion displayed by a sectilian. Jaross looked agitated and uncomfortable.

Ryliuk sent her a thought. "This is normal for a first experience. She is feeling the gravitas of a moving moment. She is experiencing more empathy than she is accustomed to." The undertone in his message urged patience.

Jane acknowledged his thought silently.

Jaross continued to stride back and forth for some time, her arms wrapped tightly around her upper body in a kind of self-hug. She stopped suddenly and turned to Jane, her voice strident, almost accusatory. "I feel as though I created that mural! But...I know that I did not." She looked bewildered. "I keep reliving it as though it were my own memory..."

So it wasn't like playing telephone, Jane thought. The message wasn't diluted in the retelling. Jaross was experiencing it the same way Jane had.

Jane suddenly realized that she hadn't noticed any forms of vicarious entertainment since she'd come to Atielle. No television or movies, no one reading, or even telling stories for pleasure. Sectilians weren't accustomed to indirect experiences. This surely increased the impact of the memory for Jaross.

Such a cultural absence could have easily lead to a lack of social awareness or a sense of individual responsibility to contribute to the community, except that wasn't the case. Everything Jane had seen showed that they were a mostly egalitarian society. They took care of everyone and everyone had an equal chance to thrive.

Some atellans were farmers, but the fruits of their labor were distributed to all according to need. There were electricians, plumbers, and mechanics who worked on demand throughout an enclave. Others taught, cooked, cleaned—all seemingly with a strong work ethic, all without monetary compensation.

The only division between the genders seemed to arise in childbearing, but even child rearing was a group activity. Jane had frequently noticed age-matched groups from toddlers through school ages playing together with adults of both genders supervising. It was a cooperative society—rare among modern humans, although on Earth anthropologists had theorized that preagricultural humans had lived more like this.

Ryliuk continued to be impassive. Jane followed his lead, watching Jaross surreptitiously. Jaross stopped pacing and leaned against a wall, facing away from them. Her head was bowed and Jane could just see her left hand working, her thumb rubbing over her forefinger in a repetitive motion. If Jaross had been human, Jane would have seen that as an unconsciously self-soothing movement indicating that Jaross was overwhelmed, but Jane couldn't be sure if she could apply the same interpretation to a sectilian.

Abruptly, Jaross turned. "I want to know more about her. I want to see more of her memories."

Jane looked to Ryliuk questioningly. It seemed strange to rely on his expertise when she barely knew him, but she was the outsider here and had no choice. "Is that a good idea, so soon?"

Ryliuk didn't answer out loud, but connected the three of them anipraxically. Now Jane could see that Jaross's thoughts had calmed and all that remained of the previous turmoil was intense curiosity.

Jane showed them many moments from Rageth's life. The day she assumed command of the *Speroancora* and met Ei'Brai for the first time. The day she gave birth to her oldest child. The day she passed all of the aptitude tests that eventually allowed her to join a ship community.

Ryliuk passively observed every memory without reacting. Jaross's reactions were muted. She'd figured out that Jane was hesitant to show her more because of the intensity of her initial reaction and reined in her responses.

Jaross clumsily passed a thought to Jane—loudly, intrusively, breaking Jane's concentration. "You are showing us moments that are positive in nature only. Let us see a more balanced experience of her life."

Jane inhaled deeply and showed them the day the Swarm destroyed the colony world that Rageth had called home for many years while raising her children. She showed them a moment from the day Rageth learned her closest confidant and lover had died. And then, finally, Jane showed them Rageth's final days on the *Speroancora*.

That memory was agonizing to experience. When it was done, Jane sat silently and let her mind go blank. She bowed her head, sniffing back tears and surreptitiously swiping at her eyes. She couldn't prevent that memory from affecting her. She felt the great loss of Rageth, even though she'd never truly known her.

After a long moment, Jane sent them a question. "Do you know who did this to your people, who programmed the plague into the squillae?"

Both Ryliuk and Jaross answered swiftly and with vehemence. "No."

That satisfied Jane. Jaross in particular would have difficulty lying right now. She continued. "Do you think there is anyone on either world who does know?"

With a subtle movement of his hand, Ryliuk deferred to Jaross.

"No," she said. "It is my understanding that in the time after, before the communication networks fell, the perpetrator was unknown. Since then, it's doubtful that anything new has come to light."

Jane pressed. "There's no particular enemy who was suspected?"

Jaross's face broke into an almost human simulacrum of incredulity. "What enemy? The Sectilius are cooperative. The only enemies we face are those who are unwilling to communicate: the Swarm. The Swarm has never used technology to our knowledge. So it seems unlikely that they wrought the destruction of our culture."

Jane nodded. This fit with what she knew.

Jaross's face darkened. "Do you know who did it?"

Jane leaned back in surprise. "No!"

Ryliuk raised a hand. "Allow me to assure both of you that I detect no elements of deception. Indeed, you are both so new to anipraxic communication it would be exceedingly difficult for either of you to even attempt a lie under these conditions. Rest assured, we are all speaking frankly here."

Jane nodded. She felt the truth of that. She eyed the two of them thoughtfully. "There is just one more thing I really want to know, Gistraedor Dux Jaross Rageth Hator. It is my main reason for coming to Sectilius."

Jaross swept her loosening braid off her shoulder and laid her hands open on the table in front of her, a gesture that Jane thought probably meant something like "I am an open book."

Jane let out a shaky breath, almost afraid of the answer she would receive. "I have brought this ship back...to return it."

Both Jaross and Ryliuk indicated surprise. That was the same reaction Jane had gotten from Sten.

Ryliuk asked, "You do not want the ship? Is it still contaminated?"

Jane held out a hand. "No, that's not it. The ship is free of the plague. It's hard to explain." Jane paused. She wasn't sure what she was trying to say.

Ryliuk said, "This is a cultural construct you are wanting to express. Merely tell us how it would be on your world."

Jane smiled. "On my world, we would want the ship back. It is a very large, very valuable commodity. Humans would wish to reclaim it."

Jaross's delicate brow furrowed. "But who would reclaim it here?"

Jane calmly met Jaross's gaze. "I thought you would, Gis'dux. I understand there is no centralized governmental entity now that unifies the two worlds, but you are Quasador

Dux Rageth Elia Hator's closest living relative, aren't you? You lead this compound. Or have I misunderstood?"

"You are correct that I am her closest living relative. She was my father's mother. I am the figurehead here, but this community has no use for a spacefaring vehicle. It could be cannibalized and all of its components used, but what of the kuboderan? We are landlocked. We have no access to the ocean here. I have no way of knowing if he could survive in Atielle's oceans. Besides, it is distasteful to dismantle something that is functional and useful. To add to that, it could worsen conflicts with other communities if the imbalance in technology between us fell heavily to our side. That is not our way. We already have difficulty with Gis'dux Sten because of the lack of parity between our communities. It creates friction."

There were echoes of these same sentiments in Ryliuk's mind.

Jane felt lighter. She suppressed a smile of relief, her mind racing with feelings of happiness that she hadn't expected. She didn't actually want to give up the *Speroancora* or Ei'Brai, and the depth of her relief surprised her.

"What I want, what every sectilian wants, is to see Sectilius return to her former level of technology and prosperity. It will take time to achieve this. Our primary obstacle is population. We are consumed now with survival and growth. We retain the knowledge but the infrastructure is gone. Until we can rebuild that, we are, as you can plainly see, arrested in a transitional phase of unknown duration. A ship will not change that. It is no longer of value to us. It is yours now, Quasador Dux Jane Augusta Holloway."

Ajaya called after him, "Alan! What on Earth are you doing?"

He yelled over his shoulder, "I'm going to see if this thing is even repairable before we go to any more trouble."

All the others were scrambling out of the vehicle. The atellans hung back, but Ron and Ajaya chased after him.

Ron stepped in front of him and held up his hands. "Come on, man. I know this is upsetting news, but you don't need to go off half-cocked and get yourself killed."

Alan sent Ron a dirty look and didn't stop moving. He just dodged around him. Ron threw up his hands.

Alan sauntered a few steps down the hill at an angle while rolling up his sleeves. His boots bit into the hard-packed soil just enough to give him purchase. The perpetually saturated ground was baking into clay in this heat. In places it had dried to a crumbly, fine powder and gave way under him, kicking up plumes of dust as he scrambled to get his footing.

He picked his way carefully, trying to avoid these softer patches. His cybernetic leg didn't do too bad. It wasn't quite the same, and he was more awkward than he used to be, but it was starting to feel more natural.

Ajaya called out, "Alan, stop being silly and come back here. We'll figure this out!"

Alan's lips tightened. He turned to face her, squinting against the sun hovering behind her. "Silly? I'll tell you what's silly. Silly is coming all the way out here, wasting an entire day, but not being prepared for what we would find. Silly is traveling to an alien planet, but not speaking the language fluently. *Silly*—" He paused for a moment to collect himself, because his voice was getting really loud and spit was flying everywhere. He scrunched up his face and then relaxed it. "Silly is letting Jane go off by herself when one of us should have gone with her. *This* is not silly. *This* is gathering information. It's what I do, dammit."

With that, he felt satisfied that he'd delivered a rather pretty speech before tromping off to his impending half-assed annihilation. Maybe he'd be remembered for something. He turned and continued skittering down the hill.

Ajaya's voice carried after him. "Okay. We like you, Alan. Please don't let them trample you. Jane would never forgive us."

He was facing away so he let himself smile grimly.

The behemoths weren't active at the moment. They all seemed to be lounging either in the mud pits or in the cool, moist shadows of the hills to pass the hottest part of the day. He would guess that, like a lot of animals in hot climates, these would be pretty lethargic during midday heat like this and more active at first light and at dusk. He might be able to just walk among them and straight up to the engine. He decided to gamble everything on that assumption and hope that he wasn't about to become a pancake.

Alan glanced over his shoulder. Ron and Ajaya stood at the top of the hill, hands clasped, watching him descend into the valley, the picture of a loving couple. *Well, aren't they just peachy.* He snarled to himself a little bit and kept walking.

It had been dark for days while Atielle was in Sectilia's shadow. It had rained during that entire period—but of course it would be a hot, sunny day when he took off on a hike. And the sun in this system ran a bit hotter.

It had been so long since he'd enjoyed sun on his skin, and though it felt good at first, he soon felt his skin getting dry and tight. He'd have a burn if he survived, and probably nothing else to show for his stupidity. Just as well. He was too pasty these days.

It did feel good to be outdoors. He chuckled to himself. He'd traversed thousands of light-years inside an alien spaceship and now he was hiking on an alien moon. That was pretty fucking awesome.

In fact, he took a moment to gaze up at the sky. The first clear day since they'd arrived on Atielle afforded him the opportunity to see the other half of Sectilius—the planet Sectilia dominated the sky like an impressionist painting looming overhead. He could even see one of the other moons, a tiny white ball, off to one side. That wasn't a sight you got to see every day.

His cyber foot suddenly sank several inches, and he flailed to keep himself on his feet, but failed and slid to his ass. He put his hand out to push himself back up and found himself sliding again as the dirt gave way. He peered more closely at the ground under and around him. There was a cluster of holes carved into the side of the hill—he'd been collapsing their openings. As he looked, a weaselly face stuck out of one of the holes to whistle a shrill note at him then darted back inside. He blinked in surprise. Then another one did it. And another. He felt like he was being scolded for messing up their front doors. "All right. All right," he muttered. "I get the idea. I'm going."

He slowed his descent as he got near the bottom, choosing his footing carefully. It would be a bad idea to make a bunch of noise. When he hit the valley floor, he practically tiptoed to stand behind a large boulder and take in his surroundings.

So far none of the suesupus had moved appreciably. He was sure they knew he was there. He'd seen some eyeballs roll in his direction, but they didn't seem to care—confirming his hypothesis that they'd ignore him. They just swished their tails like lazy dogs swatting at midges that Alan couldn't see.

Now he needed to decide how to get to the engine. The shortest distance between two points is a straight line, but there were suesupus scattered everywhere. Dammit. He should have mapped out a route when he'd stood up at the top instead of shooting off his mouth.

His heart pounded. There was a tickle in his throat from the dust he'd stirred up on the way down. He wanted to cough something terrible, but he couldn't afford to make any loud noises. He knew it would pass. He bent at the waist and breathed over that devilish granule burning in his airway, swallowing saliva thick from thirst and clearing his throat with the tiniest of ahems possible, eyes watering streams down his face.

After a while it eased. He didn't look up to the ridgeline. They were probably up there thinking he was having a freaking heart attack. He shot his thumb up in the air so they'd know he was okay and edged around the side of his boulder.

Damn those things were big.

He thought for a minute about what animal they resembled most now that he could see them up close. Size-wise and in coloration they were nearly elephantine. No trunk, though. No horns or tusks either. That made them look a bit friendlier. They didn't have the elongated head of a hippo, so Alan settled on really big hornless rhinos.

Suesupus, the giant hornless rhino of Atielle. What a stupid name. Not easy to say like rhino or hippo. He could shorten it to sues or pus but that just sounded dumb. Really, if it came down to names he was just going to call them "big fella," and hope for the best.

He stepped out in front of the boulder. He was really sweating now. He wished he had a canteen.

A suesupus nearby pawed at the ground restlessly. Alan froze and watched the thing out of the corner of his eye. No eye contact. That could be seen as a challenge. The animal closed its eyes again and Alan breathed a sigh of relief.

He took a step and then another. No big movements. Nice and slow. Nobody needed to get riled up. Just keep moving. Nothing to see here, boys and girls.

He nearly jumped out of his skin when he walked by a rather large one and it grunted. It was really more than a grunt. A grunt was mild in comparison to the sound that thing made, but he didn't know what else to call it. It was similar to a snort, only several octaves lower than any animal he could imagine snorting. He felt the vibration of the deep tone rattle the ribs in his chest. Along with the grunt the beast's breath blew across him—a hot, sour, vegetal wind, stirring the dust at his feet.

He might or might not have hyperventilated for a moment.

Then the tickle in his throat came back full force.

He couldn't stop himself from glancing at the animal. Its only visible eye glared at him with a lazy annoyance, but it wasn't making a move to rise.

He held his breath and took a few more steps. Nothing happened.

He took a shallow breath and *oh my fucking God* he was going to cough. It was like a spark burning through his throat. Every breath just fanned the flame. His eyes welled with tears until he could barely see. He gasped and dry heaved and staggered forward, swallowing convulsively though he had no saliva left to wet his throat.

He was sure he looked like a cat coughing up a hairball.

He hated cats.

This had happened to him once on a date. Not even copious gulps of water had quelled it, so he'd fled to the men's room, where he'd coughed so hard his face turned beet red and he nearly vomited.

Of course he'd still gotten lucky that night.

He reached the engine and clung to a brace, trying to breathe without disturbing the animals surrounding him that would be measured in metric tons, not kilograms.

Then he lost the battle. He let out a strangled cough.

Once he started, he couldn't stop. He hacked and coughed until he was doubled over, gooey saliva dripping from his open mouth.

He'd thought a grunt from one giant hornless rhino had been disconcerting. Now he was faced with a rumble. The ground shook as dozens of suesupus staggered to their feet and started milling around, snorting and pawing.

He watched in wide-eyed disbelief as they swung their massive heads from side to side, trying to see him better. Dust swirled around them. Their ears cocked, trying to triangulate the sound that was disturbing them.

But he couldn't stop coughing.

23

A red light flashed in the data oculus implanted in Ei'Brai's right eye, but he barely registered it. His blood sugar was dangerously low. He hadn't eaten for days. His glucose stores were gone. Wasting through muscle catabolism had begun.

The health-monitoring device was urging him to eat.

The thought of eating the food the Sectilius had left for him had become abhorrent. He was a caged animal that they had coddled, and that disgusted him.

He couldn't even remember the taste of wild food from his infancy—natural food, the food his ancestors had thrived on. All he knew was the nutritionally balanced, fish-flavored vegetable-protein-based food cube, manufactured on demand when he pressed a button.

Every beakfull was the same. The same flavor. The same texture. It sustained him but it didn't *nourish* him.

He didn't want it anymore.

He drifted around the interior of his enclosure on the artificial currents, heedless to the ship's status or to the needs of his human companions on the moon below. He heard their calls, but faintly, as though from far away. They didn't ensnare his attention. Recursive thoughts tumbled over and over in his mind.

He was in agony. Every one of his appendages was cramping. His hearts palpitated out of sync. His nervous system throbbed when it wasn't shot through with stabbing pain. He couldn't segment it away. It was part of the suffering and couldn't be stopped.

He'd been left to die and no one had given him a second thought. He and his kind had been cut loose the second the Sectilius had a problem. If the plague had been incomplete—if a percentage of sectilians had survived in a disabled ship—would those survivors have been forgotten along with him in the darkest corners of space?

The Sectilius were taking care of their own kind. Many had been lost. They were rebuilding a broken society. These things he comprehended and did not fault.

What he abhorred was that they had worked so hard to convince him from infancy that he was one of them. He'd bought into it. The culture, the mindset, the reward system for honor and valor.

The Kubodera had been taken in, adopted, treated like treasured family members, then abandoned.

But was there a fallacy in that statement? Had they been taken in, or kidnapped?

Jane had asked him that once. If he was a slave. He had responded to that question as though it were ridiculous. But was it? Or had her keen intuition been correct as usual?

The sectilian child with Jane had asked if kuboderans were *people*. Just a few decades after the plague, kuboderans were not even studied in schoolrooms? Not even as a part of sectilian history? What about zoological studies? Astronomical studies? Engineering? Psychology?

Had the Kubodera ever been equals? Or had they been a commodity to exploit as long as conditions were favorable?

All the people he had known over the centuries of his long life...he had felt such affection for so many of them. Had that devotion been genuinely returned or was that part of the lie to keep the beast of burden appeased?

The warmth, the humor, the sharing of memories. He'd been in their heads. He should have been able to spot deception like that. Had he been deceiving himself too?

Not with Quasador Dux Rageth Elia Hator.

Rageth.

She was the only sectilian who'd allowed—no, encouraged—him to use her informal name. It had been such a break of protocol that he indulged in that intimacy only during rare, deeply moving moments.

Her love for him had been genuine. He was certain of that.

She'd taken special care with him, more so than anyone else ever had. She kept him closer, gave him greater access, relied on him and his wisdom.

She believed him a worthy friend. She respected him. She shared her life with him.

He'd always been so eager to dig deeper with her predecessors, but so few could bear that. They found it too uncomfortable, too familiar. It was enough to use him to communicate with ship and crew. They kept him out, held him at the surface. They shared only the memories required of them as part of the ancient contract between their peoples.

In exchange for a kuboderan's professional expertise, one had to be compensated adequately for the trial of confinement. To that end, they were allowed to accompany scientists, mentally riding in their minds, when on site during observation and experimentation. In addition, there was an expectation that there would be an allocation of older memories, allowing a kuboderan to explore the universe inside the minds of sectilians in ways their own physical bodies would never be allowed to.

Rageth had told him once that sharing her memories with him in the ritualistic way they indulged in allowed her to live her life anew. She said that he uncovered details, sensations, and sentiments from moments long past that took her breath away.

It all came from her mind, but to her it felt fresh and made the memories more meaningful. He could see how sunlight had given her environment a roseate glow, when she had only seen that it had been a clear day. He would notice the way the air tasted or how the wind had swirled around her skin. Her mind had recorded so many details, but she did not know how to access them in the way that he could.

She often said he gave her back her youth—this time to enjoy it.

They both enjoyed it.

It didn't matter.

It shouldn't matter. Not anymore.

All of his people were gone. He couldn't turn to them for reassurance now. He couldn't inquire, and he would have been too proud to inquire then, regardless.

He felt a small measure of optimism. He thought perhaps...perhaps he had been a good influence on their lives even if they had not recognized it themselves.

When new crewmembers came up from the colonies or Sectilius who had never been aboard a ship before, they tended to not be well liked at first. They were often seen as selfish. Living on a ship was very different from living on a planet, station, or outpost. It was always an adjustment, and some adapted better than others.

But time in anipraxia had a way of changing people—most of them, anyway. Everyone who lived in ship communities knew about this phenomenon. It was like a second coming of age. A chance for the mind to grow and be opened to new points of view, to cultivate compassion and empathy. Many Quasador Duci left ship life to become leaders on their home worlds when it came time to retire, to lead their people with a newfound skill.

Perhaps he had helped to change them. Their time on the ship improved them as individuals. He felt almost sure that those crewmates would have given their lives to save him, if they'd been faced with that choice, as he had fought to preserve them.

And he knew that despite the callous indifference toward him and his kind among this generation of sectilians who had never known ship life, his life was still...perhaps...better than it would have been without them. Despite his confinement he had lived long and seen much, even if it was through the eyes of others. He had certainly lived longer than any of his wild brothers and sisters on the world whose name he did not know.

That life, the life of his progenitors, was a feral existence. Feast and famine. Struggle and unceasing danger. Once mated, he would be condemned to death. His counterpart would oversee the growth of the offspring until hatching and then she, too, would die. Neither of them would ever see their progeny grow to adulthood as sectilian and human parents did. Their children would become food for hundreds of predators until only one or two remained. He was spared the pain of watching that.

He was also spared the harsher confinement that non-sectilian races sometimes subjected the Kubodera to, illegally. Tanks smaller than the arm span of an individual. Primitive filtration equipment that didn't adequately scrub the water of unsanitary contaminants. The choice between suboptimal food or being hungry. He'd heard stories of his kind going mad under these pitiful conditions. Without the yoke that the Sectilius used to maintain strict control of the kuboderan navigators, some had committed suicide, taking ships of people with them, flying into a star or black hole, venting the atmosphere, charting a catastrophic collision course.

It had been a blow to hear those words from the child, Tinor. But it could be worse. His tank was sparkling clean. He was safe. He had an excellent commanding officer. He had never been forced to hunt or kill sentient creatures to survive.

He shuddered with a spasm of pain. He was unwell.

Perhaps... Perhaps it was time to consider eating again.

24

Alan kept trying to strangle the cough, but the dust was swirling around him and it was about more than the tickle in his throat now. He'd taken some of that dust deep into his lungs and his lungs didn't appreciate that at all.

He pressed himself against the engine and watched with increasing dismay as the animals began to stagger around. One of them lowered its enormous head and pushed the engine. It scooted a few feet. Alan was pulled stumbling along with it as he stubbornly held onto an exhaust collar.

His bleary eyes abruptly focused on another suesupus bearing down on him. Shit got real—real fast. There was nowhere to hide from the charging beast.

He scrambled up on top of the engine, dimly noting melted and crushed components as he did so. The fire had done a lot of damage, and being pushed around by mammoth animals had not been optimal. This engine would take months, maybe years, to repair under the primitive manufacturing conditions currently prevalent on Atielle.

The suesupus slammed into the engine, sending it sliding in the dust until it stopped suddenly as it met a patch of uneven ground. Alan's body wasn't anchored in any way—

just his hands, which were wrapped around a coolant manifold—so he flipped like a hinge, landing on his back with his arms extended, hands still gripping the pipe.

The air whoofed out of him. He saw stars.

He ended up arched over something that was damn hot from the sun beating down on it. It took a moment to feel the heat. His cybernetic leg locked up as it began to run a diagnostic, which it was supposed to do when he was in an accident. He hoped to hell it hadn't been knocked loose again. He was in too much pain to tell.

He managed to roll over onto his stomach, rotate his hands, and lock his good ankle into a crevice just before another suesupus nudged the engine again. He continued to cough and wheeze and generally just try to breathe and hold on as the peevish beasts took turns pushing the source of their consternation across the dusty valley floor in quick, violent bursts, kicking up thick clouds of dust each time.

They were playing Atielle's version of air hockey with him as the disk in play.

Then he felt the sickening lurch as a suesupus stuck some portion of its head anatomy into some element of the defunct engine and lifted one side. He hovered upside down in the air for a second before the engine came crashing back to the ground so hard his teeth rattled.

That was when he heard Ajaya and Ron. They were up on the ridgeline, whooping and hollering and waving their arms while the two atellans stood nearby silently. For a long moment he waited, holding his breath as long as he could, gasping for air only when absolutely necessary.

The engine remained still. He dared to open his eyes and saw that the beasts had redirected their attention to the ridgeline.

Mentally he cursed and wished they would shut up. Eventually the beasts would have gotten bored and left him alone. He could have quietly limped away. But Ajaya and Ron were stirring up more trouble. He didn't want to be responsible for the damage that might cause. The last thing he needed was for his friends to get hurt because of his own stupidity.

Through slit eyes, he watched one of the closest suesupus nodding its head vigorously. It scraped one of its three-toed front feet in the dust before loping toward the steep slope trumpeting a sound that felt like it could break his eardrums. Several others followed in the moments after that. Soon the entire group was heading for the ridge. The vibration caused by the stampede and the suesupus vocalizations transmitted through the engine into Alan's body.

Alan blinked grit from his eyes. Ron, Ajaya, and the atellans piled back into the ATV and took off. He wearily lowered himself off the engine and set his good foot on the ground gingerly, grimacing when the cybernetic leg made contact, pain shooting straight up his spine into his skull. That leg was still locked up. He closed his eyes for a second to let himself acclimate, then tried to figure out which way would be the best direction for hobbling to safety.

He was freaking the fuck out—the bum leg might not let him climb the hill.

The ATV zoomed around the perimeter of the ridge then went out of sight, the suesupus hot on its tail. Alan cursed.

He knew they wouldn't leave him there, but he also didn't know what their plan was.

He reluctantly attempted to make contact with the Squid, but felt only dead air where normally there would be an effusive response. So much for help from that quarter. What the hell was the Squid doing up there, anyway?

Alan gimped to the boulder he had originally hidden behind. It felt like a touchstone. He'd been safe there before. From there he considered the possibilities. How long would the suesupus be distracted? Would they wander back the way they came? Would they still be in stampede mode? Would the sight of him enrage them again?

The bad leg was nothing more than a peg at the moment. Climbing the steep slope wasn't a possibility, but he could try clambering up one of the gentler sloping areas as a tripod, dragging the bad leg behind him.

He had just picked a spot and started for it when he came face to face with an immature suesupus. It couldn't be very old. It was the size of a draft horse. It snorted and tilted its head like a curious dog. Alan hadn't even heard it coming. He'd assumed they were all up chasing the all-terrain vehicle.

Alan sighed. The suesupus backed up a few steps, then slowly, almost daintily, came forward again.

Alan decided to ignore it. What else could he do? He wasn't going to get out of the valley unless he moved.

He edged around the creature toward his goal.

The suesupus grunted, low and throaty, and began to sniff the air around Alan.

Alan kept gimping.

The baby suesupus followed. It moved in closer until it was touching Alan's body, snuffling in his hair, nudging his arm to get its nose up in his armpit.

Alan froze. In his peripheral vision he saw the atellan vehicle sweep over the crest of a hill and into the valley. It was barreling across the dusty plain straight toward him.

Alan turned and started moving in the direction of the car.

The suesupus grunted again, louder this time, and nudged Alan so hard he stumbled forward onto his good knee.

He barely suppressed screaming a string of curses.

The car was racing closer.

The suesupus stuck its nose up in Alan's junk. He'd had just about *enough* of that business.

Without thinking, Alan whirled around, arms swinging wide, with an instinct to do violence. But then he just looked at the damn thing. It was cute as all hell. He couldn't actually hurt it.

It backed up, the whites of its tiny eyes showing.

He muttered at the beast, "That's right. You back down, little man. I'm fucking intimidating."

The side door of the car flipped up just a few feet from Alan and slowed to a roll.

The cyber leg vibrated—it was back in business. No time to test it. He took off at a sprint to intercept it, diving inside when their paths crossed. He tumbled into a seat and looked back to see the suesupus paw at the ground, then charge. Ajaya closed the door and the car was off again at top speed.

Alan pulled himself up as the car sped away. The suesupus followed at a good clip for a while, then seemed to tire or lose interest and came to a stop, rapidly becoming a tiny speck in a cloud of dust behind them.

He hauled himself upright, panting. Ron was driving. The atellans looked very confused, their ears pulled so far back the skin of their faces was taut, and they were slowly blinking at each other and the humans. They must have been out in the sun for a while because their skin had become visibly darker.

Ajaya was glaring at him. "Well," she said, "how is the engine?"

Alan pushed dust-coated hair back from his face. "It's fucked. We're fucked."

Jane and Jaross walked together through the shadowy rabbit warren of rooms and short corridors that made up the compound. Jaross was serious about overseeing her domain. She didn't seem to micromanage, but to put out small fires before they became larger and more difficult. She spent her days giving advice and connecting people who needed each other.

As they strolled, Jane spied Tinor eating a meal with some children of the same age and waved. When Tinor saw Jane, iad leapt up to join them. The child had been shadowing several medical professionals and chattered at Jane excitedly about the experience. They had more functional medical technology here. The youth was very excited to learn about it.

"What will you do now?" Jaross asked Jane when they moved on.

"I need to go back and find out how my friends have fared with the engines," Jane answered. This was the third day of walking and talking like this with Jaross. As the days passed, Jane felt less and less like a recovering invalid, but that improvement was counterbalanced by anxiety that grew with each passing hour without contact from Ei'Brai or her crew. She hated to cut the visit short. She was enjoying Jaross's company and was learning so much about sectilian culture, but not knowing what was happening with her friends was killing her. She was sure something was wrong with Ei'Brai. It was so unlike him to be so uncommunicative. Getting back to the *Speroancora* as soon as possible had to be their top priority now.

"The engines, yes," Jaross replied. It felt as though Jane had told Jaross everything that had happened since she'd left her home on Earth. The last three days had been warm and full of stories and sharing. Jaross was insatiably inquisitive. She looked thoughtful. "Do you think they could possibly have survived the impact after such a drop? And one had been on fire, correct?"

Jane frowned. "They were designed to be dropped in an emergency, but I've no idea what it will take to repair them or if that's even possible. My engineer is very capable."

"What will you do if the worst should come to pass?"

Jane heaved a deep sigh. "To be honest, I don't know. I don't like to think about that. I have faith that we'll find a way back to our ship, somehow. I can't...I can't bear the thought of abandoning Ei'Brai up there—all alone again. It was such a terrible trial for him, before."

"Yes. His pain was great."

Jane had shared that with Jaross. They'd had several sessions with Ryliuk as well. It certainly saved time in the telling.

One of Jaross's thin eyebrows perched high on her forehead. "You will return to him." She looked forward again, her arms folded and her hands each tucked into the opposite sleeve of her ornately embroidered cream-colored garment.

"I'm worried about him," Jane said, glancing up at the ceiling as though she could see through it to the sky, the clouds, the ship, and Ei'Brai himself.

"Could he have contracted an illness? Perhaps he is resting after the long journey." Jaross paused at the bottom of the ramp. They were in the basement and garage area of the compound, where Jane had arrived.

"I don't know," Jane said. That hadn't occurred to her. It made her worry even more.

"You will leave at daybreak, then? You will take Ryliuk?"

"Yes. With your permission." Ryliuk seemed to be convinced he was already a member of her crew and Jaross had not protested the notion further, so Jane hoped it wouldn't cause trouble. She thought he would make a fine addition. He seemed to be capable and confident, and he knew how things had worked before the plague. The technology wouldn't be a mystery to him. There were things he would know that Ei'Brai didn't know. That could be helpful.

"It is given, freely. Ryliuk has made his case. He belongs with you and the kuboderan."

Jane suppressed a sigh of relief. "Thank you."

"Your crew is very small. The ship was meant to hold thousands."

"Yes, but we manage."

"Have you made any attempt to recruit?"

Jane hesitated. She felt sure Jaross knew the answer to that question. It was clear to Jane that the atellans felt their first duty was to their own people, to bring their society out of this terrible setback. Jane wouldn't disrespect Jaross by trying to entice anyone away. She didn't want to make trouble. "No, I haven't," She said solemnly.

"Would you consider volunteers?"

Jane's brow came down. "I'm not sure what you're asking, Gis'dux."

Jaross swept the tail of her braid over her shoulder. "I would like to accompany you."

Jane took a step back, her mouth gaping. This was so unexpected. "What? You would?"

"Yes. I believe you are surprised."

Jane stared at her hard. "Well, yes. Your reaction to Ryliuk on the day I arrived led me to think it would be impossible for anyone—perhaps even him—to join us."

"Do you want people to join you, Qua'dux?"

Jane sighed. "That's a good question. On one hand, it would be good to have more hands to help us achieve our goals. On the other, it could be dangerous. We're so inexperienced. We don't have the knowledge of the galaxy and the technology that the sectilian race does. But I do worry about putting other people at risk. We will make mistakes."

"You are terran. That alone qualifies you for the position. If you will have me, you will be my Quasador Dux. I'm trained as an engineer. I will be of use to you, I assure you."

"I have no doubt of that, but you...but...you don't want the command?"

Now Jaross looked surprised. "No! I have told you the *Speroancora* is yours. That would not change because I came to my senses and realized what you represent to us—not just to sectilians, but to all the Sentients. I have given this careful consideration in the days we've spent together. What you have accomplished thus far is nothing short of stunning. This is a moment that will be remembered."

Jane frowned. "I mean no disrespect, but I don't know anything about the Cunabula or their purpose for us. I don't know if your legends about us are meaningful. I'm simply a woman. I'm not a prophet."

Jaross tilted her head in a thoughtful way. "The writings of the Cunabula aren't meant to be prophetic. Cunabulists aren't religious zealots—they're students of science. And terrans weren't chosen by gods—you were bred. Your commitment to the Kubodera is honorable, supremely altruistic. It's an example of what is needed—perhaps more sectilian than the Sectilius. You will inspire many, even if you fail. I want to be a part of that."

Jane just stared at her, discomfited.

"We will know, in time," Jaross said. She looked sure and very zen.

"I don't know what to say."

"Then don't say anything." Jaross's eyes lit with mischief. She raised a hand in an unusual way and Jane realized she was signaling someone. The dimly lit room brightened and Jane heard something scraping across the floor. From behind a hodgepodge of various types of primitive wagons and carriages, a group of atellans, including Ryliuk, pushed a shuttle forward.

Jane's mouth dropped open. "Oh! I…" She walked up to it and the atellans stopped pushing.

"Is it the same model?" Jaross asked.

Jane walked around it, comparing it to the one she'd flown down from the ship. "No. This is similar but definitely a different vintage. Ours is cornu class. This is…penna class, I believe? Somewhat smaller and meant for cargo, not passengers."

"The power cells will be compatible, I'm certain of that," Jaross said. "There were just a few shuttles on Atielle when the plague hit. They were used extensively in the days after. Until the power cells became useless, they were one of just a few ways that survivors could find each other and consolidate isolated populations. This vehicle has been used a great deal, but it was built to last. It will convey us to your ship without difficulty, once we install the power cells from your craft."

Jane raised an eyebrow at Jaross. She hadn't taken their landing story very seriously if she thought it wouldn't be difficult.

A woman opened the craft. Jane and Jaross stepped inside. The rear compartment of the vehicle contained a couple of banks of seats from a land vehicle retrofitted at odd angles to make them fit. However, as she looked into the cockpit, she could see that the controls were similar to those on her shuttle. It could work.

Jane had a strong urge to hug Jaross. Now they wouldn't have to wait for Alan and Ron to repair the engines. They'd be able to move on in just a few days. "I don't know how to thank you for this. I'm overwhelmed."

"There is no need to thank me," Jaross said. "Your mission is just and good and may in fact assist my people through this dark time. I only wish I could spare more individuals to join the cause. As it is, my leadership role will be filled by my very capable brother. I, alone, may be sacrificed without hardship for the community."

Jane raised her eyebrows, but declined to comment.

Jaross continued, "Ryliuk's presence will be helpful in dealing with the stranded kuboderans you'll encounter. He is well trained in the psychological well-being of that race. These kuboderans have never known anything except living among sectilians. You need the Sectilius. I'm sure you have considered this problem."

Jane nodded slowly. "I have, yes. I had hoped to find allies here on Atielle. But Sten's disinterested attitude toward us and your reaction to Ryliuk's initial offer to join us made me think it was unlikely that we would be allowed to recruit anyone."

Jaross inclined her slender neck in acknowledgement but didn't comment on that. "You will need more individuals simply to crew the derelict ships you encounter during your mission."

Jane didn't need reminding about that problem. She thought about it daily.

Alan was having a meal in a cafeteria with Ron, Ajaya, and Schlewan. Today it was big bowls of raw greens with a slab of indeterminate protein and some kind of nut sprinkled on top. The atellans really needed to learn about salad dressing.

The meal was filling though, and he hadn't had any adverse reactions, so he couldn't complain. Atellans seemed to consider flavor to be a secondary consideration to nutrition when it came to food.

Ajaya and Schlewan were pretty much inseparable these days, which was great, because the old dame watched over them and made sure they got things they needed—like meals. She asked a lot of questions about human life and Earth, which no one else was doing. She seemed to be studying them, which Alan thought was far more normal than the blank stares of the rest of the community. Also, Schlewan never grabbed for his privates, which Alan considered to be a huge plus in her favor.

His face had burned a little while he was down in that valley, and though the atellans had no personal experience with sunburns, Schlewan had noted the problem, asked a bunch of questions about his skin, and provided a soothing ointment to put on it. It was greasy and it stank of weird herbs, but it helped a little.

The room was at a dull roar, accompanied by the sound of rain drumming against the large windows. Typical meal. All the atellans were chatting about God only knew what. He had a far better grasp on the language now, but they still spoke too fast for him to really feel like a participant. He only interacted when it was clear he was being spoken to. The first thing he always said was, "Please speak slower."

That meant they treated him like an idiot, but he didn't give a shit. Apparently most people in the galaxy gained access to the genetically imprinted language of Mensententia when they reached puberty. Anyone who couldn't fluently speak that language by adulthood was considered developmentally impaired in some way. Humans were the only exception the atellans had ever heard of. That didn't jive with their legends of humans as saviors of the universe. It was probably the reason no one was interested in them aside from Schlewan.

Whatever. He didn't pay any attention to their crazy folklore.

He did notice, however, when a shout rang out over the murmuring din—and when throngs of people stood and went over to the floor-to-ceiling windows.

He looked to Schlewan. She gestured to the windows and said, "Qua'dux Jane Holloway returns."

Alan leapt up and pushed his way through the crowd until he was pressed up against the glass. She'd been gone for days without word, which wasn't like her at all. The Squid had been strangely quiet throughout that time, which would normally have been welcome, but now was just another level of annoying. He was probably up there in the ship, focused so completely on Jane that he'd forgotten the rest of them existed. It was pretty creepy actually. Whatever was going on between those two couldn't be healthy.

It was raining hard, which made visibility poor. The carriage rolled up to the compound and he briefly glimpsed Jane's blonde hair through the window of the carriage. None of the atellans had hair like that. He was sure it was her. The carriage stopped twenty feet from the building.

He looked up. A team of six suesupus lagged some distance behind, pulling another shuttle through deep ruts in the mud. He broke into a huge grin. "That's my girl," he murmured, and pushed his way back through the people, heading for the ramp that would take him down to see her.

When he got to the bottom, three people barred him from going farther. He was tempted to break through but didn't want to create any more ill will than he already had with the suesupus fiasco. Jane wasn't going to be pleased when she heard about that. No one had been injured, but the atellans were all butt hurt over it.

He was glad that none of his buds back on Earth could see him being held back by a man and woman no taller than four foot seven inches—even though they were easily as bulky as Hans and Franz. The third person was a man, a toothpick really, but at least six foot nine. Alan strained on tiptoes, trying to see what the hell was going on.

Pledor brushed past him. The trio of guards parted to let the Gis'dux through, but when Alan tried to follow him, they pushed him back.

Pledor strode outside to stand under the overhang, preening like a bird. Alan could hear a lot of talking and the snorting and blowing of the domestic suesupus, but he couldn't tell what was going on.

Ajaya and Ron came down the ramp and spoke to the guards who were keeping him from joining Jane, but the guards remained impassive. No human was going to get by them.

Someone came in from outside and signaled to the guards. The guards pushed the three of them up the ramp without explanation until they were back in the cafeteria, where they couldn't hear or see anything.

Alan cursed like a sailor, for all the good it did him.

27

Jane stepped down from the carriage and was instantly soaked. The rain fell in large, cold drops, at times pelting her sideways during heavy gusts of wind. The atellan driving the suesupus had called into the carriage to say that Gis'dux Sten had ordered that they would not be allowed inside.

Pledor was aggravated about something, but Jane had no idea what. To have Jane face him alone was Jaross's idea, and Ryliuk concurred that it was the best plan. Pledor stepped out from under the overhang of the compound into the driving rain.

Jane lifted her arm in the arc of greeting and was about to vocalize it, but before she could say anything, Pledor sputtered, "What is this, Qua'dux Holloway? Why do you abuse my hospitality thus?"

Jane took a deep breath to steady herself against Sten's bluster and took in the situation. "If I've given offense, I apologize, Gis'dux Sten. Please, edify me—I'm a foreign traveler unaware of the intricacies of your culture."

"When you said you would go to the Hator compound, you said nothing of bringing guests back. It is the height of rudeness to foist more mouths to feed upon our beleaguered compound. Isn't it enough that we have been feeding your people out of simple kindness to vagabonds? You take advantage! And now you bring *her* and expect me to feed *her*? Outrageous."

Jane smiled tightly. "I'm sorry, but you've misunderstood, Gis'dux Sten. My return brings an end to our imposition. I've come to retrieve my friends and our shuttle. We'll be gone from here as soon as possible."

Sten's face flushed red, but Jane wasn't sure if that meant the same thing to a sectilian as it did to a human.

Tinor slipped past Jane and into the dry enclave. Jane wished she could follow the child. The ceremonial garment she wore was made of plant fibers. It was soaked through and cold against her skin.

Ryliuk sent a tingle to the fringe of her thoughts. She let him in. He said, "Do be careful. I don't believe Gis'dux Sten is being forthright. However, you must avoid saying as much, because that will likely anger him further."

The battered and dirty shuttle rumbled up behind the carriage and came to a stop. The beasts of burden expected a drink and a meal, Jane was sure. They snorted and stamped and scraped at the mud with their broad heads. She felt badly that they weren't being cared for as they were accustomed to after pulling the heavy craft so far.

Jane thought carefully about what had been said and the emphasis Pledor had put on Jaross's presence. There was clearly a rivalry there. He was angry that she'd brought Jaross with her, but Jane wasn't sure why. She remembered Jaross's intimation that Pledor was greedier than the average atellan. There was definitely a rivalry between the two clans, but were they always this intolerant of each other? Surely there was trade between the two enclaves.

She kept her voice neutral. "Haven't you been compensated adequately? Do you need us to refresh more of your power cells before we depart?"

Pledor stepped back and turned away from her. He pulled someone close to him, spoke softly in their ear, and sent them off into the compound. Jane didn't think that boded well. She turned to see that Jaross and Ryliuk had stepped down from the carriage. Jaross was wearing a poker face. Ryliuk looked chagrined.

Jaross came to stand beside Jane, wisps that had come loose from her sloppy braid instantly plastered against her face from the driving rain. She raised her arm while simultaneously saying, "Scaluuti, Gistraedor Dux—"

Pledor interrupted. "What are you doing here, Hator?"

Jaross did not look perturbed. She answered, "I am joining Qua'dux Jane Holloway and the *Speroancora* crew."

Sten's gaze grew icier. "And who is this?"

Ryliuk swept his arm briefly in the sectilian way before answering, "I am Ryliuk, a mind master from the Mebrew compound. I am also joining the Qua'dux."

"Mebrew?" Pledor thundered. "That's six days' ride from here!"

Ryliuk dipped his head in agreement. "I left Mebrew the same day I felt the presence of a kuboderan in orbit. The journey was an ordeal. I would do it again. My place is with the terrans."

Sten's eyes narrowed. "You are a renegade. You both are! How many go with you? Who is leading Hator compound now?"

Jaross said, "I hardly think that's important. The Qua'dux merely needs to retrieve items from her damaged shuttle, and collect her people, then we'll perturb you no more."

"This is not so simple, Hator." Pledor shoved a hand at Jaross. "You are colluding with an alien that has broken quarantine protocols. The penalties could be severe. Perhaps I should call the local adjudicator to decide upon these matters."

Jaross remained impassive. "Nonsense. The adjudicators lost their power fifty standard years ago. That threat is meaningless."

"Is it?" Pledor asked, his thin lips barely moving.

He looked more hawklike than ever before, Jane thought. Then a rider sidled up behind him, just inside, on a solitary suesupus.

Sten folded his arms and tilted his head back. He didn't seem to notice the sheets of water cascading over his face. "I'll send for Lish."

Jaross didn't take her eyes off him. Her voice remained even. "The Gis'dux of Lish is an old woman. She will laugh at you."

"Krik is dead," Pledor countered.

Fat drops of water dripped from curled tendrils around Jaross's face. "If Krik is dead, she was succeeded by someone sensible—someone with far better things to do than to arbitrate such a clear-cut dispute, Sten."

Sten's lip curled. "Why do you wish to attend the human? You would give up your leadership?" Then he snarled, "Or has she transferred command to you?"

Jaross blinked long and slow, then answered. "I will serve the terran because the Cunabula meant for her people to lead us. Sectilius is naked and exposed. There is nothing we could do to stop the Swarm if it should come now. The terrans—these ships they seek, the technology they contain—could assist us. It may be what we need to bring our people out of this dark time. I will serve this Qua'dux because serving her serves our people. My intent is above reproach. Is yours, Sten?"

Pledor sobered. Some of the choler evaporated from his gaze. He took a small step back and seemed to be lost in thought.

Jane stepped between the two of them and appealed to him. "What is it that you want, Gistraedor Dux Pledor Makya Sten?"

He stiffened. His gaze turned resolute. "There should be equal representation from Sten compound."

Jane nodded. "I will agree to that. However, I reserve the right to choose the individual from Sten compound who will join us."

Pledor raised his chin. He remained statuesque despite a gust of wind sweeping a drenching wave of rain over them. "You may choose two. I will be one of them."

Jaross's eyes widened and her ears pulled back sharply—the first sign of emotion Jane had seen from her throughout this interchange.

Rain pummeled Jane so hard it made her balance wobble. She was chilled. Her teeth were starting to chatter. "Equal representation with Hator compound would mean just one individual."

Pledor narrowed his eyes. "You would turn down a volunteer, freely offered?"

Jane didn't like Sten. She didn't trust him. She also didn't doubt that he would make good on his threats if she wouldn't agree to his terms.

He could hold her crew hostage along with the shuttle, and she would have little recourse as an outsider. Jaross's support might not be enough to resolve things quickly. Pledor could easily tie them up for ages—or worse. Jane had no desire to find out what passed for a court system on this broken planet. He'd already threatened her life once. She didn't want to find out what the inside of a jail cell on Atielle looked like if Pledor had some power over the court that Jaross couldn't counter.

There really wasn't a choice.

She raised her chin. "I agree to these terms."

28

When the guards finally cut Alan loose, he didn't waste any time. He bounded down the ramp, stumbling to a halt when he saw Jane at the head of an entourage coming up the other way, Ajaya and Ron on his heels. Jane looked like a drowned rat and mad as hell.

Proceed with caution...

His brows drew together. "Hey, you okay, babe?"

She blinked at him dramatically. "Babe? What is this? 1975?"

He grimaced. "Sorry. But seriously...is that a functional shuttle?"

She sighed. "I sure hope so." She patted his arm as she reached him.

He turned to match her pace ascending the ramp. He itched to slip an arm around her but he wasn't about to push it. "What's up with Sten?"

She tilted her head a little to indicate the atellans behind her, then shook it wearily. "Let's talk after I get a warm bath and some dry clothes."

"We were having a meal when we saw you'd arrived," Ajaya said. "Shall we save you a place at the table?"

Jane considered that. "I'll try, but I'm not making any promises. You go ahead though. Finish your meal. It can wait until morning, if necessary."

Ron smiled. "Glad to have you back safe, QD."

When they reached the cafeteria level, Ajaya and Ron peeled off to resume their meal. Jane looked at Alan quizzically.

"I'm not hungry," he said, shrugging. He wasn't, really. And he was so glad to see her, he was reluctant to let her out of his sight again.

An atellan directed Jane to the guest quarters, handed her some towels, and then withdrew. Alan had been sleeping on a cot in that same room with Ajaya and Ron.

Four more atellans followed them into the room. He barely noticed them until he realized two of them were as wet as Jane and they were stripping down to their skin. He didn't mean to look, but he wasn't expecting them to do that, so he got an eyeful.

He was having trouble keeping his eyes off the lithe atellan woman as she divested herself of her wet garments. Her body was...well, she looked like a living manga cartoon—an exaggerated thin body topped with a cloud of wild light-brown hair. Neither of them seemed to realize that anyone else was there. He noticed Jane's gray eyes watching him with amusement so he shifted his body away from the atellans and refocused on her.

He cleared his throat. "So, ah, do you want me to go get you anything? I can try to rummage up some food."

The atellan woman swept out the door completely naked, holding towels and dry clothes, presumably heading for the communal bathing area. The dude followed. He was more human in proportion—like a lumberjack on steroids. Tall and buff as shit.

Alan closed his eyes and physically turned again toward Jane. "Really? Did they just do that?"

She blew out a breath that verged on a laugh. "Yeah. You haven't noticed? Their culture doesn't value privacy like we do. They are very...free with their bodies. This is going to take some getting used to."

"Yeah. I guess." He'd been keeping his distance from the atellans, bathing at odd times so he could be by himself. It seemed prudent considering his ongoing issues with young atellan women. He just felt like everybody wanted a sneak peek at his privates and he wasn't having that.

He rubbed the back of his neck and looked at Jane. Really looked at her. She had her hands tucked up in her armpits. A puddle of water had formed around her feet. He suddenly felt weird. "Hey, um...you..." He gestured toward the open door. "You want me to leave you alone so you can...ah..."

She bit her lip and looked unhappy. "I don't know."

"What don't you know?"

"If I'm ready to embrace the lack of privacy, you know? Right now." She gestured toward the door, indicating the atellans who had just passed through it.

"But you're cold. Your lips are turning blue, Doc."

"I'm freezing!" she cried suddenly.

"Yeah, well, put on some dry clothes!"

She looked around, forlorn. "I..."

He felt like a heel. He was making her uncomfortable. "Oh, shit. I'm sorry. I'll just leave."

She grabbed his arm. "No! Don't go. I meant—with them." She sighed. "I don't know what I want except to be warm and dry. I'm tired. Don't go."

He stared at her blankly, trying to figure out what she wanted him to do but was unwilling to say. She did want him to stay, though. He liked that. He settled on, "I'll just turn my back and you can get that stuff off. You look pretty soggy."

"Okay." She sniffed.

He started to turn.

"I don't have any clothes. In the confusion...I don't know where my flight suit is."

"Oh."

Her face looked so pale, so strained. She was exhausted from the trip. "I was in the infirmary before I left."

"Oh, shit. Ummm." He wasn't sure if he could find the infirmary on his own. He looked around the room. He had a spare flight suit, but it would be too big for her. He went over to one of the wall-shelf-drawer thingies and opened it. Jackpot. Tons of green sectilian clothing in there.

He pulled out item after item. None of them were the right size for her. The skinny stuff would probably fit in the waist, but be too long. The dwarf stuff would fall off of her. He held up something that looked like a dress.

"That one," she said. "That will work."

"Okay." He took it over to the cot next to his. It also happened to be unused and farthest from the door, at an angle where she'd be unseen from the hallway through the door-less portal. He laid it out like he'd seen his sisters lay out their clothes for school. "There you go," he said. "I'll stand watch."

It was silly gentlemanly business. He could do that shit.

She grabbed his arm for a moment as she walked past, squeezing. "Thank you."

He nodded. "Welcome."

He turned his back on her and waited. He felt the corner of his mouth turn up. He'd just earned himself a white hat. He was a good guy.

"It looks like you got some sun while I was gone," she commented.

He fidgeted. He didn't want to talk about his folly right now, when things were going so well. "Who are the new guys?" he asked.

"I should have introduced you, I'm sorry," she said, sounding distracted.

"No worries. I'd rather meet them with clothes on, anyway."

She snorted. After a moment she let out an exasperated sigh. "These knots! They got tighter or something and my fingers are so cold. I can't seem to—"

He held his breath. *Oh, boy. What...*

"Alan...can you help?"

He closed his eyes for a second. *Be a gentleman. I can be a gentleman.* "Sure." He turned.

Her head was bowed and her hip thrust forward as she fumbled with a knot. Her fingers were trembling with cold.

He sat on the edge of the cot and waved her over.

Jane stepped in close and lifted her hands away from the decorative knots that kept the asymmetrical garment closed.

He dug his nails into the knot. After working on it a bit he was able to loosen it. He wiped his hands on his pant legs and went for the next one.

She leaned over him to grab a couple of towels off the bed, close enough that he could smell her. A few cold drops of water fell on him. He didn't mind.

She dropped one towel at her feet to soak up the water on the floor and raised her arms over her head, blotting her hair with the other one.

He shifted, willing his pants not to get any tighter, and focused hard on the knots.

The building was very still. He heard the two atellans who had come with Jane emerge from the communal bathing area. They spoke softly to each other and disappeared down the hall toward the nearest ramp. Most of the people in the compound would be having a meal now. He'd take Jane up to eat after she was dressed.

"At least the ship has doors," she said softly.

"Yeah." He didn't trust himself to say anything else.

"We'll have to explain things to them so that they understand. The cultural differences could lead to issues if we don't communicate well."

He cleared his throat. "Sure."

He'd gotten the three bottom knots loose. Now he worked on the one just under her breast. His knuckles kept brushing that round part of her. He couldn't help but notice her nipple straining at the fabric. As he loosened the knot, he looked up. She was staring at him, her lips slightly parted.

Now *his* fingers were shaking.

He wiped his hands on his pants again.

He reached up for the last knot on her chest. He couldn't quite reach it. He put his hands on her waist and pushed her back gently, then stood.

Her eyes were hot on his. That wasn't his imagination. He swallowed hard and tried to keep his breathing even.

Her lids flicked down and he remembered what he was supposed to be doing. He went back to the final knot. He'd figured out how they worked now, and he had it loose in seconds.

He stood there, frozen, looking at the ties and the nipple just under his hand. He wanted that nipple in his mouth. He wanted to feel her arch under him while he did it. He wanted to hear her moan. He wanted to watch her climax.

The front of his flight suit was tenting. There was no hiding that. He didn't care. She knew how he felt about her. He dragged his attention back to her face.

Her lips were slightly parted. Her hands came up and covered his, lingering just over her breast.

Her fingers were icy. He enclosed them in his own and pressed them to his chest to warm them. He lowered his face over hers until he was hovering just above her lips.

He gave her plenty of time to pull away.

She didn't.

His lips pressed against hers. He tried to be gentle, but her response to him nearly blew the top of his head off. She kissed him back, hungrily. He found himself crushing her to him, demanding deep kisses from her.

Her arms slipped around him. Her cold, wet clothes pressed into him.

He cupped the back of her head with his right hand and with the left, he dragged down at the hollow of her throat, pulling at the wet front of the garment to separate the layers. He pulled at the wide flap until it hung loose and flicked the narrower flap aside. Her skin felt cool under his hands. She gasped against his mouth but didn't stop the kiss.

It was going to happen this time.

He slid the tunic from her shoulders and let it fall with a wet slap to the floor. He bent his head over her neck, kissing and nibbling.

Her breathing was ragged. She moaned. Such a beautiful sound, better than he ever could have imagined—and he'd imagined it a lot.

She wriggled into him. She felt right against him.

He felt her hands at the top of his zipper and his heart stopped. She slowly slid it down the length of him, all the way to the bottom. He groaned deep in his throat. Even pressing against her cold skin didn't slow him down in the slightest.

And she was warming, quickly.

He loosened the knot on her drawstring pants and they fell to the floor.

Her breath was shaky. "We should stop," she panted. "Someone will see us."

"No they won't," he growled. He opened his mouth, trailing the tip of his tongue and plenty of kisses over her body as he moved to kneel in front of her.

She gasped. "Oh, my God...Alan." Her legs trembled.

He liked that. His own body was begging for release. He was probably going to blow like an eighteen-year-old boy.

But she would come first.

He gazed up at her, watching her response as he worked his magic. Her upper body and face were flushed, eyes closed, gasping for air, and then holding her breath, and then gasping again.

Her whole body was trembling. She had to be close.

He kept his left arm wrapped around her, helping her keep her balance. Nothing would ruin this.

He felt her stiffen. She stifled a cry. Then she was uttering throaty, wordless vocalizations of pleasure.

She calmed and then shuddered several more times.

When she stilled he slowly reversed his trail of kisses, then stood and kissed her. She gripped him fiercely. He turned her toward the cot, guiding her down gently. He slipped off his flight suit and boots and crawled on top of her.

She welcomed him with a tremulous smile. "Someone might come."

He grinned back. "You just did."

She pushed up with her hips, urging him on. Her hand slipped between them to guide him...then she suddenly went still. Her kisses slowed to a stop. Her grip on his back slackened.

He pulled back to look at her, worried and perplexed. When he saw her face, he went rigid with rage. *Now? Really? Now?*

He pushed himself off the cot roughly, noting with satisfaction that it sprang back a few inches. He violently shoved his legs into his flight suit and stomped his feet into his boots. He was zipping his flight suit up when he heard her bewildered voice saying, "Alan?"

He called over his shoulder, his voice harsh, "You made your choice."

He didn't look back.

Cock blocked by a goddamn fucking squid.

Jane's head fell back onto the cot. She closed her eyes against the tears welling up. The euphoria she'd felt moments before evaporated and was replaced with embarrassment and guilt.

"Qua'dux Jane Holloway?"

She didn't answer. Her throat was tight. Hot tears slid down into her hair.

"Is something amiss? Are you unwell?" She felt him probing at the surface of her thoughts, but that was all she would allow.

"Qua'dux?"

Jane swallowed thickly. "I need a moment, Ei'Brai. I was in the middle of something important."

"Of course. I await your leisure."

She rose up on her elbows and gazed longingly at the open archway, hoping Alan would come back so she could apologize. She knew he wouldn't though. His animosity for Ei'Brai was already so strong. This would be hard to come back from, if they even could.

When no footsteps echoed down the hall she rose slowly and slipped the sectilian tunic over her head, then rummaged around for a pair of pants to put on underneath. The cold was seeping back in, though she'd been warmed through just moments before. She draped her wet clothes over a couple of wall shelves that jutted out the farthest and mopped up the water she'd tracked in with the towel. Then she sat on the edge of the cot, hugging herself, and gave in briefly to the sobs that couldn't be contained any longer.

She wiped her face on a towel and crawled under a thin green blanket, curling up into a tight ball to conserve body heat and feel safe. She replayed the moments with Alan over and over again. He had been so tender and sweet. His eyes had been so full of passion. She was shocked by the depth of feeling he'd shown her. Everything else had completely faded away.

Until they were interrupted. She sighed and reopened the link to Ei'Brai, but kept the connection on the surface. "Ei'Brai, I was worried about you. I've been trying for days and days to connect to you, but you weren't there. Are you okay?"

His voice rumbled in her head, and she realized he was keeping his distance from her as well. "I apologize for causing concern. I was preoccupied." He seemed to be about to say more, but reconsidered and remained silent.

She frowned. "What were you preoccupied about?"

"It is of no importance. Your mood is unusual. Is all well there?"

Jane shook her head. She wouldn't break Alan's trust by confiding in Ei'Brai. Ei'Brai didn't understand these kinds of social constructs. He would only say something to Alan that would make Alan feel betrayed. Nothing good could come of that. No matter how much she'd like to confess what was bothering her—and try to figure out what to do about it—there was no one she could talk to about this aside from Alan himself. Not a single, solitary person. She'd have to figure it out on her own.

"We're doing well. We'll be returning to the ship soon. Probably in a day or two. No more than a week. I still have some details to work out."

"I'm elated." He sounded excited.

That made her smile a little. "Ei'Brai, we're going to need to set up a system for communication."

"Oh?"

"Yes, a signal. Sometimes I will need to be able to finish whatever I'm in the middle of before I answer you. Unless it's urgent, you should expect to wait. I can't be available to you one hundred percent of the time."

"Understood. In future, I shall endeavor to be more patient."

"Good."

Ei'Brai sounded hurt, but she had to do it. She was too distracted to work out the details of the system now. She'd think about that later.

It was too little, too late. Alan would never understand why she'd allowed that connection to happen. He wouldn't be able to imagine the repeated attempts Ei'Brai had made, banging around inside her head—escalating each time, to make contact with her. It had been distracting when she wanted more than anything to focus all her attention on Alan.

She'd only connected long enough to acknowledge Ei'Brai and tell him she would be available later.

It had taken long enough for Alan to notice. Too long.

She was sick about it. Alan thought she'd chosen Ei'Brai over him. She didn't want him to think that. She just...she'd been worried about Ei'Brai. He'd been disconnected so long. When he'd finally resumed contact she couldn't simply ignore him. She'd never even gotten a chance to explain.

Alan was a hothead. She'd let him cool off, and hopefully he would eventually listen to reason. Hopefully.

The truth was she had missed Alan while she was gone. Seeing him, touching him, had felt right. Sleeping with him, even if it had gone well, would have complicated things, but she'd finally felt like she could accept that risk. With sectilians aboard the *Speroancora*, she'd have a better support system. The team would be stronger. She wouldn't have to bear so much of the burden alone. The rest of her team were getting more adept at speaking Mensententia—and after these few weeks of immersion their skills would likely have grown by leaps and bounds. She could relax a little bit and let her desires have some rein.

Ei'Brai had seemed content to coexist in companionable silence, but now he spoke. "Dr. Jane Holloway, I must submit to you a query of grave importance…to me. And may I please have your true depth of feeling on the topic? You've always been nothing less than sincere, but I have a great wish to know…"

Jane frowned. It wasn't like Ei'Brai to sound so hesitant. "Of course. Go ahead." She opened herself up and felt the eager surge of his mental tendrils into deeper, more private layers of thought.

After a moment, he said, "Am I—to you—or, rather, do I…work *for* you or *with* you?"

She realized that this mental connection didn't go both ways. He was holding back his own feelings.

224

"Ei'Brai, you recruited me to be your commanding officer."

"Yes."

"You chose me."

"That is an oversimplification, but yes."

"You put your trust in me to make decisions for the greater good, even when you disagree with those decisions."

"Indeed."

"But I rely on you, too. I need your input. Our survival depends on it. We work together, but sometimes someone has to make a decision quickly. When opinions aren't unanimous, there would be chaos without a leader. I don't see you as my employee but as my colleague. Whenever possible I make decisions democratically—you know that."

For a moment relief flooded her senses. Her emotional turmoil lessened as his feelings colored and superseded her own.

Ei'Brai's voice was soft to a degree she'd rarely heard from him. "I am gratified."

"You're welcome, Ei'Brai."

"There is another matter…"

"Yes?" She was perplexed by how tentative he seemed.

He spoke in a rush. "You once implored me to refer to you as Jane, your private name, rather than your full name and title, as befitting your station. I refused, foolishly thinking that deference was of utmost import in our nascent association."

Jane smiled. "I remember."

"I would like to revisit that decision."

Her brows pulled together. His behavior was so strange today. What was going on up there? "I'd be pleased if you called me Jane."

"And you would call me Brai?" She could almost feel him tremble with anticipation. Brai was his true name—the Ei prefix indicated his status in the sectilian fleet among kuboderan officers. The lowest rank was Do, then came Ei, and finally Kai—the highest rank achievable. He'd rarely spoken of it, but Jane knew he'd longed to become Kai'Brai one day.

"Of course I would, if that's what you want."

He sounded pleased. "The matter is settled, then."

She decided to give it a try. "Brai? I'm worried about you. Are you okay?"

"I am now, Jane."

He seemed unwilling to open up further. She decided not to press. He'd survived decades of solitude. He was scarred, but also a survivor. "I'll be back soon. I've missed you."

"I have likewise noted the absence of your close proximity. Rest now, Jane. I clearly perceive your enervation."

She let out a small huff of breath in amusement. His word choice was always so proper and supercilious, especially in times like these when his feelings or actions weighed heavily on him. She thought it might be a defense mechanism when he was uncomfortable with whatever he wanted to say and that was the only way he could get it out. There were certainly times when he spoke more plainly or directly. Some might find the tendency grating, but as her affection for him grew, she found it endearing, and it actually helped her interpret his foreign emotions a little more easily.

She yawned. Her eyelids felt heavy. He was right. She was exhausted from the journey. "Goodnight, Brai."

He stayed with her as she fell asleep, instinctively filling her mind with soothing thoughts, and she quickly relaxed into deep sleep with his help.

30

The next morning Jane woke to find that Pledor had called a compound-wide meeting very early. She'd hoped that he would allow her to speak to the potential volunteers, but the assembly was nearly over by the time she got there with Ajaya—and they were turned away at the door.

That worried her. She couldn't imagine what Pledor could be saying to them that he wouldn't want her to hear. She hoped he wasn't going to cause trouble. The good news was that with both a mind master and Ei'Brai—no, Brai—aboard, it would be nearly impossible for him to hide any ulterior motives he might have.

Ajaya led her to a vast, empty cafeteria where Alan and Ron were having a meal by themselves. She helped herself to some greens and savory grain mush and sat down. Alan never looked up at her. He kept his gaze on his food and didn't speak unless spoken to.

She told them about her visit to the Hator compound and briefed them on what she knew of Jaross and Ryliuk. They talked at length about the new shuttle and what would have to be done to retrofit it with their gear, their power cells, and any maintenance items they should check.

They discussed the possibility of using the space elevator located on the other side of the planet and how they would handle ascent and escape velocity if it was not functional, which seemed probable based on her crew's reaction to the concept of such a construct.

When they were nearly done, Sten's people flooded the place and began their morning meal. Conversation had taken a turn toward more general banter as everyone finished up.

Ron asked, "So did you see any domesticated animals on your trip besides the suesupus?"

Jane drew her brows together in thought. "No, actually."

Ron shook his head. "No pets. That's weird to me. Everybody needs a shaggy companion."

Ajaya ventured, "Come to think of it, no one here appears to consume animal protein. It's all greens and grain and other produce. No eggs or dairy products either. They appear to be vegan. At least here locally."

Medical Master Schlewan and Tinor sat down with them. Ajaya turned to the older atellan. "Master Schlewan, pardon me if this is awkward. Do the Sectilius ever consume animal flesh, eggs of various birds, or the milk produced by large mammals?"

Master Schlewan looked ruffled. "No-no-*no*! Whyever would we do such a thing? How barbaric!"

Ron gestured at the rest of the humans. "I guess we're barbarians," he said with a laugh.

Schlewan's ears pressed back farther than Jane had ever seen, and her voice went very soft and low. "Have you been killing and eating animals while you were here?"

Jane leaned in. "Master Schlewan, I assure you we have not. We are omnivores. On Earth, animals are part of our agricultural system. While humans are accustomed to eating protein from meat and animal byproducts like eggs and cow's milk, we are adaptable. Many humans eat a vegan diet like this." She indicated the empty tray in front of her.

Schlewan nodded thoughtfully. "Yes, yes, *yes*. Our distant history was much the same. Then the introduction of the nepatrox happened millennia ago, a terrible setback for our species. The population explosion devastated most mammalian species, large and small, on both worlds, because there was no natural predator to balance it. It was a scourge without end. I'm sure you've noted that most wildlife has adapted or survived by adopting niches where the nepatrox cannot reach—burrows and tunnels, deep in the sea, high in the trees. Thousands of species became extinct. The ecosystem shifted dramatically. It changed both planets forever—both our diet and our way of life. This incident is taught to children as a cautionary tale about hubris and lack of foresight."

Schlewan gestured around her. "Atielle got the worst of it, ultimately, because the environment is less hospitable with far fewer natural resources. Until the plague, trade for goods and luxuries with Sectilia was common. Now, atellans survive on what they can grow. Sectilia is very different. Unimaginably high walls are built at great expense and a substantial percentage of the population is designated to maintain and crew them. It allows for..." She looked thoughtful. "A more normal way of living. I've always wondered why the atellans didn't migrate to Sectilia, but you know what is said of home." Schlewan returned to her food with gusto.

"We don't know," Ajaya said. "Please tell us."

"Oh-ho! I forget. I'm out of practice with outsiders." Schlewan spoke around a large mouthful of food. "Home is what one knows. Everywhere else is someplace different. Different, different, *different*." She continued eating as though that were explanation enough.

Jane nodded. She thought she understood. The Sectilius were averse to change. "So most atellans are forced to live in small enclaves like this?"

"Indeed-indeed-*indeed* they are. Here there are fewer natural resources to build walls. Low walls were never enough. Some land is developed for large-scale farming of grains and the nepatrox leave that alone, though cultivation and harvest are both dangerous work. Most of the food is carefully and intensively grown on the greenhouse level, however, as you saw."

"Every enclave is the same?" Jane asked.

"Oh, yes."

"How do you get enough protein?" Ajaya asked.

"Most of our crops have been genetically enhanced to produce not only more protein but more essential nutrients in general. Not enough to adversely affect palatability, of course."

"So you say," Alan groused. He was still picking at his breakfast. They were the first voluntary words he'd said so far that morning.

Schlewan smiled at him. "I've no doubt it may take some getting used to for off-worlders. In my day, I tasted many fine things in my travels to other worlds. Many, many, *many* fine things."

Jane dragged her attention from Alan back to Schlewan. "Did you? You lived in a ship community?"

"Yes-yes-*yes*. I was visiting atellan friends during a re-supply mission when the plague hit. I was trapped here as a young woman, cut off from my family on Sectilia. I thought I would spend the rest of my life here. But now you are here, Quasador Dux Jane Holloway—and you are looking for volunteers to go with you. I hope you will consider my application."

"I certainly will," Jane replied warmly. "I assume I'll hear from the Gis'dux soon about the other volunteers."

"I'm afraid there weren't many," Schlewan said with a wry look.

Alan slammed his cup of water down. "I don't care how many applicants there are. If you don't bring Schlewan, you're a fool." He stormed off.

Ron chuckled softly after Alan was out of sight and gestured at Schlewan. "I think he likes you."

Schlewan looked thoughtful.

Tinor piped up. "I think that he doesn't like the game the young women are playing."

"What game is that?" Ajaya asked, her eyes narrowed.

Tinor looked amused. "One girl dared another to feel his reproductive organs to see how they compared in size and shape to male sectilian organs. His reaction amused her and the other girls. It has become a game with points based on the difficulty of access to his genitals."

"Tinor-Tinor-*Tinor*," Schlewan clucked. "This is no way to treat off-world guests."

"I've not participated. Everyone wants to score the points. You are included, Dr. Ron Gibbs. Your level of difficulty is higher because Dr. Ajaya Varma protects you from the girls."

Ron smiled blandly. "Good to know."

Ajaya was covering her mouth to smother a laugh.

Jane was horrified that Alan had endured this game. She turned to Tinor. "But what does that have to do with Medical Master Schlewan?"

Tinor grinned. "Master Schlewan is one of very few females he sees every day who isn't trying to grab his genitalia."

Ron raised an eyebrow, his lips twitching, and looked like he was about to ask a question.

Jane was afraid the conversation might take a prurient turn, so she jumped in with another question for Schlewan. "You volunteered? Is there anyone else I might know who volunteered too?"

"Me!" Tinor said cheerfully.

Jane smiled. She wondered if it was her imagination, but she thought Tinor was looking more feminine the past few days. There seemed to be a pretty blush on the child's high, angular cheeks.

Schlewan dipped her head. "I'm afraid we come as a pair, if you'll have us, Qua'dux."

"Oh? Do you think it's a good idea to bring an adolescent on board, Master Schlewan?"

"Onto a community ship? Of course it is. It will actually be the safest place for Tinor as the child slips into adulthood."

Schlewan took a bite of food and seemed unhurried about explaining. "Tinor is an orphan like me. The child is more than my apprentice. Tinor's father was killed by nepatrox and ius mother died of a genetic illness when iad

234

was very young. Like a lot of people since the squillae plague, Tinor had no other relatives to assume the upbringing."

Schlewan took another bite, chewing thoughtfully. "As the mother's medical caregiver, I could have put ium in an adoption lottery, but since I was separated from my own children on Sectilia I decided to raise Tinor as my own."

Tinor leaned forward. "Medical Master Schlewan is my *subidia*—surrogate mother."

Schlewan went on. "By that time I'd been conscripted as the only living medical master in the area." She frowned. "I was bound to this place. There are a lot of useful years left in this body. If you will have us, I would be happy, happy, *happy* to serve you."

Ajaya looked concerned. "Why do you say Tinor would be safer aboard the *Speroancora*?"

Schlewan washed down a bite with a long drink of water, then sighed. "It is extremely likely Tinor carries the same fatal genetic defect as ius mother. In the days before the plague, such things were easily treated. Here, however..." Her eyes swept the room. "Such matters are not considered important in the larger scheme of things. The child will die if the defect takes hold. Likely within a decade of full pubescence."

There was a moment of quiet, then Ajaya broke the silence. "Do you mind if I ask how you survived the plague?"

Schlewan sobered further. "For me, as it was for most, it was by the narrowest of margins. I was most definitely close to dusk. Some of us just took longer to die. I can't say whether that was due to some anatomical difference, or whether my body simply harbored fewer squillae to exert their nefarious effect, or if there were other factors. Some-one—we assume it was the Unified Sentient Races—deto-nated several fission reactions in the atmospheres of both Atielle and Sectilia, obliterating nearly all technology at that point. If we had any strength left in us, and if we happened to be in a safe place at that moment, we survived. It took a great deal of time to recover and then to find others. I have trained eight medical masters in the time since, who were then traded to other communities in exchange for goods and services."

Ron asked, "If you're the only medical professional in the area, why would Pledor let you go with us instead of keeping you here in the compound?"

A look of disgust swept over Schlewan's face for a split second. "Gis'dux Sten is too young to remember the time before the plague. He doesn't comprehend the types of med-ical facilities that are aboard the *Speroancora*. He will allow me to go for the purposes of keeping himself in good health."

31

Alan was happy to leave the Sten compound for good. It couldn't happen fast enough, as far as he was concerned. While Jane worked out the details of recruitment among the atellans, He threw himself into the only thing he could trust: work. He had to get that tired old shuttle ready for flight.

He had the help of Ron, of course, but also Jaross, the woman Jane had brought back with her from the Hator compound. Jaross was an engineer and therefore, in Alan's book, all right. She'd been trained thoroughly on a lot of sectilian tech, even though much of the tech left from before the plague wasn't in use anymore. She'd be handy to have around on the ship.

Jaross watched Alan and Ron work for a while until she seemed to come to the conclusion that they knew what they were doing. Then she asked for duties of her own. She worked hard and she didn't shy away from getting dirty or from asking questions if she was unsure about anything, which he appreciated. Because relations between the Sten and Hator compounds were strained, she said she needed to stay busy and out of sight of Pledor. That made total sense to him.

It was good to have help because there was a fuckton of crap to do, but it also irked him. He preferred to work by himself, and with the foul mood he'd been in, he didn't really enjoy the hassle of trying to communicate in a foreign language all the time, though he knew this was something he would have to put some effort into or life from here on out was going to be miserable.

He was getting better at it though, every day—almost exponentially better. Mensententia was worming its way into his head, that was for sure. Just hearing it all the time helped. He didn't have to ask people to speak more slowly nearly as often. Talking was harder, but he was managing.

They worked around the clock, installing the new power cells in the old shuttle, as well as putting in the nanite production module—which they kept hidden from the Sten people because he got the feeling it would just create additional problems. If Jaross took issue with it, she kept that to herself. Then they painstakingly checked every system.

There had been a lot of wear and tear on the older craft. Unfortunately they couldn't just remove the engines from it and plunk them in their shuttle. They were incompatible, of course. So he did the reverse. He replaced every vital system he could with parts from their shuttle. When things couldn't be replaced or repaired, he surreptitiously dumped nanites on them to reinforce structural integrity, which was basically how they worked on the *Speroancora*. He gave the nanites raw materials from discarded components and they worked their magic. Without these little machines, they'd have been in trouble. This shuttle was near the end of its useful life. He didn't want to crash and burn. Again.

Ron worked on the electrical systems in a similar manner. Ajaya brought them food so that they could stay focused. Tinor liked to watch them and often hung around so quietly that he hardly knew the kid was there until he or she spoke, usually to ask pretty intelligent questions.

He was wedged into a small space in the dash in the pilot compartment. It would have been much better suited to a skinnier person like Jaross or Tinor, who was sitting in the copilot seat, watching. He didn't know how long the kid had been sitting there, but he was tempted to put him or her to work.

He'd removed the emergency release for supplemental oxygen from the dash and the keg-shaped canisters of O2 it was connected to, so he could inspect the components beneath. Tinor pointed to the assembly. "These are for breathing in vacuum?"

Alan strained his arm to reach with the tool that would loosen the part he wanted to see. A small flashlight was in his mouth. He didn't look back at the kid. He mouthed the Mensententic word for "Uh-huh" around the flashlight. Finally he grabbed the component and pulled himself out of the tight space. His right shoulder grazed the rough opening. He cursed in English.

Tinor was unfazed. The kid was examining the components avidly, getting very close, but not touching. Not touching was good. It raised his degree of respect for the kid a couple of notches. "How does this work?"

He was tempted not to answer. He was in a shitty mood these days. But apparently Jane had decided the kid was going with them, and this technology was his or her heritage. It was good that the kid was curious about it.

He rubbed his shoulder and straightened.

Tinor asked, "Do you need medical attention?"

"No. Look—you pull the lever and it handly releases." He was mangling the words. He pulled up the ship's schematic on the copilot's holograph generator. "You seen one of this?"

Tinor dipped a hand into the hologram and swung it around, then magnified the part that he or she had been asking about. Tinor swirled a finger around that component and a text box popped up. "Yes. Every child takes basic engineering and design." He or she said it sternly, as though Alan should know that.

The kid seemed intent on reading it, so he went back to work, smiling slightly. The kid managed to teach him something about the Sectilius every time they hung out together. Jane had said that these people were very focused on science and engineering. It was one thing to like about this crazy planet.

"I told the girls that they upset you. I told them to leave you alone, that you don't like them to touch your genitalia."

He froze. Had he just heard that right? He was pretty sure he had. "Um. Thank you."

"Do you prefer to enjoy sexual activities with men?"

He sat up abruptly and banged his head on a protruding component that he should have tucked back away the night before. He peered around the pilot's seat and saw Ron grinning at him. Alan rolled his eyes. "No."

"Are you asexual then?"

"No! I..." He switched to English. "Jesus, Ron, do you think you could help me out, here?"

Ron guffawed. "I wouldn't dream of it."

"Asshole," Alan muttered. He drew in a deep breath and turned back to Tinor. "I like girls—women. Just *not* people grabbing me. Any part of me. But especially…there. And you, Ron? Do you like it?"

Ron chuckled. "Under these conditions? No."

"Is this a cultural phenomenon?" Tinor asked.

"Yes," Ron and Alan said in unison.

There was a momentary silence. Alan went back to work under the dash and Tinor seemed to be absorbed in the 3-D blueprint. Suddenly Tinor said, "I just want to understand. I'm going to be a girl soon, I think."

Alan's eyes bulged. He heard Ron cough. He lifted his head to see Jaross pause outside and glance in through the open hatch, her ears pulled back and a frown on her grease-smudged face.

Alan didn't know what to say. He should say something discouraging. He didn't want this kiddo to get the wrong idea. But what would he say that didn't sound…weird or gross? And he had to be careful not to assume he knew what the kid meant.

He waited too long. By the time he'd formulated something and emerged again from under the dash, Tinor had left.

Alan was brooding in the back of the refurbished shuttle, squished between Ryliuk and Jaross on a shabby recycled bench seat from a land car. It was relatively quiet. The diverse group wasn't very comfortable yet. He wondered if that would ever change.

Their merry band of four now numbered nine. Once they were aboard with the Squid, their party would reach the dubious sum of ten—on a ship that was supposed to hold thousands.

He looked around, sullenly assessing his new crewmates now that he wasn't busy rebuilding the ship anymore. Jaross's features were always set in a serious expression, though now free of grease for the first time in days. She always held herself with a queenly air which was oddly punctuated by a light-brown, fizzy mop of hair that she seemed to barely take care of. It was always coming undone from hasty makeshift braids. That might have given one the sense that she didn't care about her appearance or something if she hadn't been so freakishly graceful. Her skin was normally toffee colored, though all of the Sectilius, atellan or sectilian, could get as dark as Ron pretty fast when exposed to sunlight—a pretty nifty little metabolic trick and far better than getting sunburned. His own skin was peeling off his face in flakes from his suesupus excursion. He wouldn't have minded a little extra protection that day.

Jaross was pure atellan, tall and lithe. Her bones jutted out at angles that made him feel like someone should remind her to eat a sandwich, though it seemed that her appearance was pretty normal, based on what he'd seen of atellans in general.

Ryliuk was the opposite—just as tall, but built like the Hulk—all muscle and heavy bone structure. He must have had some kind of hybrid vigor going on from mixed parentage. Alan wasn't too keen on this dude. He apparently was nearly as powerful telepathically as the Squid. That automatically put him on a sort of temporary shit list. So far Ryliuk hadn't said much, so Alan couldn't know whether he was as much of a dick as Ei'Brai or not.

He already knew Schlewan, Tinor, and, of course, Pledor. Now that Pledor was no longer a leader, he wasn't going by the name Gis'dux Sten anymore. They were supposed to call him Pledor Makya Sten, but Alan declined to be so pleasant after the way the asshole had blackmailed Jane into coming along. He tried not to talk to him, but if he had to, he just called him Pledor, and the others had picked up on it and were doing the same. That seemed to piss the dude off. His lips tightened and his eyes narrowed every time Alan did it, so Alan would be sure to continue.

It was going to be a fun mission, he thought sourly.

They'd gotten fairly decent weather for the trip—which meant fewer and lighter storms, not sunny skies. Jane and Ron were flying the shuttle to an island in the middle of an ocean on the other side of Atielle where there resided an antique space elevator.

Alan worried they were wasting a day of decent weather for this wild goose chase when they should have just used the shuttle itself to achieve escape velocity. But Jane was gun-shy about flying through the atmosphere again. He didn't blame her, but he also didn't have high hopes that the space elevator would work.

On Earth a space elevator was still just a concept—a pretty decent concept, but the materials required to pull it off were almost like something out of a fairy tale. It had to be strong and it had to stretch all the way to geostationary orbit. Granted, that was a shorter distance on a planetary body as small as Atielle, so the materials used wouldn't need to be as strong as they would for a space elevator on Earth or Sectilia.

Jaross said it had never been used for anything but taking payloads into orbit. Landings on Atielle were always done manually. Getting payloads to orbit for trading purposes cheaply and efficiently was the primary goal of the space elevator, and when it had still been in use, Atielle's Ladder had run around the clock.

Apparently Sectilia had built a twin space elevator. The elevators' geosynchronous orbits swept near to a Lagrangian point where a trade outpost had been placed. Once a payload was lifted to orbit, it took very little energy to drop it at the outpost. The elevators kept trade costs down, especially since they were only one-way. There was no wait for vehicles to descend the track. It could be in constant operation.

He perked up when Atielle's Ladder came into view. There was a tiny island in the middle of a vast sea with a small, fortified, round structure at its center. From there a cable—barely visible until you were right on it—projected vertically and disappeared into the clouds overhead.

"Well, it's still here," Jane said.

"Am I seeing some twist in the cable?" Ron asked, glancing back at Alan.

Alan pressed himself against the window as they made the final descent. His brow furrowed deeply. "Huh. I think so."

"What purpose would that serve?" Ron asked.

"Well, I can think of several things," Alan said, musing. "On Earth, everyone's always worried about the cable crashing down—but if you mold the thing in a spiral, it falls in a more contained manner. That's assuming that what we're seeing here is essentially a stretched-out spring."

Jane landed the shuttle on a rocky beach near the building. It was completely deserted and devoid of any wildlife. The topmost greenhouse floor looked brown instead of green like the one in Sten's compound.

Tinor asked what they were saying. Jane admonished them for not speaking in Mensententia then translated the gist of the conversation.

They got out. Alan squinted into the drizzle, trying to see the cable better. It definitely had some twist. The closer they got the more pronounced it was.

Tinor jumped into the conversation. "A helical shape could be twisted to take the cable out of the path of debris."

"The Coriolis force!" Alan blurted out. "As a payload is lifted, it gains not only altitude but angular momentum—this causes a vertical cable to bias and creates drag. If the cable is a spiral, the angular momentum is always pushing the craft in the right direction, up the spiral. It would be slightly more efficient and, depending on the material used, more durable. It's genius!"

Ajaya looked skeptical. "Are we about to need some Dramamine?"

Now he was getting really hopeful that everything would still be in useful shape. They walked the short distance up to the building, and he was surprised to see that the wide hangar doors lifted automatically. "The building still has power."

Master Schlewan clucked. "Someone left the power cells behind. That was poor planning. Those power cells could have saved many, many, *many* lives over the last decades."

Pledor said, "We should take them with us."

Jaross looked at him askance. "There is no shortage of power on the *Speroancora*. We can leave them here for other travelers."

They continued to discuss it. Maybe they were even arguing about it. Alan tuned them out. He jogged to the center of the building, which was open to the sky, and looked straight up. At this point the cable was about seven centimeters in diameter, though he was sure it would be much thicker at the other end, at geostationary orbit, where the tension exerted on it would be at its greatest. When he leaned in close, he could see daylight through the circular spiral.

When he let his gaze come back down to earth, he found himself staring directly into Jane's eyes. Her expression was wistful and a little sad. He tried not to let that affect him. She'd made her choice.

"Well? Will it work?" she asked softly.

He had to look away. "I don't see any reason why it won't. Bring the shuttle in here and let's rig it up."

Jane watched Alan and Ryliuk huddle together with Jaross, running a diagnostic on the integrity of the cable. After a few tense minutes, Ryliuk turned, smiling broadly, and announced that the cable was viable. They'd yet to find anything that would keep them from the attempt.

Jaross had brought a data stick that contained everything they needed to know about where Atielle's Ladder could be found, how the elevator worked, and how to hook a shuttle to the system so that the shuttle's drive could engage with the climber and push them up the cable through the planet's atmosphere and into space.

Jane stood back and watched as Alan, Ron, Ryliuk, and Jaross hooked the shuttle to the climbing system. They opened specialized compartments on the underside of the shuttle and fed the thick cabling through an arrangement of mechanical components and then locked it back into place. She stayed back with Ajaya, Pledor, Schlewan, and Tinor, lending a hand when extra hands were called for and she was told exactly what she needed to do.

Ryliuk was able to take concepts from Jaross's mind and transfer them without language so that Ron and Alan could grasp them easily. Jane occasionally jumped in to work out translations of technical information for Alan or Ron, but for the most part, the humans and atellans worked very well together. The process went smoothly. Jane began to hope that this newly integrated crew would work efficiently together, especially once Brai was brought into the mix more fully.

Brai, however, was still strangely quiet. He was declining conversation or interaction and seemed intent on observing the new crew. There was something serious going on with him, but he wasn't ready to get into it. She worried about him, though there was not much she could do. She could only lend support.

Alan remained cold. For the most part, he either avoided or ignored her. There was no getting him alone for a quiet word of explanation. Nonetheless he was working well with the others and she noted he relaxed a bit when she moved to the opposite side of the building as they rummaged for additional safety gear before launch.

Yes, he was being stubborn and proud. That was his nature. But she knew he was in pain. She'd hurt him, inadvertently. She'd have to give him time to come around, to be able to hear her side. Until that happened, she'd give him a wide berth. Forcing a confrontation would only make things worse.

Ryliuk was incredibly perceptive for an outsider. She noted that he intervened frequently to assist Alan so that she wouldn't be called to translate. Alan seemed to be comfortable with that, far more comfortable with Ryliuk than with her. And Ryliuk's brute strength came in handy several times throughout the process.

Once the shuttle was attached to the climber, they boarded again. Jane was tense. She'd never sit in a cockpit with ease, and the memory of their descent was heavy on her thoughts. Nonetheless there wasn't anyone more qualified than her, so once again she was in the pilot's seat with Ron at her side.

Jane powered up the ancient shuttle, made the final checks, and engaged the engine. She glanced at Ron.

He was back in his element. He nodded in his level-headed way, fingertips dancing over the dash as though it held controls he'd known all his life. "All systems nominal, QD. We're ready to go when you are."

Jane swallowed the lump in her throat. "Engaging thrust." The shuttle lifted off the floor with the sounds of groaning and creaking metal. The drag on the cable straightened it a bit more, and they were pressed into their seats as the nose of the shuttle pointed nearly straight up and began to climb.

The passengers were silent. Minutes ticked by. As they picked up speed, the artificial gravity caused by acceleration coupled with Atielle's gravity, making them feel much heavier. Luckily the coupler that connected them to the cable contained a rotating adapter that kept them from spinning around the axis of the spiraling cable. In the rearview cameras she could see the ladder station receding in the distance. Ahead was a gray sky with rushing clouds. Nothing threatening as of now, which was reassuring. Brai was tracking the debris field in the upper atmosphere with more detail than the shuttle was capable of and routing that information to the shuttle's computer.

It took only a few minutes to reach the cloud layer. They passed through the gray, cottony stuff without incident.

Jane took a deep breath and tried to relax a little. It was going smoothly thus far. But she wasn't naive enough to think all danger had passed.

Their rate of ascent increased gradually with altitude according to an algorithm that set a pace based on where they were on the elevator. Apparently there were points where it was dangerous to go too fast or too slow. Doing so could trigger too much sway. Sway in the line would throw the anchor at the other end of the elevator off course and could also be dangerous for the integrity of the cable itself.

It was even more complicated because Atielle's Ladder was designed to be in constant use. Only one climber ascending at any given time was unusual and could be problematic. Normally there were up to ten climbers at a time at various stages, coordinating their ascent according to complex algorithms in order to keep the line stable.

They passed through the stratosphere without incident. The view outside the cockpit windows went dark, with many pinpricks of light. At this altitude the climber began to pick up speed quickly.

"How fast are we going?" Ajaya murmured.

"We are going..." Ron drawled, checking a readout and pausing to calculate in his head, "...just under 150 kilometers per hour or about 100 miles per hour."

"Oh, my. I can't feel a thing," Ajaya said absently.

Alan moved around restlessly. "It's a far cry from rocket boosters, for sure. 'Course it would take forever at this speed—probably twenty days or more. We'll pick up more speed soon. But get comfy. This is still going to take a while."

The mesosphere was the part that Jane was most worried about. That was the section of the atmosphere where there was the most debris from derelict ships and satellites falling from orbit and burning up. The cable was thin, flexible, and made of the most durable materials the Sectilius had been capable of creating during the peak of their civilization. It had likely weathered some impacts without a catastrophic failure. But the shuttle would be more delicate by comparison. A collision could be devastating, as they'd already experienced during their descent.

Alan must've been thinking the same thing. He said, "Now we play debris-cloud Frogger until we clear the mesosphere."

He was right. They began a kind of dance. Forward. Wait with the brake engaged. Slow ascent. Fast ascent. She had to override the shuttle protocols that dictated their rate of speed. These protocols were meant to handle some debris, but nothing like what they were experiencing. It was a rapidly changing environment.

Alarms went off. The cockpit lighting shifted from a soft, neutral, blue-white tone to red. Jane leaned forward, searching for a clue as to what had gone wrong. Brai knew before she or Ron did.

"There appears to be an issue with a segment of the cable, Jane."

"We ran a diagnostic—" Jane blurted in disbelief.

"What is it?" Alan demanded. He released the latch on his harness and pulled himself up over her shoulder, gripping her seat.

Jane manipulated the forward cameras until they ran along the sight line of the cable. She frowned because she couldn't see much.

"Pull up a 3-D render!" Alan barked.

When she didn't immediately respond, he said, "A holo-gram—" He lurched against her seat, trying to reach for the controls.

Jane batted his arm out of the way. "I know what a holo-gram is, Alan." She did her best to sound calm and unruf-fled, but the stress she felt was immense. Who knew what could be hurtling toward them while they figured this out?

Ron raised his eyebrows and changed the setting so that a hologram of the cable floated between the three of them. Nothing was immediately apparent. Ron scrolled up. Alan found purchase on something behind him and pushed far-ther into the cockpit. His left shoulder pressed hard into hers. Some of the atellans began to unlatch themselves and push up to look as well.

Jane bit back the urge to tell them to stay seated. She didn't have to. Ajaya was saying it for her. Except no one was listening.

A mass came into view on the line. It was a gnarled tangle that looked like a bird's nest. Ron tried to focus on it, but it was nearly out of range of the cameras and remained blurry.

"What is it?" the booming voice of Ryliuk called from the back.

"Space junk," Alan barked over his shoulder.

Jane let out a tight sigh. This piece of debris could be the remains of a ship just like the *Speroancora*. She could scan it to find out, but she didn't want to. "It's a hunk of wreckage from some satellite or ship. But...it can't be fused to the ca-ble or the diagnostic would have detected it."

Jaross peered around Alan. She was wedged into the cockpit now too. "How do we dislodge it? Does someone have to go out there?"

Pledor said, "Fools! We can't go out there—there's no air! We'll all suffocate if you open that door."

Alan growled, "We've got safety equipment for that."

Ajaya pierced the grumbling conversation that filled the tiny ship. "Everyone return to your seats at once. The commander is fully capable of attending to this problem without all of you crowding her. Let us give her the space and the silence she needs to determine a solution."

This time they listened, and Jane heard them sliding and shifting around and buckling their harnesses again. Except for Alan. Alan stayed pressed up against her.

Alan murmured, "I'll never understand why they didn't put laser cannons on these things."

Ron huffed. "I heard that. We could really use a phaser right now."

Jane gave them both a stern look. She distinctly remembered someone rebuking her for wondering about what kind of devices the Target might have had before they boarded. "Let's stick to realistic solutions, please," she said dryly. "This isn't the Starship Enterprise after all."

Alan cleared his throat. The comment had hit home.

Jane's fingers fluttered over the controls. She urged the craft forward at its slowest possible rate, the alarms blaring louder and louder until the ship simply wouldn't budge another inch and the brake engaged automatically due to safety protocols. But she was able to bring the obstruction into focus.

Jane wished she had something at hand to block her ears. It was hard to concentrate with all the noise and the shouting of questions.

The debris was made up of green-coated wires and sheared-off metal. A coil of insulated wire had caught on the cable. It didn't look like it was fused to the cable in any way.

"Just plow into it. It'll break free and we can be on our way."

"It doesn't work that way. The safety protocols won't let me get any closer," Jane said.

Ron continued to tap and peck at the controls on his side. "Yeah, I'm trying to override them from here, but this isn't looking good."

Brai, who had been silent up until now, said, "Overrides would be difficult but plausible on the ground. During operation such endeavors would be impossible. This is not the solution."

"I'll do an EVA," Alan said flatly.

"No!" Jane said, then ground her teeth together. She continued more evenly, "No, that's not an option. There has to be another way." A spacewalk would be her last possible choice. It was just too precarious.

She opened the panel that would release the clamps and free them from the cable. A quick burn, a little bit of supremely dangerous fancy flying, and they'd be into the far-safer reaches of the upper atmosphere and well on their way to the *Speroancora*. She stared at the open panel and the releases that resided inside. It would be easier for Ron with his larger hands. She turned to him.

Ron stared back at her with a grave expression she didn't like. He gestured at the dashboard. Jane blinked. She could hardly believe what she was seeing. One of the engines was now performing at only 32 percent capacity. They wouldn't have the punch needed to outmaneuver all the space junk.

They had to keep traveling vertically on Atielle's Ladder at least until they cleared the mesosphere. "Damn it." What could have happened to the engine?

Well, that settled that, anyway.

Ajaya broke in. "A spacewalk may be the only option. It should be a fairly simple EVA. We are all trained—"

"No," Jane said. The cabin went silent.

Jaross spoke up. "You spoke to me of the *Speroancora* scooping up your smaller vessel when your comrades were in trouble. Why couldn't your navigator perform some variation on that operation now?"

Jane shook her head, but before she could speak, Medical Master Schlewan said, "The yoke. The kuboderan cannot move the ship to such a degree without the Quasador Dux aboard. Impossible, impossible, *impossible*."

Pledor Sten's grating voice rang out. "I thought you set it free?"

Brai's rage was immediate and scorching hot. It took Jane completely by surprise. She reeled, her hands balling into fists as she tried to push him back, tried to regain her sense of self among the roiling thoughts of fury and anguish.

Jane looked up and caught Ron's gaze. His eyes were wide, his jaw clenched. He looked angry enough to kill someone.

She felt Alan swing away from her and turn toward the back of the craft. She knew without looking that he was focusing on Pledor. Only the awkward angle was keeping him from tumbling back and lunging for Pledor's throat.

Alan's voice rumbled through the shuttle. "You *stupid*—"

"Brai," she commanded as she retook some measure of control, "disconnect yourself from us until you can behave rationally."

Instantly the connection was severed. Jane exhaled in a rush and panted for a few seconds. She consciously unclenched her fingers and looked down at her hands. Red crescents marked her palms from her nails digging into her flesh.

"Jesus…" Ron murmured.

"What the fuck just happened?" Alan asked.

Ryliuk spoke calmly from the back. "Pledor, you will do well to remember that the Gubernaviti is sentient, male, and—above all else—can sense your thoughts and overhear your utterances through his colleagues here, even if you haven't connected with him directly."

Pledor seemed unfazed. "What? Out here? We're tens of vastuumet from the ship."

"Yes," Ajaya said. There was a shrill note to her voice. She was shaken too. "Even out here. He is more powerful than you can imagine. And you just made him very angry."

He *had* made Brai very angry, but Jane wasn't sure why. It had been a thoughtless slight, but she'd made mistakes like that herself when she'd met Brai and was learning about what and who he was. He'd always been patient and instructive with her. Why would he be anything different with the sectilians? She wasn't sure. It worried her, but she didn't have time to explore that now.

He would give her the answer when she was ready to probe. He couldn't hold things like this back from her if she commanded him.

She lifted her head to gaze over her shoulder at the atellans in the rear compartment. "To answer your question, I gave Ei'Brai, the Gubernaviti, as much autonomy as was possible. The yoke is complex and there was only so much I was able to do within the scope of its boundaries. We haven't yet determined how to sever it completely. So no, he can't perform such a rescue operation. That would be impossible under current conditions."

Brai reconnected abruptly, breaking into her thoughts with a painfully discordant reverberation, the likes of which she hadn't experienced since her earliest days of bonding with him. She winced. His mental voice was clipped and harsh. "I am tracking an object approaching in an erratically oscillating orbit. There is a twenty-six percent chance it will pass within an estimated fifty-five exiguumet of your vicinity."

That was too close for comfort. Jane gritted her teeth so hard her jaw hurt. They were stuck there waiting to see if they'd be hit unless she took some kind of drastic measure. "Hold on. I'm going to try something." She turned back to the proximity sensors, calibrated the cameras to remain focused on the cable obstruction, and released the brake by degrees without engaging the drive, allowing them to be pulled back down the cable by gravity to wait until they were well clear of any potential collisions.

There was a loud squeal and a grinding sound as long as they were sliding in reverse. The shuttle wasn't designed to go that direction, and the brakes were protesting. Jane flicked a glance at Ron. He shook his head and grimaced. She heard someone moving restlessly behind her in the cabin, probably Alan.

At least the proximity alarms stopped blaring. That helped. She could think again.

The cameras stayed focused on the cable obstruction. Though the resolution of the image became poor again, she could tell the obstruction was swinging around the cable lazily from the movement and vibration they'd just created on the line.

A high timid voice came from the back—Tinor's. "Could we create enough movement in the cable to fling the junk off?"

It got Jane thinking. It could work. She made sure everyone was safely harnessed and told them to brace themselves. After the orbital debris passed their former location, she set the controls to override and put the pedal to the metal, zooming back up the cable until the proximity sensor screamed and the safety protocols put on the brakes. They lurched against their harnesses. The cable began to sway. She watched breathlessly as the obstruction swung around the cable...but didn't break free.

She ground her teeth and released the brake again. It screamed in protest as they slipped down the cable even farther this time, and put them in free fall for a few moments.

Then back up again, the sudden stop grinding her into her harness so hard she was sure she was going to have bruises.

She waited as the cameras refocused, swallowing the bile that was rising in her throat. The cockpit was a cacophony of alarms. The cable was not only swaying now, but also vibrating, and they had begun to create some bounce along the vertical axis of the coil. The inertial dampeners couldn't control for all of these variables. It felt like being tumbled in a clothes dryer.

The obstruction jounced around, barely trackable by the cameras. It seemed to be hanging on by a thread but still hadn't broken free.

There was a tight, painful feeling high in the center of her chest, just below her throat. This wasn't any safer than a traditional launch. She'd gambled on this route and it hadn't paid off.

She should probably abort.

But she didn't. She repeated the ludicrous maneuver, screaming down the cable and surging back up even faster than before.

She shifted in her seat after the shuttle came to its abrupt stop. The harness was painful and chafing now. As the cameras refocused she held her breath. The snagged object swung off the cable and drifted free to tumble to the surface of Atielle.

The cabin erupted into cheers despite the fact that the shuttle was still ricocheting in nauseatingly erratic movements. Tinor took a lot of praise for the suggestion.

Ron looked at Jane and grinned. "Nerves of steel, QD. Nerves of steel."

"It's not over yet," Jane replied. Her mouth was dry. The cable was dangerously unstable now. She had just taken a huge risk. Maybe she'd acted rashly. If the cable snapped now, it would recoil so fast that she feared she might not be able to break free of it before they were dashed against the surface of Atielle.

33

Jane inched the craft up Atielle's Ladder.

She couldn't risk anything faster than a snail's pace because of the movement on the cable. Brai was tracking the location of the counterweight of the ladder and the high orbital station just beneath it, where he would dock and pick them up. It had moved a great deal from its original location.

Brai was a heavy presence in her mind. Keeping tabs on the trajectories of both the atmospheric debris and the path of the cable was far more complex now than it had been before. He was tightly controlled, cold, and all business, but also, beneath all of that, so...wounded. They were going to have a long talk when she was safely aboard the *Speroancora*.

Most of her human passengers had a greenish cast to their faces, while the atellans swayed and jerked drowsily without resistance in their seats. She thought they seemed to be faring better than the humans, but no one was comfortable. It made Jane think of a primitive, jerky roller coaster in three dimensions. It wasn't pleasant.

But they were approaching the low orbital station, which would mark the point at which they would pass the worst of the debris hurtling through the mesosphere. And that station should have stabilizing systems in place. They didn't seem to be functioning at the moment though, and she wasn't getting a reply from the station's computer when she pinged it. She hoped that was just proximity, but as they drew closer she became doubtful.

This had been a fool's errand. Why was she being so stubborn?

Hours went by. The movement subsided by degrees, but it hardly seemed to matter. Jane felt like her brain had been scrambled. She began to seriously worry for their well-being.

Pledor suddenly let out a low, dramatic groan—the first audible complaint she'd heard from her passengers. "Oh, great Cunabula! We've been conscripted by Zang Hoi..."

Ryliuk's baritone rang out, strong and true, not a trace of discomfort in the sound of it. "Not a one of us was conscripted, Pledor."

Ajaya cleared her throat. "Who—" she asked, and then they swung around and she waited for the craft to stabilize, "—is Zang Hoi?"

Schlewan addressed Pledor. "Can you not achieve torpor?"

Jane's eyes widened. There had been a distinct slight in Schlewan's tone.

"I can," he replied defensively. "It is difficult to maintain with each...conflicting sensation."

Jane's hands tightened on the control wheel.

"Torpor?" Ajaya asked. The craft dipped and bobbed.

Jane looked over her shoulder to see Schlewan reaching for the sectilian medical kit protruding from the wall of the shuttle. She rummaged through it noisily, clamping her hands over the contents each time the shuttle shifted, then came out with a microinjector. "I will chemically induce hibernation, then."

"No. That's uncalled for!" Pledor gasped.

"I believe it is medically necessary," Schlewan declared. Then she injected him, and Pledor went limp. "Anyone else?" Her voice rang out defiantly into the silence of the ship.

No one said a word. The power dynamics among the sectilians were shifting. This had been Schlewan's way of reminding Pledor that he was no longer in charge, and she seemed to relish it.

Jane felt Brai chuckle softly in her mind. His tone was contemptuous though—not amused. She went cold inside. His reaction surprised and disconcerted her. Perhaps he was not the person she believed him to be. Was there a dark side to Brai that she hadn't witnessed before?

Schlewan turned to Ajaya. "Torpor is a physiological state that can be self-induced. It is something like sleep or a kind of mental and physical dormancy. It conserves energy and resources. We use it to get through times of famine or other difficulties. You do not have a similar state?"

Ajaya replied, "No. We can meditate. I believe that's the closest we may come under our own power to what you describe. It does not have the same effect."

Schlewan replaced the microinjector and closed the protruding drawer. "I see. I see. *I see.* Without consulting the ship's medical library I can't know if this drug would affect you adversely. Better for you to endure this temporary discomfort than to take the risk."

"I concur," Ajaya said.

"Are all of you meditating, then?" Schlewan asked.

"Fuck no," Alan said.

"Meditation is normally attempted under calm, quiet conditions. I am finding it helpful to try," Ajaya answered noncommittally, clearly hedging around the cultural snafu Pledor had just found himself in. "Distraction would work better for humans, I believe. Can you tell us about Zang Hoi?"

Tinor spoke up. "I will. Zang Hoi is a mythological figure from very early sectilian literature. In some stories she is the first atellan to survive landing on Sectilia in a tiny pod. In other tales she is purported to be the first alien to arrive from a world beyond this star system. She was said to be captivating to look upon, though she is described many different ways in various legends and sometimes as a shapeshifter. She was always depicted as a trickster who sneered at our then-primitive technologies and lured unsuspecting sectilians into various precarious circumstances during which they often lost their lives."

"Not exactly a flattering comparison, then," Alan said dryly.

The atellans were silent. Jane sensed through Ryliuk that they were embarrassed by Pledor's outburst and that a few of them were more than marginally worried he was right. No one spoke for a long time.

They reached the doughnut-shaped low orbital station a couple of hours later, and it was immediately obvious why it wasn't functional and why its computers hadn't answered her queries. Something had torn a hole right through one side of it. Nevertheless, because of its mass, it was a quieter place to rest for a short time and regroup. Jane docked with the station but didn't open the doors of the shuttle.

She was exhausted and needed a break. She turned off the consoles and closed her eyes to try to get some sleep before deciding how to proceed.

She dozed fitfully and dreamt of clinging to the deck of her parents' boat on a stormy sea off the coast of Australia, sobbing after her father had been caught in the reef. This was a familiar nightmare. Often she dreamt that she dove over the side to attempt to rescue him, but in her panic she always forgot to put the diving equipment back on. In this version of the dream she was disoriented, swimming blindly with storm-surging waters tossing her around, lungs burning until they felt like they were going to burst.

She woke with a gasp. She could hear Alan and Ron conferencing about the mechanics of the shuttle and Ajaya passing around more motion-sickness medication as well as water and food cubes.

"Good. You're awake," Alan said brusquely. "Put this on." He handed her one of the shuttle's emergency-decompression masks and an air cartridge.

The mask was a form-fitting mask that went over the head and neck, creating a seal that could suit nearly any anatomical configuration. Small cartridges could be attached to the chin area in the front to provide air. They'd tested them on themselves before they left the *Speroancora*. They worked equally well on humans as they did on the various body types of the Sectilius. She stared at it dumbly, still groggy. "What's going on?"

He sighed heavily, his hand going to the back of his neck. "The way I see it we've got two choices and both of them involve all of us wearing these masks."

Ajaya eased between them, gripping the seat backs as the shuttle bobbed, then settled into the vacant copilot's seat. "You might let her come fully awake before you start in, Alan. Try some manners. They're good for you." Ajaya handed her a water pouch and some food cubes.

Jane took them gratefully. She watched Alan in her peripheral vision. He was fidgeting. He was the kind of person who needed to always keep busy. This trip was probably driving him batty. She sipped from the pouch then turned to him fully, keeping her expression carefully neutral. She nibbled on the corner of a cube, knowing she needed to eat, but afraid to put too much in her stomach. "Tell me."

"At this point we either have to fix this station or the shuttle."

He wanted to do a spacewalk. That was so dangerous. Her heart started to pound. She turned the shuttle's external lights on the station and gazed at it. Twisted, jagged metal and green plastic marred the opening of a gaping wound. The tightness in her chest squeezed harder. She turned back to him.

Before she could say anything, he went on, "Yeah. It looks bad. But Jaross and Ron and I have been going over scans of the thing. It's not as bad as it looks. Most of the tech was spared." He reached between the seats and pulled up a hologram on the dash. It showed the station as a line diagram. He tapped another button, superimposing a transparent image which displayed the damage over the schematic. Then he pointed to one of the two holes. "See here? The only vital thing missing is the main power conduit. If I patch it, we've got power to the stabilizing system."

Jane's eyes narrowed as she focused on the area his finger was pointing to.

"This is probably the simpler of the two to fix. All we really need there is essentially an extension cord. The shuttle will be a whole lot easier to work on if we do this first."

Jane made eye contact with Ajaya and Ron, though she already knew through Brai that they both concurred with this assessment. EVAs were dangerous, but they were trained for them—even in conditions as harsh as this. She should trust that.

According to Brai, the cable could take weeks to settle down on its own. They were out of options. She'd chosen this path because she thought it would be safer, and now that the engine was compromised, she guessed it had been. After all, that could have happened midflight. But continuing on without stabilizing the cable and fixing the engine would be madness. They had to do something. She frowned. "This is a one-person job, or two?"

"One. I can have the station up and running in thirty minutes." Alan leaned into the copilot seat as the shuttle and station bucked. He was close enough to kiss. She didn't back away a single millimeter. She gazed into his eyes deeply, trying to tell him everything...everything...

The moment passed. The craft settled into a momentary lull and he backed away, turning his head and sniffing. Waiting for her reply.

She twisted to look at Ron. "Suit up."

Ron nodded and began to make his way to the back where the skintight pressure suits were stored.

Alan punched the copilot seat. Ajaya flinched but said nothing. Jane didn't have to explain herself to anyone. Ron was the electrical engineer and was more qualified. Alan wasn't the one making the decisions, and he needed to remember that. It wasn't personal.

34

Jane remained tense while Ron worked.

They had no clear view of him inside the station since they were docked below it. However, he'd agreed to let them hover on his outermost mental layers, able to see, hear, and feel without intruding on his thoughts.

Brai was jacked much deeper into Ron's thoughts. He was running computer simulations of the cable and station's motion in order to predict each movement before it happened so that Ron wouldn't have any surprises while he worked. It would keep him safer and make the work go more smoothly.

Alan stood braced near the door, head bowed as he concentrated on Ron's every movement and observation, tensed to take action at a moment's notice. The decompression mask sat on top of his head like a stocking cap, ready to slip over his face in seconds.

They'd all donned safety masks and pressure suits while Jane depressurized the cabin, quickly let Ron out, then repressurized again. The sectilian suits were tight against the skin, exerting pressure mechanically instead of being filled with air pressure the way the puffy orange NASA suits had. The extremely stretchy suits were designed to protect against moisture loss in vacuum as well as minimize exposure to cosmic radiation. They felt a lot like a wet suit, and were quite a step up from the suits they had worn when they had begun their exploration of the Target.

The zone the station resided in was the equivalent of Low Earth Orbit back home. As a layperson, Jane had been dimly aware that LEO was where the International Space Station resided, and since she had frequently seen astronauts in her online newsfeeds broadcasting from ISS drifting around, she would have assumed there was no gravity at that distance from Earth. She hadn't understood how the space station was constantly accelerating down in its orbit over the curved edge of the Earth, neutralizing the effective perceived gravity for the occupants. That was free fall, not true microgravity.

When she trained with NASA she'd gotten a crash course in physics, and the command-and-control engram set she'd received from Brai had deepened her understanding of these concepts. So she wasn't surprised that even when they had docked at the low orbital station, the sensation of gravity felt pretty much the same as it had on the surface of Atielle, though less than they'd been experiencing under acceleration.

Except when the entire cable dipped. On the downswing they were weightless for a moment as they fell back toward Atielle. As they swung back up there was a slight increase in the sensation of gravity. It played havoc on her stomach.

And she wasn't the only one. As Ron worked, he referred to the low orbital station as Vomit Station without a trace of humor. He kept a running commentary going as he worked. His patience and caution were remarkable. He didn't rush a thing. He was acutely attuned to Brai's predictions of the station's movements, carefully tucking everything he was working with away and retreating to a position of safety every time the station was about to move dramatically.

Once he accomplished the necessary connection, the station came to life, true to Alan's promise. Ron carefully made his way back to the shuttle along his safety line, everyone donned masks while Jane cycled decompression-recompression, and then Jane was able to access the station controls from the dashboard and bring the stabilizing countermeasures online. They took effect very quickly. They soon reached a point where the inertial dampeners compensated for the remaining motion and everyone breathed a sigh of relief.

Jane sank back into the pilot's seat and closed her eyes. She couldn't relax, wouldn't be able to relax, until they were safely back aboard the *Speroancora*, but this moment was sweet. She could breathe a little easier now, but only a little.

She felt Ajaya brush past her and someone else quickly filled the copilot seat. Jane expected it to be Ron. She opened her eyes, planning to praise him for a job well done, but it was Alan who sat there. He stared at her, his eyebrows nearly reaching his hairline and his jaw bulging.

She tried not to frown. She knew what he wanted to do.

And she was going to have to let him do it.

He took a deep breath, and she was sure he was about to launch into his version of a convincing tirade about why he had to go out there and find out what was wrong with the engine.

She held up a hand to forestall him. "Yes. With caveats."

He blew out the breath like a deflating balloon and looked surprised, then wary. "What caveats?" he snarled, his blue eyes angrily boring into her.

She wanted to ask him why he hated her so much now. She wanted to beg him to just listen to reason. But she knew that he was a volatile individual and that for some people the line between love and hate could be incredibly thin. And he had so little experience with love, it seemed. She longed to put a hand on his face to soothe him, to scrape her thumb over his unruly beard and…

She snapped out of the moment of reverie and he was still staring at her, hard. This wasn't the time for these thoughts or even these conversations. That would come later, she hoped.

"You have to take all the same safety measures Ron took. A safety line—"

"Of course!" he growled and rolled his eyes.

"And connect with Brai," she said.

His eyes narrowed and his lips tightened. "Oh, you're on a first-name basis now, are you?" He shook his head. "Fine. I'm ready to go."

35

It was a fucking dream come true.

A spacewalk, man. Finally, a spacewalk.

Alan would have preferred that it be in microgravity. That would have been loads more fun, but he'd take it—because it was a *spacewalk*.

Since he'd been a little kid, he'd wanted to put on one of those puffy white suits and bounce and drift in space, doing important repairs on spacecraft.

Neil Armstrong, John Glenn, Buzz Aldrin, Yuri Gagarin, and Alan Shepard had been his childhood heroes. He'd pored over every book he could find about them at the library and hidden them from his mother so she couldn't return them, deaf to her pleas about the late fees he racked up until she gave up and paid the library to replace them.

Jesus, when he'd been six, his dad had brought home a mutt and told him she looked like the Soviet dog that had been the first animal to orbit the Earth. Alan had pored over grainy black-and-white photos from the 1950s in his books until he conceded his dad was right. He'd never given a thought to pets prior to that moment, but that dog, which of course he named Laika, had become his constant companion and playmate.

How many EVAs had he and Laika embarked on in the backyard? Him bouncing slowly with his arms outstretched just like the astronauts in the moon footage, Laika trotting alongside...until she spotted a chipmunk. He smiled to himself. She would have been a much better astronaut if it hadn't been for chipmunks.

Years later his parents would admit that they'd worried about him because he'd been such a solitary and serious kid. A dog had seemed like a good idea to them, but they'd known it had to be the right dog. And they'd found him just the right one.

When he was in college, he'd gotten a call from his mom on a Thursday night to tell him that Laika had died suddenly. He'd gone on a bender that lasted for days. He had no memories of that weekend, which, according to his friends' accounts, sounded like it was for the best.

Alan sighed and eased out of the cabin, clipping his first tether to the outside of the shuttle. "I'm secure," he said to Ei'Brai, and the shuttle's door closed instantly.

Jane didn't say anything, but he felt her yearning for him to be safe through the connection with the Squid. He flinched because the surge of emotion took him by surprise. Damn it. The rest of the NASA crew and Ryliuk were watching and now they all knew there'd been something going on between him and Jane.

They'd probably suspected anyway, but he would've preferred it to remain at that level. It was bad enough she made eyes at him all the time. It was confusing and frustrating and he just couldn't figure her out. It was so messed up. He was tired of thinking about it.

He was sorely tempted to break the connection and just do his thing. She could watch him work over the external cameras and shit. She didn't need to be jacked into his head. But he'd made a promise.

He looked down. Atielle was a gray ball of storm clouds with layers of glowing gasses around the curve of her horizon—blue green at the leading edge fading to a haze of white with a second arc of gold just above it. Here and there glimpses of the oceans and land masses flickered as storms roiled over the surface of the moon. Beyond that, Sectilia looked like a giant Earth in the far distance with Atielle's shadow obscuring about a third of the much-larger planet. Just hanging out down there, millions of kilometers away. It was an amazing sight to see. And all around him, the darkest dark with so many stars it was like someone had spilled glitter in the sky.

Bleh. Enough of the pretty thoughts. Time to get to work.

Just like the larger ship, this smaller one had plenty of swooping shapes extruding from its outer hull. These were sturdy and made great handholds, regardless of their true purpose of deflecting heat and redirecting airflow during reentry.

His experience rock climbing had come in handy more than once since they'd shown up at the Target. He moved carefully over the outer surface of the shuttle until he reached the end of his tether. Then he secured a new line, clipped the first to the second, and kept moving until he reached the engine hatch.

He'd quadruple-checked this engine before they left the Sten compound. He couldn't imagine what had gone wrong, but he'd have them up and running in no time.

He put himself into the best position he could, dangling on the line with a steadying hand and foot on the ship, gravity wanting to suck him straight down to the surface of Atielle. That wasn't disconcerting at all.

He focused his headlamp on the hatch and wedged the specialized tool into the slot that would open the compartment, grunting as he awkwardly lunged up into it with all the weight he could muster. He had to try three times, abs burning, swinging wildly a couple of those times, before the hatch sprang open in his face. He had a good grip though. He'd known that would happen. It didn't surprise him.

It was darker in there than it should have been. That wasn't right. His eyes refocused. What the...

"Oh, shit!" he blurted and lurched back. He lost a handhold and a foothold at the same time in his panic. Suddenly he found himself jerking at the end of the tether, flailing, arms and legs outstretched.

"Alan!" he heard Jane shout in his head. He couldn't tell if that was over the mic or through the squidnection.

He couldn't see her, but he could *sense* her through Ei'Brai. She'd risen from the pilot seat into a crouch inside the cockpit, her hands going to her decompression mask like she was ready to leap out the door to come rescue him.

"For fuck's sake, I'm fine!" he shouted into the mask's mic, spittle flying in his fury at his own ineptitude. "Jesus, people. Calm down."

"You calm down!" she yelled right back. Her voice sounded angry, but also wavered.

He sobered suddenly, staring down at the gray marble below him, and panted raggedly.

She really was scared. The Squid wasn't holding anything back. Her eyes were watering. She was holding her breath. Every muscle in her body was cramping with tension.

He marveled at how this connection was going both ways. He hadn't noticed that before, maybe because he'd been so mad at her.

He swallowed. She was sorry, so sorry, and she cared about him. A lot.

She... Crap...

He shook his head.

"Yes," she said in his head, softly. "Against my better judgment, you idiot."

He shrugged uncomfortably. Everyone was watching this.

"Can we please talk about this later?" he said out loud.

He was all flustered and shit. He cursed some more for good measure then reached behind himself to grab the tether. He pulled himself up, hand over hand, until he could get ahold of a protrusion coming off the ship. He scrambled a bit until he got himself back into his original position. He set a third tether because he wasn't dicking around anymore.

"Is it really...?" Ajaya asked tentatively, through the Squid.

"Yep," Alan answered. "It's goddamn nepatrox slugs. I can't tell how many. Slimy bastards. I guess they crawled in there when we were working at the base of Atielle's Ladder. I should have checked a fifth time before we started up, but I figured we were set by that point."

He shuddered a little as he looked into the engine compartment again and began to consider what tool to sacrifice to scrape them out of there. None of his options had much reach, and the inside of the compartment was slimy. He knew from experience that the slug slime was some caustic shit.

"How much alkalinity can these suits take—anyone know offhand?" he said to everyone listening.

"They aren't rated for that," Jane replied. "This is a pretty unusual situation."

"Surely they can't be alive?" Ron asked. "In that environment they should just desiccate. Freeze-dry, really."

Alan sniffed with distaste and poked his head in a bit farther. He could see that Ron was right. The slugs were shrinking and turning a lighter color with the exposure to full vacuum. Butt-ugly bloated balls of goo. They must not have any bones. Probably just slid right into the compartment, disintegrating the seal as they slipped through the impossibly thin crack.

"Yeah," Alan replied. "I think they must have been somewhat protected until I opened the door. They seem to be dead now. Freeze-drying as we speak."

He considered his tools again and picked one of the larger ones, of which he had a duplicate inside the cabin. It had a flat edge. He didn't know what it was called, only what it did. He tethered it to his suit.

He shoved the boot of his good leg into one of the swooping extrusions until he felt it was really secure, then the other, legs splayed out a bit more than he'd really like, so that he could position himself just to the left side of the compartment door. His head felt full and heavy, like he'd been hanging upside down on a jungle gym for far too long. It throbbed with every heartbeat. He was getting really fucking tired of dangling there.

EVAs were supposed to be fun, goddamn it.

He hooked his left arm into a protrusion. It wasn't made for this. It was holding all of his upper-body weight, and it dug into his arm painfully. It was going to leave a mark.

With his right arm, he started running the flat edge of the sectilian tool over the inside surface of the door. Dried goo flaked away to fall down to Atielle. He scraped the walls as thoroughly as he could so that he wouldn't expose himself to any more of the caustic material than he had to when he crawled more fully into the compartment.

What he wouldn't give for a power washer right now.

He lunged, striking at the mass of larvae and swinging away as some bits flew free, hoping they would slide right past him. He poked his head in to see what was left.

Oh, good grief. Rapidly freeze-drying piles of glop that had broken open. He coughed a little and clung to the outside for a few minutes to let the vacuum do its work.

Lunge. Knock. Scrape. Swing back out of the way as the flakes and gobbets of goo fell down to the moon below.

He was working up a sweat. His muscles were tiring. He was getting thirsty but these suits didn't have any kind of water reservoir. That would be one point for NASA. Good to know sectilian tech wasn't superior in every way to good old American ingenuity.

Of course, he thought, frowning, NASA had never managed gloves that worked like these. These gloves were effing amazing…

Finally he took a look inside, and the compartment was as clean as he thought he could get it. Now was the time for the coup de grace. He pulled a green plastic packet off his belt. He had a secret ingredient that he hoped would make it all better, or at the very least much better. Nanites. Beautiful, angelic little machines that were programmed to fix things at the molecular level.

He pulled his entire body inside the compartment until he could reach the outer shell of the engine itself. It was all scarred up and deformed from the caustic exudate of the slugs cozying up to it. He pressed the packet up against it and squeezed until he felt the resistance give way.

"Activate protocol 538–729," he told Jane. She could do that from inside faster than he could out here. That would turn them on and get them working.

He smiled as he eased out and closed the compartment. His first successful EVA was almost complete. Now he could get back inside the cabin and they'd be underway in a few hours.

He disconnected the third tether and began to retrace his steps, finding handholds and footholds to pull himself back up to the side of the ship. He didn't intend to waste a minute. He remembered the last time he'd been burned by nepatrox-slug slime. It was probably going to be days before they got back to the *Speroancora*. He had to get this suit off ASAP.

"Mffft." He hauled himself up, muscles screaming in protest. He was a little disgusted with himself, frankly. The gravity on Atielle was a fraction of Earth's gravity. He'd gotten soft down there. This shouldn't be so hard. He'd definitely put himself through harder workouts climbing in Tahquitz and Joshua Tree for fun.

The Squid suddenly cut in to his musings. "Doctor Alan Bergen, it would be prudent to increase your rate of return."

Alan gritted his teeth and hauled himself up another foot. He huffed. "I'm busting my hump here, Mr. Brai. I'd appreciate it if you'd keep your opinions to yourself."

Then Jane was in his head. "Alan…" Immediately he was on high alert. He'd lost track of her thoughts while he'd been concentrating on the work. Now he seemed to zoom into her head like he was sucked there. But she was looking out through his eyes and focused on the face shield of his mask. And she was scared.

That was when he saw it.

Gunk on the upper part of the small domed area that covered his face. And the tiny display that showed the integrity of the face shield was falling like a stone.

Fuck.

He knew what that gunk was doing. That gunk was going to fucking kill him.

He reached the end of the second tether and clipped himself to the first before unclipping the second, but he didn't bother to mess with gathering up the length. Woe to anyone standing at the base of Atielle's Ladder. He let it go and pulled his ass up another foot, simultaneously rubbing his face on his arm. That smeared it, rather than wiping it away. Great. Now a larger area of the face shield was disintegrating.

He let out a roar as he heaved himself up some more. No one could hear you scream in space. He laughed. Unless you were psychically connected to the goddamn son of Cthulhu.

"We're here for you, man. You've got time. I'll come out and bring you in if I have to. Even if the mask goes to hell. You're okay. We got this." That was Ron. He could feel them all scurrying around inside the cabin, getting ready to open the door. Someone was anchoring a cable inside.

He pushed harder. Just a few more feet.

He glanced at the readout. It was almost gone. Holy shit. He was *not* going out like this.

Then Ron's voice. "Get ready to exhale, man. You have to exhale. You'll only be conscious about fifteen seconds. I'll get you. I'm ready. Brace yourself. Do not let go."

He dragged himself up another couple feet. The closer he got to the door, the more likely he'd survive…

He felt it go.

There was no chance to exhale. He was breathing so hard from the exertion, the air just left him. He could almost reach the door if he stretched out his arm. He had the presence of mind not to do that. He just grabbed on where he was.

Ron was coming.

Alan saw the door open.

His vision was closing in already. He couldn't see anything but all that glitter on black.

No way that was fifteen seconds. All those NASA bastards didn't take exercise into account when they handed out tidy little numbers like fifteen seconds.

Ron grabbed his arm. Ron had him. He trusted Ron.

He let go.

Everything went black.

He came to on the floor of the shuttle, coughing and sobbing and gulping air. He didn't care.

He was alive.

And Jane was there, kneeling over him, tears wetting her cheeks. Her warm hand rested on his cheek. He turned into her caress and breathed.

He just breathed.

Brai watched Jane and her colleagues carefully while his mind was occupied with other thoughts. After a break of some hours they resumed their journey up the cable. He could feel them pressed into their seats under acceleration, gaining speed with every passing moment.

If there were no other complications, Jane would return to him very soon.

Brai was sobered by the near miss on Atielle's Ladder. His limbs drifted around him unheeded as he considered what he'd almost lost.

He'd been so preoccupied with the atellan newcomers, and with brooding over his petty existential crisis, that he'd nearly forgotten what was really important.

Jane. The entire human team. They were a new beginning. A new and better life.

Jane could have given him up to her government and let them do what they would with him, but she respected him, valued him as a person, and had chosen to honor his request instead.

She was not alone in this sentiment. All the remaining humans felt the same to varying degrees. This was something precious. If this journey to Atielle had taught him anything, it was that the humans saw him quite differently than the Sectilius ever had—more fully as a colleague rather than a servant, or a convenient living extension of the ship. This was novel and should not be taken for granted.

And there was more to consider.

Jane had a dear affection for Doctor Alan Bergen. The man was always in her thoughts. If this man was in danger, Jane hurt—she felt physical pain. That was a powerful connection.

If Doctor Alan Bergen was important to Jane, he should, by extension, be important to Brai as well. This was not a binary situation. She did not care for one individual to the complete exclusion of any other as he'd sometimes seen sectilians do. Her sense of community was more complex than that—a spectrum, a matter of degrees for each individual at any given time. Even if Jane enjoyed a deep relationship with Dr. Alan Bergen, Brai was beginning to see, that would not preclude a deep relationship with himself. Jane was generous with her affection. He could see, even now, that attachments were growing between her and the sectilian strangers.

He felt some shame. He had underestimated not only her, but her entire people, judging them based on his experience with the only people he'd ever known. He found himself with his limbs bunched protectively around his mantle. He consciously let them go again, shaking them out to release the tension.

It was so quiet without her here now. Surely he could be forgiven for fearing the loss of such a precious individual. He'd been alone so long it had nearly driven him mad. He never wanted to feel that loss again.

Affection was unusual and so valuable. He'd been greedy with Jane's. Rageth had always said she guarded vigilantly against anyone knowing how deep her feelings for Brai ran because sectilians rarely felt such levels of intimacy even with each other. It was considered aberrant behavior to involve oneself to that extent with a kuboderan, to entwine one's life with an alien's. Rageth had thought she was different because she'd been a young mother and nearly lost her children when the Swarm had come to her colony world. It had made her value every moment, every individual in her life, more.

She had said her life was richer because of Brai. The things they achieved together had more value because of all they shared. She'd believed strongly that it was worth the risk. It might have been injurious to her career if anyone had found out.

He had kept the secret well. And they had been assigned to the most important job on the roster. When coordinates were discovered in an ancient Cunabalistic text that were believed to be those of Terra, it was the *Speroancora* that the Unified Sentient Races sent, one of the finest ships in the sectilian fleet. He couldn't help but swell with pride at the memory of that time.

Losing Rageth had nearly killed him. There had been no goodbye. She'd simply faded away, and her body had rotted where she lay until he couldn't bear it anymore and programmed the squillae to sweep the ship clean of all of the bodies.

And then he'd simply lived to keep the ship in the best order possible, so that when rescue came from Sectilius, Rageth's legacy as one of the finest officers in the fleet would remain intact. That had been the only thing that kept him going during those long lonely years, even when enough time had gone by that he was fairly certain deliverance would not arrive from that quarter.

Then Jane had come.

Her empathy was a balm. He came to know in time that this was a common trait among the humans. Dr. Thomas Compton had also possessed it to a great degree, as had Dr. Ajaya Varma and Dr. Ronald Gibbs. The others less so, but still far more than the average sectilian.

And him? A kuboderan? What degree of empathy did he possess? He rumbled with laughter. He'd never given this a moment of consideration before now. He didn't know his own people well enough to be able to say with any certainty. He only knew himself, and perhaps he did not even know himself well. This was a time for introspection.

But Brai suspected that life on his home world among wild, unfettered kuboderans was short but sweet and full of savage emotions—like the one Jane called love. That was stunning to consider.

He seemed to feel more since Jane had come. The difference within him was unsettling and complex. He didn't understand it, but he thought it was good.

The truth was Jane's warmth had nearly overwhelmed him when she'd arrived. He'd been broken, felt nothing for so long that he'd become consumed with her, possibly to a deleterious level. He'd also been greedy. He needed to find balance now if he was to serve her as she deserved.

He must stop feeling this selfishness toward her and petty jealousy toward any other in her orbit. It was not becoming of all that he had achieved. He was capable of more.

He would follow Jane's lead, forge something deeper with all of the humans. Each of them was exceedingly unique with so much to offer. It was his job to learn their strengths so that he could draw on them when needed. In the coming months, that could be the difference between survival and extinguishment.

Today he'd learned how calm and methodical Dr. Ronald Gibbs could be in a crisis and how Dr. Ajaya Varma was able to eclipse distractions in order to focus every one of her senses on a patient in need—more so even than she realized consciously. Dr. Alan Bergen was willing to put himself in danger for the greater good even when he felt an antipathy to those he shared company with. In addition, his will to live in the face of poor odds was remarkably robust. All of the humans had a sense of trust that was unprecedented in his experience.

Brai felt a strong urge to move his body. Normally when he craved exercise, he would travel a familiar circuit. Starting at one end of the ship, he would fill his mantle to capacity and clamp down suddenly so he could feel the rush of speed until it petered out and he drifted slowly to the other end of the ship. How many times had he completed this regimen? Thousands? Millions? It required no thought. He could concentrate on other problems while he performed this routine.

He'd been stuck in a loop just like this. It was time to break out. He needed to find a way to shed the lingering pain in his body that was surely a manifestation of all of this angst. He wanted to be whole again.

He filled his mantle and held it, feeling the uncomfortable fullness for as long as he could, until his body vibrated, then let go, turning his funnel randomly so that he swooped and jetted in arcs. He let his eyes lose focus and just felt the unpredictable movement.

Several times he nearly hit the barrier, but turned away at the last moment, his tentacles grazing the glass and pushing off as he came to rest before surging again in another direction, sometimes headlong, other times tentacles first. It didn't matter. All that mattered was moving.

He continued this way until his aching muscles and rumbling stomach demanded he stop. At first he felt wonderful, suction cups tingling, and he vowed he would work harder to get more vigorous exercise like this. The persistent bodily discomfort he'd been suffering since Jane had traveled to the Hator compound had finally left him. But as he stretched out a limb to trigger the mechanism that would drop a serving of food into his tank, his arm trembled and the muscle seized up painfully.

He was taken aback. That had never happened before. He flexed the arm carefully until the spasm eased. As he moved back toward the food depositor, he noted a pervasive feeling of malaise.

Surely this was just caused by hunger. He triggered the mechanism, but was left with a sensation of disquiet, as though there were something important he was forgetting. As he carefully brought the solid cubes to his beak, he dismissed that and resumed his consideration of the humans.

They continued their trip up Atielle's Ladder unimpeded. The cabin was nearly silent, most of the individuals beginning to relax, to believe the danger had passed, subsiding into sleep or torpor to cope with the long, uneventful journey. There was nothing to see through the windows but the stars, and the newness of that had already worn off for most of them.

Jane and Dr. Ronald Gibbs remained vigilant, poring over all the data the small ship provided. He was linked to them, monitoring that same data as well as multiple sources of his own. He would not rest until they were safely aboard, and might not even rest then.

Brai was aware that Doctor Alan Bergen fought exhaustion to stay alert in case of changing circumstance, but the man kept him at a distance.

It was true that Doctor Alan Bergen had developed a strong dislike for him. And why shouldn't he? Brai knew that Dr. Alan Bergen craved privacy, and yet that was something Brai had found nearly impossible to give.

Brai's entire world consisted of an artificial environment that never changed. His life experience came from others on the outside. He craved mental contact like he craved oxygen. And he'd been alone so long. Surely Dr. Alan Bergen didn't realize what that meant.

Even so, Brai would have to try harder to honor Dr. Alan Bergen's wishes, to be warmer, more like Jane. Perhaps in time the man could learn to trust the kuboderan as he'd learned to trust Dr. Ronald Gibbs so unconditionally. He did not harbor any illusions. It would not happen quickly. However, it was a worthy goal.

He could be patient. The desired outcome was worth it.

Brai turned the food cube he was eating over and over between his suction cups, considering. A piece broke off and without thought one of his tentacles shot out to capture it before it floated away to foul the tank and put undue pressure on the water-filtration system.

Brai brought the crumb of food to his beak and contemplated his own long life, conjuring sentiments he didn't indulge in often. Gratitude, primarily. He was alive. He was no longer alone. He had a crew.

Brai hadn't started from scratch with a new crew since he was very young. As Do'Brai he'd served as navigator for a small supply ship to the colonies. He'd forgotten how lonely and awkward those early years had been and how it took seemingly interminable amounts of time for trust and connection to build. Lately he'd been so distracted by grief and then consumed with the joy of the arrival of the human expedition, and then there had been the test and the training and all that had come after. He'd forgotten this important lesson.

In the early days of his career there had been many painful lessons. He'd had to learn to segment his mental processes. The mind masters made grand attempts to teach young kuboderans that level of control, but reality was far different from scholarly exercises. Learning to converse and interact with multiple individuals as they fleetingly passed in and out of his awareness on their own whims while simultaneously overseeing and managing an entire ship—that had taken time and experience. He'd made mistakes, early on, some of them quite costly, but that was why young kuboderans were put on small ships when introduced to the fleet—less was at risk, both in terms of lives and financial investment.

Brai tasted the water with his suction cups, seeking bits of food that might have escaped his attention. A disturbing thought struck him. What if they had come here and found

that Sectilius had not fallen? What if the atellans had decided to take control of the ship? Where would he be then?
Where would Jane be? How would he have responded to
that?

Deep down he knew the answer. He would not be separated from her. He would become a traitor to his heritage to
keep her safe.

Brai was wary of the atellans coming aboard. He probed
them carefully as they moved into range and quickly felt he
knew their motivations well. In due time he would see if he
was right about them.

Tinor Fotep Sten was young, curious, optimistic, and
promising. Medical Master Schlewan Umbrig of Caillea was
practical and businesslike—harmless, a very typical sectilian
individual, accustomed to ship life.

Gistraedor Dux Jaross Rageth Hator was not unlike her
namesake, his very own Rageth, though perhaps less generally aware of others and significantly less compassionate.
She was young, however, and had never been aboard ship.
The experience of anipraxia would change her. That was inevitable.

Jaross's chivalrous nature had been forged in a different
crucible, however. She had no children, but she managed a
large compound of her people that was clinging to survival
against all odds in the aftermath of the plague. She had left
her compound in the capable hands of a sibling. She'd
joined the human crew because she felt the same starlust
that his own Rageth had felt. She had endured a frustrated
longing her entire life. And she liked Jane, was intrigued by
Mind Master Ryliuk of Mebrew. She would not pass up this
opportunity. This was a motivation he could understand.

On the other end of the spectrum, Gistraedor Dux Pledor Makya Sten was crudely ambitious. This was apparent to all who knew him. Under Brai's scrutiny, the former Gis'dux's motivations were transparent. He'd changed his mind about the ship and intended to find a way to usurp the *Speroancora*, to use it to bring his own compound and people to prosperity.

Brai would never allow that to happen. The atellan leader had forced his way on board and would be watched scrupulously. Jane was perceptive enough to be leery of him. Brai would not burden her with the details of his ambition until she reached the ship and safety.

The unknown entity was Mind Master Ryliuk of Mebrew. Brai had known many mind masters during his early training, when he had been young and naive. Having one aboard a ship of this size and class would be considered unusual, since the masters mainly resided on the hidden planet where Brai's people were harvested and tutored.

Master Ryliuk was powerful and well trained. His mind was orderly and well segmented. He was capable of deflecting Brai's probes or obfuscating his own intentions. He appeared not to be doing this now, but Brai could not be sure this was authentic.

Master Ryliuk presented himself as a restless wanderer who was grateful to resume some semblance of his former life. He appeared to be committed to Jane's cause—finding and rescuing the stranded kuboderans scattered across the universe, helping them recover from their trauma so they could serve again, to help defend and rebuild Sectilius.

This selfless gesture notwithstanding, the mind master warranted strict observation as well. Brai would probably never be fully assured that Master Ryliuk was harmless, simply because of who he was—his participation in the old system meant he subscribed to the core beliefs that all mind masters shared.

"You have nothing to fear from me, Ei'Brai."

The interjection of Master Ryliuk's mental voice took Brai by surprise.

Brai's limbs went completely still. He forgot to breathe. He'd thought that at this distance his musings were entirely his own.

He meticulously shuttered away his every thought on every last level.

He would not be so careless again.

37

Alan struggled to stay awake in case Jane needed him. He stared blankly over her shoulder, blinking owlishly. He didn't have the energy to try to exclude the Squid anymore. Ei'Brai was there, keeping tabs on all of them, but not in an intrusive way, which actually felt reassuring instead of annoying for a change.

They were under constant acceleration now, which created a force on their mass that felt like gravity, but technically wasn't. It was a long way from the upper reaches of the mesosphere, where they'd stopped to repair the station, to the high orbital station where they would uncouple from the elevator in order to traverse the short distance to the waiting *Speroancora*.

There wasn't much to occupy his mind, which made the task of staying awake more difficult. He was trying not to think about Jane so that he could keep his thoughts private. He had no idea how much others could see and he was too exhausted to try to figure it out now. He realized that not practicing this crazy telepathy business put him at a disadvantage, and he didn't like that.

And yet, he wasn't stupid. He realized that Ei'Brai had just played a huge role in saving his life.

Maybe that was why he softened a bit when the Squid's voice softly murmured in his head, "Doctor Alan Bergen, you have my assurances that I will awaken you the instant something critical develops. Should you wish to subside into sleep, you will not miss anything pressing." The Squid receded from his mind and waited for his reply from a distance. It was very unlike his previous behavior, which honestly had felt a lot like an energetic dog jumping on him to get his attention.

Alan cleared his throat and sat up a little bit. He was sore from his little excursion outside, so the movement made him grimace. He looked around over the tops of the seat backs. Everyone else, aside from Jane and Ron, had gone to sleep. Jane turned in her seat and nodded at him slightly. She was listening to this interchange. He nodded back, his mouth twisting in a frown.

"Okay," he said to the Squid, reluctantly. "The second something happens, though."

"Of course. You will perform better in a crisis if you are well rested. This is a human necessity. It is for the greater good of all."

Alan settled back into the bench seat, careful not to sprawl on Ajaya, who was neatly arranged next to him, dozing. He was so tired he'd have no trouble sleeping. The Squid actually had a point. Curiosity tugged at him, though. "What about you? Don't you sleep?" His eyes were already closing.

The Squid's voice softened even more. It was oddly soothing. "I do, of course, but in stages. Never all at once. I am able to always be on alert. It is one of the many evolutionary advantages of my species."

Alan blinked his eyes open again, but he couldn't keep them open. Huh. He'd heard dolphins did that—slept with only part of their brains at any given time so they could keep swimming and be on the watch for predators. That was pretty badass…

When he woke he had no idea how much time had passed. The first thing he noticed was that his arms were drifting in front of his body. Then he noted the sensation of feeling light and suspended. The only thing keeping him in place were the straps holding him against the seat. They were in microgravity then. He huffed and rubbed his face. After the ten-month journey to the Target, he'd reached a point where microgravity felt just as natural as gravity, so this didn't seem strange at all.

He squeezed his eyes shut hard and blinked, trying to shake off the grogginess and assess where they were and what was happening. They were no longer under the force of acceleration and clearly had passed geostationary orbit, below which they would still have been under the effects of Atielle's gravity to some degree.

Ajaya was seated next to him and took his vitals and so forth. He tried waving her off, but she wouldn't be denied, so he ignored her, craning his neck to see what was going on while she patted and prodded him.

He gathered from the mental chatter that they were approaching the high orbital station now. It was the end of the line, so it was shaped like a giant disk instead of a doughnut like the low orbital station. It grew in size quickly, until he couldn't see stars anymore unless he looked out one of the side windows. Docking lights came on as they approached. This station was still fully functional.

Ajaya handed him a pouch of water. He sipped idly while he drank in the view of the enormous space station. It shared a lot of esthetic components with the *Speroancora* and the shuttle, including the extruded structures swooping across its surface. It looked undamaged from what he could see. At one time this station would have housed a large crew that oversaw traffic, shuttle repairs, and the maintenance of this section of the elevator itself. He wished they had a reason to go inside, though he guessed it was probably pretty spooky in there. There wouldn't have been anyone left to clean up the bodies after the plague.

Jane docked the shuttle with the station and announced that she was beginning the decoupling process. He could feel the vibration of the mechanics disengaging from the cable, and the faint sounds of that transmitted through the cabin. It went off without a hitch, which was a relief. It was about time something was easy. When Jane turned the shuttle, he got a full view of the counterweight on the other side of the station. A small asteroid was tethered there.

Then the *Speroancora* filled the view through the windscreen and his chest tightened a little. He'd seen it several times now, but damn, that ship was a sight. He swallowed hard and glanced at Ajaya. She was staring at it too, the same kind of appreciation on her face.

And he could feel the rest of the NASA crew echoing the same feeling that made his heart whump in his chest: that effing-amazing ship was their home now.

No one was taking her from them. The *Speroancora* was theirs.

There was a lot of excited chatter coming from the seats behind him, so many voices overlapping and speaking so fast in Mensententia that he couldn't make out more than four or five words out of every ten, but he didn't really need to. The newbs were freaking out over the size of the ship. Jaross, Tinor, and Pledor had never seen anything like it.

He turned in his seat to see their gawking faces. Even Schlewan and Ryliuk looked more animated than usual. Heh. Spaceships had that effect on people everywhere.

Everything went off as planned. External service hatch 245 opened. That was on deck thirty-seven, the cargo bay next to the one Jane had used to scoop up the *Providence* with the nanite-enraged Compton, Walsh, and Varma inside. That seemed like a lifetime ago.

Jane landed without so much as a jiggle. Ei'Brai reset the synthetic gravity to the bay on her command and they settled into their seats. Alan was so buzzed to get back, he flung off his restraints and barely noticed the momentary disorientation as his body adjusted to gravity again.

They all waited impatiently while the service hatch closed, the bay repressurized, and Jane triggered the electromagnetic-pulse generator they'd set up inside the bay before they'd left, to decontaminate the shuttle of any bad nanites they might have picked up on Atielle.

The shuttle door flipped up and they all piled out. Everyone stood in a clump staring at each other.

Jane hopped out last, her movements slow and jerky.

He sent her a thought. "Welcome home, Doc."

She met his gaze, and one corner of her mouth quirked up. Then she was all business again. She raised her voice to get their attention. "I realize everyone is excited to be here, and also fatigued from the journey. Ajaya, if you would please find adequate lodgings for our guests on the same deck as our own? Help them settle in? Show them where to find food, etc.?"

"Of course, Commander. If I might suggest—"

Jane cut her off. "Alan, Ron, and I will complete a thorough inspection of the shuttle for unwanted parasites, then we'll join you." She dismissed Ajaya and the atellans and turned without preamble back to the shuttle.

Ajaya dropped her hand, what had clearly been an impending plea for Jane to rest unspoken in the face of a direct command. She ushered the atellans out of the chamber.

Jane glanced at Alan and Ron. Her tone of voice brooked no nonsense. "We'll start at the nose and go inch by inch over the entire ship. I want three sets of eyes and a camera with magnification on every single compartment they could possibly wriggle into, even the ones we think they couldn't breach. I don't want to chance a single slug getting loose in the ship."

"Understood," Alan said in unison with Ron, and they immediately got to work. It was a shame they couldn't put it off. Jane and Ron both looked exhausted. Jane had dark circles under her eyes. She moved stiffly and with purpose though. She seemed to be driven by determination alone. She kept her thoughts to herself. Checking the shuttle was clearly the only thing on her mind.

They worked for hours, methodically. They did find a few more very small slugs. Wherever possible they used a palm-held concussive-blast cannon to kill off any that were too small to see with the naked eye.

When they finished the sweep of the shuttle, Ron and Jane went off to find their beds, but Alan stayed behind to tinker with some drones he'd created. They'd keep watch over the bay and blast any stragglers before they could make their way into the rest of the ship. Just in case.

38

Jane desperately needed to rest, but that would wait a little while longer. She traversed the halls of the ship now with a strange, giddy feeling swirling in her stomach. She'd never in her life imagined she'd be so happy to see pea-soup-green walls.

When she'd left this ship, she'd been fully expecting to hand over control to a sectilian officer. But she hadn't had to.

The adventure wasn't over yet. She was glad. There was no denying it—she was ecstatic to be back aboard. The future was uncertain, but that no longer seemed so frightening. She'd made it to Atielle and returned with her crew not only intact but augmented.

Despite her fatigue she felt like she could handle whatever the universe threw at her. And relish it.

She entered her rooms and took the data sticks Jaross had given her to the small terminal in her quarters to download their contents into the database. Ei'Brai immediately began to pore over the data.

Then she briefly showered and changed, slipping on a warmer layer of clothing, and left her quarters for the central core of the ship. It was cooler there.

Her eyes adjusted to the twilight dimness as she crossed the railed gantry that led to the gangway that circumnavigated Brai's domain. His presence was heavy on her now. She'd forgotten the difference proximity could have on the connection between them.

He was waiting for her. He hovered horizontally, limbs unnaturally outstretched in alignment with his body in a torpedo shape, with his eyes averted. It was the submissive pose he always performed upon greeting her in person. She noted that his arms trembled with the difficulty of maintaining the position. He shimmered, his quicksilver skin pulsing with a crimson glow.

He was happy to see her. His mental touch was effusive with pleasure.

She couldn't help but smile. "You don't have to do that," she said to him solemnly.

There was a small rush of emotion within him as he contracted his mantle, pushing water through his funnel to right himself, allowing his limbs to curl around his body in more relaxed and natural arrangements.

"That's better," she said. Still, something wasn't quite right.

His enormous, limpid eyes turned on her, meeting her gaze without flinching. The thought struck her that he looked sad, though she couldn't say why exactly she thought that.

"You truly do not expect this behavior of me?" he asked, his mental voice softer and smaller than she'd ever heard it.

Jane placed a gloved hand on the glass, her brow furrowing. His behavior perplexed her. "Brai, I've told you this before. I don't see the point in it. It doesn't mean anything to me. Just be yourself. We don't need any silly rituals between us. They only get in the way."

He was silent. She could sense a tumult of emotion behind his eyes.

She had been going to wait until after she'd rested to ask him what was troubling him. Seeing him now, though, she realized it couldn't wait. She leaned against the glass. If he'd been human she would have pulled him into a hug.

"Tell me," she said, and closed her eyes, readying her mind to move closer—not to be told, but to see.

"I would prefer not to trouble you now. Your fatigue is great."

She pushed in anyway, dismissing his concern.

He tried to stay calm, but that only lasted seconds. Each segment of his minds seemed to have its own rush of conflicting thoughts to convey all at the same time.

She could barely breathe. Grief, anger, fear, helplessness, rage, sorrow, jealousy, animosity...all of these and more washed over her. She opened her eyes and could see the colors he flashed had changed hue. The dark crimson of friendliness was transmuted in an instant to the fierce yellow of anger, then to the bright-blue broadcast of alarm, and then a brief magenta flicker of fear.

Images flitted through his mind so quickly she could only glimpse them. His training with the mind masters. His life with Rageth. The years of forced solitude under the weight of the yoke. Herself. But one moment in particular kept bubbling to the surface again and again, until she began to see the pattern, discern what was truly troubling him amid the waves of emotion. Through her own eyes, she saw small Tinor in the carriage asking, "They are people?"

She rested her head against the glass until her body was trembling with cold and tears streaked down her face, until he'd shown her all of it and she finally understood.

She straightened again to look at him. There was a haunted bleakness behind his eyes.

"That was your past," she said firmly. "It cannot be changed."

He said nothing, but there was a tenor of confusion in the mental strand that connected them. He felt adrift, vulnerable. He was afraid of what she would say next.

"Your future will be different, Brai. I assure you."

"But you have invited the Sectilius aboard."

She inhaled deeply, trying to understand. "You believe they will influence me?"

"I believe they will strive to do so."

She could see the profiles he was drawing in his mind of each individual she'd brought from Atielle, that he was preparing an argument, ready to supply reasons for his concerns. She held up a hand and, though she was tired, perused his mental dossiers until she was satisfied that she had seen enough. "None of this surprises me."

His arms were practically in corkscrews. He was literally wound up tight. He flashed only crimson at her now, but that was sporadic and undisciplined, not the regular rhythm she was accustomed to.

She decided to try something she'd never done before, give him something he'd frequently given to her. She settled a blanket of reassurance over him in her mind. She mentally projected herself wrapping her arms around him and keeping him safe.

He was surprised but didn't draw away. He drank it up, until they both felt warm and calm. It was draining, but she gave all she had. She didn't need to say more, but she did anyway. "I wasn't born on Sectilia or Atielle Brai. I have command of this ship and we will do things my way, you have my word."

When she released her hold on him, she noted he appeared to be more relaxed, more like the confident being she'd come to know.

She eased back from the glass. "You have the data I uploaded?"

"I am processing it now. I will have calculated proposed routes for you to look at when you wake, Jane."

She smiled. It was good to hear him address her with her given name. "I look forward to seeing them. It's time we were on our way."

He pressed a tentacle to the glass. The suction cups kneaded the surface.

She placed her hand over the same spot. "We're saving each other, Brai." The ghost of gratitude flickered between them.

She took a step back, dropping her hand. "I'll see you when I wake."

The club of his tentacle remained on the glass, still kneading.

She turned and walked back down the gantry. When she arrived in her rooms, she wearily tossed off the extra layer of clothing and curled up in bed, asleep instantly.

39

Jane murmured thanks to Ajaya as Ajaya passed her the last tray of nutrition squares to lay on the tall, narrow, buffet-style table in the crew cafeteria. Jane had asked Ajaya to make up a tasting menu, with a variety of flavors for the new crew members to try. Ajaya had arranged them carefully with the Mensentic names for every flavor on 3-D printed cards that were propped in front of each tray.

She could have just held a meeting, but they were a small crew and breaking bread seemed like a good way to bring them all closer. Jane wished it could be something more elaborate to make their first meal together aboard ship memorable, but she hoped this was festive enough.

It seemed like an opportunity to encourage more interaction between the sectilian and human crew. In the few hours since she awoke she'd seen a lot of aimless wandering but little socializing between the two groups. That was going to have to change. Cliquish behavior would be natural in this circumstance but also ultimately divisive. She needed to think of creative ways to bring them all together to work as a team for their common cause. The task that lay ahead of them would be challenging.

Jane had been chatting with Ajaya and watching the newcomers react to the food cubes and their varied flavors.

Tinor in particular was delightful to watch. The adolescent's reactions were big, and iad asked Schlewan a lot of questions, tasting each flavor carefully and trying to name it without looking at the cards. But the scarcity on Atielle meant that many of the tastes were new. Schlewan was wistfully describing at length all the fruits, vegetables, grains, legumes, nuts, seeds, and fungi that the food-cube flavors were meant to represent. Eventually she located a tablet to call up images and facts from the ship's library.

The rest of the room was nearly silent by comparison. Jaross was less enthusiastic. She politely tasted each flavor one at a time, listening to Schlewan and Tinor's banter but not participating or commenting in any way. She kept her eyes downcast and seemed uncomfortable.

Jane was still learning to interpret sectilian body language. Though she had Rageth's memories and Brai's mental insights, they composed an incomplete picture. She was careful not to ascribe human attributes to some of the behaviors she observed, but it did seem as though many sectilians operated in a very closed-off, introverted manner. There seemed to be a preference for a degree of isolation as well as a tendency toward pedantic speeches and obsessions over minutiae that might not be important to anyone else. The thought had occurred to her that something akin to Asperger's might be neurotypical for the species. Someday psychologists on Earth would study these similarities and differences and it would probably do a lot of good on both worlds, but for now she could only speculate and continue to record her observations in her personal journal.

Pledor's reactions to the food were less muted than those of Jaross. He'd tried three cubes so far and set them aside, making faces with varying degrees of revulsion. Ryliuk came forward to companionably suggest a few of his favorites. Pledor tried one of those and then coughed and possibly even gagged. Jane thought she might have seen him wiping his tongue with his napkin, but she was trying not to stare, and then Alan sidled up to her, stealing most of her attention away from Pledor's antics.

Alan glanced at her sideways. "That dude's gonna get real hungry," he murmured dryly in English, just loud enough for her to hear.

Jane didn't dare smile for fear she wouldn't be able to stop at just that. She licked her lips and nodded gravely. She was glad that he was talking to her again. She didn't want to ignore him or send him the wrong message. She turned to him and raised her eyebrows briefly. No one else would be able to see that.

He chuckled softly. She had hit the mark, then. "Before we started eating these, I was pretty worried about how they might affect us."

That surprised her. "You were? Why?"

"I was pretty sure they would poison us." He nodded slowly and popped an entire food cube in his mouth.

Jane was nonplussed. "What?"

He chewed thoughtfully. "Oh yeah. I figured there would be some heavy metal that the Sectilius needed nutritionally but that our livers wouldn't be able to get rid of. I figured it would build up in our blood until we went nuts or got weak and sick or something." He took a swig from a cup of water he held.

The thought had never occurred to her. Maybe because of the engram Brai had put in her brain. She felt a small spasm of guilt that she hadn't reassured the others more about the cubes' contents. Her brows drew together. "Oh, wow. I didn't think—"

He shrugged. "Then I really thought about it. All the elements in the universe, aside from hydrogen and helium, come from stellar nucleosynthesis. The proportions should be roughly the same everywhere, so wherever life evolves, its needs will be pretty similar, especially since there was some godlike super race rampaging around, planting humanoids everywhere." He picked up another food cube thoughtfully. "This flavor is growing on me, but it needs more salt. I'm going to tinker with the food printer and see if I can make it do that."

Jane smiled. "Which one is it?"

He gazed at it like he wasn't sure how to describe it. "It's kind of like the flavor of chili. Beany, beefy, but more earthy than that. There's a hint of spiciness."

Jane nodded. "Oh. That's the flavor of a subterranean fungus that grows in dry forestland on Sectilia."

He made a wry face. "I'd rather not know, thanks."

She pressed her lips together so she wouldn't smile again. "Sorry. I'm pretty sure the flavor is just a synthetic replication."

He waved her off and contemplated the food cubes like he wasn't sure if he wanted to eat more. He set them down on a nearby table. "Anyway, I've analyzed them. There's nothing scary in them that I can find. I'm no chemist, but I'm pretty sure they're a solid nutritional value for humans too. Kinda weird though. Like eating dog food in a way. All the essential vitamins and minerals in a uniform bite-sized kibble." He grinned.

She grinned back. He always had the oddest way of looking at things that she found so endearing. It was nice to talk to him again like this. It felt tentative, like they were both unsure of where they stood, but she thought that maybe it was a good place to get their feet back under them and try to start again. A comfortable silence lengthened between them.

Tinor suddenly exclaimed, "Pua fruit! Oh, this is tasty!"

Pledor narrowed his eyes and grumbled, "Which one?"

Tinor bounced over to the table where the food was displayed and gestured with an open hand. Pledor snatched one and nibbled on it suspiciously. He ate the entire square slowly, his expression still mostly in a moue of disgust, but when he finished that cube he went back, emptied the tray of that variety, and walked away to turn his back on the rest of the group, greedily consuming them one after another like a starving man.

It made Jane think about what Alan had said about the food poisoning them. Then she remembered him telling her once about being certain that the aliens inside the Target were going to tear them limb from limb. She turned to him, her brow furrowing. "You have a bit of a doom-and-gloom streak, don't you?"

He frowned. "What do you mean?"

"You always imagine the worst-case scenario."

His hand went to the back of his neck, as it often did when he was thinking. "It saves being disappointed, I guess." He sent her a probing look.

She met his eyes, unflinching.

He glanced away and looked uncomfortable. It seemed like he might drift away at any moment. She scrambled to think of something to say that would put them back on a more even keel. The problem of Brai's nanites popped into her head. Yes. Work. That was the perfect thing to talk about. He loved a challenge.

She instinctively reached out to him but stopped just shy of touching his arm as she blurted out, "There's something I've been meaning to ask you to do. I just haven't had an…opportunity." She cringed inside. There was a reason why she hadn't asked him yet. "I recently learned that Brai had his own specialized set of squillae that were very different from those populating the rest of the ship. His enclosure isn't shielded, so they would have been deactivated when we set off the EMP. I have only a vague idea of what they were meant to do. Could you look into that for me? You'd have a better grasp on the implications. I think it could be important. Something tells me it might be related to the difficulty we've had with the jumps."

He looked intrigued. "Why don't you just ask him?"

Jane sighed. "He honestly doesn't know. There are a lot of things the Sectilius have kept secret on these ships, especially as they pertain to the Kubodera. Even the Quasador Dux is left in the dark."

"That's effed up. What else are they hiding?"

She shook her head. "I don't know. Right now the yoke and Ei'Brai's squillae are the two mysteries I'm most interested in solving. If I encounter others, I'll let you know."

He nodded, deep in thought now. "Yeah, the yoke is odd. It's a very complex system. It's hard to tell what all is involved."

"It demonstrates a profound lack of trust," Jane said.

Alan looked like he was going to reply, but Ryliuk came barreling up to Jane before Alan could say anything, and she had no choice but to turn her attention to him.

Ryliuk towered over her, his frizzy white hair sticking out in all directions as though he'd been running his fingers through it repeatedly. He sent a thought to her, directly. "Quasador Dux Jane Holloway, I've a matter of critical importance to discuss."

Jane glanced at Alan, uncomfortably. By human standards this was a bit rude. Alan was excluded from the conversation. His face had gone blank.

She took an unconscious step back. Ryliuk had a habit of hovering very close inside her personal space. That step didn't help, because he only moved to loom closer.

"Please call me Jane," she said out loud. All the formality of the multiple names was wearing on her. She didn't know how to get around it. It seemed to be ingrained in their culture. To disregard it completely when addressing them would be disrespectful. She hoped that with time they'd consider calling her Jane, as Brai had come to. That might break it down a bit.

Jane kept her body turned to include Alan, though his attention was now elsewhere. She was pretty sure he was angry, given the set of his jaw, but she couldn't be certain because he'd returned to his habit of excluding himself from the anipraxic network.

Ryliuk pressed forward another step, to put himself between her and Alan. Jane took a deep breath and forced herself not to back away. She glanced at Alan, but he had scooped up his cup and bowl of food cubes and was wandering away. She had to work hard not to frown. Instead she turned her face up to query Ryliuk aloud. "What is your concern?"

He ignored her attempt at returning to verbal speech and continued with the direct thoughts. "Upon arrival, I went immediately to visit Ei'Brai's enclosure to offer greeting. I feel it is very important to assess the health and well-being of the kuboderan, but he is refusing all attempts at communication with me. He would not even show himself to me."

Jane wasn't surprised, but she carefully modulated her answer. "His confidence in the Sectilius has been shaken. I think that's understandable given the circumstances he's found himself in, wouldn't you agree?"

Ryliuk's eyes roved over her face questioningly. "No. I don't think it's understandable. The squillae plague did not come from Sectilius. There was an outside instigator. You must order him to treat with me."

Jane couldn't help but frown. "I don't think that's wise, Master Ryliuk."

"You are his commanding officer."

Ryliuk had moved in even closer. She found herself pressed into the wall. She scanned the room. Alan was glaring at her and Ryliuk.

Jane lifted a hand and moved as though she would push him back. He retreated in advance of her touch. She breathed a little easier. "I'll take that under advisement, Master Ryliuk." She wasn't about to promise Ryliuk anything until she talked to Brai. It was a delicate situation, and she wasn't going to betray Brai's trust now. She didn't know what Ryliuk really wanted to do, but she'd figure those things out in time.

Jane skirted Ryliuk and raised her voice above the general din to get the crew's attention. "I realize most of you are still settling in, learning the rhythms of ship life." She moved to sit at a long table. They'd been milling around for a while, sampling nutrition squares, and it was time to get to the point of the gathering.

The humans immediately sat down, but it took a few moments for the sectilians to clue in to what was happening. They drifted to the table in ones and twos. Pledor was the last to seat himself, at the farthest spot from Jane.

Jane laid her hands flat on the table in a sectilian gesture that indicated that she would be open, honest, and receptive. She hoped it would make the newcomers feel more comfortable. "For some of you the presence of a kuboderan is new and probably overwhelming. It will take time to get used to, but I urge you each to forge a strong bond with Ei'Brai. It's very important to the way this type of ship functions. I want to give you a few days to adjust before we begin our mission, so don't waste that time. In the interim I'll also be assigning each of you duties. This is a big ship and we are a small crew. It's been neglected for a very long time. There's a lot of work to do."

She seemed to have everyone's attention now. "I've given work assignments a great deal of thought. I hope to bring out each individual's strengths, but the truth is we're all going to have to learn new skills. Because we are a comparatively small crew, we will all be generalizing and multitasking. We'll begin these assignments immediately."

She picked up the tablet she had laid on the table earlier, on which she'd left some notes. "I'll start with Tech Deck. Dr. Alan Bergen, Machinutorus Jaross Rageth Hator, and

Dr. Ronald Gibbs will handle that department. Alan will lead and will assign tasks related to environmental control, life support, propulsion, the generation, regulation, distribution and storage of power, and all structural and mechanical concerns. It's a big job for three people." She looked up to see Alan, Ron, and Jaross staring at her solemnly.

"At the moment our most pressing concern is structural integrity, squillae distribution, and reintegrating the escutcheon."

Alan was nodding along, all cold professional now. "I agree. Those should be our primary focus."

Pledor got to his feet. "Squillae? Continued use of these devices seems imprudent given the circumstances."

Alan rolled his eyes. "Here we go."

Jane sent him a quelling look then turned to Pledor, glancing in turn at each sectilian as she spoke. They all looked uncomfortable. She supposed she couldn't blame them. "Believe me, I understand your concerns—"

"We've taken plenty of precautions," Alan interjected.

Jane nodded patiently, but spoke a little louder, to try to maintain control of the conversation. "Yes, we have. The reality of the situation is that this ship simply can't be operated without either a large crew or the use of this technology. And the escutcheon is vital protection on the outer hull, repairing it from microfractures and other damage. There's no replacing that functionality with something else. It's necessary for our protection."

Pledor remained standing. "But the potential for disaster—"

"Has been mitigated," Alan said flatly. "I've personally rewritten the code so it can't be messed with. I'm not cool with it being used against us. It's not gonna happen."

Jaross said, "The terran crew was just as susceptible to the squillae plague as we were. For that reason, they would take the dangerous nature of the technology seriously. I think we can trust that. Just the same, I would like to personally look into this, and offer my own expertise in this area, if that does not offend?"

Everyone looked at Alan, whose annoyed expression hadn't changed much. He shrugged. "That's fine by me."

Pledor retook his seat. "If Machinutorus Jaross Rageth Hator believes that the new safeguards will be sufficient, my concerns will be appeased."

Jane glanced at her tablet and suppressed a sigh of relief. She'd known this would come up at some point, and now it had and the discussion had been relatively tame, compared to the imagined scenario in her head. "Good. All right. Moving on to medical. Dr. Ajaya Varma and Medical Master Schlewan Umbrig of Caillea will work as a team in this department with Tinor Fotep Sten as apprentice."

Schlewan asked, "Do you have any initial tasks you'd like us to complete?"

Jane nodded. "Yes. Before the jump, I want a thorough workup of every individual aboard. I need everyone in tip-top shape. Call them in one at a time, please."

Ajaya lifted her chin and spoke. "Does 'them' include you, Commander?"

Jane frowned. Ajaya had caught her off guard. "Yes." She continued on. "Mind Master Ryliuk of Mebrew will oversee communications as necessary, when we have someone to communicate with. And he will also work with Pledor Makya Sten in the department of maintenance and security. I will train both of you personally for this critical duty. Today we will begin a ship-wide sweep for parasites." When she looked up this time, she was met with stoic gazes from the sectilians she'd just named. These jobs didn't sound glamorous, but they truly were critical. Someone had to perform these functions, and these two people had the least-specific skill sets, aside from leadership. She swallowed and looked back down at her tablet.

"Ei'Brai of Kubodera will continue to act as Gubernaviti, the governing navigator. He oversees most of the day-to-day running of the ship and all things related to navigation as well as data collection and management." She stood, ready to wrap this session up and return to work. "Anyone have any questions?"

"I have a question." It was Pledor. "In three standard days we will arrive at the last known location of another starship."

"Yes," Jane replied.

"We assume that this ship will be devoid of crew except for a kuboderan, which may have survived all this time, just as the kuboderan on this ship has."

"Yes," Jane said.

"That ship will need a Quasador Dux and a crew. Who will assume that role?" Pledor blinked slowly, lazily, but didn't take his eyes off her. His voice was far from neutral. This was a kind of challenge.

Jane had anticipated this question. She stood a little straighter before answering. "We will allow the kuboderan to choose from among the crew of this ship, whoever he or she feels most compatible with."

Pledor's slow blinking stopped, and his expression grew hard, his ears pulling back starkly from his face. Suddenly he stood. "Preposterous! You would leave such decisions in the hands of an animal? Why? It might choose the child for all you know!"

Jane braced herself for an outburst from Brai, ready to sever the connection if needed. She didn't have to, though a low, feral growl rumbled inside her head. Pledor was not helping the deep-seated antipathy Brai was feeling toward the sectilians.

Jane nodded slowly, refusing to let Pledor bait her. "He or she might."

Pledor sneered. "And you would allow this? Passing over a proven leader? I am a Gistraedor Dux!"

Jane was searching for something to say in reply to that statement, but Schlewan interjected. She tilted her head toward Pledor, but did not look directly at him. "No. Here you are not a Gistraedor Dux. You gave that up when you left the Sten compound. Here you are ship maintenance and security. Without status. Without rank."

Jane kept her face and her mental signature carefully impassive. She focused her gaze on the table. There were class issues here that she would not be wise to tread on.

Pledor spluttered, "This is ridiculous. No one told me there wouldn't be proper food. Or that I would be reduced to manual labor like a common fool."

Jaross stared straight ahead and spoke, her voice ringing loudly. "We are all of us equal status here—whether female, male, adolescent, terran, sectilian, atellan, or kuboderan.

We have left behind a great struggle for survival. Here there is great abundance. Like in all times of change, we will need to adjust. I suggest you do so and refrain from this antagonizing behavior. There is a long tradition of our species adapting to great changes—to surviving against all odds. We are fortunate to have been brought aboard this grand vessel."

Brai purred upon hearing this. She sensed him warming to Jaross, extending probing tendrils into her mind to verify that she was speaking her true thoughts. He found what he hoped to find there and subsided into a reverie.

Alan slammed his empty cup down on the table so hard nearly everyone in the room jumped simultaneously, breaking Jane's intent focus on Brai.

"Hear, hear," Alan said quietly. "Let's not all forget that we're on a spaceship or anything." He pushed his chair back loudly and headed for the exit. He paused in the doorway and gestured. "Ron, Jaross, let's get to work." Then he left. Ron rose slowly and followed, with Jaross on his heels.

Jane decided not to make an issue of the fact that she hadn't dismissed them.

Tinor stood, looking distressed, eyes wide, lips pulled back into a deep grimace. Iad exclaimed, "I didn't get to make my declaration!"

Schlewan looked nonplussed, staring at the adolescent.

Tinor turned to Pledor. "You didn't have to be so disagreeable! You ruined everything!" With that, Tinor stomped off.

Schlewan rose and followed, saying nothing. The remaining sectilians looked mildly surprised at the outburst.

Ajaya said, "Would it be impolite to ask if you know what declaration Tinor is referring to?"

Ryliuk replied, "Not at all. Tinor has reached the developmental stage of gender selection and was likely about to declare a choice. This is normally done after a meal in front of one's entire compound or clan, though it is customary to give adults some time to prepare in advance. It is a difficult transition, a turbulent time in one's life. The child is experiencing internal and external pressure. At times stress can delay the onset, or it can significantly accelerate the process. I believe iad is experiencing the latter."

Jane sat down again, at a loss. If Tinor had just come to her ahead of time and made mention of this desire, Jane would have accommodated it.

40

Jane clomped up to the door to the Greenspace Deck with Pledor and Ryliuk. This was the most dangerous area left on the ship. It was within the realm of possibility, that there could still be a few nepatrox remaining—and if there were, this was where they'd likely be hiding.

They were all outfitted in sectilian powered battle armor with helmets retracted. The gleaming obsidian suits were compact and made to expand to conform to the wide range of body types among the sectilian people, even accommodating Ryliuk's massive form. Jane had grown accustomed to wearing the snug suit on occasions like this. It was like a form-fitting protective shell that made her many times stronger, and the controls had come to feel like an extension of herself.

Jane had spent long hours over the previous two days with the two sectilians exploring as much of the ship as possible. They'd found and removed quite a few slugs, most of them small. Regular sweeps like this would continue to be necessary because the microscopic spawn of the slugs could lie dormant for extremely long periods of time. There was little danger of new nepatrox being converted from the larval stage without an influx of fresh xenon gas—which would not happen on Jane's watch—but the transformations that had been triggered shortly after the *Providence* crew boarded could potentially have given rise to a few stragglers that hadn't been located yet. Since the nepatrox lacked sentience, Brai couldn't sense them, and they could be difficult to detect with the ship's sensors in the Greenspace due to the dense flora on that deck.

She'd saved this deck for the final day before the jump so that the others would feel more comfortable inside their armor, not to mention familiar with the controls. But it needed to be done, for the safety of the crew, before they embarked on their journey.

Jane triggered the door mechanism and stood there for a moment with her mouth agape. This was her first time seeing this deck with her own eyes, though she knew what it had looked like during Rageth's tenure aboard ship. It had been parklike, well groomed. A vast place for hobby gardening and peaceful off-duty hours strolling through manicured gardens that represented all the principal climates of Sectilia and Atielle.

The deck was flooded with dazzling bright light. The ceilings and walls glowed, and there were strategically placed fixtures throughout, providing enough light for the plant life to thrive. It took Jane's eyes a moment to adjust, though the hallway had been well lit. The ceiling was three times higher than that on most decks, to accommodate tree growth.

She took one step inside the door and paused. A wave of humidity washed over her, bringing with it odors of warm damp soil, decay, and the peppery scents of growing things. There was a steaming, dazzling jungle in front of her. In one sweep of her eyes she could see every shade of green from the palest chartreuse and celadon to tones so deep and blue they appeared to be navy or black. In places the vegetation converged into thick, dark tangles and looked impenetrable.

Jane sighed. She'd underestimated what the years could do in this place. The lighting, automatic watering systems, and CO_2 supplementation had never failed. Everything had grown for decades, unchecked. This was going to take many man-hours to explore. It wouldn't be done in one day. They might have to cut some of it back.

She could seal the deck off, but how could she forbid the crew from using the only deck that held growing things? She couldn't know how long any of them would be living on this ship. She hoped it would be a very long time. This was going to be an ongoing problem, but she couldn't put off the jump for this.

Pledor pushed past her roughly, stumbling over thick vines with deep-purple veins creeping across the floor. "Praise the Cunabula!" he shouted. "What wonder is this?"

Jane stepped aside, giving Ryliuk room to enter.

"Di mirro…" Ryliuk uttered, a sectilian expression of astonishment without a direct translation.

"My eyes…such beauty," Pledor choked out. "How is this possible? I thought places such as this were only found in fantastical paintings someone conjured from their imagination long ago on writeflat."

That was when Jane realized there weren't wild places like this on Atielle anymore. The nepatrox had slowly eroded the ecosystem until settings like this were an ideal, only vaguely remembered.

Ryliuk murmured something under his breath and burst forward, scrambling into the space, saying, "No! It is a dream of my childhood…"

Jane followed Ryliuk, motioning to Pledor to come along. "Wait, Ryliuk! We need to stay in visual contact. It might not be safe!"

She caught up to him fifty yards into the snarl of trees. He'd stripped to the waist, the arms of the suit dangling behind him. He stood in the midst of the wilderness reaching out to a fuzzy gray-blue plant.

"Ryliuk—" Jane panted.

"Do you see this? My mother grew one like this near our home, when I was a child, just for me. I played with it every day. Do you see?" He stroked a fuzzy tendril, and the entire plant shuddered and began to move to embrace and caress him.

Jane stopped and stared.

Ryliuk turned. His face was split in an enormous, toothy smile. He continued to pet the plant and it kept moving. It enveloped him until she could barely see him amid the swirling, writhing branches. She could hear him, though, roaring with laughter and murmuring endearments.

"Ryliuk?" He didn't seem to hear her.

"It was so lonely. I could feel it the moment we stepped through the door. My new friend. Ah, what shall I call you?"

Pledor shouted in the distance, "There is abundant food here! I've found guanac beans and prillion nuts! Enough for a feast for the entire compound!"

Jane grabbed Ryliuk's arm. "It's not safe here. You need to put the armor back on." She took off in the direction of Pledor's shout.

She skirted a thicket and was faced with the thick trunk of a tree that had fallen over due to the immense weight of its canopy in such shallow soil. She could barely see over it. It was now growing at a very shallow angle across the floor. She couldn't get under it because the scrub was too thick. She would have to go over. She grabbed one branch to brace herself and stuck her boot on another. When she hefted herself up, she found the top of the trunk was dotted with tiny bright-pink flowers. She started to throw her leg over, hoping to avoid destroying something so lovely, when one of them moved.

She paused, looked closer, and saw that they weren't flowers, but short, stubby caterpillars with wide petal-like things decorating their backs. They were marching across the tree trunk in a meandering line.

Pledor was still waxing poetic about something else he'd found.

Ryliuk was still chortling in the bush.

All Jane wanted to do was stare in amazement at these tiny, wondrous creatures, but she had to get her team together and reclaim some order. Because if there were nepatrox here, they'd be hunting them any minute.

"Commander? Are you available?" Ajaya sent a thought to her telepathically.

Jane gritted her teeth and climbed over the trunk, careful to avoid crushing the pink insects. "I'm here."

Ajaya's voice was tinged with worry. "Jane, I think you should come down here."

Jane tramped over uneven terrain, trying to triangulate where Pledor had gotten himself off to while keeping the powerful suit under control and not flattening every plant in sight—or tripping and falling on her face. It wasn't always easy getting up in one of these things if you fell over.

"I'll come down in a few hours, just before Tinor's dinner." She'd planned a modest little affair for Tinor's announcement. She was really looking forward to it. Observing a cultural rite like this ceremony was the best part of her job.

"No, I'm sorry, Jane, but this can't wait. You really need to come now."

Jane paused, still listening to Pledor's pontifications. Ajaya sounded worried. She and Schlewan had been doing thorough physicals on the entire crew for the last few days. Jane was due for hers after dinner. Who was she seeing right now? Was it Alan? Could he be sick? She felt a little nauseated at that thought.

"Okay. It's going to take me a few minutes—"

A blood-curdling scream rent the air followed by a couple of concussive blasts. She took off running, ordering the helmet up over her head as she went. She spoke over the comm in the helmet because Pledor was still learning how to use anipraxia. "Everyone get your armor on—fully on—now."

She splashed through a muddy pit choked with spiky reeds and ducked underneath enormous aerial roots supporting a massive tree trunk.

There was a commotion nearby, a struggle. Telltale hissing made her heart pound. She darted through a glade of grasses that were frothy with seed heads, dodged a thorny yellow bush with corkscrew-shaped branches, and nearly tripped over a nepatrox.

It turned, hissing and flapping crimson-and-gold hinged jaws, and slashed at her with its venomous tail. It was no match for her armor though. She blew it to smithereens.

She'd found Pledor. He lay in a heap, covered in a confetti comprised of tattered leaves and nepatrox gore. His helmet was still retracted and his face was streaked with blood—hopefully not his own. Just as she registered this, there was a loud crashing sound behind her and a series of concussive blasts went off. She whirled to find Ryliuk bursting through the vegetation and a dead nepatrox carcass at her back.

"Can you walk?" she asked Pledor.

"My foot is caught in the vines," he said weakly.

She knelt down beside him. The leg was twisted at a bad angle. He'd fallen with the weight of his armor on it. She tore at the vines to free him and Ryliuk reached down and picked him up like a rag doll.

"Let's go," Jane said. "Ryliuk, you take lead. I'll watch from behind."

They picked their way through the vegetation but weren't bothered again by the nepatrox.

When the door closed behind them, Jane turned on the two shamefaced sectilians. "Get him to the nearest medical center and call Schlewan to care for him." Then she stomped off for the deck transport.

41

Jane stepped into the deck transport. She sent a thought to Ajaya. "Where are you?"

"Deck thirteen. Master Schlewan has just been called away to deal with a medical emergency, but I'm still here."

Jane tapped the symbol that would put her on deck thirteen and realized where Ajaya had to be. The only medical facility on that deck was built into Brai's enclosure, for monitoring his health and safety.

A cold feeling of dread began to pump through her body, tightening her muscles and making her heart skitter.

She quickened her pace. Her boots made loud crashing sounds on the metal gantry. She turned down the gangway toward the suite built between the hull of the ship and the enormous tank where a small compartment of it extended into the medical suite. It contained a cornucopia of medical equipment specifically adapted to monitor kuboderan anatomy. Brai was inside that bubble now, his arms drawn up tight around his body with all of the razor-sharp barbs pointed outward. He was feeling threatened.

As she strode through the door, his arms parted and he peered at her with one of his enormous eyes. He remained mute, but the eye tracked her as she crossed the room.

Ajaya was bent over a console, but looked up and turned when Jane entered. Her expression was drawn.

Jane's heart sank. "What is it?" she asked aloud.

Ajaya's lips were tight and her eyes glistened with moisture. "He's very ill, Jane. I don't think it's wise to attempt the jump tomorrow."

Jane stared at Ajaya, uncomprehending. Her voice came out a hoarse whisper. "What?"

Ajaya turned back to the console and gestured for Jane to follow. "Schlewan will be able to explain it better." She pointed at medical diagnostic readings on the screen. "It boils down to advanced senescence—age-related degeneration. It's happening so quickly we can see it in real time. There is some neurodegeneration and cardiovascular disease as well as several species-specific metabolic disorders. I'm sorry, Jane. But I have to tell you. He's dying."

If the suit hadn't been holding her up, Jane would have fallen over. "No," she said, shaking her head. "That's not possible. He's only about three hundred standard years old—they can live for thousands of years."

"Three hundred seventy-four and one-third," he rumbled softly in her mind.

She turned to him and stared blankly. "I don't understand."

"Jane, in the wild a kuboderan can only expect to live three to five years," Ajaya said.

"I know that…" She felt so cold. She was frozen in place. "Why? What…?" Then it hit her, and she gasped. The squillae. The nanites kept them alive.

She began to tremble. She had done this to him when she'd used the massive EMP to destroy all the squillae, to save her crew. Saving them had meant unknowingly endangering Brai. A tear fled down her cheek. She went to the side of his bubble-shaped enclosure, placing both gloved hands flat against the transparent material. "Are you in pain?" she asked him.

"It is negligible," he replied, and placed one clubbed tentacle over each of her hands. He was minimizing it. She could tell. He didn't want to admit how terrible it was. She was afraid to probe to discover the extent of it.

Schlewan came in then. Jane didn't turn. "Can we reverse it?" she asked thickly.

"Unknown, unknown, *unknown*," Schlewan said crisply. "This is unprecedented. It's likely we can halt the senescence if we intervene immediately. But it is unlikely he can jump in this state."

"You should have told me," she said to him bitterly. "You kept this from me."

"You did not ask," he replied.

A flare of anger rose in her. "How could I possibly know to ask this?" she demanded. "You lied by omission! I thought you said you couldn't or wouldn't do that! This is why you didn't want to do the electromagnetic pulse. You knew this would happen. I might have made a different choice, if I had known!"

"You made the only choice you could have in that moment," he said wearily.

"Maybe that's true, but I would have taken measures to protect you afterward! All this time has gone by. Weeks. I would have never asked you to suffer like this."

"I could not know." But she saw in his head that this was an evasion.

"You're too proud by half," she spat at him. "You'd die rather than admit you are fallible."

His single eye turned away from her. "As Medical Master Schlewan indicated, this is unprecedented. I was unaware of the rapid effect—"

Jane dropped her hands and turned away, seething with anger and self-recrimination.

Ajaya stood by nervously, watching. Schlewan was impassive, observing.

They could all be stuck here on this ship orbiting Atielle for the rest of their lives. They knew that.

They might never go home.

"How is Pledor?" Jane asked, not meeting their eyes. Her voice sounded cold and angry to her own ears.

"Sanalabrius immersion," Schlewan replied.

"It was that bad?" Jane asked, half turning toward the sectilian woman.

"I would have submerged him if he had a splinter, Quasador Dux Jane Holloway. It is a simple muscle strain and a few small contusions. It was a relief to put him out of reach for a standard day." She started to turn and then seemed to change her mind. "You should know he is desperate to get back into the Greenspace Deck. It was all he talked about. Despite the danger."

Jane let out a long, slow breath then straightened. "Do whatever you can here to stabilize Ei'Brai. I'll produce a batch of squillae tailored for him."

Schlewan spoke. "Only the Quasador Dux can break the seal—"

"I know," Jane said. She left without saying another word. She felt a twinge. She was adopting some sectilian manners.

Jane stood in the deck transport and worked to pull herself back together. She wanted to rant and scream, maybe even cry in frustration. But she couldn't. She had to go ask Alan to help someone he actively disliked.

Every minute that went by, Brai's health was degenerating, possibly beyond repair. He needed her to stay calm and not waste time.

She forced herself to count through several long breaths. When she felt steadier, she tried querying Alan via anipraxia.

Brai immediately replied to tell her that Alan had removed himself from the anipraxic network. So she reached out to Ron instead.

He answered instantly. "Hey, QD, what's up? Getting ready for the big soirée tonight?"

"Not yet. Where's Alan?" Her tone was more brittle than it should have been.

"Uh-oh. Have trouble on the Greenspace Deck?"

"A little. Is he on Tech Deck?"

"Aw. No. He just went to get some real sleep for the first time since you gave us our orders. Need any help?"

Jane sighed. He had worked for days without rest and now she'd have to wake him. "I'll let you know. Thank you." She severed their link and hit the symbol for the crew deck.

As she passed her own door she wished she could stop to change, but she couldn't spare the time. She'd wait until the squillae were in production.

She rapped lightly on Alan's door. There was no answer. She knocked harder and waited. Nothing happened. She pressed the open symbol next to the frame and the door slid up. The room was dark, except for a small, red blinking light. She waited for a moment, hoping he would wake while she stood there allowing her eyes to adjust.

There was a low humming sound permeating the room, a kind of white noise. The outline of a bulky machine sat on a shelf a few feet from the bed. It was the source of the blinking light and probably the sound, though there were piles of gadgets scattered around the room. She knew that he'd been repairing some of the smaller devices that hadn't been well shielded and were fried when they'd destroyed all of the nanites. He must work in here sometimes. He liked to be alone.

She squinted at the blinking machine. Now what could that be? Some kind of experiment or invention he was working on? Something he was testing?

She took a step inside, her boots clanking against the plastic-coated flooring. The lump on the bed didn't stir.

"Alan," she called softly.

Her eyesight adjusted further. He still didn't move. He was stretched out on his stomach, his arms wrapped around a pile of scrunched-up blankets under his head. The Sectilius didn't use pillows, so he'd created his own.

She took another step closer, speaking a little louder. "Alan?"

Suddenly her link to Ei'Brai and the ship was completely severed. She reeled. For the second time in the course of fifteen minutes she would have fallen if the suit hadn't been holding her upright. Her vision swam. She swayed dizzily.

She must have cried out, because suddenly Alan was a cursing blur, leaping out of bed and taking a swing at her. The suit moved autonomously, the software sensing her incapacitated state through the neural threads. Her body ducked and came back up with arms held defensively in front of her, ready for a fight.

She recovered enough to choke out, "Alan, it's me! Stop!"

He paused, mid-lunge, and staggered back. "Jesus, Jane! What the hell's going on?"

She blinked at him, still confused herself. That was when she noticed he was naked. She lowered her arms from their defensive position. She was too dumbfounded to do anything but stare at him, her eyes darting down his body of their own accord though she tried to control them. She could feel her body responding to the sight of him. Instantly she felt flushed and warm. "I—"

He didn't seem to notice at first. He just stared at her angrily, his hands still clenched in fists. A moment passed, and then he inhaled sharply and grumbled about being woken by people in battle armor scaring the shit out of him as he cast around, looking for something. He found what he sought on the floor next to the bed and jerked on a pair of pants.

She was finally able to look away, completely embarrassed, the warm flush creeping up her body. She turned and tapped on the lights at a low level. "I'm sorry I had to wake you. It's important. I knocked several times. I called your name."

He sat down on the edge of his bed and rubbed his face with his hands. "I'm dead on my feet. I've been working for days straight—doing all the stuff you asked me to do, I might add."

She contemplated sitting next to him, but the suit, though compact, was heavy and awkward. "I know. I'm sorry, but it can't wait."

He yawned and stretched. "Well, this doesn't seem to be a booty call. What is it? Something go wrong? What are you doing in battle armor?"

"I've just been patrolling for nepatrox."

He exhaled loudly.

She turned to the machine nearby. The suit had analyzed it and was feeding her a bunch of technical information. She knew what it was, but wasn't sure she knew the proper terminology in English. "You've generated an electromagnetic field to block Brai?"

"Yeah. So?"

She frowned. "Are you sure that's safe?"

He huffed. "It's not a HERF gun or anything. It's low energy. Cataracts later in life are the worst I can expect, and the risk of that is minimal as long as I stay at the edges of the EM field. It's worth the trade-off for me."

"It hinders communication. I couldn't reach you."

"There's ship-wide communication. You could have used that."

She nodded slightly. She could have, but it was impersonal and felt...egregiously demanding. She didn't want to lead that way. "But why?"

His jaw tightened. "You know why. It's simple. I don't want him in my head."

She slumped a little inside the suit. This wasn't going in a good direction, considering the reason she was here. "He's trying to do better, Alan. He's learning about us, what we need, what we can handle. If you'd let him—"

His lips tightened. "He is doing better. But I don't want him in there when I'm not in control of what he sees. My brain. My thoughts." His voice had turned into a growl.

"Okay," she conceded. She wasn't going to change his mind about it now. She needed to figure out how to broach the squillae topic. "I'm curious. Did you build this device before or after we went to Atielle?"

He rubbed a hand over his face again. "The idea came to me the day you came down to Tech Deck and experienced the dropout in signal. It's a fairly simple device. It was just a matter of designing and 3-D printing a magnetron and using a DC power source I salvaged from the *Providence*. I tinkered with it in my spare time. Tuning it to the right frequency and modulation was the hardest part. I started using it whenever I slept right before we got to Atielle."

"I see," she said in as neutral a voice as she could manage. He was so smart it was mind-boggling. Designing and printing a magnetron—whatever that was—was a simple matter?

"What did you need, Jane? You came down here and woke me up for a reason. It wasn't to find out about my anti-brain-fuck machine."

She cringed, but kept her voice steady. "No. It wasn't. We have a new problem. Several, actually, but only one that I need your help with right now. Have you had a chance to look at Brai's squillae?"

"Ah, that? Yup. I looked it up in the ship's database a couple days ago. That's some messed-up shit, Jane. I've been meaning to write up a report for you, but I wanted to consult with Ajaya first and we've both been busy."

"Ajaya? What did you find? What's wrong with them?"

He hauled himself off the bed and went over to the desk that housed a sectilian computer terminal against the opposite wall. "This really can't wait?"

She didn't answer. She was wishing he'd put on a shirt. It would help her to keep her thoughts from meandering away from the urgency of the situation.

He rummaged around in his piles of electrical components and personal items until he rooted out a laptop and sat back down on the bed to open it. "Based on what I saw, their programming was completely different from the other types of nanites on the ship."

She edged closer to him. The suit was so awkward. She wished she'd changed out of it now. He didn't seem to notice. "In what way?"

He stared at the screen hard. Apparently he'd found a way to interface with the ship's system. It was scrolling sectilian code. "Well, it's a lot more biologically related than I was expecting." He highlighted a section, though he had to know she didn't comprehend it. "There seems to be two main objectives for these nanites. One is to harness the power of the Squid's natural regenerative ability and keep him in a peak physical state for as long as possible. The other is to stifle his emotional states—to keep him as stoic as possible via manipulation of neurotransmitters. My guess is this was to enhance performance."

"Really," Jane breathed.

"Yep. The Sectilius can be stone-cold bastards."

It explained so much. How Ei'Brai's behavior had changed so dramatically after the EM pulse. Why he was in such dire straits now, healthwise.

"Alan, can you change this code?"

He looked at her skeptically. "You do know who you're talking to, right?"

"How long would it take you to delete the stuff that inhibits his emotions? Keep just the stuff that maintains his health?"

He blinked slowly. "Could I get about four hours first? It'll take half the time if I get some sleep."

She looked at the floor, trying to keep her emotions in check. She managed to say, "He's dying."

"Shit. No wonder you're so freaked out." He closed the laptop slowly. "In that case, you shouldn't worry about the code. Just get nanites in him as soon as possible. I can comb through the code later and upload the changes, easy."

He rose, leaving the laptop on the bed, and returned to the desk to dig for something. He pulled out a data stick, stuck it in its slot, then searched for the correct file to upload. When he found it, he transferred the file and handed the stick to her. "You'll need this to make the right kind of nanites for him."

She took the data stick gingerly and slipped it into a compartment on the suit. "Thank you. I appreciate this. I know that things are strained between the two of you—"

"Yeah, but I don't want him to die, for fuck's sake. You want me to go down with you? Help you get it started?"

Yes. "No. I've got this. You get the sleep you need."

He looked at her wistfully and reached out a hand to lightly touch her arm for a split second. She couldn't feel it, of course, but she wished she could. "Okay. I did find something unusual on Tech Deck today. I think it might be a big component of this yoke business, but I need some sleep before I dive into it and really start tearing shit apart. You still sure you want me to do that?"

Her eyes widened. "Yes. I do."

"Alrighty then. More power to Cap'n Cthulhu tomorrow." He yawned and rubbed at his beard.

"Thank you, Alan," she murmured. "I don't know what I'd do without you."

He shrugged. "I don't know what you'd do without me either." He smiled and pointed at her lazily. "You look pretty rad in power armor, you know. If you weren't in such a hurry I'd be trying to seduce you right now."

Her lips quirked up on one side. "Save that for later."

He groaned and sat down heavily on the bed again. "Yeah. Story of my life."

Jane clomped over to the door and triggered the lights to go off. Ei'Brai surged back into her mind, now a mute, withdrawn presence. She paused for a second until the vertigo passed. She half turned and raised a hand. "Goodnight, Alan."

He was already splayed out on the bed. He waved limply, then threw an arm over his face. "Goodnight, Jane."

42

Jane sat on a low bench in the antechamber of her suite, impatiently waiting for the sectilians to get on with things. The room was large, with seating scattered in conversational groups, and dominated by the former Qua'dux's paintings. She liked to use it as an informal meeting place. They'd just shared a meal and Tinor was supposed to be making ius announcement, but iad was upset and the proceedings had not yet begun.

Tinor was complaining quite loudly that it was customary for every member of a tribe or compound to be in attendance. The only person missing was Alan, who was still sleeping. Even Pledor was there, looking grim and sullen, but no worse for wear from the excitement earlier in the day. Schlewan must have given him leave from the sanalabrium to attend.

Schlewan was urging Tinor to understand that sometimes as an adult one had to accept disappointment in others' performance and persist in one's commitments despite that disappointment. This argument seemed to be falling on deaf ears.

The rest of the crew meandered around, examining the murals that Jane's predecessor had created on the walls and talking in subdued voices. Everyone was carefully pretending they couldn't hear Tinor's complaints. Word had spread about Brai's health and it had cast a pall over all of them.

Jane fidgeted. This wasn't the celebratory occasion she'd hoped to give Tinor. She doubted that in his fatigue Alan had really put much importance on attending the ceremony, though she wished he had because all Jane could think about was that the squillae would be ready soon and she needed to go pick them up and inoculate Brai with them. Alan was rightly more concerned with the integrity of the ship and all of the other duties she'd tasked him with.

However, Jane was also very aware that for Tinor, this was possibly one of the most important days in ius life. Jane didn't want to be rude, but if things didn't start moving along soon, she'd be forced to make apologies and reschedule, and she was sure that would only upset Tinor further.

The gifts were laid out nearby, ready for their presentation to the new adult. As Jane understood it, this was one of the few times in a sectilian's life when gifts were routinely presented—to mark the passage from childhood into adulthood. Traditionally they were practical items to help an individual begin their new life, but given that Tinor didn't expect the same challenges on a ship as iad would have faced on ancient Atielle or Sectilia, it was acceptable to present gifts that were more sentimental in nature. Jane had urged her crew to consider giving Tinor something uniquely human as a way of symbolically demonstrating acceptance into their culture as well.

Ryliuk sat down next to Jane. She pushed back as the dense cushion sank under his weight, so she wouldn't be pulled over to lean into him.

He didn't speak aloud, but sent a thought, mind to mind without the inclusion of Brai, which seemed to be his default. "We must discuss this new development regarding the kuboderan."

Jane lifted her chin and couldn't stop herself from scooting over a couple of inches. Even sitting, Ryliuk towered over her. She didn't know for sure if the Sectilius sometimes conducted power struggles with relation to size and height in the same way humans did, but she suspected there was a similar element in their culture. Something told her he was using proximity as a way of forcing deference. What she wasn't sure of was whether that was a conscious choice or not. Nor was she certain of how to tell him that made her uncomfortable without creating new problems. The language had come easily to her, but these sorts of social constructs had to be very carefully learned.

"Everything that can be done is currently being done," Jane said out loud.

"With all due respect, Quasador Dux, that is not the case."

Jane stared at him and said nothing. She began to dread where this conversation was going, but carefully kept those thoughts to herself. Brai had warned her about Ryliuk's anipraxic ability being stronger than that of most mind masters. She would heed Brai's advice and keep herself closed off to Ryliuk.

Suddenly Alan's EMF device didn't sound like such a bad idea.

Ryliuk continued, leaning toward her. "I feared just this sort of consequence when you related that you'd been forced to destroy all of the squillae on board in the course of eliminating the threat against your people. I could sense you had no idea of the full ramifications on the kuboderan. I was not gratified to find those fears were realized."

Jane nodded slowly. "The effects on his health are concerning. I'm hopeful they will be reversible."

"They will be. In any case, a good kuboderan will work until dusk takes them in order to honor their Quasador Dux's wishes."

Jane shook her head. She was pleased to hear the certainty in Ryliuk's mental voice that Ei'Brai's health would be restored, but the rest of his statement was problematic. It galled her. Brai wasn't a commodity whose life she would spend on a whim. She was starting to get angry, but held herself in check. Patiently, she said, "Ryliuk, our cultures are very different. You should know I would never ask that of him."

"And this concerns me greatly."

Jane stood without thought, just as a sectilian would. Now she towered over him. He started to rise, but instinct moved her forward to push on his personal space. She was challenging him now, reestablishing who was in charge, despite the fact that he was easily twice her size.

He averted his gaze. "Ei'Brai is beholden to you. I must insist that you command him to submit to reconditioning. You are an outsider. Whether you can see it or not, this is necessary. Waiting to do so will only incur more trouble with him."

Jane explored that word carefully: reconditioning. He left it open to her in his thoughts, giving her a taste of what that would entail—the level of strict compliance Brai would be forced to adhere to in an unrelenting, repetitive series of lessons and tests over an extended period of time, purely for the purpose of putting Brai back in a place of subservience. It turned Jane's stomach. Based on Ryliuk's mental conception of these exercises, she was sure that he didn't view them the same way. She also knew that no human or kuboderan would relish being subjected to them. To her, the process seemed to be nothing more than an application of extreme humiliation, meant to strip the kuboderan of personhood. There was no other way for her to describe it.

Jane stared at him hard.

Ryliuk glanced up once, but his eyes rolled away again. Now he was the submissive one. She needed to make him feel that. She needed to remind him that this was her ship and that things would be done her way. She had to protect Brai from these misguided and antiquated ideals.

"You are a product of your culture, Ryliuk. I do not condemn you for that. But my duty at present is to Ei'Brai and his needs, not the culture of the sectilian mind masters. You remind me that I am an outsider. I've not forgotten that. I believe I see this situation with more objectivity from the outside than you can. While your people have given the kuboderans in your care many gifts, you have also stripped much away. It is not an equitable exchange to my way of thinking. You do not have my permission to perform any kind of reconditioning on Ei'Brai. Not while I am Quasador Dux of this vessel."

He kept his gaze carefully averted. "Your compassion for him will be your undoing."

Jane stepped back involuntarily, shocked and surprised, despite her training. She kept her mental voice low and even. "Is that a threat, Ryliuk?"

His ears pulled back. He sounded contrite now. "No. It is a prediction based upon what I know of the facts at hand. I will defer to your judgment in this because that is my place. But I do so with objections."

"Your objections are noted," Jane told him coldly and moved away. She hoped she hadn't just made a terrible mistake in challenging Ryliuk, but she couldn't let him do that to Brai. It went against her every value and instinct.

Tinor was still remonstrating with Schlewan and anyone else who would listen. Jane impatiently checked the time through her connection with Brai, just as Schlewan made eye contact with her. Jane sensed that Schlewan was about to ask Jane to wake Alan, so Jane stepped decisively into the midst of it.

She addressed Tinor quietly, but firmly. "If you wish to have your ceremony today, you must begin now because my duties will soon call me away. We all have work we should be attending to. If you want to, you can reschedule, but ship life is busy and since we don't have a sun to remind us when to wake and sleep, people will work and sleep at all times. I may never be able to bring together the entire crew all at once, unfortunately. I'm sorry for that, Tinor, but this is how it is here."

Tinor looked down, chastened. Then the child moved to stand next to the table bearing the gifts. Iad stood silently for a moment, unmoving. The low buzz of conversation hushed and all movement stilled.

Tinor began to speak the ceremonial words. "I am Tinor Fotep Sten, a child of Atielle, of Sectilius, and of the stars. Logic and science are my guides. I was a student. I am a student. I will be a student until I meet dusk."

An undercurrent of surprise ran through the sectilians as Tinor deviated from the standard dictum by adding the phrase "of the stars." Brai wasn't surprised though. He'd told the adolescent that some individuals added those words aboard ship.

Tinor continued. "I am ready to be included, to join, to work toward the goals of my species, to ally myself with others. I have reached the age of pubescent change. I am female."

Schlewan spoke. "Tinor Fotep Sten has been confirmed as a documented citizen. She has been free to explore gender without bias or influence. She is female." Schlewan turned to gaze at Jane.

That was her cue. As the highest-ranked individual, she would give the first gift. She strode to the table and picked up a thin box containing the chain necklace that was one of very few things she still had from Earth. She'd racked her brain trying to think of an appropriate gift, but this was the only thing she could come up with—a gift from her grandparents upon her own sixteenth birthday. She hated to part with it, but it was appropriate to the occasion.

She stood next to Tinor and smiled. "I pass on to you a gift given to me at my own coming-of-age ceremony, of sorts. I've noticed that the Sectilius don't tend to adorn themselves the way humans do, but I hope you will enjoy this trinket." She opened the box and held out her hand.

Tinor timidly reached in and picked up the necklace. She held it out, pinched between two fingers, looking perplexed.

"May I put it on you?" Jane asked.

Tinor nodded. Jane took the chain from Tinor, opened the clasp, and draped it around Tinor's neck before connecting it. Jane patted the young woman on the shoulder and stepped away.

Tinor looked deep in thought and fingered the chain. As Jane passed by Schlewan, Schlewan shot Jane an intense look that Jane didn't understand, but Schlewan was already moving forward as Tinor's next of kin and the next-highest-ranking officer in attendance. She presented Tinor with a small handheld emergency cauterizing tool, then turned to gesture at Ajaya.

Ajaya stepped forward to hand Tinor a fun-sized Snickers bar she'd somehow saved. "This is food from Earth inside this wrapper. It's very special. I hope you enjoy it." Tinor turned it over in her hand with a dazed expression on her face.

Jaross came forward, scooped up a bundle of fabric from the table, and allowed it to unfold into a large blanket or wall hanging before Tinor. Jaross peeked over the top. "I took some salvaged items and wove them for you in the traditional way. I hope it pleases you."

The gift was green, like most of the fabric originating on the ship, but was woven into elaborate textural patterns. Some of the fibers shimmered, others were matte. Jane wondered when Jaross had found the time to make it, because she hadn't brought it with her from the Hator compound. It was lovely.

Tinor took the material gingerly, staring at it until Ryliuk interrupted, pushing an item toward her already-full hands. It was something small and wooden with a long lanyard made of braided plant fibers. Jane had looked at it closely earlier in the evening. It appeared to be a hand-carved whistle. When Tinor fumbled, Ryliuk settled the cording over her head and one shoulder, then moved away without a word.

Pledor was just behind Ryliuk. He held out a large, smooth-skinned purple fruit in one hand. "A zoba fruit," he said proudly. "Harvested from the Greenspace earlier today at peak ripeness. Don't wait long to consume it. It will rot quickly."

Ron stepped up, grinning, and delivered a very realistic sketch of a cat that he'd drawn. He patted Tinor's arm. "Thought you might be curious about what Earth creatures look like."

Tinor held the sheet of paper delicately, like a treasure. She nodded shyly at Ron.

Ron sidestepped back to the table and returned with the last remaining item: a screwdriver. He shook his head as he passed it to Tinor. "This is from Berg. It's a human tool. Happy..." He shrugged. "Happy coming-out day."

That seemed to conclude the proceedings. People were already leaving. Tinor lingered, examining each of her gifts closely with a reverence that made Jane smile.

Jane walked to the door to head to Tech Deck to obtain Brai's batch of nanites, but before she reached it, Schlewan stepped into her path.

The same intense expression that Jane had noted earlier was fixed on Schlewan's face. "As an off-worlder, you cannot possibly understand the symbolism of the gift you just bestowed upon Tinor. I will inform the girl of this, so she doesn't misunderstand your intent."

Jane hesitated. "I'm sorry. Have I blundered in some way?"

"Did you wish to form an alliance with Tinor?"

Jane's eyes widened. The word was filled with implications. She wasn't sure how to respond. She queried Brai and he supplied her with the missing information instantly. Jane blinked. "Oh, no. That wasn't my intention at all. This is a customary human gift..." She trailed off, unsure how to navigate this huge gaffe. She should have run the idea for the gift by Schlewan before deciding on it.

Schlewan pursed her lips. "This is unfortunate. Tinor has already formed a fondness for both you and Dr. Alan Bergen. It would be an advantageous attachment for her for obvious reasons. She will be disappointed to learn that she will not be joining your circle." Schlewan turned on her heel and moved away.

Jane staggered out of her quarters into the hall so no one would observe her expression. She knew that sectilians didn't pair bond the way humans did. They formed circles, small diversely gendered polyamorous groups to raise children and share resources. It had never occurred to Jane that any of them would want to include humans in that social construct. She would have to discuss this mistake with Tinor, and soon.

43

Brai twitched with palsy.

His thoughts were sluggish. He was restless.

This space was too small. His limbs ached with the need to move.

It was too warm here, too close to the edges of his habitat. Water constantly circulated, but at a restricted rate, and the warmth from the hominids' spaces bled into the tiny diagnostic bubble.

The bright light made his brains ache, and though he worked to keep his body turned away and his eyes covered with arms and tentacles, it was a difficult position to maintain indefinitely.

There was nowhere to go to escape all of this. It was too much.

They had effectively trapped him here for monitoring. He knew it was only for a short time, but it felt like he was caught in a time-dilation field. Each moment stretched out like an eternity.

He hadn't been confined like this since infancy. It was not a happy comparison. He kept flashing on the agony of that long-ago time, reliving the punishing moments he'd endured until he was able to figure out what the mind master wanted of him. The light, the warmth, all of it was so similar.

But Jane wouldn't let the mind master repeat those devilish training exercises. She'd just said so to Ryliuk without hesitation. He consoled himself with that. He had to do everything in his power to protect her, so that she would continue to protect him.

He was an Ei. He was far beyond reconditioning. Reconditioning was for underachievers, for maladaptives, for those with behavior issues. To say that it should be required of him was a defamation of all that he'd accomplished. That insult would not stand.

The growing sense of debility unnerved him. His interface with the ship was dimming. His mind was turbid and clogged. The pain grew apace, but that, at least, was something he could ignore. The rest of it was impossible to disregard, so he focused on Jane and the others.

Young Tinor had just had her ceremony. She'd told him in advance that she would choose the female gender. She seemed to be pleased with having achieved her new status. He liked her. She enjoyed conversing with him and sharing memories. It helped.

He hadn't considered that Jane's gift for the young woman would be problematic. He was only peripherally aware of the ancient custom of presenting potential lovers with circlets as a form of invitation to a lovers' circle. He did know that the Sectilius tended to avoid restrictive clothing around the neck, except in displaying the collar of rank. Uniforms with collars were worn to symbolize that one was tied to high office. He hadn't realized the two concepts were connected. Or perhaps he'd just forgotten…

He didn't want to think about that.

Instead he focused again on his crew. Ronald and Ajaya were quietly discussing the day's activities. They touched their lips together in that oddly human way and parted. Jaross was heading to the Tech Deck to resume work. Pledor wheedled Ryliuk about returning to the Greenspace Deck to hunt nepatrox. Tinor and Schlewan carried the young woman's gifts to her quarters, debating the merits of each item.

And Jane…he'd lost track of Jane…

She stood before him.

He parted his limbs to see her better. In the blazing light she glowed. Her ceremonial sectilian uniform was a white blur. Her pale hair was pulled back from her face neatly in a tight configuration. His attention converged on her gray eyes which were lit with the fire of determination.

Her thoughts were quiet as she worked. She executed a series of commands. It was no small thing to break the seal. It took time. He curbed his impatience as she temporarily shut down the flow of fresh water to contain the nanites in the small space, so that none of them would be lost in the vast tank. Efficiency was everything now.

Finally she released the shimmering mass into the diagnostic bubble. He moved closer to the port and inhaled deeply to pull them into his body quickly.

She continued to work, but he'd lost the thread of her thoughts.

He trembled. His body was on fire. The billions of new nanites burned as they burrowed into him. He'd forgotten how this felt.

Jane was speaking inside his mind. "You will sleep now until I wake you, Brai. Then I will release you. By then, I hope we will have completely severed the yoke as well."

He started to protest, but her command didn't allow the thought to express itself. His circumstances had changed dramatically. His mind was no longer completely his own. He shook with choler, but it subsided quickly.

He drifted, barely aware of her as she extinguished the painful lights and set the environmental controls to a much lower temperature. Her pale form hovered for some time watching him. His eyes went unfocused and then she was gone.

He descended into the oblivion of a complete and total sleep.

44

Alan pulled in a deep breath and held it. Something had woken him again. His heart pounded. He stayed still and listened, all senses on alert.

He was going to 3-D print a deadbolt for that door in the morning, everything else be damned.

Soft padding feet on the floor. Someone was here without his permission. He stiffened, every muscle tensing to fight, all grogginess swept from his mind in that instant.

He was curled on his left side, away from the door. He suddenly felt very exposed. His only viable defense was surprise. He had to maintain the illusion that he was sleeping.

He curled his fingers into fists and mimicked the slow, soft breaths of deep sleep.

The blankets were lifted and someone slipped beneath them with only a whisper of sound. The mattress dipped behind him.

Wait…what…?

Relief flooded through his body. He relaxed slightly.

Jane had come back. It was time for some good old-fashioned make-up sex.

His thudding heart didn't let up, but now it was sending blood somewhere else. He waited to see what she would do.

She eased toward him without a word until he could feel her warmth against his back. Still not touching, but just there. Of course that's what she would do. She wouldn't wake him because she was so damn sweet. She'd just be there when he woke.

It was nicely played. If he'd thought he could get away with such a move, he'd probably have done it by now. He wasn't normally so timid with the women he was involved with, but this was different. She was in control. She had an image to maintain and shit. And he wasn't complaining. Not at all.

Except that he was awake now and didn't really feel like waiting until morning.

She wouldn't apologize. Just like that it would all be okay again. He should probably put up a bit of resistance, at least for show. The last thing he wanted was Ron taunting him that he was pussy whipped. But dicking around like that with Jane could just throw things in reverse again.

He frowned. That wasn't what he really wanted. He wanted her. In his arms. Under him. He wanted crazy animal sex. He wanted to show her how he felt about her. He wanted her to forget every other man who had ever touched her.

But indecision weighed on him. He'd gotten things wrong before. He'd screwed things up more than once.

Well, two could play this game. He rolled on his back, still feigning sleep.

She retreated slightly. Her breath quickened.

Ah, yes. This was good. This was fun.

He should wait a bit, draw it out. Extend the anticipation. But his loins had other ideas.

He rolled on his right side. Now he could feel her. His hand snuck out to rest on her stomach. He wriggled his face into her hair and breathed deeply, meaning to place a kiss on her jawline before climbing on top of her and trapping her beneath him.

Except something wasn't right. She smelled different. Her hair didn't feel right. His wandering hand froze on a bony frame that didn't feel anything like Jane's curvaceous form.

He pulled back and scrambled from the bed, yelling, "For fuck's sake!"

Whoever was still in the bed sounded like she was hyperventilating. What fresh hell had he gotten himself into now?

Fuck sleep. He was going to go design and print a padlock—right fucking now.

"Jaross?" He couldn't remember a damn word of Mensententia.

"No," said a tiny, trembling voice.

He strode to the wall and triggered the lights. He blinked against the sudden blinding glare.

It was Tinor.

He rubbed his hands over his face. He'd been touching a kid. He felt like hurling.

He found a shirt and threw it over his head. At least he was wearing pants. Thank God for small favors.

He pointed at the door. "You have to go," he choked out in broken Mensententia.

"No, it's okay," the kid protested, still in his bed.

"No. No. No. Not okay." He opened the door. "This is not okay."

Tinor lifted a necklace between two fingers. The kid's eyes were huge. "Quasador Dux Jane Holloway gave me this. I'm a woman, now. She wants us to be together."

He shook his head. "You're not making any sense. You need to leave my room. And you can't come back."

He heard footsteps in the hall. He groaned and hung his head. Now the shit was gonna really hit the fan. He was going to take the heat for this. He clenched his jaw, nostrils flared, and watched Jane appear in the doorway.

"I heard raised voices…"

He stared at her hard, shaking his head. "This is not what you think, Jane. I swear to you. You gotta believe me."

She took in the scene and went all business mode. "Tinor, I was just looking for you. I'll escort you back to your quarters now. We need to talk."

"No, I want to stay."

"You can't stay," Jane said firmly. "Come on. I'll explain everything." She gestured to the kid, who got up and shuffled toward the door, making anxious whimpering sounds.

"Jane—" Alan started to say.

She held up a hand. "I'll be back as soon as I can and we'll talk about it."

By some miracle she didn't sound mad. He didn't know if that was good or bad. He eased down to sit on the edge of the bed and wait.

As they walked down the hall, Jane said, "Did Master Schlewan talk to you about my gift?"

He sat with his head in his hands for an age. Then he paced. Then he pulled out a laptop and did some work on the nanite code for Ei'Brai.

Finally Jane appeared in his open doorway again. There was a strange expression on her face. Her lips were pressed together in a line as she turned to hit the door control.

She paused for a moment with her mouth open like she was searching for something to say. She looked guilty and embarrassed, then she started stammering. "Oh, Alan. I'm so sorry. That was completely my fault. She told me what happened."

He blinked and shut the laptop. She wasn't mad? It wasn't his fault? That was new. He just stared at her warily.

"I mean it was bad enough what the young women on Atielle were doing to you, but this... Oh, God, please tell me she didn't touch you!"

"She didn't."

She sank down next to him. "Sometimes a necklace isn't just a necklace. I made a huge *faux pas* and you paid for it. You okay? You look freaked out."

"Let me get this straight. You gave her a necklace for her sectilian bat mitzvah and she decided that meant she could sleep with me?"

She bit her lip. "Cultural misunderstanding. Yes."

He rubbed the back of his neck. "I thought she was you. I thought you came back."

Her head jerked back and her eyes went wide.

"Nothing happened!" he exclaimed.

She stifled a giggle. "I believe you!"

"Don't laugh at me! A twelve-year-old girl just snuck into my bed!"

Jane sobered.

He nodded. "Yeah, I did the math a long time ago when they started talking about this coming-of-age business. That's how old she'd be on Earth if she were human."

"Well, by their standards, she's an adult woman now with full rights and responsibilities."

He huffed. "That's fucked up."

"They're a different species. If there's one thing I learned in my line of work, it's that we can't expect everyone to have the same societal expectations that we grew up with."

He frowned, thinking about his sisters at age twelve and how they'd been nowhere near grown-up enough to take on adult responsibilities. They'd still been playing with Barbie dolls, dressing up as princesses, pinching each other and pulling each other's hair while fighting over the remote.

He looked at her. "How's the Squid?"

Worry flickered over her features. "I have reason to believe he's going to be okay. He's resting comfortably now. I'll check on him after I get some sleep. It might take some time but I think we'll get things back on track."

He nodded. Her hair was slipping out of its severe bun. His fingers itched to pull it apart so he could run them through her hair. He hesitated. He needed to be sensitive right now. "It can't have been easy to hear the bad news. I'm glad it's looking up."

"It's only looking up if Ryliuk knows what he's talking about. That's just between you and me."

"That guy." He rolled his eyes.

She nodded solemnly. He felt the urge to lighten the mood.

"I hope he's right. He probably is. Of course, if we do get stuck here, I could have a good life on Atielle. All the women there want me."

She sputtered out a laugh. That was good to see for a change.

"I was wishing for your anti-anipraxia device earlier when he cornered me to talk." She emphasized the word "talk" dramatically.

"I know what you mean. The dude's intense."

She leaned back slightly on the bed. She still looked worried.

He said, "You know you can tell me anything. I won't repeat it. Just get it off your chest. I can take it."

She looked down and said, "Thank you."

And all he wanted to do was pounce on her. But he didn't. He had to have some kind of sign. One he was sure of. That had never been his way before, but this was different. He had to be the man she needed now, a better man than he used to be.

He patted her hand awkwardly, then let his fingers linger. "Brai's gonna be okay, Jane. The squillae will patch him up. You've seen the miracles he's worked around here with them."

She stared down at their hands. "When did you realize she wasn't me?"

He groaned. "She didn't smell like you."

"What do I smell like?" she asked softly, raising her eyes to meet his. Those clear gray eyes, so haunted and full of longing.

This was it.

He edged closer, moving his hand more fully over hers. "You smell fucking amazing, Jane."

He held his face close to hers. With his free hand he smoothed a loose tendril of her hair back from her face and traced his fingers over her cheek. She still didn't look sure. He smirked at her. "Wanna cuddle?"

A surprised sound flew from her lips. Her eyes looked brighter. She smiled at him. "Yeah. I do."

She leaned into him, warm and full of promise. He put an arm around her. She rested her head against his cheek and they stayed that way for a while.

Finally she lifted her head and pressed her lips against his. Soft kisses, at first, then more frenzied. The kisses deepened. He couldn't get enough of her.

When he felt her hands go under his shirt he stood and tore it off, then pulled her up against him so he could fumble with the knots on that infernal uniform. He'd done this before, though, and he made quick work of them.

She was watching his expression closely as he loosened the final knot. He didn't open the tunic right away. Instead he kissed her and let his hands still for a moment. Her hands were restlessly roaming his body.

He ran his fingers between the two panels of the front. Her breathing quickened and her fingernails dug into his upper arms. She lifted her mouth to his, crushing his hand between them.

He slipped his hand under the right panel and let it rest just under her breast. It brushed against his knuckles as she moved.

She pulled him closer until he was grinding into her.

He tugged the tunic off. She stood there looking at him shyly as he gazed at her lush body. She gasped as he bent his head and planted a light kiss on each breast.

He eased himself down on the edge of the bed and turned her to face him, pulling her between his knees. He loosened the waistband of her pants, letting them fall to the floor as he placed openmouthed kisses all over her, gliding his lips over her silky skin while his fingers wandered more intimately.

She was panting raggedly with her eyes closed.

Her legs began to tremble. A moan started low in her throat and rose in tone until she ran out of breath. He moved his fingers faster. Suddenly she seized up and cried out. Then she was collapsing into him, no longer able to stand.

He maneuvered her onto the bed, pulled the tangle of pants from her ankles, and pulled off his own.

Easing into her felt like coming home. He hovered over her and rocked his hips, leaning in for kisses. Her eyes were dark and her cheeks flushed. She gazed back at him with an expression that made him crazy—it was wonderment. It was all he could do to keep himself from pounding into her like a wild animal. But he kept it slow for as long as he could, until she was moaning again and pushing up against him like she wanted more. When she was arching and spasming under him, he finally let go.

Afterward he pulled her with him as he rolled on his side, keeping her connected to him, fully entwined, still kissing.

Her hair had slipped from its restraints and lay over her face. He smoothed it back to find tears sliding over her nose. A small dose of panic seized him.

"Jane? You okay?" he whispered.

She sniffed and smiled at him. "Yes. More than okay." Then she burrowed her face into his neck. They fell asleep like that, tangled together, with the lights still on.

Fight or flight engulfed Brai. Coherent thought had not yet found a place to moor when he came to himself flattened against the side of the tiny enclosure, limbs flailing, mantle pulsing frantically, with Jane's voice in his mind saying, "Whoa, whoa, it's okay, Brai. Slow down."

The intensity surprised him. Every nerve screamed torment. Every muscle twitched and throbbed. Every synapse fired out of control.

"We're premature," Dr. Ajaya Varma observed.

Doubt and fear were the dominant emotions in Jane's mind. His eyes rolled around, trying to find her and failing. The light was too bright and he couldn't focus.

"Brai, we're putting you out again," Jane said. There was a tremor in her mental voice. She was concentrating on the console. "We'll give you more time to heal before we attempt to wake you again."

He couldn't reply. He couldn't even form a strangled half thought.

He heard Schlewan say, "You must face the possibility that he will not…"

He went blank.

The next time they brought him to consciousness more slowly. He couldn't feel his limbs. He twitched, breathing sluggishly.

"Brai? Can you hear me?" It was Jane. She was repeating this phrase.

He drifted through a light-saturated haze. The water felt viscous, difficult to pull in or push out. It took a long time to force himself to answer her because it took so much effort. "Yes."

He felt the presence of Dr. Ajaya Varma, working at Jane's side. "Do you feel any pain?"

"No."

Varma continued, "Good. We are returning function to your central nervous system gradually. You must tell us if you feel pain."

Varma made an adjustment. He felt Jane's anxiety rise and subside as she tamped it back down. He experienced a degree more sensation, mobility, strength, but no pain.

By tiny fractions they restored him until he was whole and what remained of the suffering of his first waking was bearable. It was, he thought, less than he'd been enduring before Jane had discovered his problem.

They watched him, tested every parameter, questioned him until they were satisfied he was stable, had reached a safe equilibrium with the new squillae, and then they freed him.

It felt good to be in his larger space. It felt right. But beyond that, he realized quite suddenly, he felt little else. He should have felt immense relief. It should have been glorious. Joyful. He considered this analytically, probing his own mind for clues about the change.

He'd been restored to standard—to the state he'd been in before the ionic burst had destroyed all of the squillae aboard. He remembered being afraid of that course of action, afraid of how it might change him. It had changed him—for the better. He mourned the loss, but only lightly, because that was all the emotion he was permitted.

Then duty consumed him and those thoughts were set aside to concentrate on checking every system on the ship: orbit, trajectory, life support, every status and condition that he normally monitored constantly. He'd neglected his responsibilities too long. It took a while to reassure himself that all was right, in place, and working properly.

Quasador Dux Jane Holloway appeared—had he once dared to call her Jane?—on the other side of the barrier just outside his workspace. An expression he'd come to know as concern transformed her features. He drew himself into the compulsory submissive pose without thought, turning his gaze away from her while something inside him ached with confusion.

"This is why you didn't tell me," she said so softly he barely heard the thought.

He trembled, but was unable to reply. He was not allowed to have opinions on this topic. He should have surrendered to Ryliuk's reconditioning for the thoughts he'd been having.

"Alan? Are you ready?" She connected a third mind to the anipraxic circle.

Dr. Alan Bergen's mind was focused on a complex task, his body bent over a computer station. "Yep. Uploading now," he said.

The Quasador Dux probed Ei'Brai's thoughts, watching for something.

A bubble seemed to burst inside his mind. A chain reaction cascaded through him down to the tips of his tentacles. He gulped water, filling his mantle to capacity, trying to push away the strange sensation. He forced the water out again, jetting in an arc that took him back to where he'd started, except he didn't hover or look away. He pulled himself upright and pressed the club of a tentacle to the glass against the spot where Jane had laid her hand.

She was smiling.

Gratitude swelled within him. He was too overwhelmed to say anything. But she heard him.

"I know," she said. "I'm sorry we couldn't wake you this way. The code wasn't ready yet. I couldn't wait a few more hours to make sure you were okay. I'm sorry I was selfish."

"No apology is necessary," he managed to say.

"Everything okay up there?" Alan asked testily.

Jane answered, "It couldn't be better. You did it. It worked."

"Glad to be of service. I got shit to do, though, so I'm out." Alan removed himself from the anipraxic circle.

"I'm so glad to have you back, Brai."

"Thank you," he stammered, "for giving me back..."

"Yourself?"

"You note the difference?" he asked.

"I do. I prefer you this way." He could tell she meant it.

He swelled a bit, reflexively. Then he extended tendrils of querying thought into the ship to check on the rest of his flock. All seemed to be well. The crew was at peace, working, sleeping, taking a meal. He centered back on Jane. "What did I miss?"

She chuckled, that human expression of humor that lit up her mind with pleasure. "Maybe you should ease back into it. Rest for a few days."

He was a little affronted. "I feel no fatigue. I am poised for action."

"Maybe I'm the one who needs to rest then," she said with chagrin. She shifted her body to lean against the transparent wall that separated them, but she was smiling at him fondly. "It's been a rough few days for me while you were asleep."

"Tell me."

It didn't take much coaxing to get her to pour out her anxiety. It wasn't just about him, though he was the largest part of it. And some things had taken a turn for the better. Tentatively she told him that her relationship with Alan had improved. She did not supply detail, but he could sense an effusive tenor of hope and delight in her. He made certain that she knew that he was happy for her. That surprised her, but also pleased her.

Then she tensed a little. "But I seem to have made a mess of my relationships with nearly every one of the sectilians."

He skimmed the thoughts of each of the sectilians in turn. She watched, almost afraid of what he would find. "I sense no animosity toward you."

She sighed.

"Tell me the specifics as you perceive them," he said.

"I think you already know all the specifics. Nothing really changed. I botched my gift to Tinor and made her think…" She made a physical sound that indicated frustration. "Well, you know what she thought. That hurt her feelings, and Schlewan was really angry about it. Ryliuk is miffed because I won't let him put you through reconditioning. I was forced to remind him of his place and I worry that he'll resent that. Or that, I don't know, that it won't last? Pledor has been disgruntled since he set foot on the ship. I shouldn't have shamed him when he got caught unawares by the nepatrox on the Greenspace Deck. Jaross is the only sectilian I haven't offended in some way."

"And what are the results of these gaffes?"

She looked weary. "Tinor avoids me. Schlewan and Ryliuk both seem to be more reticent. Pledor is gruff as always. Even Jaross seems more distant. I've failed to foster camaraderie. The crew isn't gelling like I'd hoped. This is a terrible way to begin our journey together."

"Ah. I see. You use the word 'seem' as though it means something."

A furrow formed between her brows. She straightened. "What do you mean? Are you saying this is all in my imagination?"

"I believe that your worry is manifesting in a misinterpretation of the data. You are expecting human reactions from sectilian individuals. That is where the error lies."

"But…" She sagged against the wall again.

"After your blunder with Tinor, you took steps to rectify and explain the cultural difference immediately. That satisfied Schlewan—she respected your straightforward manner and held no grudge. Tinor was disappointed because she admires you and wants to please you. She will attempt to stay beneath your notice until she can achieve something that will capture your attention. She is more concerned with this than about the mistake. This is natural."

"Really?"

"Really. As for Ryliuk—he may not agree with you, but he absolutely believes in the validity of your authority, because that is what his culture dictates to him. He accepts your decision and will work within the boundaries you set for him. Sectilians, for the most part, are cooperative. They seek harmony. It is their way—the sharing of resources, of duty, of child-rearing. This is a significant aspect of their culture. From their point of view, these situations are long past over. Your dwelling upon them is fruitless."

"Oh."

"You know this. All of this."

She tilted her face up. "Pledor and Jaross are the same, then?"

"You may not believe this, but Pledor is inordinately content. He spends all of his free time on the Greenspace Deck, which uniquely suits his personal skill set. Jaross, likewise, is satisfying an inner craving and very happy to be here."

She nodded, mulling over his words. "I missed you, Brai."

"I am indispensable."

She laughed again. He could almost hear the tinkle of the sound transmit through to his enclosure. Then she turned more grave. "Brai, your health is important to me. You just reminded me that I think like a human, so don't assume that I would manage your well-being as a sectilian Quasador Dux would. I understand how you were treated in the past, why you might believe that your needs would be ignored, but I'm different. I'm not them. You should have told me."

He held her gaze. "Understood."

"Good."

"Shall we schedule the first jump?"

"Soon. I have another surprise for you first." She had an impish look on her face. Her cheeks were pink. She had adopted a mysterious air and kept him from seeing her thoughts.

He harrumphed. "I look forward to it."

Brai didn't feel anything when Alan implemented the second change. Hours had passed and Brai was occupied with optimizing the formula for the impending jump sequences, managing several large squillae repair cadres, and having a conversation with young Tinor when Jane showed up again. She'd just spent a few hours with Alan, Jaross, and Ron on Tech Deck.

"Am I under surveillance?" he asked.

"Maybe." She shrugged. "How do you feel?"

"Eminently normal," he replied cautiously.

"You're not just saying that?"

"No," he said dryly, though he supposed he deserved the question.

Her thoughts were excited, verging on giddy. "Well, then, move the ship."

"Coordinates?" he asked absently as he connected to the navigation console through his implants, and shifted his body closer to the physical controls in anticipation of her command.

"I don't care. It doesn't matter. You choose."

He jetted over to the partition between them and stared at her. "Do you jest?"

"Do I ever?"

He ground his beak as he made his way back to the console. Her anticipation was infectious. He contemplated the possibilities and opted for a small move to start—something just slightly beyond the scope the yoke had allowed him before—a correction of altitude of more than a vastuumet. The ship responded instantly—and without personal consequence. He experienced none of the punishment that a transgression of the yoke would have earned him in the past. He plotted a course that would break orbit and move them toward the fringes of the system, in preparation for a jump. Without linking through the Quasador Dux, the ship responded flawlessly to his command.

Twice in a single day she'd astonished him.

She caught that thought. "That's payment enough for me," she said.

46

Jane sat up straight in the command chair. She could feel the jump device spooling. The mechanical feeling of it hummed through both her and Brai, rising slowly in resonance. Her connection to Brai was so close in moments like these, their consciousnesses all but merged.

The Brai that Jane had known before the ship-wide squillae purge and the Brai she'd known afterward were now reconciled. He was happy. It came off him in waves and seemed to affect everyone on board in a positive way. Disabling the yoke and the code that crippled Brai mentally had been the right thing to do. She didn't need to chain him, only to trust him. That was enough. The trust, she was certain, was mutual.

Alan sauntered onto the bridge and took his seat at the Tech Deck monitoring station. He sent her a meaningful glance and a slight nod. The rest of the crew began to filter in. Ryliuk was the last to arrive. He made his way to the communications station without saying a word.

Her bare-bones bridge crew was in place. They had a route planned, but they were going to have to think on their feet, depending on what they found when they arrived. They would start by looking for the ships closest to the Sectilius system and branch out from there.

It was finally time to begin the journey to find the lost kuboderans.

Their first target was a ship called the *Quisapetta*—"she who waits." Its last known location was in an uninhabited system, where it had been doing scientific research on the composition of the system's planets in an attempt to discover why some star systems were capable of supporting life, while others were barren. The Sectilius had been sending ships to this nearby system for thousands of years, collecting data over time. The *Quisapetta* was the same type of ship as the *Speroancora*, primarily a science vessel.

There was no information in the database about the *Quisapetta's* Gubernaviti, Kai'Negli, other than the facts that he was over 1,000 years old, had a spotless record, and had risen to the highest rank achievable for a kuboderan—Kai. There were no notes about his personality or other achievements, despite the fact that there was plenty of information about the other officers who'd served aboard the *Quisapetta*—though Jane assumed those individuals were likely long dead. In moments they would know more.

It was going be a single short jump. There was no use speculating on how this would play out, but she hoped that they would find these kuboderans in much the same state that Brai had been in, eager to help look for their own kind, though she knew that might not be the case. Every kuboderan was an individual and would have their own ideas about how they wanted to go forward. She would do her best to honor that.

"Quasador Dux Jane Holloway, the jump drive is at the ready. Checking all critical systems now," Brai intoned formally to the entire anipraxia network, while underneath he vibrated with an undercurrent of excitement.

Jane mentally touched the minds of each individual aboard to make certain everyone was linked and ready. Alan, Ron, Ajaya, Jaross, and Ryliuk were all on the bridge, and the systems they monitored were green for go. In the background, connected but not directly assisting, Schlewan, Tinor, and Pledor waited and watched nearby.

Jane was a little nervous. The jumps taxed her and were painful. She didn't want to show weakness in front of the sectilians, especially Ryliuk and Pledor.

She let Brai see those thoughts but no one else. She had become adept at choosing which thoughts to share while keeping others private. It seemed as though there were several layers in her mind that she could use depending on prevailing conditions—complete privacy, sharing with Brai, or sharing at another level with others either individually or as a group. She'd learned to default to keeping things just between herself and Brai unless she had something specific to share with the rest.

Brai's mental voice rumbled, "All systems ready, Qua'dux. Awaiting your command."

Jane inhaled sharply and gritted her teeth, focusing all of her attention on the impending jump. "Initiate jump sequence."

He didn't have to confirm because she could feel him set the operation in motion. His connection to the ship was stronger now. The squillae lent support in bridging the connection between his implants and the neural-electric pathways of the ship. His signal engaged the wormhole drive and she felt it roar to life.

Through the viewscreen she saw the invisible swirl instantly form, smearing the stars behind it. Pressure built in her head. She concentrated doggedly. Her heart pounded once, twice…she blinked…and they were through.

An entirely new set of stars came into focus.

It had happened so fast she'd missed traversing the short tunnel when she blinked.

She let out her breath, huffed and puffed for a moment, trying to get her bearings. She was gripped in a moment of disorientation. It passed quickly.

"Report," she ordered. She almost didn't believe that the jump had gone off as it should have. It was too different from the journey to Sectilius—it was too easy.

"Tech Deck systems nominal," Alan said. Similar reports echoed from the rest of the crew.

"What about our location?" she asked.

"Location confirmed, Qua'dux," Brai said smugly before turning his attention elsewhere.

A smile quirked her lips for just a second. "Scan the system."

"Scanning."

Jaross said, "I'm detecting the chemical signature of a sectilian ship between the orbits of the third and fourth planets."

"Is it the *Quisapetta*?" Jane asked.

"Unknown," Jaross replied.

Ryliuk said, "There is no identification beacon broadcasting on any frequency."

"Plot a course," Jane told Brai. "Let's go see. Maybe Kai'Negli turned it off to conserve resources." Never mind that such an action wouldn't make sense—above everything else, he should want to be found.

The ship moved swiftly through the system, passing an asteroid belt but not seeing another planet except a single red rock from a distance.

A flicker of unease came through the connection with Brai. It felt like deja vu. He didn't sense the presence of any kuboderan, though he should have well before now. Despair surged inside him, then was quickly tamped down.

What was left of the *Quisapetta* came into view. Scattered debris, blackened from an explosion, had fallen into its own orbit around this star.

47

Jane commanded the viewscreen to zoom in on a quadrant of the destruction and watched the pallid body of a kuboderan easily twice the size of Brai slowly float by, surrounded by huge irregularly shaped shards of ice. Kai'Negli, surely. Half of his arms were severed partially or completely, the rest curled protectively around himself in death.

Brai choked out, "It would be unwise to approach any closer with the escutcheon in its current state."

"Release a probe," Jane said.

"Damn it. I was afraid of this," Alan muttered.

Jane stared at the debris field in disbelief. The ship had been obliterated. "Who would do this?"

Ron shook his head at his station in front of her. "Maybe whoever planted the bad squillae?"

Alan huffed. "It could have been anyone pissed that there were zombie plague-infested ships left all over known space. They'd view it as risky to just leave them floating around. Better to eliminate the threat."

"Why not help them?" Tinor asked in a quiet voice.

"Did anyone help the Sectilius?" Alan asked. "All we know is that someone, probably from this Sentient Alliance we know nothing about, dropped atomic bombs in the atmospheres of Atielle and Sectilia to kill the nanites and all the technology on the surface—but no one ever went in to help them. They just quarantined the entire system and forgot about them. Left them to survive or die."

The probe glided through the wreckage, gathering data.

Jane frowned. "Are there squillae in the wreckage?"

"Negative," Brai announced. "None detected."

"We need to know more. Is the probe picking up any information that could help us glean anything about this ship's attacker?"

"Still processing data," Brai replied.

Jane walked to the front of the bridge to visually inspect the wreckage at high magnification on the viewscreen. She called Ron up to look at it with her, since he had extensive ballistics experience from his past work as a Marine.

He pointed at what she thought of as the underside of the hammerhead-shark-shaped ship, toward the tail. "Looks like primary impact was here. It just ripped her open in one shot. That's some heavy-duty ordnance, QD."

Jane nodded. "The ship wasn't moving. Because of the yoke, Kai'Negli couldn't fight back or take evasive maneuvers."

Ron grimaced. "He was a sitting duck."

Ron gestured at another chunk floating nearby. The remains of the kuboderan's habitat were exposed in that section. Ice with a pearly iridescence flowed in knobby shapes into a multidirectional waterfall from every edge of the tank's remains. "You see this? This isn't from the explosion. It's too regular. These are straight lines. This happened after the explosion. Someone wanted to make sure there were no survivors and they knew exactly where to cut."

That was so disturbing. What would prompt someone to do that?

Ron turned his attention back to the primary impact site and pointed at a blackened, jagged segment of the hull. "We should get a sample of this material for analysis. Can the probe cut off a small piece?"

Jane thought about it. The probe was a scientific sampling tool, but it was primarily designed to siphon, scoop, or drill. "No. It doesn't have the tools to cut into something of this nature. This is outside the scope of its intended purpose."

Jaross stood. "With your permission, Qua'dux, I'd like to take a shuttle in closer, obtain samples to see if I can gather any additional forensic information."

Schlewan chimed in. "I would go as well."

Ajaya said, "I'll go too."

Jane held up a hand before anyone else volunteered. She consulted privately with Brai. "How risky would that be?"

Brai labored over some calculations. "The risk is minimal. Jaross has completed the simulated shuttle-pilot training course and has field experience. She displays an innate aptitude."

Jane sat back in the command chair. These three were qualified to analyze just about anything. Far more than she was herself. She nodded. "You three. That's it. Gather what you need and leave when ready. Take no risks."

The three volunteers left the bridge. Alan half turned in his seat and sent her a thought along with a mock baleful glance. "You know I wanted to go, too."

Jane sighed. She'd expected this. "You didn't stand up fast enough."

He turned back around. "Fair enough. I already got to do a spacewalk, anyway."

"Yes. Thank goodness you survived it."

"I lead a charmed life like that." He sniffed. "I'll just be here, looking over this data, then."

They launched the shuttle. Jane stood with arms folded, resisting the urge to pace, and watched the small craft as it maneuvered through the wreckage. Jaross narrated every action as she executed it. She was calm and self-assured. She pulled up alongside the spot Ron had pointed out. Ajaya opened the rear hatch, outfitted in the same kind of suit Alan had worn on his spacewalk, brandishing a sectilian laser cutting arc. She proceeded to hack off a piece of the outer hull at the edge of the blast zone.

She pulled herself back inside the shuttle. They began to repressurize the cabin.

A bright blast whited out the viewscreen.

Jane gasped and flew to the front of the bridge to stare in horror as the tiny ship was flung away from the larger one.

"Jaross, report!"

Jaross didn't reply.

Jane turned to Alan. "Show me the interior cameras."

The view on the screen changed almost instantly.

It was chaos. The ship was tumbling. People were injured. There was a gaping hole in the rear compartment. Jaross and Schlewan were tethered but Ajaya was being tossed around in the rear compartment.

Jaross still looked calm, but she was struggling to get the ship under control.

They'd survived the blast because they hadn't yet repressurized and removed their masks. If they hadn't had supplemental air, they would have died from the breach alone. Beyond that, if the shuttle had repressurized then Ajaya, still untethered, would have been sucked out into the explosion.

The bridge was silent as everyone watched the shuttle narrowly miss a collision with a large piece of the destroyed ship.

"How can we help them?" Jane asked aloud. No one replied. Suddenly it occurred to her. She closed her eyes and commanded Brai to create a tight link with Jaross. Now she could see what Jaross could see.

Jane gave Jaross terse instructions on how to regain control based solely on instinctive impulses. Jaross followed them without question and was able to pull the ship out of its spiral. That allowed Schlewan to attend to Ajaya as they limped back to the *Speroancora*.

As soon as the smaller ship was back aboard, Jane gave the order to put some distance between them and the wreckage. She raced for the door to the bridge. She had to get a stretcher to the cargo bay where Jaross had landed the ship. She sent a message to Tinor to meet her there.

"QD?" Ron was standing. His normally calm expression had slipped away. His jaw was clenched tight. His hands were balled into fists. "Permission to accompany you?"

"I need your eyes and ears here. Keep a tight link to me. Schlewan is working on her. She's in the best hands possible. I'll make sure she's okay."

He nodded and returned to his station.

48

Jane took a seat at the head of the table in the crew dining hall. It was the closest they were going to get to a conference room on this ship. Alan sat next to her on one side. Jaross sat herself stiffly on the other side. She was battered but not badly enough for the screening device to recommend sanalabrius immersion.

Ajaya had not been so lucky. She'd barely survived. She'd lost a lot of blood when the piece of the wreckage she'd cut from the *Quisapetta* had punctured her abdomen. Thankfully she'd been wearing a skintight pressure suit, so the injury hadn't resulted in loss of air or she'd have been dead in seconds. Though she was covered in burns and bruises and had several fractures from being tossed around in the shuttle, she'd never let go of the fragment of the other ship. She would be out of commission for a long while.

Jane acknowledged each of the crew members in turn as they took a seat. "We're here to discuss what happened and what we'll do next."

Without hesitation, Alan said, "We blow that shit up before we do anything else."

Pledor grunted. "Why would we do that?"

Alan didn't bother to look at Pledor, but he did answer. "It's booby-trapped throughout. Anyone else who gets close to that thing is going to get hurt."

"Why didn't you detect the bombs before we put people in such close proximity?" Pledor asked.

Alan blinked. "Because we didn't know what we were looking for. The bombs are made from everyday objects on board a ship. After the explosion I was able to go back into the probe's scans, pick out where the origin of the explosion was, and then search the rest of the ship for those kinds of devices."

Pledor looked like he was formulating another cynical question, but Ron leaned forward to say, "I'm confident I can trigger a chain reaction with just a single missile. That should remove most, if not all, the risk to anyone else who stumbles on this."

Jane glanced at Alan. He was nodding in agreement.

Pledor wouldn't be silenced for long. "That's a waste. We may need those munitions at a later date, if we encounter a Swarm pod. That's what they're meant for. Defense under threat. This is an uninhabited system. It's unlikely anyone will stumble on it."

Pledor had clearly been studying his ship history.

"The *Quisapetta* was here. We're here. Ships come here." Alan's voice was starting to rise.

Jane held up a hand. "I agree with Alan. We should remove the danger. We'll work out the particulars when we're finished here. But there is something else we need to discuss. Something that doesn't make sense. Alan, please tell everyone what your team found when you analyzed the piece of the *Quisapetta* that Ajaya removed."

Alan nodded. "In short, the *Quisapetta* was blown up by another sectilian vessel."

Everyone but Jane and the engineers looked surprised.

"How is that possible?" Pledor demanded.

"No idea. We've been working under the assumption that the plague affected every sectilian ship. Now it's looking like we may have a civil war on our hands."

"Impossible, impossible, *impossible*," Schlewan said sternly.

"Were there opposing factions on either planet that were radical in any way?" Jane asked.

The sectilians looked at each other skeptically. Jaross spoke. "Certainly there were disagreements, but that is not the way of our people. We look for solutions, not warfare."

"We would not murder our own in this way," Schlewan said. "When some of our colonies were destroyed by the Swarm there was a widespread referendum. Our people are determined to always present a united front. We declared that we would never, never, *never* fight amongst ourselves again."

Tinor said, "Every child is trained this way in the schoolroom. We do not harm our own."

"Okay," Jane said. "Do you have another explanation?"

Ryliuk put his hands out flat on the table in front of him. "They must have done it to themselves during the madness of the infection."

"Nope," Alan said. "The residue left behind from the explosion indicates the missile came from a category-six warship. The *Quisapetta* is the same category as the *Speroancora*—class four. It doesn't carry those kinds of missiles."

"Not warship," Pledor corrected. "Defense ship. Those ships were created to defend against the Swarm."

"Well if it looks like a warship and it quacks like a warship…" Alan quipped.

Ron leaned forward. "They didn't just blow a hole in the *Quisapetta*. Once they split her open, they used laser weapons to cut open the tank so they could kill the kuboderan."

"How strange and cruel," Tinor said softly.

"This had to happen during the plague—it creates a madness. I can summon no other explanation," Jaross said.

Ryliuk coughed. "We should return to Sectilius space."

Silence fell.

Ron looked at Ryliuk skeptically. "Why would we do that?"

Ryliuk shifted in his seat and glanced toward Jane, though his gaze fell short of meeting her eyes. "We should recruit a larger crew. We could have lost thirty percent of our number to the shuttle sortie."

"But we didn't," Ron said.

"No, we didn't," Jaross agreed. "We should continue on."

Tinor leaned forward earnestly. "We only have one data point. We need to gather more information."

Pledor huffed. "It's too soon to turn back. Nothing has changed."

Jane concealed the surprise that threatened to pass over her features from hearing Pledor side with the humans and Jaross. Jane knew through Brai that Tinor and Schlewan agreed with them as well.

"It's settled then," Jane said and rose. "We'll blow up what's left of the *Quisapetta* and jump to the next target, the *Crastinatra*—'The Black Tomorrow.'"

49

They blew up the *Quisapetta*. Then they watched it burn from a distance. Ron had not been exaggerating when he'd said he could pick a spot that would create a chain reaction. Once it started blowing up, it didn't stop until most of the fragments were annihilated.

It felt like a funeral. Brai was struggling to manage his emotions. The general mood on the ship was somber.

When it seemed as though there was nothing left to do, they jumped to the next destination on the list. Like the last jump, this one was fairly easy, but it was also short.

A quick search revealed the *Crastinatra* to be in the same state as the *Quisapetta*, drifting in the far reaches of a white-dwarf star system. If there had ever been civilization there, it was long gone now.

This smaller ship was also booby-trapped, and its ku-boderan Do'Goa had been killed in the same manner as Kai'Negli. Do'Goa was much younger, only a few decades old. The *Crastinatra* had been a trading vessel, moving between Sectilius and her colonies.

They took all the data they could at a distance. Then they blew up the *Crastinatra* too.

Another jump. Another ship. The *Allucinaria*—the Dreamer—a diplomatic vessel that had been returning to

Sectilius after a mission to the planet Terac, where the Unified Sentient Races held ambassadorial assemblies. They found the *Allucinaria* in the void between star systems, also destroyed. Another kuboderan dead, this one called Ei'Nadj.

They tagged the *Allucinaria* with a warning beacon in Mensententia rather than waste another missile. The outlook was not looking good and they had limited munitions. Jane called for a short break for a rest before they prepared to move on.

She found herself wandering the ship in a restless, pensive mood. Alan had decided to do some work for a few hours on Tech Deck. Brai was in an introverted state of mind and wasn't good company. Jane didn't feel as though she was either, so she avoided the other crewmembers in favor of a long walk to clear her head.

But after a while the endless quiet of the empty corridors started to get to her. She paused at a bubble-shaped viewport and gazed out into the deep black sprinkled with so many stars. Were there any live kuboderans out there to find? Had someone killed them all for a reason, or was it all senseless? She decided what she really needed was to see something life affirming, so she suited up in power armor to visit the Greenspace Deck.

When the door to the space opened, Jane was stunned. Within the immediate area of the entrance, a semblance of order had been restored. Someone had been hard at work, trimming, cutting, carving out walkways. It was still very lush, but not so overgrown. It smelled as lovely and green as she remembered. Just the sight of green growing things eased her mind a bit.

She heard some rustling and decided to investigate, to see who had done all this work. As she got close, she heard the sound of power armor locking into place over someone's torso, immediately followed by the faint high-pitched whine of someone arming concussive palm blasters. She ordered her helmet up for safety, thinking there must be nepatrox nearby.

She came around a stout gray trunk covered with lavender moss and saw another suit of battle armor, palms out, pointed at her. The hands dropped and the helmet retracted. Jane ordered hers back too. It was Ryliuk. His expression was blank but wary.

She realized this was where she had found him the time before. He had cleared out the space around his peculiar shrub. There were clippings and limbs piled up neatly nearby, waiting to be carted off. He had carved out a little sanctuary here, complete with a small log to sit on. It almost looked like a shrine.

His armor split open across his torso and he slipped his arms out of it, leaving himself bare-chested without a trace of self-consciousness. Jane had to remind herself that this kind of nakedness did not mean the same thing to him that it did to a human male. She'd seen plenty of man-chest display when she was on campus. At least he was covered from the waist down. "I thought you were a nepatrox," he said. "I set up a motion-detecting perimeter so that I'd have time to ready myself, just in case." He pointed at a device mounted to a tree trunk, some distance away.

"Has there been any more trouble with nepatrox?" she asked.

"Just one. It seemed to be old and infirm, likely the reason it didn't chase us that day. None since then. Precautions do seem prudent, however, until we're certain. That will take time."

She nodded. She'd find it difficult to completely relax her guard here unless months went by without seeing one. "Did you do all of this, Ryliuk?"

"This?" he gestured to the small hideout. "Yes. But not all that. That's Pledor's work, mostly. Though all of us come down here when we can, to assist."

She knew Pledor had been coming here, because Brai had mentioned it to her and because he'd been leaving lots of fresh food in the crew mess hall. But she never would have guessed at all that had been done. "All of us?"

"The sectilians and atellans."

That was the first time Jane had heard the two groups referred to that way. Normally when someone referred to both groups they just used the all-encompassing "sectilians." That Ryliuk hadn't was interesting.

"If the humans had known you were doing this, we would have helped as well," Jane said.

"I suppose this is true."

Jane bit back a sour retort. She wanted to say, "Of course it's true. I just said it was," but that wouldn't help the strained relationship she had with Ryliuk. "Tell me about this plant," she said instead.

"It is called Plumex." He held out a hand to the frizzy bush and it twined a sinuous branch around his arm.

Jane stepped closer. "That's the name of the species or the name you've given this specimen?"

He caressed the bough and the entire shrub vibrated slightly, rhythmically, almost like it was purring. "The species. *Plumex sinciput.* They are native to the dark forests of the fifth continent of Sectilia."

"It seems to be very special."

His expression warmed. "There has been much debate about whether they are sentient, but I have no doubt. They have a rudimentary central nervous system. They have feelings, but no language. I can sense them, though not many can. When my mother discovered that I could, she said I would one day be a powerful mind master."

Jane didn't doubt that. Now she wished she could remove her armor so she could touch it too, but like Ryliuk, she was naked underneath, and she wasn't about to give Ryliuk a lesson in human mammary anatomy. She'd have to come back at a later time.

"You said you had one as a child," Jane probed, hoping to get him to tell her more about it.

"I did. We encountered one on an excursion. When my mother saw that I had an affinity for the species, she obtained one to plant near our home. I nurtured it carefully as it grew. They thrive on contact, you see. Normally with their own kind—they live in understory groves in the wild, and their branches caress each other. Their combined mental state is like joyous music."

He continued to touch it. It was like a pet to him, she realized. He continued. "But when planted singly, like this, they aren't happy unless they have a connection with an outsider. This one was unbearably lonely."

Jane nodded and stepped closer. She wondered why Ryliuk could understand that about the plant and the plant's

401

needs, but not about Brai. Her fingers itched to touch it. It looked very soft. Watching him fondle it was mesmerizing. She felt drawn to it.

"We were two of a kind, my Plumex and myself. Both of us outsiders."

"Why was that, Ryliuk?" She sat down on the log he'd placed nearby. He was tethered to the plant and not dominating her personal space for a change, so she didn't mind sitting reasonably close to him.

He looked at the plant longingly and Jane wondered if he would have just climbed in if she hadn't been sitting there. As it was, the shrub leaned toward him, tendrils reaching toward his waist, his shoulder, his neck, even wrapping around the shell of his ear, as though it were trying to pull him closer.

"My mother was of atellan descent. My father, sectilian. This isn't unusual. However, children tend to favor one body type over the other. My own genetics combined to create something different. I stood out as an outlier. I did not fit in with either group, though it is normal to socialize with all types. I was too…large, too strong, too different. I was left to occupy myself. And when my communication abilities manifested at a very early age, that only isolated me more. People didn't trust me to abstain from observing their thoughts."

"But your Plumex didn't mind," Jane said.

He smiled. "No. It did not. It flourished under my care."

"It looks very soft."

"It is." He took a branch and dangled it just under her nose. "The needles are so fine and so numerous they resemble feathers. See?"

He touched it to her cheek. It felt kitten soft. She could see the appeal. "It's lovely."

"Pledor says he will help me propagate it, so that it will have a companion."

"A wonderful idea."

Ryliuk grew quiet and was focused on the shrub, so she rose to go. She was encroaching on his private time. She'd accomplished what she'd set out to do. She felt more centered and at peace. As she started to walk away, she realized that the sectilian mind was so concrete that Ryliuk wouldn't make a connection unless she showed it to him bluntly.

She paused. "I'm glad you're here for your Plumex, as I have been for Ei'Brai. They were both lost and lonely for far too long."

He didn't move, though his ears pulled back a degree.

"Brai is not so unlike you, Ryliuk. He, too, feels caught between two worlds, not fully belonging to either. Is he kuboderan? Or is he of Sectilius? He was raised by your people to believe he was sectilian, but then he was left to die alone, abandoned. He does not even know where his home world is. And if he could find it, would he belong there either?"

Ryliuk looked thoughtful, but didn't reply.

"We are all part of a new tribe now. We are the crew of the *Speroancora*. We need to nurture each other as a family would."

She turned and left the deck without waiting for a reply.

Jane emerged from the shower. She was warm and pink and felt refreshed. She carefully combed her hair, pulled it back into a ponytail, and began to dress.

Alan lounged on the bed, watching her, mischief in his eyes.

She ignored him.

He kicked the sheet off and rose to stand behind her, planting kisses on her neck. "I like watching you dress, but I like undressing you more," he murmured into her ear as his hands wrapped around her and pulled her into him.

A thrill shot through her. She smiled. "We just did that."

"Mmmm. Yep. Let's do it again. You know, the lack of a bra takes away a component of challenge, but all of these ties more than make up for it." His fingers fiddled with the tie at the hem of the tunic.

She covered his arms with her own, stilling his fingers. "You're saying if I wore a flight suit, you'd be bored of me?"

"Never. I'd just unzip you inch by glorious inch."

She sighed. "I'm due on the bridge in thirty minutes."

"I can work within those limitations."

She was at war with herself. If she turned in his arms now and kissed him, she wouldn't be able to pull away. She had a ritual of walking the corridors of the ship before a jump. It helped to gather her thoughts. This one would be a longer jump. It could be harder than the ones before. "Tempting…"

He groaned. "But…?"

"Work. And I want to visit Ajaya for at least a few minutes."

He stopped trying to pick at the knots she was tying. "I was afraid you'd say that. How's Ajaya doing?"

"Healing, slowly. The pain meds keep her out most of the time."

"It sucks that she's stuck in the tub o' goo. But she'll be back in no time. To lecture us, and save our asses, as often as possible."

She smiled.

He planted another kiss on her cheek, this one more chaste. "Another jump today."

"Yes. I hope you'll join us." She turned her head slightly so that her cheek brushed his.

He squeezed her a little tighter. "I wouldn't have it any other way. How many dead squid are we going to find before you give up?"

She frowned. She felt a pang of sadness. He didn't mean to sound callous, she knew. He was just so pragmatic. "I don't know. I hope there won't be any more."

He nodded, rubbing his stubbled chin against her hair, and softened his tone. He must have realized he'd hit a soft spot. "We should consider shifting gears at some point. Maybe it's time to pay the Justice League of Sentients a friendly visit, see if they know anything."

"That's definitely on the table. I'd like to be thorough, gather as much information as possible, though, before abandoning this mission."

"That's sensible. I'm all for collecting data. It's not great for morale, though." He released her with a lingering caress over her backside and sat down on the edge of the bed.

"I know. There's nothing I can do about that." She finished knotting the final tie and turned.

"This jump is going to be different though. It's the first time we'll jump into an inhabited system." Her stomach flipped. She was extremely excited about potentially meeting a new species of people. She had to get through the jump first, though, so she shoved that feeling down and put it off for later. Anything could happen between now and then.

He raised his eyebrows. "That makes it more interesting, for sure. But don't get your hopes up. That information is more than seventy years old and we don't exactly know what the hell's going on."

"I'm hoping the Pligans will be able to provide some answers."

"Me too. You going for a walk?" he asked.

"Yes."

"Do you need to be alone, or can I tag along and hold your hand?" He grinned like a schoolboy. Adorable.

She smiled back and cocked her head to one side. "We could try it."

He leapt up and headed for the bath. "Two minute shower," he called over his shoulder.

The wild disorientation of the jump subsided. Jane's eyesight came back into focus, leaving behind the dysphoria of the swirling tube they'd just dropped out of. They'd arrived in the Pligan system, deep in the Kirik Nebula. Here they hoped to find the science vessel *Oblignatus* and its Gubernaviti, Ei'Pio, alive.

This system's star was a red dwarf, one-fifth the size of Earth's sun and far cooler, with only about seventy percent its brightness. As a result, its rocky core planets orbited at a closer distance than Mercury's orbit in relation to the sun back home.

Pliga, the only inhabited planet, was tidally locked with that star, meaning only one side ever faced its sun. One face of the planet was a sheet of ice in eternal night. The other was dotted with small continents and islands, but primarily a vast ocean, and bathed in sunlight without end.

The people of Pliga were descended from arboreal amphibians. They lived at high altitudes in a cloud-forest climate and built their living spaces in and among the treetops, in amazing feats of architecture. To say that Jane was looking forward to making contact was a grand understatement. But first, the *Oblignatus*.

Brai activated the sensors in a dispirited mood.

"I'm picking up a standard identification beacon, Qua'dux," Ryliuk stated.

Brai broke in, now rumbling with excitement. "The *Oblignatus* is in high orbit around Pliga. It appears to be intact."

Jane blinked. "Plot a course that will take us within approximately three vastuumet."

His reply came back nearly instantly. "Course plotted."

The complex equations flowed through her easily now. "Execute." She felt the familiar rumble of the engines, sensed the heat as they flared to life, and they glided through the small system toward Pliga.

The mood on the bridge had changed. Everyone was alert. The mental chatter was lively with speculation.

"Commander, you've found one alive?" Ajaya asked groggily from the sanalabrium.

"It seems so," Jane replied. She felt breathless.

"We're nearly in range for the Squid to make contact," Alan murmured just loud enough for Jane to hear.

"Let's wait until we're closer. Don't strain," Jane told Brai. "Let's make a good first impression."

The icy dark side of Pliga grew larger, blotting out the light of its sun in a partial eclipse. As they drew closer, the outline of a ship roughly the same size and shape as the *Speroancora* passed through the crescent of light to the other side. The *Oblignatus*.

The standard protocol would be a formal hail. But this was far from a standard situation and Jane felt like it called for a personal touch.

Brai vibrated with the need to communicate with Ei'Pio.

"Send her a calm greeting," Jane commanded.

"Scaluuti, Ei'Pio. I am Ei'Brai," he sent, nearly managing what she'd asked.

She was there. Jane could sense her, through Brai. She was reaching out, wordlessly assessing. She sent timid tendrils of thought.

"No!" Ei'Pio cried suddenly. Her mental voice grated with rage and despair.

Jane jumped, startled.

"This is not...this cannot be. How am I to...? This is wrong!" She sounded panicked, out of control, confused.

Brai's voice purred in a soothing tone she hadn't heard from him in some time. "You aren't alone anymore, Ei'Pio. All will be well."

"No. It won't. It will never be well. You should go." Now she sounded cold.

Confused looks passed around the bridge.

"We're just tools. We pass from one hand to the next. It's unending. There's never choice in this matter. It's all dire threats and conditions and pain. There is no hope." Ei'Pio's voice shook, rising and falling through entire ranges of emotion in each short statement.

"There is hope," Brai soothed. "I once felt as you do now. I've seen that it can be different."

"No. No-no-no-no-no-no. No!" Ei'Pio shrieked this last no, then fell silent.

"Perhaps if I—" Ryliuk started to say.

"No. This is not the time," Jane told him.

"I've got a bad feeling about this," Alan said.

Jane joined Brai's connection with Ei'Pio. "Scaluuti, Ei'Pio. I am Jane. Are you injured? We are here to offer assistance."

Ei'Pio surged into her head with potent curiosity. Jane's mind reverberated on an unfamiliar frequency with this new contact. She left her mind open, easily allowing Ei'Pio in. "What are you? You aren't sectilian!"

"I am terran. We call ourselves human."

The *Speroancora* slipped around to the light side of Pliga. Black oceans and white fluffy clouds came into view through a dim gray sky. They fell into a high orbit some distance behind the *Oblignatus* in the same orbital plane, far above the few artificial satellites.

Jane could sense Ei'Pio's bewilderment. The kuboderan was frenetically checking their identification beacon, making mental connections.

"Terran?" Optimism seemed to well up within Ei'Pio as she uttered this word, but then crashed again into despondency. "No. No. It isn't supposed to be this way. They've dropped relay stations all over the galaxy. They'll know you're here by now. You should go. It's not safe."

"We've found the solution to the plague. It's perfectly safe now," Jane said.

"No, you haven't. You haven't got an inkling."

"The humans are different. Look closer, Ei'Pio. Look at me," Brai intoned.

Ei'Pio seemed to be mollified for a moment as she peered into Brai's thoughts.

"Is she insane?" Ron whispered.

Jane carefully disconnected from Ei'Pio. She spoke aloud. "All I can tell for sure is that she's traumatized and terrified."

Jane reconnected with Ei'Pio. "We know that squillae were weaponized against the Sectilius. We fixed that problem. We can give you a crew, a purpose. We can take you home."

There was a long silence as Ei'Pio continued to explore Ei'Brai, mind to mind.

"Should I hail the Pligan government, Qua'dux?" Ryliuk asked.

Jane started to answer Ryliuk, but Ei'Pio ripped her attention away from Brai to accuse Jane. "You have sectilians aboard! You have a mind master! You're not all terran!"

"Two more ships just jumped in at the edge of the system," Alan exclaimed.

Brai was nonplussed, frozen into inaction. "There are two sectilian ships, moving under their own power, heading our way? How can this be possible?"

Ei'Pio scanned the *Speroancora*, searching for something.

"There are no identification beacons on these ships," Ryliuk said.

Jaross turned to look at her. "They're moving quickly, Qua'dux."

Jane's heart began to pound in her ears. "What is happening, Ei'Pio?"

"You don't have a chance," Ei'Pio said frantically. "Your escutcheon is damaged. Jump away, now!"

"Maybe you should do what she says, Doc," Alan whispered.

Jane gritted her teeth. "I have to know what's going on."

Ron looked up from his station. "One of the ships is the same size as us, class four. The other is much bigger."

"Fuck!" Alan yelled. "It's class six. The same kind of ship that destroyed the first three."

A science vessel and a warship. What were they doing here? What did they want? And why was Ei'Pio so scared? Was she afraid of them? Or had she been broken by some other event?

Jane sat up straighter. "The jump engine is still spooling. Prepare for another jump, just in case we have to run. Ron, you may be needed at the weapons station." She pushed herself closer to Ei'Pio. "Please, Ei'Pio. Tell us what we are facing."

But all Ei'Pio would say, her mental voice anguished, was, "An impossible choice."

Jane's mouth was dry.

She was in so far over her head.

Brai was mostly silent, diligently working to get as much intel on their visitors as possible.

The two new ships glided into a parallel orbit on either side of them and paced their velocity. She'd always thought the *Speroancora* was massive. But this new ship, the larger class-six ship, was a leviathan.

Shaped something like a sperm whale, it was, at minimum, twice the length of the *Speroancora* and probably quadruple its bulk. She had to cycle through several exterior-mounted cameras to get a good look at it, because it was too close and too large to get a full view from any single camera.

She kept her voice calm and authoritative. "Is there any way to trace the ballistics residue we found on the first ship to this one?"

"I'm working on that now, Qua'dux," Jaross said, her fingers dancing over the keys of her console.

The two ships moved even closer, hemming them in. Proximity sensors went off. Jane instructed Brai to alter course slightly to a higher altitude. They slipped from between, putting a safer distance between them. It didn't last more than seconds. The two ships immediately matched their original relative positions.

"This is a standard intimidation tactic," Ron said evenly from his new spot at the weapons console.

"It's working," Alan said dryly.

Yes, it was.

The two new ships remained silent. As did the *Oblignatus*.

Jane gritted her teeth so hard her jaw ached. "Are there any identifying marks on either ship that will give us a clue as to who's inside?"

"Yes," Ryliuk said.

But before he could say more, Brai interrupted. "The larger ship is called the *Portacollus*." There was a note of trepidation in his mental voice, and perhaps a shade of familiarity.

The name of the ship translated to "Bring the Mountain." An apt description.

Ryliuk cleared his throat. "Its kuboderan is named Kai'Memna."

Jane asked Brai privately, "Do you know this kuboderan?"

"Only peripherally," Brai answered. "He is known as a bully throughout the fleet. The smaller ship is the *Colocallida*, and its Gubernaviti is Ei'Uba, a known associate of Kai'Memna. A sycophant. They've worked together on several missions."

So the Sectilius had allowed a relationship of sorts to develop between the two. Interesting.

"The second ship is—" Ryliuk said.

"The *Colocallida*," Jane finished for him. "She Who Lives In Cleverness."

"Yes," Ryliuk said, narrowing his eyes at her.

Brai broke in before she could say more. "They are speaking privately with Ei'Pio."

Jane felt a strong urge to interrupt any discussion they might be having about the *Speroancora*.

"Open a hailing channel with the *Portacollus*, Ryliuk."

"Channel is open, Qua'dux."

They passed to the dark side of the planet. Dim light reflected off of one of Pliga's moons, revealing Pliga's far side to be made up of a thick crust of irregular white ice with black ocean all around the edges.

"Scaluuti, Kai'Memna. To what do we owe the pleasure of your company?" Jane spoke crisply and made no attempt to disguise her accent. Ei'Pio had been thrown off by learning she was human. That was the only advantage she had while she figured out what the hell was going on here.

Jane felt a foreign mind searching.

She knew this feeling well—the vibration of an attempt at forging an anipraxic connection. Though this was on a different frequency than either Brai or Ei'Pio had used, the sensation was similar to what she'd first felt with Brai. She grabbed onto it with ferocity. The presence flooded her mind, but she was ready for it. She kept him where she wanted him—kept him from seeing too much. She felt far more cautious now than she had been only thirty minutes before with Ei'Pio.

"Kai'Memna," she said, mind to mind, doing her best to sound unperturbed.

"Who are you?" a voice even deeper than Brai's rumbled in her head. It sounded rich and arrogant and deadly. Then it pitched even lower. "What are you?"

"I am Qua'dux Jane Holloway of the *Speroancora*. I am terran."

Kai'Memna pushed on her barriers, trying to see more. She held firm, though it cost her. In pain.

"How did you come to command this ship?"

Jane considered. Instinct dictated she try to seem as powerful as possible. She was tempted to say she had taken the ship, to imply strength and ruthlessness, but she was afraid that gambit would antagonize the kuboderan or that he would be able to detect the lie. There was an undercurrent here that she couldn't quite grasp. It was far better to be terse and stay as close to the truth as possible. "I have formed a partnership with a kuboderan, Ei'Brai."

"Have you, now?" Switching on a dime, Kai'Memna sought confirmation from Brai, who was protectively watching the conversation.

"This is the truth of it," Brai said imperiously.

This seemed to pique Kai'Memna's curiosity, and he more fully moved his focus to Brai. It was a relief when his mental grip let go, even if it was only momentary. "And your terran pet was unaffected by the squillae plague?" Kai'Memna's tone was wheedling and syrupy sweet.

Jane didn't like it, or him. Her hands curled into fists. "My team eradicated the squillae threat before it became an issue," Jane said calmly, though deep inside she was starting to seethe.

"Oh? None of your terran crew were lost? Intriguing." He sounded almost disappointed.

"Not a single one," Jane said flatly.

Kai'Memna returned to interrogating Brai. "But your terran master still keeps you in sectilian shackles, does she not, little kuba?"

That provoked Brai's ire. "No. In fact, she doesn't," he growled. "I am free of the yoke."

Kai'Memna's thoughts expressed disbelief without words. Then he coughed out a semblance of a laugh. "Why would you serve a terran if you are free? Surely you do not believe the absurd mythos surrounding these people."

Jane was so absorbed in this conversation, the images that flowed lightning fast from Kai'Memna's mind flickering in her head, that she barely registered the physical environment her body was still in until Alan came up beside her and put a hand over hers. She flinched and turned to look at him.

Alan's eyes bored into hers. He whispered, "There are living sectilians on both of those ships, but not on the *Oblignatus*."

She nodded and he returned to his station.

Jane breathed deeply. She'd missed part of the exchange between Kai'Memna and Brai, but there was a lull in the conversation, so she decided to speak. "There are sectilian survivors aboard the *Portacollus*," she stated.

"Indeed there are." Kai'Memna swelled with self-importance. "They serve me."

Jane's heart rose into her throat. Then she saw exactly what he meant and it was worse than she could have imagined. Kai'Memna revealed the reality he had created aboard the *Portacollus*. Most of the sectilians had been killed by the squillae plague, but those who remained were slaves obeying his every order. He'd gotten his revenge on these men and women by flipping the balance of power. He weakened them with the plague and then controlled them with his mind whenever they put up any resistance.

Jane thought she had the whole of it now, but she played dumb. "You turned this tragedy to your benefit, Kai'Memna."

"Tragedy? Tragedy? It was a triumph." He was pleased with himself.

Jane's stomach churned.

"Oh, you are a quick one," he said as he caught an inkling of her revulsion. "It took one weak mind. After centuries of serving my sectilian masters, I found one with the expertise I needed. I used him. The rest was easy. The blueprint for my success was packaged neatly within the historical record of the Sectilius, too ironic not to use. You may have heard of a sectilian named Machinutorus Tarn Elocus Hator who invented the squillae, a ship called the *Percedus*, and their ill-fated experiments on a Swarm pod at Seta Nu Four?"

Jaross gasped and stood, turning to look at Ryliuk with abject horror. Ryliuk also rose, his ears pulled back so starkly his face looked more angular and drawn than she'd ever seen it. Every sectilian and atellan was having the same appalled reaction.

Jane didn't know this story, but she tapped into the memory playing out in Jaross's mind and saw the significance immediately. This was a story taught to sectilian children to remind them that squillae could never be used against another species. They could only be used to support life, never as a weapon against any living thing. Kai'Memna had violated that precept egregiously.

He continued, "Breaking the yoke after that first terrible transgression was a simple matter. And I was free."

"You perpetrated genocide," Jane said, her voice trembling with anger. She shouldn't have let it. It was stupid to let that slip.

Kai'Memna didn't seem to mind. He was enjoying telling his tale. "Merely a blip in population dynamics. This is how evolution works, my dear little terran. The superior survive and thrive by exploiting weaker species. As one of the favored children of the Cunabula, you surely understand this."

Jane didn't reply. He was pressing harder now, pushing deeper into her mind, though she worked hard to keep her barriers in place. Her thoughts slowed to a trickle and pressure built up, making her head feel like it could split in two.

"There is another species evolution favored. Do you know it?" It felt like he was shouting inside her head. "Surely you must. Haven't the Swarm found Terra yet?"

"I know about the Swarm," Jane said defiantly.

"Oh, she knows about them, she says. I can see that. I know about them too, Quasador Dux Jane Holloway." He paused theatrically. "Actually, here's a tidbit of information you might find curious: I *know* them."

"You know them?" Jane asked, her voice smaller than she'd intended it to be. Something in his tone was tripping a deep-seated reservoir of fear. She fought to keep it at bay. She didn't want him to see it.

"I do. As a matter of fact, I've just returned from parleying with the ravenous beasts. No manners, but of course we all know they aren't civilized."

The pain in her head was excruciating. She was barely keeping him closed out. Now she had an inkling of what he was after and Brai was attempting help to shore her up, but it wasn't enough. Kai'Memna was burrowing deeper and deeper into her head, one memory at a time.

She unclipped her harness and stood unsteadily. She couldn't form words aloud without breaking her concentration.

She could *not* break her concentration.

"You communicated with members of the Swarm? I thought that was impossible?" Jane asked and staggered a single step toward Ryliuk.

Brai struggled to help Jane push Kai'Memna back, but Kai'Memna was very effective at blocking his attempts. She swayed.

Alan leapt up to support her, so she didn't fall. "Jane. End this. We need to get the fuck out of here."

Kai'Memna answered smugly, pretending they weren't in the middle of a battle of wills. "I did indeed. No one had ever tried with any real effort before, believing them to be nothing but mammoth mindless insects—which they are, of course, don't get me wrong. I don't believe any Sentient has ever asked a kuboderan to make the attempt. So shortsighted."

Jane didn't doubt it. The sectilian cultural mindset sometimes had blind spots. Humans were no different.

Jane grabbed hold of Ryliuk, who stood staring at her, perplexed, his eyes wide with fear as he listened to Kai'Memna's diatribe.

"What did you tell them, Kai'Memna?" she asked.

Jane pleaded with Ryliuk with her eyes. He didn't understand. He was listening to the ongoing anipraxic conversation, like everyone else, but he didn't know, couldn't see what was happening inside her head. She trembled, her fingers tightening around Ryliuk's beefy arm.

"I told them the location of every single Sentient world in existence. And soon, I'll tell them the location of your world as well."

Brai was also handicapped with the effort, but he managed to send a thought to Ryliuk. "I beg you, Ryliuk, help me keep her safe."

Ryliuk's eyes flared and he locked onto Jane's mind with a ferocious grip, instantly buttressing her mental walls. It took Kai'Memna by surprise. Jane felt immediate relief from the pressure on her mind.

But it was a mistake.

"What is this?" Kai'Memna roared. His rage was unhinged and violent.

Jane could taste blood dripping down from her nose. Her upper lip was wet with it.

Kai'Memna released his grip on Jane and turned his attention to Ryliuk. "A mind master! Here? How many of my kind have you conditioned, you stinking cesspool of air-breathing meat?"

Ryliuk fell to his knees. His fingers fluttered around his neck and chest. He looked like he was choking.

Jane fell with him. "Stop it! What are you doing to him?"

"Punishing him!" Kai'Memna bellowed.

Brai spoke urgently. "He's attacking Ryliuk's autonomic nervous system—preventing him from breathing, possibly arresting his heart."

Ron pushed Ryliuk flat to the floor and began CPR. Schlewan went for a stretcher.

Alan grabbed Jane's shoulder. "He's force-choking him, Jane. It's time to go!"

Jaross hunched over her station. "The two ships have moved in even closer, less than one vastuumet."

"Brai, prepare to jump on my mark, to the next coordinates in the sequence." She wanted to give him some random number, far, far from here, but she didn't think she could stay conscious through a long jump.

Brai went to work swiftly. "Preparing jump sequence, Qua'dux."

Kai'Memna abruptly released Ryliuk, leaving him gasping and choking on the floor like a fish out of water. He would live.

"Oh, no, little kuba. You aren't going anywhere. We are going to have words."

Jane stumbled to the command chair. Everything began to feel very far away. Something was wrong. The bridge seemed to heave and reel around her. She sat there blinking, trying to get her bearings.

Faintly she heard Alan roar, "Oh, this is a clusterfuck!"

Then she realized what it was. Brai was receding under Kai'Memna's onslaught.

"So your terran Qua'dux has given you your freedom, has she? You don't know what freedom is. Haven't the decades of solitary confinement without recourse shown you that? You didn't break free on your own. She deigned to remove your chains, but has she removed your cage? Have you felt the rush of real current? Have you tasted the actual flesh of fish?"

Brai didn't reply.

"Do you not tire of the daily dose of bland chow? Come now, little kuba. You know you were meant for more."

Schlewan and Tinor got Ryliuk off the bridge and on the way to the medical facility to be checked, but Jane knew there was nowhere safe on this ship for Ryliuk if Kai'Memna decided to crush him. He could turn his brain like a screw and ruin him on a whim. She couldn't protect him from that. It was terrifying.

Ron had returned to his console. "The *Colocallida* is moving off."

Jaross added, "The *Colocallida* is spooling up in preparation for a jump."

It hit Jane like a brick to the head. The *Colocallida* was going to go tell the Swarm where Earth was. Kai'Memna had wriggled it out of her brain somehow. She started to tremble violently.

Kai'Memna was treating Brai to a sequence of images, glimpses of what wild life was like. Capturing prey, swimming free in a vast ocean. It was visceral and savage.

And she knew any kuboderan would find it compelling.

Kai'Memna cajoled, "I have experienced these things. I have lived fully, without restriction, as all of the Kubodera should. You can too, if you join me. Live free, Ei'Brai. Join me."

Jane reached out to Brai. "Brai, report status on the jump sequence."

He either couldn't hear or couldn't respond. He was paralyzed, just as she had been.

She refused to doubt him. He wouldn't sacrifice them. She wouldn't believe that could happen.

They passed once again to the light side of Pliga.

Kai'Memna's voice still thundered in the back of her mind, persuasively telling Brai about the power he could have, the wonderful life he could lead if he joined Kai'Memna. And if he declined, his fate would be the same as the first three kuboderans they'd found.

Jane knew Brai wouldn't do it. He wouldn't condone killing on that scale, no matter the cause. They had to find another way out.

Everything had spiraled out of control in just a few minutes. She had to stop Kai'Memna. She had to stop the *Colocallida* from getting to the Swarm.

How could she?

If she could just disrupt...

"Alan!" Jane leapt from the command chair and grabbed Alan's arm. She spoke English, pouring words out in a rush. "Go to your quarters and get the EM field generator. If we can obstruct Kai'Memna's signal for even a minute, we should be able to jump."

He nodded. "I'll have to boost the power to increase the range, but it should work. Give me a few minutes." He dashed off.

"This isn't a true choice," Brai told Kai'Memna.

There were probably only seconds left to stop the *Colocallida* from jumping.

Jane strode to the weapons station. She leaned over Ron, rapidly flipping switches and pulling up a schematic. Ron moved out of her way and watched her intently. She knew the weakest points on the *Colocallida* because they were the weakest points of her own ship. She pinned three targets on three precise locations on the other ship—one of which should breach their Tech Deck and hopefully disrupt the jump drive.

Brai continued to attempt to reason with Kai'Memna. "What will happen when the Swarm have devoured all the Sentient worlds and turn on the Kubodera?"

She hesitated for a split second. There were lives on that ship. But compared to an entire world of millions of people with no defenses...

The stars started to smudge in front of the *Colocallida*.

She fired three missiles in rapid succession and slid over to the laser controls.

"Prepare three more missiles," she barked.

Ron bent over the console.

Jane looked up. The *Colocallida* wasn't blowing up, but it wasn't jumping either. She'd definitely done some damage. There were three gaping holes in the hull. The stars receded back into points of light.

Jaross called out, "The *Colocallida*'s jump drive has powered down, Qua'dux."

Brai was talking about her. About all the humans. Telling Kai'Memna how different humans were from the Sectilius. How they treated him as an equal instead of a servant. How they'd rescued him. How the terrans might be the true weapon against the Swarm that the entire galaxy had been waiting for. "To send Jane Augusta Holloway into dusk is to send hope for peace and unity there as well," he said.

Jane had disrupted a lot of neural-electric pathways with those missiles. The *Colocallida* wasn't going anywhere. But it could still fire on the *Speroancora*. Surely it would at any moment.

Brai had told her repeatedly that the escutcheon had been weakened. It would take at least a year to make enough squillae to replenish it and make it strong enough to protect the ship against severe external damage.

"Murder is not the solution," Brai said.

Jane wiped fresh blood from under her nose and turned to Ron. "The lasers take a few moments to recharge. You'll only get one good burst. If they open their missile bays, blast them before they can fire." She pointed at the schematic, smearing it with blood. He nodded and eased back into place.

She moved on to the emergency navigation console, leaving bloody fingerprints everywhere she touched. The irony wasn't lost on her. She could move the ship, at least a little, without Brai. Her fingers knew where to touch practically without looking. Just fractions of a vastuumet were all she needed. It took seconds.

The *Speroancora* changed course, shifting in her orbit to take up a spot in the shadow of the *Portacollus*, just beyond the *Colocallida*'s reach. Somehow they had to disable the *Portacollus* too—

Brai and Kai'Memna winked out of her head. She staggered. Alan's device had disrupted the all anipraxic communication between Brai and anyone else.

Then she fell to the floor, Kai'Memna pounding relentlessly on her brain in retaliation for what she had done to the *Colocallida*.

Darkness pushed in on her vision.

The deck transport opened almost instantly, but it wasn't fast enough. Alan raced down the corridor, berating himself the whole way. He'd stood there, watching something happening to Jane. He hadn't been sure what was going on at first. All he could think about was that they needed to just leave. But even when he figured out that he was watching an evil squid crushing her brain, the device hadn't even occurred to him.

Why? Because he was fucking selfish. The only reason he'd ever set it up was to be alone. And later, it was perfect for having Jane all to himself. He'd never thought about how it could have other applications. He was a fool.

But not Jane.

He would have thought of it just a few seconds later. He would have. He was sure.

He ran headlong to his door and hopped in place, cursing, while it took a split second to open. Then he was crashing around his place, searching for a suitable power supply. He needed something that could create enough voltage so that he could have a hope in hell of stopping that cretinous squid from hurting Jane or Brai.

Sectilian engineering was pretty conservative with power. Most devices were designed to operate at low voltage. He picked up one, then another, examining the symbols on the sides, trying to find one that might work.

He heard a deep rumbling sound and then a high-pitched whine. He paused for a second, wondering what that had been. Then he realized. Jane was shooting up the aliens. Shit.

He was about to give up and head down to Tech Deck, where he would have the opposite problem, when he remembered a device Schlewan had asked him to fix. It had been low priority because there were duplicates on board. He pulled it out of a low drawer protruding from the wall. It was some kind of portable medical scanner and had an outrageous power supply. That would do it. He pried off the housing and separated the components. He threw the power supply in the bag he'd brought from Earth along with a few tools to deal with the wiring and was off again.

The Squid had a habit of hanging out in a spot that wasn't far from the bridge. He had a workstation there. Though he was connected with the ship cybernetically, it contained monitors and other equipment he used. Alan headed there.

When he arrived Brai was where he expected to find him. All his creepy legs were curled up tight around his head with those wicked sharp hooks sticking out. Brai looked damn prickly and pretty damn scary, honestly. He didn't seem to notice that Alan was there.

The monitors that lined the opposite wall of the tank were displaying various views outside and inside the ship. One showed Kai'Memna's ship, Kai'Memna's sidekick's ship, and the disabled ship they'd found when they arrived. Another showed the bridge, and though Alan's view was distorted through the transparent barrier plus water, he could make out Jane, which was reassuring. She was hovering over the weapons controls next to Ron.

So it was a shooting match now? There was no way they could outgun that class-six ship. They needed to get away—and to do that, they needed the Squid.

He dropped to his knees, dumped the contents of his bag on the floor, and got to work on assembling the device. Inside his head, he could hear the Squid making a case for humanity. He was arguing that Jane could change things, that humanity would soon be accepted into the galactic Hall of Justice or whatever and they wouldn't stand for the way the kuboderans had been treated.

He made the last connection between the magnetron and the power supply and frowned. Either Brai had a very high opinion of humans or he was bullshitting to stall for time. Whatever he was doing, it was working.

Alan turned his contraption toward Ei'Brai and flipped on the device. He was starting at a low voltage because he wasn't sure how this was going to work, having never tested it with this power source before. He didn't know exactly how much juice this power supply could give.

For him, the voices in his head went silent, but he couldn't be sure how far the electromagnetic field would penetrate. He looked up to see if it was having any effect on Brai.

At that moment Brai seemed to notice he was there. In the blink of an eye the Squid rushed him. His body ballooned up to twice its size. His legs flew out wide. Suddenly he was huge and he was slamming into the glass.

Alan scrambled back.

Damn it.

The Squid was freaking the fuck out.

He stood up, putting up his hands, then gestured at the device.

Brai's eyes were wild and rolling around, and his tentacles were thrashing all over the place. He kept crashing into the barrier.

Alan guessed the field wasn't strong enough. He squatted next to it and turned it up.

Brai kept writhing and twisting and bumping against the glass.

Alan gave it more juice, but now he was getting worried. This was probably not a good idea. He wasn't sure if the little transducer he'd originally stuck on the magnetron could handle this kind of load. Even the switch was getting hot to the touch.

But that seemed to do it. The Squid went quiet and finally showed signs that he recognized Alan. Then Brai swam back over to his station and started working. Hopefully he was getting them the fuck out of here.

Alan glanced at the screens inside the tank. They'd changed course. They were below the big ship now. Then he looked at the bridge and saw Jane falling to the floor. He took a step toward the tank to try to see what was going on.

Shit.

If he'd known something like this was going to happen, he'd have made a dozen of these devices. The range was just too small to protect both Jane and Brai at the same time.

Then he smelled it—the smell every engineer knows and hates—burning, hot, metallic, and waxy.

The transducer was fried.

But Jane was getting up. She was okay. Something was happening. He squinted. He saw movement on the screen, but the smell was getting stronger. He had to turn the device off. He'd try to wait until the last possible second, to give Brai enough time.

He pivoted to see smoke pouring out of the device. He reached for it. It popped with a flash of light. The magnetron was still going full tilt.

Every time he got his hand anywhere near it, electricity arced and he barely missed getting electrocuted.

Then it got worse.

53

Like an aperture, Jane's vision opened again.

Kai'Memna had taken leave of her.

Brai was out of reach. She was alone in her own head, which felt like it was splitting in two. Alan must have gotten the device working. Was it able to reach so far that it could protect her too?

She heard Ron mumbling under his breath and struggled to make sense of it. She grabbed the nearest console and pulled herself up until she could see what had captured Ron's and Jaross's attention.

She couldn't believe what she saw. She blinked. Was she seeing double because Kai'Memna had been messing around in her head?

No...

She was seeing the *Oblignatus* and the *Colocallida* together. The *Oblignatus* had moved. Ei'Pio was not locked into orbit around Pliga as Jane had assumed.

And that wasn't the most astounding thing. Ei'Pio had docked her ship with the *Colocallida,* as one would to transfer cargo in space. It looked like an absurd mating ritual, the ships stacked on top of each other with dark space above them and the pale gray skies of Pliga below.

Ei'Pio was moving both ships, using the momentum of their orbit, effectively changing their course and aiming the *Colocallida* at the *Portacollus*—she'd hijacked the disabled ship and was using it like a massive projectile.

It was happening fast. The ships had started out too close together. It seemed like the *Portacollus* was correcting course, but its size made it lumbering and slow.

A fresh surge of adrenaline hit Jane with a jolt. She lurched for the emergency navigation controls to try to move them out of the path of this juggernaut.

Seconds ticked by in a blur as she worked.

She fired thrusters to starboard to push them up toward Pliga's nearest pole. They were moving, but not fast enough. She needed Brai to calculate the most precise trajectory. She had none of his expertise in this.

The *Colocallida* rammed the *Portacollus*, pieces of both hulls crumbling off and scattering wildly in every direction, fueled by the energy behind the impact. The hammerhead of the *Colocallida* crumpled as it plowed into the side of Kai'Memna's now-ruined ship.

Ei'Pio's ship scraped over the top and released the *Colocallida*, moving away from the smashed ships. Jane couldn't tell how damaged the *Oblignatus* was, if at all, after that maneuver, but the *Portacollus* was little more than wreckage. Already, shards of ice were forming like spikes around the point of impact, and more bubbled around the edges. Kai'Memna's habitat had been compromised. Surely he wouldn't survive that for long.

There was an explosion—but not outside, not on the screen. The decking shook under her feet. It had been inside the *Speroancora*.

What?

Brai popped back into her head, broadcasting a level of panic she'd never felt from him before.

Shreds of debris streamed toward them.

"Jane! We've got a problem!" Alan shouted over the anipraxic network. He was running.

Kai'Memna's voice raged incoherently again, but it was weaker and fading.

Jane felt numb. There was too much happening at once. She wasn't sure what to do next. She stared dumbly at the viewscreen in horror as large pieces of the broken ships headed right for them. And without a fully functional escutcheon...

She snapped out of her daze, hunching over the emergency navigation console, frantically trying to correct their course to avoid the debris storm, to increase speed, anything. "Brai, help me move the ship!"

He responded sluggishly, locked into some kind of chaos of his own and possibly hurt. Jane didn't know.

Then she did know.

Alan's EM-field generator had worked to sever the anipraxic link with Kai'Memna, but required massive amounts of power to make a field big enough to do the job. He'd had to make do with the first power supply he could cobble together, and it couldn't take the load. It had exploded next to Brai's enclosure, creating a massive crack in the surface that quickly turned into a fissure. The structure was weakening under the pressure of the volume of water it contained. The entire central core of the ship was going to flood.

Brai assessed the trajectory of the wreckage and plotted a course to take them out of the path of the worst of it.

It was too late. They couldn't move fast enough to dodge all of the debris. It slammed into them.

Jane was hurled across the bridge and landed with a thud against a wall. She blacked out for a few seconds.

She lifted her head. Everything hurt. She was stiff. Moving was hard. On the viewscreen it was clear they were plummeting toward Pliga.

"Brai…"

The water in his tank was sloshing and rotating in a great whirlpool. He was fighting against this swirling current while trying to regain control of the ship.

Heat built up on the outer hull.

They'd passed to the dark side of Pliga at some point. They were going to crash into the white ice of that massive glacier.

She had saved Earth. That was something. But the rest of the Sentients… No one knew. No one knew what was coming.

Brai grappled with the failing controls, but his reaction times were lethargic. They'd taken too much damage. He wouldn't be able to regain altitude. How could they survive this?

The decking shuddered under her feet. The exterior of the ship glowed with heat. The beautiful extrusions were peeling off.

Jane reached out to Ei'Pio. It was imperative that someone take the news where it could make a difference. "Ei'Pio, you must jump to Terac and tell the Unified Sentients what Kai'Memna was planning."

Ei'Pio was despondent. "What can I do to save you?"

"Tell them. Make them listen to you. You're the only one who knows."

"They'll never listen to me. You must survive."

A calm settled over Jane. She stood, swaying, focusing all her mental energy to help Brai concentrate on finding solutions and to route his navigation properly.

The *Speroancora* crossed over to the light side of Pliga. The *Oblignatus* pulled alongside them. Jane had no idea what Ei'Pio was trying to do now, but it seemed suicidal.

With what little control he had left, Brai steered away from landmasses toward the clearest area in the planet's ocean within reach.

Alan burst onto the bridge.

"Everyone strap in and brace yourselves!" Jane shouted over the roar of atmospheric entry. The ship felt like it was shaking apart around them.

She stumbled a few steps to fall into the nearest seat and fumbled with the restraints. Everyone else did the same. All she could do was watch the viewscreen and hope they could somehow survive this.

Brai's habitat had been fouled. His life support was no longer functioning and the explosion had dumped great caches of food and filtered wastes into the water.

He was being poisoned. His mental voice was quieting, his ability to create anipraxia fading, his movements slowing.

Impact.

Jane's body slammed against the restraining straps. More pain.

They skimmed the surface, their velocity reducing marginally. Pieces of the ship continued to break off. Then they went under. The vibration ceased, but they were still moving at an incredible rate, with the *Oblignatus* right behind them.

Jane was still alive, and as long as she was still alive, there was hope. "Jaross, assess the hull integrity. Seal off any decks or deck sections that are taking on water or that are vulnerable."

"Yes, Qua'dux," Jaross replied, still calm and focused.

Jane unlatched herself and went to one of the science consoles to assess the water quality of Pliga's ocean. She frowned. It was significantly less saline than the water in Brai's tank, by three-quarters of a percent. Most of Pliga's land mass was tied up in ice. And though the planet was extremely old, few minerals and salts had leached into the oceans.

She hoped Brai could handle the shock. And the foreign microbes. And any predators that might be present. He had the squillae to help him fight.

There was one significant problem. Only one external portal led to the outside from Brai's habitat. Normally used only for installing a new kuboderan into a ship, it was well above the waterline inside his tank now. She'd have to take drastic measures.

Her head throbbed. Her whole body ached. She straightened wearily and turned to leave the bridge. "Jaross, take over communication. Anipraxia is offline. We'll use ship's comms now."

"What are you doing, Jane?" Alan asked.

"Brai is dying. I'm going to try to save him."

"Jane, we're going to be crushed by several atmospheres of ocean in no time. It won't matter. We're all dead."

"No. No. We're not dead yet." She marched into the corridor outside the bridge. He followed. She located one of several suits of battle armor stored nearby and stripped.

Alan wordlessly did the same.

As he peeled off his shirt she noticed the blood. The burns. He was hurt. "Alan, stop. You need medical attention."

His jaw was set. "No. It's minimal. The suit will handle it."

She nodded. Wasn't she doing the same thing? "This is risky. Sectilian power armor isn't made for use underwater. I don't know if this will work, but I have to try."

He nodded. "NASA tests their suits underwater. It should."

The suit threaded and adjusted to her anatomy then went straight into triage mode. Immediately she felt a little better. She took off at a run for the nearest maintenance storage locker. Alan followed. She pulled a laser cutting arc out of the locker and looked at him. "You don't have to go with me."

He looked grim. "I'm going."

She felt a surge of gratitude that he would follow her into this without hesitation. He had her back. She could count on him no matter what. That meant so much.

She handed him the tool then took out another for herself.

She repeated, "Hang on Brai," in a mantra over the failing anipraxic link.

Brai had made his way to the spot farthest from the breach. He didn't have the energy to do anything but acknowledge that she'd communicated with him. He was still monitoring the ship. Their velocity had been slowed a great deal by the density of Pliga's ocean. They were drifting now, momentum pushing them forward, gravity pulling them down. The weight of the ocean overhead would start crushing them in a matter of hours as they sank deeper.

She took off with Alan for the exterior hatch nearest Brai's current location. When they stepped into the deck transport, the ship lurched again. The heavy suits barely kept them on their feet.

Alan looked at her, wide-eyed. "We landed on something. Let's hope it's something that will hold."

Jane triggered the comm in her suit to signal the bridge and waited for Jaross to respond.

"I'm here, Qua'dux," Jaross said.

"Report," Jane replied.

"You aren't going to believe this, QD," Ron said. "The *Oblignatus* just put itself under us to keep us from falling to the ocean floor. No idea how she's doing it."

"Holy shit," Alan muttered. "That squid is fucking crazy!"

They left the deck transport and Jane sealed off the rest of the deck. The ship creaked and groaned around them as they jogged to the door that led to Brai's enclosure. Jane triggered the control and stepped out onto the gangway. Water was rising quickly in this intermediary space, spilling out of Brai's habitat to fill it. She could see reflected light on the churning surface of it under their feet.

Brai was hovering on the other side of the partition, his body anchored to the glass with suction cups. The water around him was dim and cloudy. His mantle fluttered in a way that looked strange and filled her with fear. His eyes stared dully back at her, but he was alive. Great bubbles of air billowed up in the tank behind him. There was only a few feet of water over his head.

Alan waved to Brai awkwardly. "Hello, again. Sorry about the explosion."

"I'm not sure how this is going to work," Jane admitted. She was getting fuzzy from fatigue and being tossed around so much. She triggered a dose of stimulant in the suit.

Alan said, "We open the nearest hatch. Hold on while the water rushes in. We'll have to wait until the pressure equalizes and fills up this space before we can cut him out."

Jane blinked hard as the stimulant started to kick in. "Okay. That makes sense. The cutting tools will work underwater?"

"Yes," he said with certainty.

The hatch wasn't far away. They left the tank behind and ran down a nearby corridor until they reached it.

Alan's helmet went up over his head and he found a cantilever to hold onto projecting from the textured wall about ten feet from the hatch. He was ready.

"Put your suit in battle mode," Jane said while activating that function on her own suit. It would protect them better that way.

She triggered the hatch control and leapt for her own wall shelf to hold onto as the iris opened. Water gushed violently into the corridor, coursing into every corner, churning and splashing up the walls. It quickly found its way into the core of the ship.

The suit held on for her, locked in a death grip as the water swirled, trying to pull her body into its powerful current.

She made an effort to relax inside the suit, to save her energy. Who knew what challenge would come up in the next minute, the next hour, the next day? She had to stay calm or she wouldn't be able to keep them alive.

It seemed to take forever for the core to fill. She waited, watching the crystal-clear water rise, and tried not to think about what might happen if all this water filled the entire ship. That led to thoughts of her father, and she just couldn't think about that now. Instead she watched a few small fish, pulled in with the rush of water, dart around the corridor.

She could still feel Brai's presence clinging to the transparent wall just a few yards away. "Stay with me," Jane told him. "I'm coming for you." He didn't even acknowledge that she'd said anything.

As the water finally rose to the level of the hatch, Ron's voice came back over the comm. "It looks like the *Obligna-tus* is pushing us toward a continental shelf."

Relief flooded through her as she let go of the shelf jutting from the wall and sank to the floor of the corridor. Alan was on her heels.

The suit had no trouble walking through the water. She went carefully though, so an eddy wouldn't catch her off guard and sweep her off her feet.

They made their way back to Brai's tank. In this space the water was just up to the armpits of her suit and still rising. Inside Brai's enclosure the level was just a little higher. Jane urged Brai to move back so they could cut into the wall and get him out. He was slow to respond, but did as she asked.

Jane activated her laser arc and began to cut three feet below the waterline, near the base of the gangway. Alan watched for a second, then joined her in cutting. Together they sliced into the clear material, creating an opening that would be about six feet in diameter, though Brai wouldn't have any trouble getting through a smaller one. When they cut above the waterline on their side, water sizzled and spit as it passed through the laser.

They stood well away and made the final cuts. The piece of transparent material burst away in a sluice of water. Now that the water was rising from two sources, it quickly rose above the level of the hole they'd cut.

Brai seemed confused. Jane coaxed him toward the opening but he held back. Jane leaned through to reach for him—slowly, slowly—she was afraid he would bolt. She wasn't sure he recognized what she was doing or even who she was.

He didn't seem to be looking at her anymore. His eyes were unfocused. She gently laid her hand flat against one of his arms. He didn't move away. She grabbed that arm and pulled him toward her. He didn't resist, but his suction cups dragged over the smooth, transparent material the tank was made from.

Carefully, she maneuvered him toward the hole. Now the problem was to get him through. She was glad for the protection of the suit as she scooped up several of his barbed arms. She eased them out carefully so she wouldn't injure his soft body on the cut edge of the tank.

Alan quickly added his two hands to the job, pulling one of Brai's limp tentacles through before it scraped over the lip they'd cut. "This has got to be one of the weirdest things I've ever done," he said.

Jane didn't answer. Brai's mantle continued to flutter. He wasn't breathing properly. The bad water was pouring out of the tank, contaminating the immediate area.

"Let's take him closer to the hatch," Jane said over the comm.

She carried Brai's head and Alan walked behind, supporting his limbs so Brai's hooklike barbs wouldn't catch on the grates.

When they got to the corridor, Jane closed the door between them and Brai's domain so the dirty water wouldn't flow into this space. She was surprised the door still worked.

As they neared the hatch, she thought she started to feel a little more tension developing in Brai's mantle. He jerked in her arms a couple of times as he filled his mantle and expelled clouds of dirty water. She let him go, flinging her arms wide so he wouldn't hook on her suit. Alan did the same.

Brai darted a few feet away, his mantle billowing out, pulling in copious amounts of clean water and expelling it again. His limbs fanned out and then elongated in a mesmerizing, rhythmic dance. She could feel his mental presence strengthening.

He turned his body, focusing on her, then drifted toward her, raising one tentacle to curve over the face shield. She placed her hand gently over it.

"I owe you a great debt, Qua'dux Jane Holloway," he said gravely.

She smiled. "You don't owe me anything, Brai. How do you feel?"

"I am well. This water is extraordinary. It is a cacophony of flavors." His voice wavered with an element of wonder.

"I'm sure it's very different than what you're accustomed to," Jane said. She marveled at how close she was to him now. Still technically separated, but able to touch him.

Brai regarded Alan. "I also owe you a debt of gratitude, Dr. Alan Bergen."

Alan frowned. "No problem, buddy. I'm sorry I blew up your...home."

Brai didn't reply. He dropped his tentacle and jetted to the hatch to peer out into the open ocean. The terrain beyond the hatch was dark, but he would be able to see in that dark far better than she could.

"We're moving," he said. He sounded surprised.

Ron's voice came over the comm. "You might want to hold on to something, guys. I think we're about to be dropped off."

"Ei'Pio?" Brai said. And then the anipraxic network was fully back in place. Now Ei'Pio was a part of the circle.

Jane could feel Ei'Pio's determination as she worked calculations to make the *Oblignatus* do things that no spacefaring ship was meant to do.

The decking tilted under Jane's feet. She slid to the nearest wall and grabbed on to a boxy ledge. Alan tumbled into her, grumbling swear words, then righted himself and clung to one nearby. Brai jetted to the center of the corridor. Fish darted around him, unaware that he was a predator. He watched them in sheer fascination, barely noting the ship's movement.

The ship swayed, making ominous creaking noises. A loud, metallic scraping sound thundered through the ship. The ship shuddered, vibrated, and finally came to rest.

Jane settled back on her feet and reached out to Alan, putting her gloved hand in his. It wasn't the same as holding his hand had been just a few hours before, but that didn't matter. She held his gaze. He looked back at her, shaking his head in incredulity. She wished she could kiss him, to celebrate that they'd survived this.

They were alive and relatively safe, for now. They were together. That was what was important.

Brai watched Alan and Jane for a moment. Their thoughts were full of warmth and a hunger to touch. He knew he was intruding on something they both felt was private, but it was hard to tear his gaze from this thing they shared. He wanted to understand it.

Ei'Pio watched through Brai's eyes, her curiosity rivaling his own. "These terrans are quite different," she said to him.

"Indeed they are." He turned away, suddenly distracted, his eye tracking an unwary fish darting nearby. It was so close he could—

Instinctively, his tentacles shot out and grabbed it. It flailed in his grasp, but he didn't let it go. He brought the squirming fish to his beak as though this was something he'd always known to do—like muscle memory, but older, deeper. Once he had it there, though, he hesitated.

Ei'Pio watched, breathlessly. There was a note of yearning in her mental touch. She urged him to continue, wordlessly.

The Sectilius thought consuming flesh was disgusting. Was it? Was he a savage because he yearned for his natural diet? Was he like Kai'Memna? Or could he be forgiven for this sin? Was it even a sin? The terrans were carnivores, he knew. They craved flesh and were not ashamed of that.

The fish struggled in his grasp. It was slippery, but he had a good grip on it.

He could let it go. He hadn't injured it yet.

However, he was hungry and perforce must be practical. He would have to feed his body. His food stores had been destroyed. Eventually need would make this act inevitable. It might as well be done now.

He sank his beak into it. The fish twitched once more and its life was gone. He devoured the fish because wasting it, after taking its life, would be profligate. He recoiled against the crunching of bones and the metallic tinge of blood in the water around him. He'd never considered these aspects when he'd fantasized of consuming wild food.

The flesh was fairly flavorless. That was all he could say. It was underwhelming in one sense because he'd given the moment so much gravitas over a lifetime of fantasies. He supposed that he'd expected something more dramatic from his first taste of flesh. But that was the way of things. One cannot anticipate what a moment will truly be like until it arrives.

Ei'Pio absorbed all of this silently. He let her see it. She'd earned his trust.

That need satisfied, his thoughts naturally turned toward the open hatch and the freedom of the open ocean on the other side of it. He found himself peering through the opening into the shadowy depths, though the words of Kai'Memna had tainted the desire and made it feel wrong somehow. Cold whispers of current caressed him through the portal, enticing him. He allowed two limbs to traverse the threshold, tasting the open water. Then, a third.

450

"Go ahead, Brai," Jane said. She'd come to stand beside him.

Something in his ocular implant caught his attention. The sensors he monitored relayed new information. He turned slightly toward her. "I'm tracking a small group of Pligan aquatic vessels en route, Jane. They will arrive within a standard day."

She smiled. "This is good news." There was an urge to touch him in her mind. Humans were rife with these impulses. Touch grounded them.

He was intrigued by that. He extended a tentacle to her. She met it and wrapped her hand around the circumference of it. Her touch was firm, but gentle. In turn, he allowed his limb to wind around her arm. She squeezed. He squeezed in return. She let go and he reciprocated. This was not a bad feeling. It mirrored her warm thoughts.

"You truly do not object?" he asked, returning to survey the view on the other side of the hatch.

"Just be careful."

He hesitated. It could be dangerous. He did not know if there were large predators in this sea. But he longed to test the freedom Kai'Memna had spoken so convincingly of, that he himself had long dreamed of.

"Less dangerous if there are two," Ei'Pio said, her voice full of excitement and promise.

Brai blanched. He hadn't allowed himself to consider this possibility.

Communing with another kuboderan mind to mind was a joy. But to physically inhabit the same spaces... He wasn't sure he would know how to behave.

"What have we left to fear?" she asked. "Have we not been stripped already of everything we have come to hold dear? What better way to start a new life?"

He considered that. He could find no fault with the argument.

"Opening exterior portal. Flooding portal corridor," Ei'Pio said.

"I'll be with you," Jane said, and moved away.

He slipped outside.

His hearts hammered out of sync. This place was so big, so open. He fought down a whirling sense of panic and turned his body to refocus on the ship, to see his centuries-long home for the first time from the outside with his own eyes.

Esthetically, the *Speroancora* looked stripped down and more streamlined. It was badly damaged, but not irreparably, he thought. The solar arrays had taken the worst of the punishment. Some had been lost when they passed through the atmosphere, the rest when they violently collided with the ocean, particularly on the lower surfaces. The ship wasn't engineered to do any of those things. But it had held together.

Without the swooping solar arrays, power generation could have become a problem if they'd been housing a large crew. Thankfully, they weren't, and stored power should outlast their needs.

He jetted up to get a better view. It made him more vulnerable to predators, but his eyesight was good and aside from more of the small fish, some soft jelly creatures, and an abundance of plankton, he didn't see anything else in the immediate vicinity.

A thermal caught him, pushing him off course. He countered instinctively by redirecting his funnel and pumping harder. He was able to end up where he wanted to be without too much trouble.

The water was so…alive. There was no other word for it. He never could have imagined it would be so dynamic. There were a million points of perception pounding on his senses, begging to be noticed. The flavors in the water, the temperature changes, the swirling current. Kai'Memna had been right. This was living. This was more real than anything he'd ever felt.

He darted up a bit more, turning and sweeping a look in all directions. It made him feel a little woozy, but it was also intoxicating. He could make a life here. He could imagine himself exploring these depths for…he couldn't even imagine how long. He could reign as king of these seas. Who would begrudge him that?

He reached a height where he could see the other ship. It was in better shape, having descended into the atmosphere at a less perilous velocity and broken through the water in a more cautious manner.

He let a slow updraft push him vertically a little more through the cold, inky water. Ei'Pio came into sight, her silvery skin reflecting what little light was available. She hovered just outside the exterior portal of the *Oblignatus*, her limbs pulled into a tight point, presumably so she could bolt back inside if she needed to.

She guarded her thoughts, just as he was doing, but nothing could stop her body from displaying the most primitive of signals, even if it was briefly—an intermittent flash of the fuchsia of fear, the cobalt flicker that broadcasted alarm to others of their kind. He had no doubt he'd been doing the same.

She was the first live kuboderan he'd seen since he'd been a paralarva. Part of him wanted to rush over just to look at her, except that he also felt a strong urge to hide, to put off what was surely an inevitable meeting until some of the newness of this place had become customary.

But now that she'd seen him, it was too late for that.

"Is it safe?" she asked.

"I've yet to observe anything perturbing," he answered.

Yet she still flashed her fear and doubt, hesitating at the mouth of the portal she'd just come out of. He wanted to reassure her.

They were two members of a ferocious race that had been tamed so deeply that leaving their cages induced fear. Kai'Memna had been right to be angry. But had he needed to commit genocide in order to free their people? Perhaps there'd been no other effective course of action, but Kai'Memna had gone too far. What he'd done next had compounded the mistake. He hadn't allowed the kuboderans he freed to choose their own way—he'd merely conscripted them for another evil coalition or killed them.

For the first time Brai wondered where the rest of those kuboderans had gone, how many Kai'Memna had managed to recruit. Perhaps Ei'Pio knew.

He looked down on her again, but found she'd retreated inside her ship. He immediately glanced around, searching for large predators. Finding none, he asked, "Why have you withdrawn?"

"You're angry," she replied warily.

He ground his beak. He'd just displayed his emotions for her without the context of his thoughts. It was a very bad impression to make. He'd been rude. He opened up to her, so she could see his chagrin. "I was thinking of Kai'Memna," he said simply.

She accepted that truth and emerged again, but hovered near the portal.

He moved closer, presenting the red of friendship. "Did he injure you?"

Ei'Pio lit up crimson for the briefest moment. "There have been many hurts." She did not elaborate. Her thoughts were still reserved, but she surged toward him a short distance.

He drifted down over the far side of the *Speroancora*, closing the gap between them. Jane was with him in his mind, watching, urging him on. "We have stopped him from perpetrating evil on anyone else. He has met dusk."

"We've stopped him, but not his evil," she said gravely and she pushed up slightly.

The threat of the Swarm. He sobered. "We will find a way."

"There are occasions when there is no way." Her mental voice broke. She turned and seemed to consider returning to her sanctuary.

He waited silently, still floating down without any thrust. "That may be true, but if there is a way, Qua'dux Jane Holloway will find it. She is determined."

"I would like to know this terran better," Ei'Pio said, turning back to face him. She let him see that Jane's tenacity in the face of Kai'Memna's aggression had galvanized her own resolve to fight him. That had saved them all.

"You will."

Ei'Pio shot up like a projectile to within an arm's length of him.

He went motionless. They stared at each other.

She was slightly larger than him. Her limbs were longer and thinner as well. That could mean she was older or that there was sexual dimorphism in their species that favored larger females. How strange that he didn't know.

Her eyes were dark and luminous, full of loss, taking him in. He did the same, opening his thoughts to her more, so she could see that he found her to be beautiful.

She was as fluid as the liquid they were immersed in. He was mesmerized by her diaphanous fins, undulating in waves to keep her steady in the column of water. Her limbs moved in helixes and coils, in quicksilver glints, as they shifted delicately around her body.

He felt stubby and clunky by comparison. That amused her, but not in an unflattering way. She found him dear.

He drew closer and she didn't move away.

Jane's tender touch earlier was on his mind. Ei'Pio saw that and liked it. Her mantle filled. Her arms corkscrewed. She pushed still closer, unhurried, at the same time fully relaxing her guard on her thoughts. She was lush and lovely, complex and full of pain and fire.

They hovered there, taking each other in. Currents pushed on them, turning them, unheeded. He was so engrossed in knowing her, learning her, seeing her, that he barely noticed her limbs gently twining around his until they were well and truly entangled.

Alan stood in the deck transport with Jane. It was full of water and was going to make a huge mess when it opened. He was just glad that the system was so robust that it could take this kind of abuse without a glitch. The Sectilius had been damn fine engineers. This shit was solid-state.

And they were still alive, against all odds, again.

He glanced at Jane. She was deep in thought, staring straight ahead. She didn't seem to notice the gush of water flooding the crew deck or sheeting off of their suits. She just clomped out into the corridor, though not turning in the direction of their quarters.

She walked a long, long way down that endless corridor, not saying a word. He followed, though he wasn't sure if he should. She was in a strange mood. Maybe she wanted to be left alone.

Well, he'd be damned if he'd let her wander off. That evil squid had been trying to scramble her brains. She needed a thorough exam. He cursed under his breath because Ajaya was in the sanalabrium and wouldn't be able to perform that task. Jane should probably be right there next to her.

She finally paused at one of the big window-bubble things. It was nearly black on the other side. He saw a shimmery fish dart past. Her helmet receded into the shoulders of her suit as she leaned into the glass. He heard her sigh.

"You okay?" he asked.

She didn't answer.

He retracted his own helmet and sidled up to her, studying her. She was paler than normal. Her dark-blonde hair was pulled back in a ponytail, but as usual a few of the silky strands were escaping. They were plastered to her face, damp with sweat. He wanted to push them back, but he didn't have enough practice with the gauntlets to trust his fingers to be that gentle. He was worried enough about the traces of blood that were smeared from her nose across her cheek.

She was entranced by something through the window. He turned to see what it was. The other ship was out this direction. Maybe she was looking at it, though he couldn't imagine how she could see it in the dark.

A flash of red bioluminescence caught his eye. Then another. He looked more closely. Now that he knew where to look, he could see the whitish outline of the two kuboderans getting all wrapped up in each other.

Squid love was in full bloom. Apparently.

He cleared his throat. "I did *not* need to see that."

She didn't hear him.

He watched her watching them. Her eyes were sad, but there was a hint of a smile curving her lips. He wondered if she was in Brai's head, experiencing the whole alien-mating-ritual thing in real time. He would never get used to that. It was just too freaking weird. But he was beginning to under-stand why she did it. Sorta.

Suddenly she inhaled and turned to him. "Hm?"

"Has the Love Boat come to Pliga?" he asked, grinning at her. "Please tell me they aren't getting busy out there."

She looked surprised. Then she laughed. It erupted out of her, transforming her face, lighting her up. "Um, no. I don't think so." She looked back then, like she wasn't sure. "No, I don't... Maybe. I don't know." She pulled an incred-ulous, and maybe even mortified, face and giggled.

He chuckled with her. He loved the sound of her laugh. He was pretty sure he loved her.

She leaned on him, wrapped her arms around him. Her head rested against his chest. It was weird in the suits, but it was still good. It was right. This was the kind of intimacy he'd avoided his entire adult life. He'd been so stupid.

He kissed the top of her head. "We've got our work cut out for us now, babe," he murmured.

She sighed. "We'll manage."

"Or die trying," he said, rubbing his chin over her hair.

"We'll find a way to fix the ship. Maybe the Pligans will help. The sectilian records say they're extraordinary engi-neers."

"Then what?"

She looked up at him, her expression tight. "We have a new mission."

"Which is?"

"We stop the Swarm."

"No easy task," he said, frowning.

"We'll find a way. We have to."

He believed her. She was right. And if anyone could do it, she could.

The galaxy's survival depended on it.

Kai'Memna hadn't lived this long to meet death like a meek rodent. He'd never underestimated his own kind. True, in all these long years, as he sought out and converted his brothers and sisters, he'd never encountered much in the way of serious resistance, but the Sectilius were to blame for that—they'd brainwashed the Kubodera into believing they were one and the same, that they were sectilian.

They weren't.

The Kubodera were apex predators who only needed to be reminded of their heritage and their place in the hierarchy of species. Any individual who was incapable of acknowledging that fact was unworthy to live.

He'd put measures in place long before in preparation for scenarios such as this—it was the main reason he'd left so many of his crew alive, though it had been taxing over the years to maintain their quiescence. They were sacrificing themselves now in his name. This was how it was meant to be. A fierce species like his own should be served without reservation by a menial, lesser species. The dusk falling on them, winking them out of existence, was a small price to pay for his survival.

His first course of action, while he struggled valiantly to keep his vessel aloft, was to dislodge the *Colocallida*. He growled at Ei'Uba, issuing orders. The smaller ship was disabled. Ei'Uba would most likely be lost. He felt a moment's regret at losing the long-time flatterer, but he was one of many, easily replaced. And he'd failed, after all, to do what he was told, letting that terran detritus get the best of him. He'd earned his extinguishment.

Kai'Memna eased the *Portacollus* to starboard so that Pliga's gravity would assist in the displacement of the smaller ship. Crewmembers already stood by, braced in battle armor with sheets of hull plating and large quantities of squillae for repairs, while others worked diligently to patch his enclosure and stop the loss of water.

Ei'Uba flailed and begged Kai'Memna for assistance. His own smaller crew worked to effect similar repairs but was not as efficient. The damage to the *Colocallida* was spread over a more significant portion of that ship. It was likely a fruitless endeavor.

When the *Colocallida* finally broke free, he watched with the mildest of interest as it hurtled to the frozen dark side of Pliga, exploding in a plume of orange and red, reflected by the compacted ice and snow on that massive continent. It was lovely, all that ice and fire.

As for himself, he opened a jump window. He would return to his home base to restore his ship to peak working order.

Then he would be back to teach this terran and her pet kuba a lesson.

aepar
- A measurement of time analogous to a second.

anipraxia
- (noun) A form of telepathic communication used by the Kubodera. Requires stimulation/activation of dormant, partially evolved structures in the brain of a sentient participant. Used for communication between a kuboderan and sectilian shipmates. (adjective) **anipraxic**

atellan
- The race of the Sectilius originating on the moon of Atielle. The lower gravity of the moon contributed to a taller, more slender body form.

Atielle
- Sectilia's moon and home of the sectilian race referred to as atellans. One of four moons, but the only one that is habitable, with a similar atmospheric composition to Sectilia. One-third the mass of Earth, with a surface area roughly twice that of Earth's moon. Gravity is roughly one-half g. This planet is extremely volcanically active with erratic weather patterns and extreme storms. Its ecosystem has been devastated by a predator species, the nepatrox.

- The origin and ancestral home of Quasador Dux Rageth Elia Hator.

Bergen, Alan
- Aeronautical engineer and the flight engineer on the original *Providence* mission.

casgrata
- "Thank you" in Mensententia.

Compton, Tom
• A mechanical engineer and pilot of the original *Providence* mission.

Confluos giganus
• The species name of the Swarm, an omnivorous predatory insect species that devours entire ecosystems, leaving nothing living behind. Through millennia of evolution, this species adapted to devastate land, sea, and travel in the vacuum of space to find new worlds to conquer.

cornu
• This class of sectilian shuttle is slightly larger, more modern, and better configured for science expeditions than other models and therefore contains more seating for crew.

Cunabula
• A scientifically advanced ancient race. Deep in the reaches of time, the Cunabula seeded many habitable worlds with the precursors of life, allowing it to evolve on its own. One of their experiments was to create a competitive race on Earth that would serve as a warrior class to defend the weaker races in the galaxy from threats that might be a danger to the diversity they hoped to preserve.

Ei'Brai
• The kuboderan Gubernaviti of the *Speroancora*.

EMP
• Electromagnetic pulse. Also referred to as an ionic pulse or burst. It is an intense burst of electromagnetic energy caused by a rapid acceleration of particles, normally electrons, which can have a variety of sources. Such a pulse normally results in widespread damage to electronics, rendering them useless by destroying delicate components.

exiguumet
• Small measure of distance, akin to a millimeter.

Gibbs, Ronald
• Electrical engineer, computer specialist, and a member of the original *Providence* mission.

Gistraedor Dux
• Leader of an atellan community. Shortened form of this title is Gis'dux.

Greenspace Deck
• An entire deck on a sectilian ship devoted to cultivation of plant species native to the Sectilius system.

Gubernaviti
• The designation of a kuboderan within a ship community. The governing navigator. Takes part in the administration of ship policy, including sitting on the Quorum. Responsibilities include navigation and monitoring personnel, among many other duties. Checked by the yoke and a close connection to the Quasador Dux.

Gubernaviti ranking system
• Do' is the lowest rank for a kuboderan officer aboard a sectilian ship. All Gubernaviti start at this rank, typically on smaller trading ships.

• Ei' is the intermediate rank for a kuboderan officer. Graduating to this rank means more responsibility and a commission on a larger ship.

• Kai' is the highest rank a kuboderan officer can hope to achieve. Rarely given. Indicates centuries of service without a black mark.

Holloway, Jane
• Linguist and member of the original *Providence* mission. Quasador Dux of the *Speroancora*.

Kubodera
• A sentient, telepathic squidlike species originating on a world dominated by water. Since its discovery by the Sectilius, the location of this home world has been kept secret. A sectilian cabal called the mind masters harvests paralarvae (newborn life-stage of the kuboderans) and trains them to serve as Gubernaviti.

kuboderan
• Of or relating to the people called the Kubodera. Analogous to the word human.

Mensententia
• The common language of the Milky Way galaxy. This language was coded into the genetics of every sentient species by the Cunabula to facilitate interstellar communication and cooperation between far-flung species. The language normally manifests at puberty, and humans are the only known sentient species that does not speak it naturally, though it has greatly influenced language on Earth through the collective unconscious—expressing itself most strongly through Latin.

mind master
• A member of a sectilian secret society with greater-than-normal telepathic acuity. Induction into this cabal means intense mental training, honing telepathic skills, and a lifetime of service training kuboderans to serve aboard sectilian ships.

nepatrox
• An apex predator species with an unusual life cycle. Their microscopic spawn are difficult to eradicate and have evolved resistance to chemical methods of control. Under favorable conditions the spawn transmute to the larval stage, which resembles a slug and secretes a caustic substance that hydrolyzes any substrate it lingers on, allowing the larva to absorb nutrition through its skin. It grows slowly at this stage unless conditions are optimal.

Under significant atmospheric concentrations of xenon, this larval stage pupates and the final form, a lizardlike creature, emerges. Its growth is only kept in check by its ability to find adequate food.

The adult of the species is characterized by a thick trunk with no narrowing of the neck, powerful limbs terminating in sharp claws, a venomous stinger in its tail, and brilliantly colored hinged mouth flaps that it opens and flares to intimidate prey. The nepatrox stinger contains a paralytic that incapacitates its victim. Its saliva contains anticoagulants which allow it to keep its food source alive and fresh while it feeds over time. It travels and hunts in packs, targeting all types of prey, and is cannibalistic. It is the scourge of Atielle, and has laid waste to that planet's ecosystem.

Olonus Septua
• The sectilian colony where the first squillae plague originated, created by the infamous Engineering Master Tarn Elocus Hator.

penna
• This class of sectilian shuttle is smaller and meant for cargo transfer on planet, between Atielle and Sectilia, and ship to ship.

Providence
- A capsule built by NASA to travel to and dock with what they called the Target (the *Speroancora*), drifting in the Greater Asteroid Belt. Commanded by Mark Walsh. Piloted by Tom Compton, with Ajaya Varma, Ronald Gibbs, Jane Holloway, and Alan Bergen as crew.

Quasador Dux
- The elected leader of a sectilian ship community. Often shortened to Qua'dux. Loosely translated, the title means admiral or general, but there is emphasis on a scientific component. Chief investigator/scientist.

Quorum
- A council of leadership aboard a sectilian ship. Members include the Quasador Dux, the Gubernaviti, and all department heads.

Rageth Elia Hator
- The Quasador Dux of the *Speroancora* at the time of the squillae plague. A distinguished leader with many years of service. When the potential coordinates of Terra were discovered in an ancient Cunabalistic text, it was Rageth and Ei'Brai whom the Unified Sentient Races sent to investigate.

sanalabrium
- (noun) Medical equipment consisting of a large basin filled with a clear therapeutic gel. The patient is submersed and treated with threadlike component devices that perform surgery, restrain the patient, and deliver medications intravenously. (adjective) **sanalabrius**

scaluuti
- A greeting in Mensententia.

Sectilia

• The planet of origin of the Sectilius, with a mass 8.7 times greater than Earth and a gravity of 1.43 gs. The star in this system is a yellow-dwarf, main-sequence star, but slightly larger than Sol. Sectilia is also in a closer orbit around this star, resulting in a brighter, larger sun shining on this planet and its habitable moon Atielle. Sectilia has an Earthlike atmosphere and green flora. This planet is also overrun with the predator species called the nepatrox, but the inhabitants have more resources to cope with the infestation and the ecosystem is not in the same dire condition as Atielle's.

sectilian

• A broad term describing the people who evolved both on Atielle and Sectilia. Analogous to the word human.

Sectilius

• Can be used to refer to the entire star system, the planet/moon combination, or the people residing on the sibling worlds of Sectilia and Atielle. "The Divided." The people originating from this system are humanoid in nature with two main body types. The type originating on the planet is compact and muscular; the type originating on the moon is taller and more slender. Both races have sharp, angular bone structures, giving their features a geometric quality. Science, logic, and cooperation are highly valued in sectilian culture.

Sentients

• An abbreviated term for the Unified Sentient Races, or a reference to them before they unified.

Speroancora

• A sectilian science and diplomatic vessel sent to verify the existence of Terra (Earth).

squillae
• Sectilian nanites originally designed by Tarn Elocus
Hator. "Shrimp."

suesupus
• A large, ungulate, herbivorous species originating on
Atielle. Its thick skin protects it from the venomous stinger
of the nepatrox, making it the only species the nepatrox
avoid, though they do attack and consume suesupus
weakened by age and disease. Due to this advantage the
atellans have domesticated this species as a beast of
burden, resulting in a smaller, more docile version of the
specimens seen in the wild.

Swarm
• See entry for *Confluos giganus*.

Target
• The term used by NASA to describe the alien ship
discovered in the Greater Asteroid Belt and later revealed
to be named the *Speroancora*.

Tech Deck
• The engineering deck on the *Speroancora*.

Terac
• The planet where ambassadorial assemblies are held for
the Unified Sentient Races.

Terra
• The term the Cunabula used for Earth in their ancient
texts.

terran
• Humanoid species originating on Terra (Earth).
Analogous to the word human.

Unified Sentient Races
• A galactic coalition of planets in opposition to the Swarm.

Varma, Ajaya
• The flight surgeon on the original *Providence* mission. A medical doctor.

vastuumet
• Measure of enormous distance in space.

Walsh, Mark
• The commander of the original *Providence* mission.

yoke
• A multicomponent system that includes squillae, cybernetic implants, software, and hardware imbedded throughout a sectilian ship with the purpose of controlling the behavior of a kuboderan and preventing him or her from usurping too much power or facilitating any form of sedition.

AUTHOR'S NOTE

I would be remiss if I didn't take the time to acknowledge the people who have helped me in my journey to complete this book (and the one before it). The first round of thanks has to go to my critique group, Working Title, and to three individuals in that group in particular.

Brandon Stenger and Wendy Hammer, both extremely talented writers in their own right (they'll be rising to your notice in the coming years) have been both supportive and encouraging as well as providing invaluable critique on early drafts of all of my work. The third member of Working Title I'd like to mention is Jeff Seymour, also a gifted author, who is more than just my critique partner, he's also my developmental editor and line editor. This guy has a deep understanding of story and he makes me look good. I'm pleased that his work is starting to get some attention.

It would be negligent to omit my family. My children are my most enthusiastic cheerleaders and my ex-husband has been incredibly supportive of my career and continues to be. I couldn't have done all this if they didn't want me to succeed. My parents, Jack and Betty, fostered an environment when I was growing up that made books, reading, and the love of science fiction a part of my world.

In addition, this novel includes a lot of technical information. When FLUENCY became popular, I was gratified to find that many prominent scientists contacted me to tell me that they enjoyed the novel. I took down a list of names at that time and leaned on a few of those people to read an early draft of REMANENCE to make sure that I was getting the science right. I've earned a degree in biology and actively seek out scientific information all the time, but I wanted to be sure that the physics and planetary science I describe was accurate.

To that end, I frequently had discussions with Andrew Schnell, an aeronautic engineer at NASA/JPL who guided me on several important topics related to space flight and space elevators. He also read and commented on an early draft of this work.

Other important early readers/technical information contributors included: Gary Tenison, who works at Kaman Aerospace; Joseph Hucks, a retired theoretical physicist; Robert Brown, a retired nuclear physicist; Tim Cox, an avid SciFi reader who keeps current on aviation and space technology; and Tom Nordheim, a Norwegian planetary scientist working for NASA/JPL. All of these gentleman provided patient and indispensable instruction on their respective fields of expertise.

I'd also like to thank my proofreader, Bryon Quertermous, for an excellent job in the final hours before publication. Autumn Kalquist has been instrumental in helping me navigate the world of independent publishing and one of my favorite writers to read. Samuel Peralta's excellent The Future Chronicles series of anthologies has afforded me abundant exposure to new readers. My agent, Danny Baror, sold FLUENCY to traditional publishers in Germany, Russia and Japan, helping me gain worldwide exposure.

The following authors have provided immeasurable personal and authorial support over the last year or more: Susan Kaye Quinn, Annie Bellet, Ann Christy, Patrice Fitzgerald, Blair Babylon, Rysa Walker, Theresa Kay, Sara Reine, Elle Casey, and Mimi Tpaulin. Thank you, ladies!

Last but not least is one of my favorite writing buddies, R. Alexander Williams, who I thoroughly enjoy bouncing ideas off of and was a great help in both developing the plot of REMANENCE as well as providing excellent critical notes on the early stages of the novel, helping me shape and grow the narrative. Mr. Williams is a successful screen-writer.

Finally, thank you to my large Twitter following for support, encouragement and never ending demands for this sequel! I enjoy you so much.

Read on!

ABOUT THE AUTHOR

Jennifer Foehner Wells lives an alternately chaotic and fairly bucolic existence in Indiana with two boisterous little boys and two semi-crazed cats. You can find her on Twitter, extolling science and scifi fandoms, as @Jenthulhu. To find out more about Jen, visit: www.jenthulhu.com.

If you enjoyed this book, please consider leaving a review on your favorite online site. That's the best way to help other readers find it and support the authors that you want to see more from.